PENGUIN BOOKS

2787

OVER THE RIVER

John Galsworthy, the son of a solicitor, was born in 1867 and educated at Harrow and New College, Oxford. He was called to the Bar in 1890; while travelling in the Far East he met Conrad, who became a lifelong friend. In 1897 he published *Four Winds* (short stories) under another name, and later two novels. *The Man of Property* (1906), the first book in *The Forsyte Saga*, together with his first play, *The Silver Box*, established him in the public mind. Other novels and plays followed, but it was not until after the First World War that he completed the first Forsyte trilogy with *In Chancery* (1920) and *To Let* (1921). The complete edition of *The Forsyte Saga*, first published in 1922, has since been through fifty-six impressions. The second Forsyte trilogy, *A Modern Comedy*, appeared in 1929, and the third, *End of the Chapter*, posthumously in 1934. Galsworthy was the first president of the P.E.N. Club, was awarded a Nobel Prize, and received the Order of Merit in 1929. He lived on Dartmoor for many years and afterwards at Bury on the Sussex Downs. He died in 1933. All nine volumes of the *Forsyte Chronicles* are now available in Penguins.

John Galsworthy

OVER THE RIVER

◄◄►►

BOOK THREE OF
End of the Chapter

PENGUIN BOOKS
in association with William Heinemann Ltd

Penguin Books Ltd, Harmondsworth, Middlesex, England
Penguin Books Australia Ltd, Ringwood, Victoria, Australia

—

First published by William Heinemann Ltd 1933
Published in Penguin Books 1968
Reprinted 1968

—

Made and printed in Great Britain
by Hazell Watson & Viney Ltd,
Aylesbury, Bucks
Set in Linotype Granjon

—

Over the River is Book Three of *End of the Chapter*,
which comprises the last three volumes of
The Forsyte Chronicles (nine volumes)

TO
Rudolf and Viola Sauter

Chapter One

❈

CLARE, who for seventeen months had been the wife of Sir Gerald Corven of the Colonial Service, stood on the boat deck of an Orient liner in the river Thames, waiting for it to dock. It was ten o'clock of a mild day in October, but she wore a thick tweed coat, for the voyage had been hot. She looked pale – indeed, a little sallow – but her clear brown eyes were fixed eagerly on the land and her slightly touched-up lips were parted, so that her face had the vividness to which it was accustomed. She stood alone, until a voice said:

'Oh! *here* you are!' and a young man, appearing from behind a boat, stood beside her. Without turning, she said:

'Absolutely perfect day! It ought to be lovely at home.'

'I thought you'd be staying in Town for a night at least; and we could have had a dinner and theatre. Won't you?'

'My dear young man, I shall be met.'

'Perfectly damnable, things coming to an end!'

'Often more damnable, things beginning.'

He gave her a long look, and said suddenly:

'Clare, you realize, of course, that I love you?'

She nodded. 'Yes.'

'But you don't love me?'

'Wholly without prejudice.'

'I wish – I wish you could catch fire for a moment.'

'I am a respectable married woman, Tony.'

'Coming back to England because –'

'Of the climate of Ceylon.'

He kicked at the rail. 'Just as it's getting perfect. I've not said anything, but I know that your – that Corven –'

Clare lifted her eyebrows, and he was silent; then both looked at the shore, becoming momentarily more and more a consideration.

When two young people have been nearly three weeks together on board a ship, they do not know each other half so well as they think they do. In the abiding inanity of a life when

7

everything has stopped except the engines, the water slippi
along the ship's sides, and the curving of the sun in the sk
their daily chair-to-chair intimacy gathers a queer momentu
and a sort of lazy warmth. They know that they are getti
talked about, and do not care. After all, they cannot get off t
ship, and there is nothing else to do. They dance together, a
the sway of the ship, however slight, favours the closeness
their contacts. After ten days or so they settle down to a life t
gether, more continuous than that of marriage, except that th
still spend their nights apart. And then, all of a sudden, t
ship stops, and they stop, and there is a feeling, at least on o
side, perhaps on both, that stocktaking has been left till too lat
A hurried vexed excitement, not unpleasurable, because suspe
ded animation is at an end, invades their faculties; they a
faced with the real equation of land animals who have been
sea.

Clare broke the silence.

'You've never told me why you're called Tony when yo
name is James.'

'That *is* why. I *wish* you'd be serious, Clare; we haven
much time before the darned ship docks. I simply can't bear t
thought of not seeing you every day.'

Clare gave him a swift look, and withdrew her eyes to t
shore again. 'How clean!' she was thinking. He had, indeed,
clean oval-shaped brown face, determined, but liable to goo
humour, with dark grey eyes inclined to narrow with h
thoughts and darkish hair; and he was thin and active.

He took hold of a button of her coat.

'You haven't said a word about yourself out there, but yo
aren't happy, I know.'

'I dislike people who talk about their private lives.'

'Look!' he put a card into her hand: 'That club always fin
me.'

She read:

MR JAMES BERNARD CROOM

The Coffee House,
St James' Street.

'Isn't the Coffee House very out of date?'

'Yes, but it's still rather "the thing." My Dad put me down when I was born.'

'I have an uncle by marriage who belongs — Sir Lawrence Mont, tall and twisty and thin; you'll know him by a tortoise-shell-rimmed eyeglass.'

'I'll look out for him.'

'What are you going to do with yourself in England?'

'Hunt a job. That's more than one man's work, it seems.'

'What sort of job?'

'Anything except schoolmastering and selling things on commission.'

'But does anybody ever get anything else nowadays?'

'No. It's a bad look-out. What I'd like would be an estate agency, or something to do with horses.'

'Estates and horses are both dying out.'

'I know one or two racing men rather well. But I expect I shall end as a chauffeur. Where are you going to stay?'

'With my people. At first, anyway. If you still want to see me when you've been home a week, Condaford Grange, Oxford-shire, will find me.'

'Why did I ever meet you?' said the young man, with sudden gloom.

'Thank you.'

'Oh! you know what I mean. God! she's casting anchor. Here's the tender! Oh! Clare!'

'Sir?'

'Hasn't it meant anything to you?'

Clare looked at him steadily before answering.

'Yes. But I don't know if it will ever mean any more. If it doesn't, thank you for helping me over a bad three weeks.'

The young man stood silent, as only those can be silent whose feelings are raging for expression. . . .

The beginnings and endings of all human undertakings are untidy: the building of a house, the writing of a novel, the demolition of a bridge, and, eminently, the finish of a voyage. Clare landed from the tender in the usual hurly-burly, and, still attended by young Croom, came to rest in the arms of her sister.

9

'Dinny! How sweet of you to face this bally-hooley! My sister, Dinny Cherrell – Tony Croom. I shall be all right now, Tony. Go and look after your own things.'

'I've got Fleur's car,' said Dinny. 'What about your trunks?'

'They're booked through to Condaford.'

'Then we can go straight off.'

The young man, going with them to the car, said 'Good-bye' with a jauntiness which deceived no one; and the car slid away from the dock.

Side by side the sisters looked at each other, a long and affectionate scrutiny; and their hands lay, squeezed together, on the rug.

'Well, ducky!' said Dinny, at last. 'Lovely to see you! Am I wrong to read between the lines?'

'No. I'm not going back to him, Dinny.'

'No, never, non?'

'No, never, non!'

'Oh! dear! Poor darling!'

'I won't go into it, but it became impossible.' Clare was silent, then added suddenly, with a toss back of her head: 'Quite impossible!'

'Did he consent to your coming?'

Clare shook her head. 'I slipped off. He was away. I wirelessed him, and wrote from Suez.'

There was another silence. Then Dinny squeezed her hand and said:

'I was always afraid of it.'

'The worst of it is I haven't a penny. Is there anything in hats now, Dinny?'

' "All British" hats – I wonder.'

'Or, perhaps, I could breed dogs – bull terriers; what d'you think?'

'I don't at present. We'll inquire.'

'How are things at Condaford?'

'We rub on. Jean has gone out to Hubert again, but the baby's there – just a year old now. Cuthbert Conway Cherrell. I suppose we shall call him "Cuffs." He's rather a duck.'

'Thank God I haven't that complication! Certain things have their advantages.' Her face had the hardness of a face on a coin.

'Have you had any word from him?'

'No, but I shall, when he realizes that I mean it.'

'Was there another woman?'

Clare shrugged.

Again Dinny's hand closed on hers.

'I'm not going to make a song of my affairs, Dinny.'

'Is he likely to come home about it?'

'I don't know. I won't see him if he does.'

'But, darling, you'll be hopelessly hung up.'

'Oh! Don't let's bother about me. How have you been?' And she looked critically at her sister: 'You look more Botticellian than ever.'

'I've become an adept at skimping. Also, I've gone in for bees.'

'Do they pay?'

'Not at present. But on a ton of honey we could make about seventy pounds.'

'How much honey did you have this year?'

'About two hundredweight.'

'Are there any horses still?'

'Yes, we've saved the horses, so far. I've got a scheme for a Condaford Grange bakery. The home farm is growing wheat at double what we sell it at. I want to mill and bake our own and supply the neighbourhood. The old mill could be set going for a few pounds, and there's a building for the bakery. It wants about three hundred to start it. We've nearly decided to cut enough timber.'

'The local traders will rage furiously.'

'They will.'

'Can it really pay?'

'At a ton of wheat to the acre – *vide Whitaker* – we reckon thirty acres of our wheat, plus as much Canadian to make good light bread, would bring us in more than eight hundred and fifty pounds, less, say, five hundred, cost of milling and baking. It would mean baking one hundred and sixty two-pound loaves a day and selling about 56,000 loaves a year. We should need to supply eighty households, but that's only the village, more or less. And we'd make the best and brightest bread.'

'Three hundred and fifty a year profit,' said Clare. 'I wonder.'

'So do I,' said Dinny. 'Experience doesn't tell me that ever estimate of profit should be halved, because I haven't had any but I suspect it. But even half would just tip the beam the righ way for us, and we could extend operations gradually. We coul plough a lot of grass in time.'

'It's a scheme,' said Clare, 'but would the village back you?'

'So far as I've sounded them – yes.'

'You'd want somebody to run it.'

'M'yes. It would have to be someone who didn't mind wha he did. Of course he'd have the future, if it went.'

'I wonder,' said Clare, again, and wrinkled her brows.

'Who,' asked Dinny suddenly, 'was that young man?'

'Tony Croom? Oh! He was on a tea plantation, but they closed down.' And she looked her sister full in the face.

'Pleasant?'

'Yes, rather a dear. *He* wants a job, by the way.'

'So do about three million others.'

'Including me.'

'You haven't come back to a very cheery England, darling.'

'I gather we fell off the gold standard or something while I was in the Red Sea. What is the gold standard?'

'It's what you want to be on when you're off, and to be off when you're on.'

'I see.'

'The trouble, apparently, is that our exports and carrying-trade profits and interests from investments abroad don't any longer pay for our imports; so we're living beyond our income. Michael says anybody could have seen that coming; but we thought "it would be all right on the night." And it isn't. Hence the National Government and the election.'

'Can they do anything if they remain in?'

'Michael says "yes"; but he's notably hopeful. Uncle Lawrence says they can put a drag on panic, prevent money going out of the country, keep the pound fairly steady, and stop profiteering; but that nothing under a wide and definite reconstruction that will take twenty years will do the trick; and during that time we shall all be poorer. Unfortunately no Government, he says, can prevent us liking play better than work, hoarding to pay these awful taxes, or preferring the present to the future. He also says that if we think people will work as they did in the war to save the country, we're wrong; because, instead of being one people against an outside enemy, we're two peoples against the inside enemy of ourselves, with quite opposite views as to how our salvation is to come.'

'Does he think the socialists have a cure?'

'No; he says they've forgotten that no one will give them food if they can neither produce it nor pay for it. He says that communism or free trade socialism only has a chance in a country which feeds itself. You see, I've been learning it up. They all use the word Nemesis a good deal.'

'Phew! Where are we going now, Dinny?'

'I thought you'd like lunch at Fleur's; afterwards we can take the three-fifty to Condaford.'

Then there was silence, during which each thought seriously about the other, and neither was happy. For Clare was feeling in her elder sister the subtle change which follows in one whose springs have been broken and mended to go on with. And Dinny was thinking: 'Poor child! Now we've both been in the wars. What will she do? And how can I help her?'

Chapter Two

'W H A T a nice lunch!' said Clare, eating the sugar at the bottom of her coffee cup: 'The first meal on shore is lovely! When you get on board a ship and read the first menu, you think: "My goodness! What an enchanting lot of things!" and then you come down to cold ham at nearly every meal. Do you know that stealing disappointment?'

'Don't I?' said Fleur. 'The curries used to be good, though.'

'Not on the return voyage. I never want to see a curry again. How's the Round Table Conference going?'

'Plodding on. Is Ceylon interested in India?'

'Not very. Is Michael?'

'We both are.'

Clare's brows went up with delightful suddenness.

'But you can't know anything about it.'

'I *was* in India, you know, and at one time I saw a lot of Indian students.'

'Oh! yes, students. That's the trouble. They're so advanced and the people are so backward.'

'If Clare's to see Kit and Kat before we start,' said Dinny, 'we ought to go up, Fleur.'

The visit to the nurseries over, the sisters resumed their seats in the car.

'Fleur always strikes me,' said Clare, 'as knowing so exactly what she wants.'

'She gets it, as a rule; but there've been exceptions. I've always doubted whether she really wanted Michael.'

'D'you mean a love affair went wrong?'

Dinny nodded. Clare looked out of the window.

'Well, she's not remarkable in that.'

Her sister did not answer.

'Trains,' Dinny said, in their empty third-class compartment, 'always have great open spaces now.'

'I rather dread seeing Mother and Dad, Dinny, having made such an almighty bloomer. I really must get something to do.'

'Yes, you won't be happy at Condaford for long.'

'It isn't that. I want to prove that I'm not the complete idiot. I wonder if I could run an hotel. English hotels are still pretty backward.'

'Good idea. It's strenuous, and you'd see lots of people.'

'Is that caustic?'

'No, darling, just common sense; you never liked being buried.'

'How does one go to work to get such a thing?'

'You have me there. But now's the time if ever, nobody's going to be able to travel. But I'm afraid there's a technical side to managing hotels that has to be learned. Your title might help.'

'I shouldn't use his name. I should call myself Mrs Clare.'

'I see. Are you sure it wouldn't be wise to tell me more about things?'

Clare sat silent for a little, then said suddenly: 'He's a sadist.'

Looking at her flushed face, Dinny said: 'I've never understood exactly what that means.'

'Seeking sensation, and getting more sensation when you hurt the person you get it from. A wife is most convenient.'

'Oh! darling!'

'There was a lot first, my riding whip was only the last straw.'

'You don't mean –!' cried Dinny, horrified.

'Oh! yes.'

Dinny came over to her side and put her arms round her.

'But, Clare, you must get free!'

'And how? My word against his. Besides, who would make a show of beastliness? You're the only person I could ever ever speak to of it.'

Dinny got up and let down the window. Her face was as flushed as her sister's. She heard Clare say dully:

'I came away the first moment I could. It's none of it fit for publication. You see, ordinary passion palls after a bit, and it's a hot climate.'

'Oh! heaven!' said Dinny, and sat down again opposite.

'My own fault. I always knew it was thin ice, and I've popped through, that's all.'

'But, darling, at twenty-four you simply can't stay married and not married.'

'I don't see why not; *mariage manqué* is very steadying to the blood. All I'm worrying about is getting a job. I'm not going to be a drag on Dad. Is his head above water, Dinny?'

'Not quite. We were breaking even, but this last taxation will just duck us. The trouble is how to get on without reducing staff. Everyone's in the same boat. I always feel that we and the village are one. We've got to sink or swim together, and somehow or other we're going to swim. Hence my bakery scheme.'

'If I haven't got another job, could I do the delivering? suppose we've still got the old car.'

'Darling, you can help any way you like. But it all has to be started. That'll take till after Christmas. In the meantime there's the election.'

'Who is our candidate?'

'His name is Dornford – a new man, quite decent.'

'Will he want canvassers?'

'Rather!'

'All right. That'll be something to do for a start. Is this National Government any use?'

'They talk of "completing their work"; but at present they don't tell us how.'

'I suppose they'll quarrel among themselves the moment a constructive scheme is put up to them. It's all beyond me. But I can go round saying "Vote for Dornford." How's Aunt Em?'

'She's coming to stay tomorrow. She suddenly wrote that she hadn't seen the baby; says she's feeling romantic – wants to have the priest's room, and will I see that "no one bothers to do her up behind, and that." She's exactly the same.'

'I often thought about her,' said Clare. 'Extraordinarily restful.'

After that there was a long silence, Dinny thinking about Clare and Clare thinking about herself. Presently, she grew tired of that and looked across at her sister. Had Dinny really got over that affair of hers with Wilfrid Desert of which Hubert had written with such concern when it was on, and such relief when it was off? She had asked that her affair should never be spoken of, Hubert had said, but that was over a year ago. Could one venture, or would she curl up like a hedgehog? 'Poor Dinny!' she thought: 'I'm twenty-four, so she's twenty-seven!' And she sat very still looking at her sister's profile. It was charming, the more so for that slight tip-tilt of the nose which gave to the face a touch of adventurousness. Her eyes were as pretty as ever – that cornflower blue wore well; and their fringing was unexpectedly dark with such chestnut hair. Still, the face was thinner, and had lost what Uncle Lawrence used to call its 'bubble and squeak.' 'I should fall in love with her if I were a man,' thought Clare, 'she's *good*. But it's rather a sad face, now, except when she's talking.' And Clare drooped her lids, spying through her lashes: No! one could not ask! The face she spied on had a sort of hard-won privacy that it would be unpardonable to disturb.

'Darling,' said Dinny, 'would you like your old room? I'm afraid the fantails have multiplied exceedingly – they coo a lot just under it.'

'I shan't mind that.'

'And what do you do about breakfast? Will you have it in your room?'

'My dear, don't bother about me in any way. If anybody does, I shall feel dreadful. England again on a day like this! Grass is really lovely stuff, and the elm trees, and that blue look!'

'Just one thing, Clare. Would you like me to tell Dad and Mother, or would you rather I said nothing?'

Clare's lips tightened.

'I suppose they'll have to know that I'm not going back.'

'Yes; and something of the reason.'

'Just general impossibility, then.'

Dinny nodded. 'I don't want them to think you in the wrong. We'll let other people think that you're home for your health.'

'Aunt Em?' said Clare.

'I'll see to her. She'll be absorbed in the baby, anyway. Here we are, very nearly.'

Condaford Church came into view, and the little group of houses, mostly thatched, which formed the nucleus of that scattered parish. The home-farm buildings could be seen, but not the Grange, for, situated on the lowly level dear to ancestors, it was wrapped from the sight in trees.

Clare, flattening her nose against the window, said:

'It gives you a thrill. Are you as fond of home as ever, Dinny?'

'Fonder.'

'It's funny. I love it, but I can't live in it.'

'Very English – hence America and the Dominions. Take your dressing-case, and I'll take the suitcase.'

The drive up through the lanes, where the elms were flecked by little golden patches of turned leaves, was short and sweet in the lowered sunlight, and ended with the usual rush of dogs from the dark hall.

'This one's new,' said Clare, of the black spaniel sniffing at her stockings.

'Yes, Foch. Scaramouch and he have signed the Kellogg Pact, so they don't observe it. I'm a sort of Manchuria.' And Dinny threw open the drawing-room door.

'Here she is, Mother.'

Advancing towards her mother, who stood smiling, pale and

tremulous, Clare felt choky for the first time. To have to come back like this and disturb their peace!

'Well, Mother darling,' she said, 'here's your bad penny! You look just the same, bless you!'

Emerging from that warm embrace, Lady Cherrell looked at her daughter shyly and said:

'Dad's in his study.'

'I'll fetch him,' said Dinny.

In that barren abode, which still had its military and austere air, the General was fidgeting with a gadget he had designed to save time in the putting on of riding boots and breeches.

'Well?' he said.

'She's all right, dear, but it *is* a split, and I'm afraid complete.'

'That's bad!' said the General, frowning.

Dinny took his lapels in her hands.

'It's not her fault. But I wouldn't ask her any questions, Dad. Let's take it that she's just on a visit; and make it as nice for her as we can.'

'What's the fellow been doing?'

'Oh! his nature. I knew there was a streak of cruelty in him.'

'How d'you mean – knew it, Dinny?'

'The way he smiled – his lips.'

The General uttered a sound of intense discomfort.

'Come along!' he said: 'Tell me later.'

With Clare he was perhaps rather elaborately genial and open, asking no questions except about the Red Sea and the scenery of Ceylon, his knowledge of which was confined to its spicy offshore scent and a stroll in the Cinnamon Gardens at Colombo. Clare, still emotional from the meeting with her mother, was grateful for his reticence. She escaped rather quickly to her room, where her bags had already been unpacked.

At its dormer window she stood listening to the coorooing of the fantails and the sudden flutter and flip-flap of their wings climbing the air from the yew-hedged garden. The sun, very low, was still shining through an elm tree. There was no wind, and her nerves sucked up repose in that pigeon-haunted stillness, scented so differently from Ceylon. Native air, deliciously sane, fresh and homespun, with a faint tang of burning leaves.

She could see the threading blue smoke from where the gardeners had lighted a small bonfire in the orchard. And almost at
once she lit a cigarette. The whole of Clare was in that simple
action. She could never quite rest and be still, must always move
on to that fuller savouring which for such natures ever recedes. A
fantail on the gutter of the sloped stone roof watched her with
a soft dark little eye, preening itself slightly. Beautifully white
it was, and had a pride of body; so too had that small round
mulberry tree which had dropped a ring of leaves, with their
unders uppermost, spangling the grass. The last of the sunlight
was stirring in what yellowish-green foliage was left, so that the
tree had an enchanted look. Seventeen months since she had
stood at this window and looked down over that mulberry tree
at the fields and the rising coverts! Seventeen months of foreign
skies and trees, foreign scents and sounds and waters. All new,
and rather exciting, tantalizing, unsatisfying. No rest! Certainly
none in the white house with the wide verandah she had occupied at Kandy. At first she had enjoyed, then she had wondered
if she enjoyed, then she had known she was not enjoying, lastly
she had hated it. And now it was all over and she was back!
She flipped the ash off her cigarette and stretched herself, and
the fantail rose with a fluster.

Chapter Three

DINNY was 'seeing to' Aunt Em. It was no mean process. With
ordinary people one had question and answer and the thing was
over. But with Lady Mont words were not consecutive like that.
She stood with a verbena sachet in her hand, sniffing, while
Dinny unpacked for her.

'This is delicious, Dinny. Clare looks rather yellow. It isn't a
baby, is it?'

'No, dear.'

'Pity! When we were in Ceylon everyone was havin' babies.
The baby elephants – so enticin'! In this room – we always
played a game of feedin' the Catholic priest with a basket from

the roof. Your father used to be on the roof, and I was the priest. There was never anythin' worth eatin' in the basket. Your Aunt Wilmet was stationed in a tree to call 'Cooee' in case of Protestants.'

' "Cooee" was a bit premature, Aunt Em. Australia wasn't discovered under Elizabeth.'

'No. Lawrence says the Protestants at that time were devils. So were the Catholics. So were the Mohammedans.'

Dinny winced and veiled her face with a corset belt.

'Where shall I put these undies?'

'So long as I see where. Don't stoop too much! They were all devils then. Animals were treated terribly. Did Clare enjoy Ceylon?'

Dinny stood up with an armful of underthings.

'Not much.'

'Why not? Liver?'

'Auntie, you won't say anything, except to Uncle Lawrence and Michael, if I tell you? There's been a split.'

Lady Mont buried her nose in the verbena bag.

'Oh!' she said : 'His mother looked it. D'you believe in "like mother like son"?'

'Not too much.'

'I always thought seventeen years' difference too much, Dinny. Lawrence says people say: "Oh! Jerry Corven!" and then don't say. So, what was it?'

Dinny bent over a drawer and arranged the things.

'I can't go into it, but he seems to be quite a beast.'

Lady Mont tipped the bag into the drawer, murmuring: 'Poor dear Clare!'

'So, Auntie, she's just to be home for her health.'

Lady Mont put her nose into a bowl of flowers. 'Boswell and Johnson call them "God-eat-yers". They don't smell. What disease could Clare have – nerves?'

'Climate, Auntie.'

'So many Anglo-Indians go back and back, Dinny.'

'I know, but for the present. Something's bound to happen. So not even to Fleur, please.'

'Fleur will know whether I tell her or not. She's like that. Has Clare a young man?'

'Oh! no!' And Dinny lifted a puce-coloured wrapper, re-calling the expression of the young man when he was saying good-bye.

'On board ship,' murmured her Aunt dubiously.

Dinny changed the subject.

'Is Uncle Lawrence very political just now?'

'Yes, so borin'. Things always sound so when you talk about them. Is your candidate here safe, like Michael?'

'He's new, but he'll get in.'

'Married?'

'No.'

Lady Mont inclined her head slightly to one side and scruti-nized her niece from under half-drooped lids.

Dinny took the last thing out of the trunk. It was a pot of antiphlogistine.

'That's not British, Auntie.'

'For the chest. Delia puts it in. I've had it, years. Have you talked to your candidate in private?'

'I have.'

'How old is he?'

'Rather under forty, I should say.'

'Does he do anything besides?'

'He's a K. C.'

'What's his name?'

'Dornford.'

'There were Dornfords when I was a girl. Where was that? Ah! Algeciras! He was a Colonel at Gibraltar.'

'That would be his father, I expect.'

'Then he hasn't any money.'

'Only what he makes at the Bar.'

'But they don't – under forty.'

'He does, I think.'

'Energetic?'

'Very.'

'Fair?'

'No, darkish. He won the Bar point-to-point this year. Now, darling, will you have a fire at once, or last till dressing time?'

'Last. I want to see the baby.'

'All right, he ought to be just in from his pram. Your

bathroom's at the foot of these stairs, and I'll wait for you in the nursery.'

The nursery was the same mullion-windowed, low-pitched room as that wherein Dinny and Aunt Em herself had received their first impressions of that jigsaw puzzle called life; and in it the baby was practising his totter. Whether he would be a Charwell or a Tasburgh when he grew up seemed as yet uncertain. His nurse, his aunt and his great-aunt stood, in triangular admiration, for him to fall alternatively into their outstretched hands.

'He doesn't crow,' said Dinny.

'He does in the morning, Miss.'

'Down he goes!' said Lady Mont.

'Don't cry, darling!'

'He never cries, Miss.'

'That's Jean. Clare and I cried a lot till we were about seven.'

'I cried till I was fifteen,' said Lady Mont, 'and I began again when I was forty-five. Did you cry, Nurse?'

'We were too large a family, my lady. There wasn't room like.'

'Nanny had a lovely mother – five sisters as good as gold.'

The nurse's fresh cheeks grew fresher; she drooped her chin, smiling, shy as a little girl.

'Take care of bow legs!' said Lady Mont: 'That's enough totterin'.'

The nurse, retrieving the still persistent baby, placed him in his cot, whence he frowned solemnly at Dinny, who said:

'Mother's devoted to him. She thinks he'll be like Hubert.'

Lady Mont made the sound supposed to attract babies.

'When does Jean come home again?'

'Not till Hubert's next long leave.'

Lady Mont's gaze rested on her niece.

'The rector says Alan has another year on the China station.'

Dinny, dangling a bead chain over the baby, paid no attention. Never since the summer evening last year, when she came back home after Wilfrid's flight, had she made or suffered any allusion to her feelings. No one, perhaps not even she herself, knew whether she was heart-whole once more. It was, indeed, as if she had no heart. So long, so earnestly had she resisted its aching, that it had slunk away into the shadows of her inmost being, where even she could hardly feel it beating.

'What would you like to do now, Auntie? He has to go to sleep.'

'Take me round the garden.'

They went down and out on to the terrace.

'Oh!' said Dinny, with dismay, 'Glover has gone and beaten the leaves off the little mulberry. They were so lovely, shivering on the tree and coming off in a ring on the grass. Really gardeners have no sense of beauty.'

'They don't like sweepin'. Where's the cedar I planted when I was five?'

They came on it round the corner of an old wall, a spreading youngster of nearly sixty, with flattening boughs gilded by the level sunlight.

'I should like to be buried under it, Dinny. Only I suppose they won't. There'll be something stuffy.'

'I mean to be burnt and scattered. Look at them ploughing in that field. I do love horses moving slowly against a skyline of trees.'

' "The lowin' kine," ' said Lady Mont irrelevantly.

A faint clink came from a sheepfold to the East.

'Listen, Auntie!'

Lady Mont thrust her arm within her niece's.

'I've often thought,' she said, 'that I should like to be a goat.'

'Not in England, tied to a stake and grazing in a mangy little circle.'

'No, with a bell on a mountain. A he-goat, I think, so as not to be milked.'

'Come and see our new cutting bed, Auntie. There's nothing now, of course, but dahlias, godetias, chrysanthemums, Michaelmas daisies, and a few pentstemons and cosmias.'

'Dinny,' said Lady Mont, from among the dahlias, 'about Clare? They say divorce is very easy now.'

'Until you try for it, I expect.'

'There's desertion and that.'

'But you have to *be* deserted.'

'Well, you said he made her.'

23

'It's not the same thing, dear.'

'Lawyers are so fussy about the law. There was that magistrate with the long nose in Hubert's extradition.'

'Oh ! but he turned out quite human.'

'How was that?'

'Telling the Home Secretary that Hubert was speaking the truth.'

'A dreadful business,' murmured Lady Mont, 'but nice to remember.'

'It had a happy ending,' said Dinny quickly.

Lady Mont stood, ruefully regarding her.

And Dinny, staring at the flowers, said suddenly: 'Aunt Em, somehow there must be a happy ending for Clare.'

Chapter Four

THE custom known as canvassing, more peculiar even than its name, was in full blast round Condaford. Every villager had been invited to observe how appropriate it would be if they voted for Dornford, and how equally appropriate it would be if they voted for Stringer. They had been exhorted publicly and vociferously, by ladies in cars, by ladies out of cars, and in the privacy of their homes by voices speaking out of trumpets. By newspaper and by leaflet they had been urged to perceive that they alone could save the country. They had been asked to vote early, and only just not asked to vote often. To their attention had been brought the startling dilemma that whichever way they voted the country would be saved. They had been exhorted by people who knew everything, it seemed, except how it would be saved. Neither the candidates nor their ladies, neither the mysterious disembodied voices, nor the still more incorporeal print, had made the faintest attempt to tell them that. It was better not; for, in the first place, no one knew. And, in the second place, why mention the particular when the general would serve? Why draw attention, even, to the fact that the general is made up of the particular; or to the political certainty that promise is never performance? Better, far better, to make large loose assertion, abuse the other side, and call the electors the sanest and soundest body of people in the world.

Dinny was not canvassing. She was 'no good at it,' she said; and, perhaps, secretly she perceived the peculiarity of the custom. Clare, if she noticed any irony about the business, was too anxious to be doing something to abstain. She was greatly helped by the way everybody took it. They had always been 'canvassed,' and they always would be. It was a harmless enough diversion to their ears, rather like the buzzing of gnats that did not bite. As to their votes, they would record them for quite other reasons – because their fathers had voted this or that before them, because of something connected with their occupation, because of their landlords, their churches, or their trades unions; because they wanted a change, while not expecting anything much from it; and not a few because of their common sense.

Clare, dreading questions, pattered as little as possible and came quickly to their babies or their health. She generally ended by asking what time they would like to be fetched. Noting the hour in a little book, she would come out not much the wiser. Being a Charwell – that is to say, no 'foreigner' – she was taken as a matter of course; and though not, like Dinny, personally known to them all, she was part of an institution, Condaford without Charwells being still almost inconceivable.

She was driving back from this dutiful pastime towards the Grange about four o'clock on the Saturday before the election, when a voice from an overtaking two-seater called her name, and she saw young Tony Croom.

'What on earth are you doing here, Tony?'

'I couldn't go any longer without a glimpse of you.'

'But, my dear boy, to come down here is too terribly pointed.'

'I know, but I've seen you.'

'You weren't going to call, were you?'

'If I didn't see you otherwise. Clare, you look so lovely!'

'That, if true, is not a reason for queering my pitch at home.'

'The last thing I want to do; but I've got to see you now and then, otherwise I shall go batty.'

His face was so earnest and his voice so moved, that Clare

felt for the first time stirred in that hackneyed region, the heart.

'That's bad,' she said; 'because I've got to find my feet, and I can't have complications.'

'Let me kiss you just once. Then I should go back happy.'

Still more stirred, Clare thrust forward her cheek.

'Well, quick!' she said.

He glued his lips to her cheek, but when he tried to reach her lips she drew back.

'No. Now Tony, you must go. If you're to see me, it must be in Town. But what is the good of seeing me? It'll only make us unhappy.'

'Bless you for that "us".'

Clare's brown eyes smiled; their colour was like that of a glass of Malaga wine held up to the light.

'Have you found a job?'

'There are none.'

'It'll be better when the election's over. *I'm* thinking of trying to get with a milliner.'

'You!'

'I must do something. My people here are as hard pressed as everybody else. Now, Tony, you said you'd go.'

'Promise to let me know the first day you come up.'

Clare nodded, and re-started her engine. As the car slid forward gently, she turned her face and gave him another smile.

He continued to stand with his hands to his head till the car rounded a bend and she was gone.

Turning the car into the stable yard, she was thinking 'Poor boy!' and feeling the better for it. Whatever her position in the eyes of the law, or according to morality, a young and pretty woman breathes more easily when inhaling the incense of devotion. She may have strict intentions, but she has also a sense of what is due to her, and a dislike of waste. Clare looked the prettier and felt the happier all that evening. But the night was ridden by the moon; nearly full, it soared up in front of her window, discouraging sleep. She got up and parted the curtains. Huddling into her fur coat, she stood at the window. There was evidently a frost, and a ground mist stretched like fleece over the fields. The tall elms, ragged-edged, seemed to be sailing slowly along over the white vapour. The earth out there was un-

known by her, as if it had dropped from that moon. She
shivered. It might be beautiful, but it was cold, uncanny; a
frozen glamour. She thought of the nights in the Red Sea, when
she lay with bedclothes thrown off, and the very moon seemed
hot. On board that ship people had 'talked' about her and Tony
– she had seen many signs of it, and hadn't cared. Why should
she? He had not even kissed her all those days. Not even the
evening he came to her state-room and she had shown him
photographs, and they had talked. A nice boy, modest and a
gentleman! And if he was in love, now, she couldn't help it –
she hadn't tried to 'vamp' him. As to what would happen, life
always tripped one up, it seemed, whatever one did! Things
must take care of themselves. To make resolutions, plans, lay
down what was called 'a line of conduct', was not the slightest
use! She had tried that with Jerry. She shivered, then laughed,
then went rigid with a sort of fury. No! If Tony expected her
to rush into his arms he was very much mistaken. Sensual love!
She knew it inside out. No, thank you! As that moonlight, now,
she was cold! Impossible to speak of it even to her Mother,
whatever she and Dad might be thinking.

Dinny must have told them something, for they had been
most awfully decent. But even Dinny didn't know. Nobody
should ever know! If only she had money it wouldn't matter.
'Ruined life', of course, and all that, was just old-fashioned
tosh. Life could always be amusing if one made it so. She was
not going to skulk and mope. Far from that! But money she
must somehow make. She shivered even in her fur coat. The
moonlight seemed to creep into one's bones. These old houses
– no central heating, because they couldn't afford to put it in!
The moment the election was over she would go up to London
and scout round. Fleur might know of something. If there was
no future in hats, one might get a political secretaryship. She
could type, she knew French well, people could read her hand-
writing. She could drive a car with anybody, or school a horse.
She knew all about country house life, manners, and precedence.
There must be lots of Members who wanted somebody like her,
who could tell them how to dress, and how to decline this and
that without anybody minding, and generally do their cross-
word puzzles for them. She'd had quite a lot of experience with

27

dogs, and some with flowers, especially the arrangement of them in bowls and vases. And if it were a question of knowing anything about politics, she could soon mug that up. So, in that illusory cold moonshine, Clare could not see how they could fail to need her. With a salary and her own two hundred a year she could get along quite well! The moon, behind an elm tree now, no longer had its devastating impersonality, but rather an air of bright intrigue, peeping through those still thick boughs with a conspiring eye. She hugged herself, danced a few steps to warm her feet, and slipped back into her bed. . . .

Young Croom, in his borrowed two-seater, had returned to Town at an unobtrusive sixty miles an hour. His first kiss on Clare's cold but glowing cheek had given him slight delirium. It was an immense step forward. He was not a vicious young man. That Clare was married was to him no advantage. But whether, if she had not been married, his feelings towards her would have been of quite the same brand, was a question he left un-examined. The subtle difference which creeps into the charm of a woman who has known physical love, and the sting which the knowledge of that implants in a man's senses – such is food for a psychologist rather than for a straightforward young man really in love for the first time. He wanted her as his wife if possible; if that were not possible, in any other way that was. He had been in Ceylon three years, hard-worked, seeing few white women, and none that he had cared for. His passion had, hitherto, been for polo, and his meeting with Clare had come just as he had lost both job and polo. Clare filled for him a yawning gap. As with Clare, so with him in the matter of money, only more so.

He had some two hundred pounds saved, and would then be 'bang up against it' unless he got a job. Having returned the two-seater to his friend's garage, he considered where he could dine most cheaply, and decided on his club. He was practically living there, except for a bedroom in Ryder Street, where he slept and breakfasted on tea and boiled eggs. A simple room it was, on the ground floor, with a bed and a dress cupboard, look-ing out on the tall back of another building, the sort of room that his father, coming on the Town in the 'nineties, had slept and breakfasted in for half the money.

On Saturday nights the Coffee House was deserted, save for a certain number of 'old buffers' accustomed to week-ending in St James's Street. Young Croom ordered the three-course dinner and ate it to the last crumb. He drank Bass, and went down to the smoking-room for a pipe. About to sink into an armchair, he noticed standing before the fire a tallish thin man with twisting dark eyebrows and a little white moustache, who was examining him through a tortoiseshell-rimmed monocle. Acting on the impulse of a lover craving connexion with his lady, he said:

'Excuse me, sir, but aren't you Sir Lawrence Mont?'

'That has been my lifelong conviction.'

Young Croom smiled.

'Then, sir, I met your niece, Lady Corven, coming home from Ceylon. She said you were a member here. My name's Croom.'

'Ah!' said Sir Lawrence, dropping his eyeglass: 'I probably knew your father – he was always here, before the war.'

'Yes, he put me down at birth. I believe I'm about the youngest in the Club.'

Sir Lawrence nodded. 'So you met Clare. How was she?'

'All right, I think, sir.'

'Let's sit down and talk about Ceylon. Cigar?'

'Thank you, sir, I have my pipe.'

'Coffee, anyway. Waiter, two coffees. My wife is down at Condaford staying with Clare's people. An attractive young woman.'

Noting those dark eyes, rather like a snipe's, fixed on him, young Croom regretted his impulse. He had gone red, but he said bravely:

'Yes, sir, I thought her delightful.'

'Do you know Corven?'

'No,' said young Croom shortly.

'Clever fellow. Did you like Ceylon?'

'Oh! yes. But it's given me up.'

'Not going back?'

'Afraid not.'

'It's a long time since I was there. India has rather smothered it. Been in India?'

'No, sir.'

'Difficult to know how far the people of India really want to cut the painter. Seventy per cent peasants! Peasants want stable conditions and a quiet life. I remember in Egypt before the war there was a strong nationalist agitation, but the fellaheen were all for Kitchener and stable British rule. We took Kitchener away and gave them unstable conditions in the war, and so they went on the other tack. What were you doing in Ceylon?'

'Running a tea plantation. But they took up economy, amalgamated three plantations, and I wasn't wanted any more. Do you think there's going to be a recovery, sir? I can't understand economics.'

'Nobody can. There are dozens of causes of the present state of things, and people are always trying to tie it to one. Take England: There's the knock-out of Russian trade, the comparative independence of European countries, the great shrinkage of Indian and Chinese trade; the higher standard of British living since the war; the increase of national expenditure from two hundred-odd millions to eight hundred millions, which means nearly six hundred millions a year less to employ labour with. When they talk of over-production being the cause, it certainly doesn't apply to us. We haven't produced so little for a long time past. Then there's dumping, and shocking bad organization, and bad marketing of what little food we produce. And there's our habit of thinking it'll be "all right on the night," and general spoiled-child attitude. Well, those are all special English causes, except that the too high standard of living and the spoiled-child attitude are American too.'

'And the other American causes, sir?'

'The Americans certainly have over-produced and over-speculated. And they've been living so high that they've mortgaged their future – instalment system and all that. Then they're sitting on gold, and gold doesn't hatch out. And, more than all, they don't realize yet that the money they lent to Europe during the war was practically money they'd made out of the war. When they agree to general cancellation of debts they'll be agreeing to general recovery, including their own.'

'But will they ever agree?'

'You never know what the Americans will do, they're looser-jointed than we of the old world. They're capable of the big thing, even in their own interests. Are you out of a job?'

'Very much so.'

'What's your record?'

'I was at Wellington and at Cambridge for two years. Then this tea thing came along, and I took it like a bird.'

'What age are you?'

'Twenty-six.'

'Any notion of what you want to do?'

Young Croom sat forward.

'Really, sir, I'd have a shot at anything. But I'm pretty good with horses. I thought possibly I might get into a training stable; or with a breeder; or get a riding mastership.'

'Quite an idea. It's queer about the horse – he's coming in as he goes out. I'll talk to my cousin Jack Muskham – he breeds bloodstock. And he's got a bee in his bonnet about the re-introduction of Arab blood into the English thoroughbred. In fact he's got some Arab mares coming over. Just possibly he might want someone.'

Young Croom flushed and smiled.

'That would be frightfully kind of you, sir. It sounds ideal. I've had Arab polo ponies.'

'Well,' murmured Sir Lawrence thoughtfully, 'I don't know that anything excites my sympathy more than a man who really wants a job and can't find one. We must get this election over first, though. Unless the socialists are routed horse-breeders will have to turn their stock into potted meat. Imagine having the dam of a Derby winner between brown bread and butter for your tea – real "Gentleman's Relish!"'

He got up.

'I'll say good-night, now. My cigar will just last me home.'

Young Croom rose too, and remained standing till that spare and active figure had vanished.

'Frightfully nice old boy!' he thought, and in the depths of his armchair he resigned himself to hope and to Clare's face wreathed by the fumes of his pipe.

Chapter Five

◄-◄-►►

O N that cold and misty evening, which all the newspapers had agreed was to 'make history,' the Charwells sat in the drawing-room at Condaford round the portable wireless, a present from Fleur. Would the voice breathe o'er Eden, or would it be the striking of Fate's clock? Not one of those five but was solemnly convinced that the future of Great Britain hung in the balance; convinced, too, that their conviction was detached from class or party. Patriotism divorced from thought of vested interest governed, as they supposed, their mood. And if they made a mistake in so thinking, quite a number of other Britons were making it too. Across Dinny's mind, indeed, did flit the thought: 'Does anyone know what will save the country and what won't?' But, even by her, time and tide, incalculably rolling, swaying and moulding the lives of nations, was ungauged. Newspapers and politicians had done their work and stamped the moment for her as a turning point. In a sea-green dress, she sat, close to the 'present from Fleur,' waiting to turn it on at ten o'clock, and regulate its stridency. Aunt Em was working at a new piece of French Tapestry, her slight aquililinity emphasized by tortoise-shell spectacles. The General nervously turned and re-turned *The Times* and kept taking out his watch. Lady Charwell sat still and a little forward, like a child in Sunday School before she has become convinced that she is going to be bored. And Clare lay on the sofa, with the dog Foch on her feet.

'Time, Dinny,' said the General; 'turn the thing on.'

Dinny fingered a screw, and 'the thing' burst into music.

' "Rings on our fingers and bells on our toes," ' she murmured, ' "We have got music wherever we goes." '

The music stopped, and the voice spoke:

'This is the first election result: Hornsey ... Conservative, no change.'

The General added: 'H'm!' and the music began again.

Aunt Em, looking at the portable, said: 'Coax it, Dinny. That burrin'!'

32

'It always has that, Auntie.'

'Blore does something to ours with a penny. Where is Hornsey – Isle of Wight?'

'Middlesex, darling.'

'Oh! Yes! I was thinkin' of Southsea. There he goes again.'

'These are some more election results. . . . Conservative, gain from Labour. ... Conservative, no change. ... Conservative, gain from Labour.'

The General added: 'Ha!' and the music began again.

'What nice large majorities!' said Lady Mont: 'Gratifyin'!'

Clare got off the sofa and squatted on a footstool against her mother's knees. The General had dropped *The Times*. The 'voice' spoke again:

'... Liberal National, gain from Labour. ... Conservative, no change. ... Conservative, gain from Labour.'

Again and again the music spurted up and died away; and the voice spoke.

Clare's face grew more and more vivid, and above her Lady Charwell's pale and gentle face wore one long smile. From time to time the General said: 'By George!' and 'This is something like!'

And Dinny thought: 'Poor Labour!'

On and on and on the voice breathed o'er Eden.

'Crushin',' said Lady Mont: 'I'm gettin' sleepy.'

'Go to bed, Auntie. I'll put a slip under your door when I come up.'

Lady Charwell, too, got up. When they were gone, Clare went back to the sofa and seemed to fall asleep. The General sat on, hypnotized by the chant of victory. Dinny, with knees crossed and eyes closed, was thinking: 'Will it really make a difference; and, if it does, shall I care? Where is *he*? Listening as we are? Where? Where?' Not so often now, but quite often enough, that sense of groping for Wilfrid returned to her. In all these sixteen months since he left her she found no means of hearing of him. For all she knew he might be dead. Once – only once – she had broken her resolve never to speak of her disaster, and had asked Michael. Compson Grice, his publisher, had, it seemed, received a letter from him written in Bangkok, which said he was well and had begun to write. That was nine months

ago. The veil, so little lifted, had dropped again. Heartache —
well, she was used to it.

'Dad, it's two o'clock. It'll be like this all the time now
Clare's asleep.'

'I'm not,' said Clare.

'You ought to be. I'll let Foch out for his run, and we'll all
go up.'

The General rose.

'Enough's as good as a feast. I suppose we'd better.'

Dinny opened the French window and watched the dog Foch
trotting out in semblance of enthusiasm. It was cold, with a
ground mist, and she shut the window. If she didn't he would
neglect his ritual and with more than the semblance of enthusiasm trot in again. Having kissed her father and Clare, she
turned out the lights and waited in the hall. The wood fire had
almost died. She stood with her foot on the stone hearth, thinking. Clare had spoken of trying to get a secretaryship to some
new Member of Parliament. Judging by the returns that were
coming in, there would be plenty of them. Why not to their
own new member? He had dined with them, and she had sat
next him. A nice man, well read, not bigoted. He even sympathized with Labour, but did not think they knew their way
about as yet. In face he was rather notably what the drunken
youth in the play called: 'A Tory Socialist.' He had opened out
to her and been very frank and pleasant. An attractive man,
with his crisp dark hair, brown complexion, little dark moustache and rather high soft voice; a good sort, energetic and
upright-looking. But probably he already had a secretary. However, if Clare was in earnest, one could ask. She crossed the hall
to the garden door. There was a seat in the porch outside, and
under it Foch would be crouched, waiting to be let in. Sure
enough, he emerged, fluttering his tail, and padded towards the
dogs' communal water-bowl. How cold and silent! Nothing on
the road; even the owls quiet; the garden and the fields frozen,
moonlit, still, away up to that long line of covert! England
silvered and indifferent to her fate, disbelieving in the Voice o'er
Eden; old and permanent and beautiful, even though the pound
had gone off gold. Dinny gazed at the unfeverish night. Men
and their policies — how little they mattered, how soon they

passed, a dissolving dew on the crystal immensity of God's toy! How queer – the passionate intensity of one's heart, and the incalculable cold callousness of Time and Space! To join, to reconcile? . . .

She shivered and shut the door.

At breakfast the next morning she said to Clare:

'Shall we strike while the iron's hot, and go and see Mr Dornford?'

'Why?'

'In case he wants a secretary, now he's in.'

'Oh! Is he in?'

'Very much so.' Dinny read the figures. The usual rather formidable Liberal opposition had been replaced by a mere five thousand Labour votes.

'The word "national" is winning this election,' said Clare. 'Where I went canvassing in the town they were all Liberals. I just used the word "national," and they fell.'

Hearing that the new Member would be at his headquarters all the morning, the sisters started about eleven o'clock. There was so much coming and going round the doors that they did not like to enter.

'I do hate asking for things,' said Clare.

Dinny, who hated it quite as much, answered:

'Wait here and I'll just go in and congratulate him. I might have a chance of putting in a word. He's seen you, of course.'

'Oh! yes, he's seen me all right.'

Eustace Dornford, K.C., new member elect, was sitting in a room that seemed all open doors, running his eye over the lists his agent was putting on the table before him. From one of those doors Dinny could see his riding boots under the table, and his bowler hat, gloves and riding whip upon it. Now that she was nearly in the presence it seemed impossible to intrude at such a moment, and she was just slipping away when he looked up.

'Excuse me a moment, Minns. Miss Cherrell!'

She stopped and turned. He was smiling and looking pleased.

'Anything I can do for you?'

She put out her hand.

'I'm awfully glad you've won. My sister and I just wanted to congratulate you.'

He squeezed her hand, and Dinny thought: 'Oh! dear! this is the last moment to ask him,' but she said:

'It's perfectly splendid, there's never been such a majority here.'

'And never will be again. That's my luck. Where's your sister?'

'In the car.'

'I'd like to thank her for canvassing.'

'Oh!' said Dinny, 'she enjoyed it;' and, suddenly feeling that it was now or never, added: 'She's at a loose end, you know, badly wants something to do. Mr Dornford, you don't think – this is too bad – but I suppose she wouldn't be of any use to you as a secretary, would she? There, it's out! She does know the county pretty well; she can type, and speak French, and German a little, if that's any use.' It had come with a rush, and she stood looking at him ruefully. But his eager expression had not changed.

'Let's go and see her,' he said.

Dinny thought: 'Gracious! I hope he hasn't fallen in love with her!' and she glanced at him sidelong. Still smiling, his face looked shrewd now. Clare was standing beside the car. 'I wish,' thought Dinny, 'I had her coolness.' Then she stood still and watched. All this triumphal business, these people coming and going, those two talking so readily and quickly; the clear and sparkling morning! He came back to her.

'Thank you most awfully, Miss Cherrell. It'll do admirably. I did want someone, and your sister is very modest.'

'I thought you'd never forgive me for asking at such a moment.'

'Always delighted for you to ask anything at any moment. I must go back now, but I'll hope to see you again very soon.'

Gazing after him as he re-entered the building, she thought: 'He has very nicely cut riding breeches!' And she got into the car.

'Dinny,' said Clare, with a laugh, 'he's in love with you.'

'What!'

'I asked for two hundred, and he made it two hundred and fifty at once. How did you do it in one evening?'

'I didn't. It's you he's in love with, I'm afraid.'

'No, no, my dear. I have eyes, and I know it's you; just as you knew that Tony Croom was in love with me.'

'I could see that.'

'And I could see this.'

Dinny said quietly: 'That's absurd. When do you begin?'

'He's going back to Town today. He lives in the Temple – Harcourt Buildings. I shall go up this afternoon and start in the day after tomorrow.'

'Where shall you live?'

'I think I shall take an unfurnished room or a small studio, and decorate and furnish it gradually myself. It'll be fun.'

'Aunt Em is going back this afternoon. She would put you up till you find it.'

'Well,' said Clare, pondering; 'perhaps.'

Just before they reached home Dinny said:

'What about Ceylon, Clare? Have you thought any more?'

'What's the good of thinking? I suppose he'll do something, but I don't know what, and I don't care.'

'Haven't you had a letter?'

'No.'

'Well, darling, be careful.'

Clare shrugged: 'Oh! I'll be careful.'

'Could he get leave if he wanted?'

'I expect so.'

'You'll keep in touch with me, won't you?'

Clare leaned sideways from the wheel and gave her cheek a kiss.

Chapter Six

＜‹‑›＞

THREE days after their meeting at the Coffee House, young Croom received a letter from Sir Lawrence Mont, saying that his cousin Muskham was not expecting the Arab mares till the spring. In the meantime he would make a note of Mr Croom and a point of seeing him soon. Did Mr Croom know any vernacular Arabic?

'No,' thought young Croom, 'but I know Stapylton.'

Stapylton, of the Lancers, who had been his senior at Wellington, was home from India on leave. A noted polo player, he would be sure to know the horse jargon of the East; but, having broken his thigh-bone schooling a steeplechaser, he would keep; the business of finding an immediate 'job of work' would not. Young Croom continued his researches. Everyone said: 'Wait till the election's over!'

On the morning after the election, therefore, he issued from Ryder Street with the greater expectation, and, on the evening after, returned to the Coffee House, with the less, thinking: 'I might just as well have gone to Newmarket and seen the Cambridgeshire.'

The porter handed him a note, and his heart began to thump. Seeking a corner, he read:

DEAR TONY—

I have got the job of secretary to our new member, Eustace Dornford, who's a K.C. in the Temple. So I've come up to Town. Till I find a tent of my own, I shall be at my Aunt Lady Mont's in Mount Street. I hope you've been as lucky. I promised to let you know when I came up; but I adjure you to sense and not sensibility, and to due regard for pride and prejudice.

Your shipmate and well-wisher,
CLARE CORVEN

'The darling!' he thought. 'What luck!' He read the note again, placed it beneath the cigarette case in his left-hand waistcoat pocket, and went into the smoking-room. There, on a sheet of paper stamped with the Club's immemorial design, he poured out an ingenuous heart:

DARLING CLARE—

Your note has perked me up no end. That you will be in Town is magnificent news. Your uncle has been very kind to me, and I shall simply have to call and thank him. So do look out for me about six o'clock tomorrow. I spend all my time hunting a job, and am beginning to realize what it means to poor devils to be turned down day after day. When my pouch is empty, and that's not far away, it'll be even worse for me. No dole for this child, unfortunately. I hope the pundit you're going to take in hand is a decent sort. I always think of M.P.'s as a bit on the wooden side. And somehow I can't see you among Bills and petitions and letters about public-house licences and so forth. However, I think you're splendid to want to be independent. What a thumping majority! If they can't do things with that behind them, they can't do things at all. It's quite impossible for me not to be in love with you, you know, and to long to be with you all day and all night, too. But I'm going to be as good as I can, because the very last thing I want is to cause you uneasiness of any sort. I think of you all the time, even when I'm searching the marble countenance of some fish-faced blighter to see if my piteous tale is weakening his judgement. The fact is I love you terribly. Tomorrow, Thursday, about six!

Good night, dear and lovely one,

YOUR TONY

Having looked up Sir Lawrence's number in Mount Street, he addressed the note, licked the envelope with passion, and went out to post it himself. Then, suddenly, he did not feel inclined to return to the Coffee House. The place had a grudge against his state of mind. Clubs were so damned male, and their whole attitude to women so after-dinnerish – half contempt, half lechery! Funk-holes they were, anyway, full of comfort, secured against women, immune from writs; and men all had the same armchair look once they got inside. The Coffee House, too, about the oldest of all clubs, was stuffed with regular buffers, men you couldn't imagine outside a club. 'No!' he thought. 'I'll have a chop somewhere, and go to that thing at Drury Lane.'

He got a seat rather far back in the upper boxes, but, his sight being very good, he saw quite well. He was soon absorbed. He had been out of England long enough to have some sentiment about her. This pictorial pageant of her history for the last thirty years moved him more than he would have confessed to anyone sitting beside him. Boer war, death of the Queen, sinking of the *Titanic*, Great War, Armistice, health to 1931 – if anyone asked him afterwards, he would probably say: 'Marvellous! but gave me the pip rather!' While sitting there it seemed more than the 'pip'; the heartache of a lover, who wants happiness with his mistress and cannot reach it; the feeling of one who tries to stand upright and firm and is for ever being swayed this way and that. The last words rang in his ears as he went out: 'Greatness and dignity and peace.' Moving and damned ironical! He took a cigarette from his case and lighted it. The night was dry and he walked, threading his way through the streams of traffic, with the melancholy howling of street-singers in his ears. Skysigns and garbage! People rolling home in their cars, and homeless night-birds! 'Greatness and dignity and peace!'

'I must absolutely have a drink,' he thought. The Club seemed possible again now, even inviting, and he made towards it. '"Farewell, Piccadilly! Good-bye, Leicester Square!"' Marvellous that scene, where those Tommies marched up in a spiral through the dark mist, whistling; while in the lighted front of the stage three painted girls rattled out: '"We don't want to lose you, but we think you ought to go."' And from the boxes on the stage at the sides people looked down and clapped! The whole thing there! The gaiety on those girls' painted faces getting more and more put-on and heart-breaking! He must go again with Clare! Would it move her? And suddenly he perceived that he didn't know. What did one know about anyone, even the woman one loved? His cigarette was scorching his lip, and he spat out the butt. That scene with the honeymooning couple leaning over the side of the *Titanic*, everything before them, and nothing before them but the cold deep sea! Did that couple know anything except that they desired each other? Life was damned queer, when you thought about it! He turned up the Coffee House steps, feeling as if he had lived long since he went down them....

It was just six o'clock when he rang the bell at Mount Street on the following day.

A butler, with slightly raised eyebrows, opened the door.

'Is Sir Lawrence Mont at home?'

'No, sir. Lady Mont is in, sir.'

'I'm afraid I don't know Lady Mont. I wonder if I could see Lady Corven for a moment?'

One of the butler's eyebrows rose still higher. 'Ah!' he seemed to be thinking.

'If you'll give me your name, sir.'

Young Croom produced a card.

' "Mr James Bernard Croom," ' chanted the butler.

'Mr Tony Croom, tell her, please.'

'Quite! If you'll wait in here a moment. Oh! here is Lady Corven.'

A voice from the stairs said:

'Tony? What punctuality! Come up and meet my Aunt.'

She was leaning over the stair-rail, and the butler had disappeared.

'Put your hand down. How can you go about without a coat? I shiver all the time.'

Young Croom came close below her.

'Darling!' he murmured.

She placed one finger to her lips, then stretched it down to him, so that he could just reach it with his own.

'Come along!' She had opened a door when he reached the top, and was saying: 'This is a shipmate, Aunt Em. He's come to see Uncle Lawrence. Mr Croom, my Aunt, Lady Mont.'

Young Croom was aware of a presence slightly swaying towards him. A voice said: 'Ah! Ships! Of course! How d'you do?'

Young Croom, aware that he had been 'placed', saw Clare regarding him with a slightly mocking smile. If only they could be alone five minutes, he would kiss that smile off her face! He would –!

'Tell me about Ceylon, Mr Craven.'

'Croom, Auntie. Tony Croom. Better call him Tony. It isn't his name, but everybody does.'

'Tony! Always heroes. I don't know why.'

'This Tony is quite ordinary.'

'Ceylon. Did you know her there, Mr – Tony?'

'No. We only met on the ship.'

'Ah! Lawrence and I used to sleep on deck. That was in the "naughty nineties". The river here used to be full of punts, I remember.'

'It still is, Aunt Em.'

Young Croom had a sudden vision of Clare and himself in a punt up a quiet backwater. He roused himself and said:

'I went to *Cavalcade* last night. Great!'

'Ah!' said Lady Mont. 'That reminds me.' She left the room.

Young Croom sprang up.

'Tony! Behave!'

'But surely that's what she went for!'

'Aunt Em is extraordinarily kind, and I'm not going to abuse her kindness.'

'But, Clare, you don't know what –'

'Yes, I do. Sit down again.'

Young Croom obeyed.

'Now listen, Tony! I've had enough physiology to last me a long time. If you and I are going to be pals, it's got to be platonic.'

'Oh, God!' said young Croom.

'But it's got to; or else – we simply aren't going to see each other.'

Young Croom sat very still with his eyes fixed on hers, and there passed through her the thought: 'It's going to torture him. He looks too nice for that. I don't believe we ought to see each other.'

'Look!' she said, gently, 'you want to help me, don't you? There's lots of time, you know. Some day – perhaps.'

Young Croom grasped the arms of his chair. His eyes had a look of pain.

'Very well,' he said slowly, 'anything so long as I can see you. I'll wait till it means something more than physiology to you.'

Clare sat examining the *glacé* toe of her slowly wiggling shoe; suddenly she looked straight into his brooding eyes.

'If,' she said, 'I had not been married, you would wait cheerfully and it wouldn't hurt you. Think of me like that.'

'Unfortunately I can't. Who could?'

'I see, I am fruit, not blossom – tainted by physiology.'

'Don't! Oh! Clare, I will be anything you want to you. And if I'm not always as cheery as a bird, forgive me.'

She looked at him through her eyelashes and said: 'Good!'

Then came silence, during which she was conscious that he was fixing her in his mind from her shingled dark head to her *glacé* kid toe. She had not lived with Jerry Corven without having been made conscious of every detail of her body. She could not help its grace or its provocation. She did not want to torture him, but she could not find it unpleasant that she did. Queer how one could be sorry and yet pleased, and, withal, sceptical and a little bitter. Give yourself, and after a few months how much would he want you! She said abruptly:

'Well, I've found rooms – a quaint little hole – used to be an antique shop, in a disused mews.'

He said eagerly: 'Sounds jolly. When are you going in?'

'Next week.'

'Can I help?'

'If you can distemper walls.'

'Rather! I did all my bungalow in Ceylon, two or three times over.'

'We should have to work in the evenings, because of my job.'

'What about your boss? Is he decent?'

'Very, and in love with my sister. At least, I think so.'

'Oh!' said young Croom dubiously.

Clare smiled. He was so obviously thinking: 'Could a man be that when he sees *you* every day?'

'When can I come first?'

'Tomorrow evening, if you like. It's 2, Melton Mews, off Malmesbury Square. I'll get the stuff in the morning, and we'll begin upstairs. Say six-thirty.'

'Splendid!'

'Only, Tony – no importunities. "Life is real, life is earnest".'

Grinning ruefully, he put his hand on his heart.

'And you must go now. I'll take you down and see if my Uncle's come in.'

Young Croom stood up.

'What is happening about Ceylon?' he said, abruptly. 'Are you being worried?'

Clare shrugged. 'Nothing is happening so far.'

'That can't possibly last. Have you thought things out?'

'Thinking won't help me. It's quite likely he'll do nothing.'

'I can't bear your being –' he stopped.

'Come along,' said Clare, and led the way downstairs.

'I don't think I'll try to see your Uncle,' said young Croom.

'Tomorrow at half-past six, then.' He raised her hand to his lips, and marched to the door. There he turned. She was standing with her head a little on one side, smiling. He went out, distracted.

A young man, suddenly awakened amid the doves of Cytherea, conscious for the first time of the mysterious magnetism which radiates from what the vulgar call 'a grass widow', and withheld from her by scruples or convention, is to be pitied. He has not sought his fate. It comes on him by stealth, bereaving him ruthlessly of all other interest in life. It is an obsession replacing normal tastes with a rapturous aching. Maxims such as 'Thou shalt not commit adultery', 'Thou shalt not covet thy neighbour's wife', 'Blessed are the pure in heart', become singularly academic. Young Croom had been brought up to the tinkling of the school bell: 'Play the game!' He now perceived its strange inadequacy. What *was* the game? Here was she, young and lovely, fleeing from a partner seventeen years older than herself, because he was a brute; she hadn't said so, but of course he must be! Here was himself, desperately in love with her, and liked by her – not in the same way, but still as much as could be expected! And nothing to come of it but tea together! There was a kind of sacrilege in such waste.

Thus preoccupied he passed a man of middle height and alert bearing, whose rather cat-like eyes and thin lips were set into a brown face with the claws of many little wrinkles, and who turned to look after him with a slight contraction of the mouth which might have been a smile.

Chapter Seven

→←→←

AFTER young Croom had gone Clare stood for a moment in the hall recollecting the last time she had gone out of that front door, in a fawn-coloured suit and a little brown hat, between rows of people saying: 'Good luck!' and 'Good-bye, darling!' and 'Give my love to Paris!' Eighteen months ago, and so much in between! Her lip curled, and she went into her Uncle's study.

'Oh! Uncle Lawrence, you *are* in! Tony Croom's been here to see you.'

'That rather pleasant young man without occupation?'

'Yes. He wanted to thank you.'

'For nothing, I'm afraid.' And Sir Lawrence's quick dark eyes, like a snipe's or woodcock's, roved sceptically over his pretty niece. She was not, like Dinny, a special favourite, but she was undoubtedly attractive. It was early days to have messed up her marriage; Em had told him and said that it wasn't to be mentioned. Well, Jerry Corven! People had always shrugged and hinted. Too bad! But no real business of his.

A subdued voice from the door said:

'Sir Gerald Corven has called, Sir Lawrence.'

Involuntarily Sir Lawrence put his finger to his lips. The butler subdued his voice still further.

'I put him in the little room and said I would see if Lady Corven was in.'

Sir Lawrence noted Clare's hands hard pressed down on the back of the chair behind which she was standing.

'*Are* you in, Clare?'

She did not answer, but her face was hard and pale as stone.

'A minute, Blore. Come back when I ring.'

The butler withdrew.

'Now, my dear?'

'He must have taken the next boat. Uncle, I don't want to see him.'

'If we only say you're out, he'll probably come again.'

Clare threw back her head. 'Well, I'll see him!'

Sir Lawrence felt a little thrill.

'If you'd tell me what to say, I'd see him for you.'

'Thank you, Uncle, but I don't see why you should do my dirty work.'

Sir Lawrence thought: 'Thank God!'

'I'll be handy in case you want me. Good luck, my dear!' And he went out.

Clare moved over to the fire; she wanted the bell within reach. She had the feeling, well known to her, of settling herself in the saddle for a formidable jump. 'He shan't touch me, anyway,' she thought. She heard Blore's voice say:

'Sir Gerald Corven, my lady.' Quaint! Announcing a husband to his wife! But staff knew everything!

Without looking she saw perfectly well where he was standing. A surge of shamed anger stained her cheeks. He had fascinated her; he had used her as every kind of plaything. He had — !

His voice, cuttingly controlled, said:

'Well, my dear, you were very sudden.' Neat and trim, as ever, and like a cat, with that thin-lipped smile and those daring despoiling eyes!

'What do you want?'

'Only yourself.'

'You can't have me.'

'Absurd!'

He made the quickest kind of movement and seized her in his arms. Clare bent her head back and put her finger on the bell.

'Move back, or I ring!' and she put her other hand between his face and hers. 'Stand over there and I'll talk to you, otherwise you must go.'

'Very well! But it's ridiculous.'

'Oh! Do you think I should have gone if I hadn't been in earnest?'

'I thought you were just riled, and I don't wonder. I'm sorry.'

'It's no good discussing what happened. I know you, and I'm not coming back to you.'

'My dear, you have my apology, and I give you my word against anything of the sort again.'

'How good of you!'

'It was only an experiment. Some women adore it, if not at the time.'

'You are a beast.'

'And beauty married me. Come, Clare, don't be silly, and make us a laughing-stock! You can fix your own conditions.'

'And trust you to keep them! Besides, that's not my idea of a life. I'm only twenty-four.'

The smile left his lips.

'I see. I noticed a young man come out of this house. Name and estate?'

'Tony Croom. Well?'

He walked over to the window, and after a moment's contemplation of the street, turned and said:

'You have the misfortune to be my wife.'

'So I was thinking.'

'Quite seriously, Clare, come back to me.'

'Quite seriously, no.'

'I have an official position, and I can't play about with it. Look at me!' He came closer. 'I may be all you think me, but I'm neither a humbug nor old-fashioned. I don't trade on my position, or on the sanctity of marriage, or any of that stuff. But they still pay attention to that sort of thing in the Service, and I can't afford to let you divorce me.'

'I didn't expect it.'

'What then?'

'I know nothing except that I'm not coming back.'

'Just because of –?'

'And a great deal else.' The cat-like smile had come back and prevented her from reading what he was thinking.

'Do you want me to divorce you?'

Clare shrugged. 'You have no reason.'

'So you would naturally say.'

'And mean.'

'Now look here, Clare, this is all absurd, and quite unworthy of anyone with your sense and knowledge of things. You can't be a perpetual grass widow. You didn't dislike the life out there.'

'There are some things that can't be done to me, and you have done them.'

'I've said that they shan't be done again.'

'And I've said that I can't trust you.'

'This is going round the mulberry bush. Are you going to live on your people?'

'No. I've got a job.'

'Oh! What?'

'Secretary to our new Member.'

'You'll be sick of that in no time.'

'I don't think so.'

He stood staring at her without his smile. For a moment she could read his thoughts, for his face had the expression which preludes sex. Suddenly he said: 'I won't stand for another man having you.'

It was a comfort to have seen for once the bottom of his mind. She did not answer.

'Did you hear me?'

'Yes.'

'I meant it.'

'I could see that.'

'You're a stony little devil.'

'I wish I had been.'

He took a turn up and down the room, and came to a stand dead in front of her.

'Look at me! I'm not going back without you. I'm staying at the Bristol. Be sensible, there's a darling, and come to me there. We'll start again. I'll be ever so nice to you.'

Her control gave way and she cried out: 'Oh, for God's sake, understand! You killed all the feeling I had for you.'

His eyes dilated and then narrowed, his lips became a line. He looked like a horse-breaker.

'And understand *me*,' he said, very low, 'you either come back to me or I divorce you. I won't leave you here, to kick your heels.'

'I'm sure you'll have the approval of every judicious husband.'

The smile reappeared on his lips.

'For that,' he said, 'I'm going to have a kiss.' And before she could stop him he had fastened his lips on hers. She tore herself away and pressed the bell. He went quickly to the door.

'*Au revoir!*' he said, and went out.

Clare wiped her lips. She felt bewildered and exhausted, and quite ignorant whether to him or to her the day had gone.

She stood leaning her forehead on her hands over the fire, and became aware that Sir Lawrence had come back and was considerately saying nothing.

'Awfully sorry, Uncle; I shall be in my digs next week.'

'Have a cigarette, my dear.'

Clare took the cigarette, and inhaled its comfort. Her uncle had seated himself and she was conscious of the quizzical expression of his eyebrows.

'Conference had its usual success?'

Clare nodded.

'The elusive formula. The fact is, human beings are never satisfied with what they don't want, however cleverly it's put. Is it to be continued in our next?'

'Not so far as I'm concerned.'

'Pity there are always two parties to a conference.'

'Uncle Lawrence,' she said suddenly, 'what is the law of divorce now?'

The baronet uncrossed his long thin legs.

'I've never had any particular truck with it. I believe it's less old-fashioned than it was, but see *Whitaker*.' He reached for the red-backed volume. 'Page 258 – here you are, my dear.'

Clare read in silence, while he gazed at her ruefully. She looked up and said.

'Then, if I want him to divorce me, I've got to commit adultery.'

'That is, I believe, the elegant way they put it. In the best circles, however, the man does the dirty work.'

'Yes, but he won't. He wants me back. Besides, he's got his position to consider.'

'There is that, of course,' said Sir Lawrence, thoughtfully; 'a career in this country is a tender plant.'

Clare closed the *Whitaker*.

'If it weren't for my people,' she said, 'I'd give him cause tomorrow and have done with it.'

'You don't think a better way would be to give partnership another trial?'

Clare shook her head.

'I simply couldn't.'

'That's that, then,' said Sir Lawrence, 'and it's an awkward "that". What does Dinny say?'

'I haven't discussed it with her. She doesn't know he's here.'

'At present, then, you've no one to advise you?'

'No. Dinny knows why I left, that's all.'

'I should doubt if Jerry Corven is a very patient man.'

Clare laughed.

'We're neither of us long-suffering.'

'Do you know where he is staying?'

'At the Bristol.'

'It might,' said Sir Lawrence slowly, 'be worth while to keep an eye on him.'

Clare shivered. 'It's rather degrading; besides, Uncle, I don't want to hurt his career. He's very able, you know.'

Sir Lawrence shrugged. 'To me,' he said, 'and to all your kin, his career is nothing to your good name. How long has he got over here?'

'Not long, I should think.'

'Would you like me to see him, and try to arrange that you go your own ways?'

Clare was silent, and Sir Lawrence, watching her, thought: 'Attractive, but a lot of naughty temper. Any amount of spirit, and no patience at all.' Then she said:

'It was all my fault, nobody wanted me to marry him. I hate to bother you. Besides, he wouldn't consent.'

'You never know,' murmured Sir Lawrence. 'If I get a natural chance, shall I?'

'It would be lovely of you, only –'

'All right, then. In the meantime young men without jobs – are they wise?'

Clare laughed. 'Oh, I've "larned" him. Well, thank you frightfully, Uncle Lawrence. You're a great comfort. I was an awful fool; but Jerry has a sort of power, you know; and I've always liked taking risks. I don't see how I can be my mother's daughter, she hates them; and Dinny only takes them on principle.' She sighed. 'I won't bore you any more now.' And, blowing a kiss, she went out.

Sir Lawrence stayed in his armchair thinking: 'Putting my oar in! A nasty mess, and going to be nastier! Still, at her age something's got to be done. I must talk to Dinny.'

Chapter Eight

❮❮❯❯

FROM Condaford the hot airs of election time had cleared away, and the succeeding atmosphere was crystallized in the General's saying:

'Well, those fellows got their deserts.'

'Doesn't it make you tremble, Dad, to think what *these* fellows' deserts will be if they don't succeed in putting it over now?'

The General smiled.

' "Sufficient unto the day", Dinny. Has Clare settled down?'

'She's in her diggings. Her work so far seems to have been writing letters of thanks to people who did the dirty work at the cross-roads.'

'Cars? Does she like Dornford?'

'She says he's quite amazingly considerate.'

'His father was a good soldier. I was in his brigade in the Boer War for a bit.' He looked at his daughter keenly, and added: 'Any news of Corven?'

'Yes, he's over here.'

'Oh! I wish I wasn't kept so in the dark. Parents have to stand on the mat nowadays, and trust to what they can hear through the keyhole.'

Dinny drew his arm within hers.

'One has to be careful of their feelings. Sensitive plants, aren't you, Dad?'

'Well, it seems to your mother and me an extraordinarily bad look-out. We wish to goodness the thing could be patched up.'

'Not at the expense of Clare's happiness, surely?'

'No,' said the General, dubiously, 'no; but there you are at once in all these matrimonial things. What is and will be her happiness? She doesn't know, and you don't, and I don't. As a rule in trying to get out of a hole you promptly step into another.'

'Therefore don't try? Stay in your hole? That's rather what Labour wanted to do, isn't it?'

'I ought to see him,' said the General, passing over the simile, 'but I can't go blundering in the dark. What do you advise, Dinny?'

'Let the sleeping dog lie until it gets up to bite you.'

'You think it will?'

'I do.'

'Bad!' muttered the General. 'Clare's too young.'

That was Dinny's own perpetual thought. What at the first blush she had said to her sister: 'You must get free,' remained her conviction. But how was she to get free? Knowledge of divorce had been no part of Dinny's education. She knew that the process was by no means uncommon, and she had as little feeling against it as most of her generation. To her father and mother it would probably seen lamentable, doubly so if Clare were divorced instead of divorcing – that would be a stigma on her to be avoided at almost all cost. Since her soul-racking experience with Wilfrid, Dinny had been very little in London. Every street, and above all the park, seemed to remind her of him and the desolation he had left in her. It was now, however, obvious to her that Clare could not be left unsupported in whatever crisis was befalling.

'I think I ought to go up, Dad, and find out what's happening.'

'I wish to God you would. If it's at all possible to patch things up, they ought to be.'

Dinny shook her head.

'I don't believe it is, and I don't believe you'd wish it if Clare had told you what she told me.'

The General stared. 'There it is, you see. In the dark.'

'Yes, dear, but till she tells you herself I can't say more.'

'Then the sooner you go up the better.'

Free from the scent of horse, Melton Mews was somewhat strikingly impregnated with the odour of petrol. This bricked alley had become, indeed, the haunt of cars. To right and to left of her, entering late that afternoon, the doors of garages gaped or confronted her with more or less new paint. A cat or two stole by, and the hinder parts of an overalled chauffeur bending over the carburettor could be seen in one opening; otherwise life was at a discount, and the word 'mews' no longer justified by manure.

No. 2 had the peacock-green door of its former proprietress, whom, with so many other luxury traders, the slump had squeezed out of business. Dinny pulled a chased bell-handle, and a faint tinkle sounded, as from some errant sheep. There was a pause, then a spot of light showed for a moment on a level with her face, was obscured, and the door was opened. Clare, in a jade-green overall, said:

'Come in, my dear. This is the lioness in her den, "the Douglas in her hall!"'

Dinny entered a small, almost empty room hung with the green Japanese silk of the antique dealer and carpeted with matting. A narrow spiral staircase wormed into it at the far corner, and a subdued light radiated from a single green-paper-shaded bulb hanging in the centre. A brass electric heater diffused no heat.

'Nothing doing here so far,' said Clare. 'Come upstairs.'

Dinny made the tortuous ascent, and stepped into a rather smaller sitting-room. It had two curtained windows looking over the mews, a couch with cushions, a little old bureau, three chairs, six Japanese prints, which Clare had evidently just been hanging, an old Persian rug over the matted floor, an almost empty bookcase, and some photographs of the family standing on it. The walls were distempered a pale grey, and a gas fire was burning.

'Fleur gave me the prints and the rug, and Aunt Em stumped up the bureau. I took the other things over.'

'Where do you sleep?'

'On that couch – quite comfy. I've got a little bath-dressing-room next door, with a geyser, and a what-d'ye-call-it, and a cupboard for clothes.'

'Mother told me to ask what you wanted.'

'I could do with our old Primus stove, some blankets and a few knives and forks and spoons, and a small tea-set, if there's one to spare, and any spare books.'

'Right!' said Dinny. 'Now, darling, how are you?'

'Bodily fine, mentally rather worried. I told you he was over.'

'Does he know of this place?'

'Not so far. You and Fleur and Aunt Em – oh! and Tony Croom – are the only people who know of it. My official address is Mount Street. But he's bound to find out if he wants to.'

'You saw him?'

'Yes, and told him I wasn't coming back; and I'm not, Dinny; that's flat, to save breath. Have some tea? I can make it in a brown pot.'

'No, thank you, I had it on the train.' She was sitting on one of the taken-over chairs, in a bottle-green suit that went beautifully with her beech-leaf-coloured hair.

'How jolly you look, sitting there!' said Clare, curling up on the sofa. 'Gasper?'

Dinny was thinking the same about her sister. Graceful creature, one of those people who couldn't look ungraceful; with her dark short hair, and dark, alive eyes, and ivory pale face, and not too brightened lips holding the cigarette, she looked – well, 'desirable'. And, in all the circumstances, the word appeared to Dinny an awkward one. Clare had always been vivid and attractive, but without question marriage had subtly rounded, deepened, and in some sort bedevilled that attraction. She said suddenly:

'Tony Croom, you said?'

'He helped me distemper these walls; in fact, he practically did them, while I did the bathroom – these are better.'

Dinny's eyes took in the walls with apparent interest.

'Quite neat. Mother and Father are nervous, darling.'

'They would be.'

'Naturally, don't you think?'

Clare's brow drew down. Dinny suddenly remembered how strenuously they had once debated the question of whether eyebrows should be plucked. Thank heaven! Clare never had yet.

'I can't help it, Dinny. I don't know what Jerry's going to do.'

'I suppose he can't stay long, without giving up his job?'

'Probably not. But I'm not going to bother. What will be will.'

'How quickly could a divorce be got? I mean against him?'

Clare shook her head, and a dark curl fell over her forehead, reminding Dinny of her as a child.

'To have him watched would be pretty revolting. And I'm not going into court to describe being brutalized. It's only my word against his. Men are safe enough.'

Dinny got up and sat down beside her on the couch.

'I could kill him!' she said.

Clare laughed.

'He wasn't so bad in many ways. Only I simply won't go back. If you've once been skinned, you can't.'

Dinny sat, silent, with closed eyes.

'Tell me,' she said, at last, 'how you stand with Tony Croom.'

'He's on probation. So long as he behaves I like to see him.'

'If,' said Dinny slowly, 'he were known to come here, it would be all that would be wanted, wouldn't it?'

Clare laughed again.

'Quite enough for men of the world, I should think; I believe juries can never withstand being called that. But you see, Dinny, if I begin to look at things from a jury's point of view, I might as well be dead. And, as a matter of fact, I feel very much alive. So I'm going straight ahead. Tony knows I've had enough physiology to last me a long time.'

'Is he in love with you?'

Their eyes, brown and blue, met.

'Yes.'

'Are you in love with him?'

'I like him – quite a lot. Beyond that I've no feeling at present.'

'Don't you think that while Jerry is here –?'

'No. I think I'm safer while he's here than when he goes. If I don't go back with him he'll probably have me watched. That's one thing about him – he does what he says he'll do.'

'I wonder if that's an advantage. Come out and have some dinner.'

Clare stretched herself.

'Can't darling. I'm dining with Tony in a little grubby restaurant suited to our joint means. This living on next to nothing is rather fun.'

Dinny got up and began to straighten the Japanese prints. Clare's recklessness was nothing new. To come the elder sister! To be a wet blanket! Impossible! She said:

'These are good, my dear. Fleur has very jolly things.'

'D'you mind if I change?' said Clare, and vanished into the bathroom.

Left alone with her sister's problem, Dinny had the feeling of helplessness which comes to all but such as constitutionally 'know better'. She went dejectedly to the window and drew aside the curtain. All was darkish and dingy. A car had drawn out of a neighbouring garage and stood waiting for its driver.

'Imagine trying to sell antiques here!' she thought. She saw a man come round the corner close by and stop, looking at the numbers. He moved along the opposite side, then came back and stood still just in front of No. 2. She noted the assurance and strength in that trim over-coated figure.

'Good heavens!' she thought: 'Jerry!' She dropped the curtain and crossed quickly to the bathroom door. As she opened it she heard the desolate tinkling of the sheep-bell installed by the antique dealer.

Clare was standing in her underthings under the single bulb, examining her lips with a hand-glass. Dinny filled the remains of the four feet by two of standing room.

'Clare,' she said, 'it's *him!*'

Clare turned. The gleam of her pale arms, the shimmer of her silk garments, the startled light in her dark eyes, made her even to her sister something of a vision.

'Jerry?'

Dinny nodded.

'Well, I won't see him.' She looked at the watch on her wrist. 'And I'm due at seven. Damn!'

Dinny, who had not the faintest desire that she should keep her rash appointment, said, to her own surprise:

'Shall I go? He must have seen the light.'

'Could you take him away with you, Dinny?'

'I can try.'

'Then do, darling. It'd be ever so sweet of you. I wonder how he's found out. Hell! It's going to be a persecution.'

Dinny stepped back into the sitting-room, turned out the light there, and went down the twisting stair. The sheep-bell tinkled again above her as she went. Crossing that little empty room to the door, she thought: 'It opens inwards, I must pull it to behind me.' Her heart beat fast, she took a deep breath, opened the door swiftly, stepped out and pulled it to with a slam. She was chest to chest with her brother-in-law, and she started back with an admirably impromptu: 'Who is it?'

He raised his hat, and they stood looking at each other.

'Dinny! Is Clare in?'

'Yes; but she can't see anyone.'

'You mean she *won't* see *me*?'

'If you like to put it that way.'

He stood looking intently at her with his daring eyes.

'Another day will do. Which way are you going?'

'To Mount Street.'

'I'll come with you, if I may.'

'Do.'

She moved along at his side, thinking: 'Be careful!' For in his company she did not feel towards him quite as in his absence. As everybody said, Jerry Corven had charm!

'Clare's been giving me bad marks, I suppose?'

'We won't discuss it, please; what ever she feels, I do too.'

'Naturally. Your loyalty is proverbial. But consider, Dinny, how provocative she is.' His eyes smiled round at her. That vision – of neck, and curve, and shimmer, dark hair and eyes! Sex appeal – horrible expression! 'You've got no idea how tantalizing. Besides, I was always an experimentalist.'

Dinny stood still suddenly: 'This is my sister, you know.'

'You're sure, I suppose? It seems queer when one looks at you both.'

Dinny walked on, and did not answer.

'Now listen, Dinny,' began that pleasant voice. 'I'm a sensualist, if you like, but what does it matter? Sex is naturally aberrational. If anyone tells you it isn't, don't believe them. These

things work themselves out, and anyway they're not importan
If Clare comes back to me, in two years' time she won't eve
remember. She likes the sort of life, and I'm not fussy. Marriag
is very much a go-as-you-please affair.'

'You mean that by that time you'll be experimenting wit
someone else?'

He shrugged, looked round at her, and smiled.

'Almost embarrassing this conversation, isn't it? What
want you to grasp is that I'm two men. One, and it's the on
that matters, has his work to do and means to do it. Clare shoul
stick to that man, because he'll give her a life in which she won'
rust; she'll be in the thick of affairs and people who matter
she'll have stir and movement – and she loves both. She'll hav
a certain power, and she's not averse from that. The other ma
– well, he wants his fling, he takes it, if you like; but the wors
is over so far as she's concerned – at least, it will be when we'v
settled down again. You see, I'm honest, or shameless if yo
like it better.'

'I don't see, in all this,' said Dinny drily, 'where love come
in.'

'Perhaps it doesn't. Marriage is composed of mutual interest
and desire. The first increases with the years, the latter fades
That ought to be exactly what she wants.'

'I can't speak for Clare, but I don't see it that way.'

'You haven't tried yourself out, my dear.'

'No,' said Dinny, 'and on those lines I trust I never may. I
should dislike alternation between commerce and vice.'

He laughed.

'I like your bluntness. But seriously, Dinny, you ought to
influence her. She's making a great mistake.'

A sudden fury seized on Dinny.

'I think,' she said, between her teeth, 'it was you who made
the great mistake. If you do certain things to certain horses
you're never on terms with them again.'

He was silent at that.

'You don't want a divorce in the family,' he said at last, and
looked round at her steadily. 'I've told Clare that I can't let her
divorce me. I'm sorry, but I mean that. Further, if she won't
come back to me, she can't go as she pleases.'

'You mean,' said Dinny, between her teeth, 'that if she does come back to you she can?'

'That's what it would come to, I daresay.'

'I see. I think I'll say good night.'

'As you please. You think me cynical. That's as may be. I shall do my best to get Clare back. If she won't come she must watch out.'

They had stopped under a lamp-post and with an effort Dinny forced her eyes to his. He was as formidable, shameless, and mesmerically implacable as a cat, with that thin smile and unflinching stare. She said quietly: 'I quite understand. Good night!'

'Good night, Dinny! I'm sorry, but it's best to know where we stand. Shake hands?'

Rather to her surprise she let him take her hand, then turned the corner into Mount Street.

Chapter Nine

SHE entered her Aunt's house with all her passionate loyalty to her own breed roused, yet understanding better what had made Clare take Jerry Corven for husband. There *was* mesmerism about him, and a clear shameless daring which had its fascination. One could see what a power he might be among native peoples, how ruthlessly, yet smoothly, he would have his way with them; and how he might lay a spell over his associates. She could see, too, how difficult he might be to refuse physically, until he had outraged all personal pride.

Her aunt's voice broke her painful absorption with the words: 'Here she is, Adrian.'

At the top of the stairs her Uncle Adrian's goatee-bearded face was looking over his sister's shoulder.

'Your things have come, my dear. Where have you been?'

'With Clare, Auntie.'

'Dinny,' said Adrian, 'I haven't seen you for nearly a year.'

'This is where we kiss, Uncle. Is all well in Bloomsbury, or has the slump affected bones?'

'Bones *in esse* are all right; *in posse* they look dicky – no money for expeditions. The origin of *Homo sapiens* is more abstruse than ever.'

'Dinny, we needn't dress. Adrian's stoppin' for dinner. Lawrence will be so relieved. You can pow-wow while I loosen my belt, or do you want to tighten yours?'

'No, thank you, Auntie.'

'Then go in there.'

Dinny entered the drawing-room and sat down beside her Uncle. Grave and thin and bearded, wrinkled, and brown even in November, with long legs crossed and a look of interest in her, he seemed as ever the ideal pillar-box for confidences.

'Heard about Clare, Uncle?'

'The bare facts, no whys or wherefores.'

'They're not "nice". Did you ever know a sadist?'

'Once – at Margate. My private school. I didn't know at the time, of course, but I've gathered it since. Do you mean that Corven is one?'

'So Clare says. I walked here with him from her rooms. He's a very queer person.'

'Not mentally abnormal?' said Adrian, with a shudder.

'Saner than you or I, dear; he wants his own way regardless of other people; and when he can't get it he bites. Could Clare get a divorce from him without publicly going into their life together?'

'Only by getting evidence of a definite act of misconduct.'

'Would that have to be over here?'

'Well, to get it over there would be very expensive, and doubtful at that.'

'Clare doesn't want to have him watched at present.'

'It's certainly an unclean process,' said Adrian.

'I know, Uncle; but if she won't, what chance is there?'

'None.'

'At present she's in the mood that they should leave each other severely alone; but if she won't go back with him, he says she must "look out for herself".'

'Is there anybody else involved, then, Dinny?'

'There's a young man in love with her, but she says it's quite all right.'

'H'm! "Youth's a stuff —" as Shakespeare said. Nice young man?'

'I've only seen him a for a few minutes; he looked quite nice, I thought.'

'That cuts both ways.'

'I trust Clare completely.'

'You know her better than I do, my dear; but I should say she might get very impatient. How long can Corven stay over here?'

'Not more than a month at most, she thinks; he's been here a week already.'

'He's seen her?'

'Once. He tried to again today. I drew him off. She dreads seeing him, I know.'

'As things are he has every right to see her, you know.'

'Yes,' said Dinny, and sighed.

'Can't your Member that she's with suggest a way out? He's a lawyer.'

'I wouldn't like to tell him. It's so private. Besides, people don't like being involved in matrimonial squabbles.'

'Is he married?'

'No.'

She saw him look at her intently, and remembered Clare's laugh and words: 'Dinny, he's in love with you.'

'You'll see him here tomorrow night,' Adrian went on. 'Em's asked him to dinner, I gather; Clare too, I believe. Quite candidly, Dinny, I don't see anything to be done. Clare may change her mind and go back, or Corven may change his and let her stay without bothering about her.'

Dinny shook her head. 'They're neither of them like that. I must go and wash, Uncle.'

Adrian reflected upon the undeniable proposition that everyone had his troubles. His own at the moment were confined to the fact that his step-children, Sheila and Ronald Ferse, had measles, so that he was something of a pariah in his own house, the sanctity attaching to an infectious disease having cast his wife into purdah. He was not vastly interested in Clare. She had always been to him one of those young women who took the bit between their teeth and were bound to fetch up now and again with broken knees. Dinny, to him, was worth three of her. But if Dinny were going to be worried out of her life by her sister's troubles, then, indeed, they became important to Adrian. She seemed to have the knack of bearing vicarious burdens: Hubert's, his own, Wilfrid Desert's, and now Clare's.

And he said to his sister's parakeet: 'Not fair, Polly, is it?'

The parakeet, who was used to him, came out of its open cage on to his shoulder and tweaked his ear.

'You don't approve, do you?'

The green bird emitted a faint chattering sound and clutched its way on to his waistcoat. Adrian scratched its poll.

'Who's going to scratch her poll? Poor Dinny!'

His sister's voice startled him:

'I can't have Dinny scratched again.'

'Em,' said Adrian, 'did any of *us* worry about the others?'

'In large families you don't. I was the nearest – gettin' Lionel married, and now he's a judge – depressin'. Dornford – have you seen him?'

'Never.'

'He's got a face like a portrait. They say he won the long jump at Oxford. Is that any good?'

'It's what you call desirable.'

'Very well made,' said Lady Mont. 'I looked him over at Condaford.'

'My dear Em!'

'For Dinny, of course. What do you do with a gardener who *will* roll the stone terrace?'

'Tell him not to.'

'Whenever I look out at Lippin'hall, he's at it, takin' the roller somewhere else. There's the gong, and here's Dinny; we'll go in.'

Sir Lawrence was at the sideboard in the dining-room, extracting a crumbled cork.

'Lafite '65. Goodness knows what it'll be like. Decant it very gently, Blore. What do you say, Adrian, warm it a little or no?'

'I should say no, if it's that age.'

'I agree.'

Dinner began in silence. Adrian was thinking of Dinny, Dinny of Clare, and Sir Lawrence of the claret.

'French art,' said Lady Mont.

'Ah!' said Sir Lawrence: 'that reminds me, Em; some of old Forsyte's pictures are going to be lent. Considering he died saving them, they owe it to him.'

Dinny looked up.

'Fleur's father? Was he a nice man, Uncle?'

'Nice?' repeated Sir Lawrence: 'It's not the word. Straight, yes: careful, yes – too careful for these times. He got a picture on his head, you know, in the fire – poor old chap. He knew something about French art, though. This exhibition that's coming would have pleased him.'

'There'll be nothing in it to touch "The Birth of Venus",' said Adrian.

Dinny gave him a pleased look.

'That was divine,' she said.

Sir Lawrence cocked his eyebrow.

'I've often thought of going into the question: Why a nation ceases to be poetic. The old Italians – and look at them now!'

'Isn't poetry an effervescence, Uncle? Doesn't it mean youth, or at least enthusiasm?'

'The Italians were never young, and they're enthusiastic enough now. When we were in Italy last May you should have seen the trouble they took over our passports.'

'Touchin'!' agreed Lady Mont.

'It's only a question,' said Adrian, 'of the means of expression. In the fourteenth century the Italians were expressing themselves in daggers and verse, in the fifteenth and sixteenth in poison, sculpture and painting, in the seventeenth in music, in the eighteenth in intrigue, in the nineteenth in rebellion, and in the twentieth their poetry is spelled in wireless and rules.'

'I did get so tired,' murmured Lady Mont, 'of seein' rules I couldn't read.'

'You were fortunate, my dear; I could.'

'There's one thing about the Italians,' continued Adrian;

'century by century they throw up really great men of one sort or another. Is that climate, blood, or scenery, Lawrence?'

Sir Lawrence shrugged. 'What do you think of the claret? Put your nose to it. Dinny. Sixty years ago, you two young women wouldn't be here, and Adrian and I would be soppy about it. It's as near perfect as makes no matter.'

Adrian sipped and nodded.

'Absolutely prime!'

'Well, Dinny?'

'I'm sure it's perfect, dear – wasted on me.'

'Old Forsyte would have appreciated this; he had wonderful sherry. Do you get the bouquet, Em?'

Lady Mont, who was holding her glass with her elbow on the table, moved her nostrils delicately.

'Such nonsense,' she murmured, 'almost any flower beats it.'

The remark caused complete silence.

Dinny's eyes were the first to come to the level.

'How are Boswell and Johnson, Auntie?'

'I was tellin' Adrian: Boswell's taken to rollin' the stone terrace, and Johnson's lost his wife – poor thing. He's a different man. Whistles all the time. His tunes ought to be collected.'

'Survivals of old England?'

'No, modern – he just wanders.'

'Talking of survivals,' said Sir Lawrence, 'did you ever read *Ask Mamma*, Dinny?'

'No; who wrote it?'

'Surtees. You should. It's a corrective.'

'Of what, Uncle?'

'Modernity.'

Lady Mont lowered her glass; it was empty.

'So wise of them to be stoppin' this picture exhibition at 1900. D'you remember, Lawrence – in Paris, all those wiggly things we saw, and so much yellow and light blue – scrolls and blobs and faces upside-down? Dinny, we'd better go up.'

And when presently Blore brought the message – Would Miss Dinny go down to the study? She murmured :

'It's about Jerry Corven. Don't encourage your Uncle – he thinks he can do good, but he can't.' . . .

'Well, Dinny?' said Sir Lawrence: 'I always like talking to Adrian; he's a well-tempered fellow with a mind of his own. I told Clare I would see Corven, but it's no good seeing him without knowing what one wants to say. And not much then, I'm afraid. What do *you* think?'

Dinny, who had seated herself on the edge of her chair, set her elbows on her knees. It was an attitude from which Sir Lawrence augured ill.

'Judging from what he said to me today, Uncle Lawrence, his mind's made up. Either Clare must go back to him or he'll try to divorce her.'

'How will your people feel about that?'

'Very badly.'

'You know there's a young man hanging around?'

'Yes.'

'He hasn't a bean.'

Dinny smiled. 'We're used to that.'

'I know, but no beans when you're out of bounds is serious. Corven might claim damages, he looks a vindictive sort of chap.'

'D'you really think he would? It's very bad form, nowadays, isn't it?'

'Form matters very little when a man's monkey is up. I suppose you couldn't get Clare to apply the closure to young Croom?'

'I'm afraid Clare will refuse to be dictated to about whom she sees. She thinks the break-up is entirely Jerry's fault.'

'I,' said Sir Lawrence, emitting a slow puff, 'am in favour of having Corven watched while he's over here, and collecting a shot, if possible, to fire across his bows, but she doesn't like the idea of that.'

'She believes in his career and doesn't want to spoil it. Besides, it's so revolting.'

Sir Lawrence shrugged.

'What would you? The law's the law. He belongs to Burton's. Shall I waylay him there and appeal to him to leave her here quietly, and see if absence will make her heart grow fond again?'

Dinny wrinkled her brows.

'It might be worth trying, but I don't believe he'll budge.'

'What line are you going to take yourself?'

'Back Clare in whatever she does or doesn't do.'

Sir Lawrence nodded, having received the answer he expected.

Chapter Ten

◄◄-►►-

THE quality which from time immemorial has made the public men of England what they are, tempted so many lawyers into Parliament, caused so many divines to put up with being bishops, floated so many financiers, saved so many politicians from taking thought for the morrow, and so many judges from the pangs of remorse, was present in Eustace Dornford to no small degree. Put more shortly, he had an excellent digestion; could eat and drink at all times without knowing anything about it afterwards. He was an indefatigably hard worker even at play; and there was in him just that added fund of nervous energy which differentiates the man who wins the long jump from the man who loses it. And now, though his practice was going up by leaps and bounds since, two years ago, he had taken silk, he had stood for Parliament. And yet he was the last sort of man to incur the epithet 'go-getter'. His pale-brown, hazel-eyed, well-featured face had a considerate, even a sensitive look, and a pleasant smile. He had kept a little fine dark moustache, and his wig had not yet depleted his natural hair, which was dark and of rather curly texture. After Oxford he had eaten dinners and gone into the Chambers of a well-known Common Law Junior. Being a subaltern in the Shropshire Yeomanry when the war broke out, he had passed into the Cavalry, and not long after into the trenches, where he had known better luck than most people. His rise at the Bar after the war had been rapid. Solicitors liked him. He never fell foul of judges, and as a cross-examiner stood out, because he almost seemed to regret the points he scored. He was a Roman Catholic, from breeding rather than observance. Finally, he was fastidious in matters of sex, and his presence at a dinner-table on circuit had, if not a silencing, at least a moderating effect on tongues.

He occupied in Harcourt Buildings a commodious set of chambers designed for life as well as learning. Early every morning, wet or fine, he went for a ride in the Row, having already done at least two hours' work on his cases. By ten o'clock, bathed, breakfasted, and acquainted with the morning's news, he was ready for the Courts. When at four those Courts rose, he was busy again till half-past six on his cases. The evenings, hitherto free, would now be spent at the House: and since it would be seldom that he could go to bed without working an hour or so on some case or other, his sleep was likely to be curtailed from six hours to five, or even four.

The arrangement come to with Clare was simple. She arrived at a quarter to ten, opened his correspondence, and took his instructions from ten to a quarter past. She remained to do what was necessary, and came again at six o'clock, ready for anything fresh or left over.

On the evening after that last described, at the hour of eight-fifteen, he entered the drawing-room in Mount Street, was greeted, and introduced to Adrian, who had again been bidden. Discussing the state of the pound and other grave matters, they waited, till Lady Mont said suddenly: 'Soup. What have you done with Clare, Mr Dornford?'

His eyes, which had hitherto taken in little but Dinny, regarded his hostess with a faint surprise.

'She left the Temple at half-past six, saying we should meet again.'

'Then,' said Lady Mont, 'we'll go down.'

There followed one of those discomfortable hours well known to well-bred people, when four of them are anxious upon a subject which they must not broach to the fifth, and the fifth becomes aware of this anxiety.

They were, indeed, too few for the occasion, for all that each one of them said could be heard by the others. It was impossible for Eustace Dornford to be confidential with either of his neighbours; and since he instinctively felt that without a pre-liminary confidence he would only put his foot into it, he was careful to be public-minded and keep to such topics as the

Premier, the undiscovered identity of certain poisoners, the ventilation of the House of Commons, the difficulty of knowing exactly what to do with one's hat there, and other subjects of general interest. But, by the end of dinner he was so acutely aware that they were burning to say things he mustn't hear, that he invented a professional telephone call, and was taken out of the room by Blore.

The moment he had gone Dinny said:

'She must have been waylaid, Auntie. Could I be excused and go and see?'

Sir Lawrence answered:

'Better wait till we break, Dinny; a few minutes can't matter now.'

'Don't you think,' said Adrian, 'that Dornford ought to know how things stand? She goes to him every day.'

'I'll tell him,' said Sir Lawrence.

'No,' said Lady Mont. 'Dinny must tell him. Wait for him here, Dinny. We'll go up.'

Thus it was that, returning to the dining-room after his trunk call to someone whom he knew to be away from home, Dornford found Dinny waiting. She handed him the cigars and said:

'Forgive us, Mr Dornford. It's about my sister. Please light up, and here's coffee. Blore, would you mind getting me a taxi?'

When they had drunk their coffee, and were standing together by the fire, she turned her face to it and went on hurriedly:

'You see, Clare has split from her husband, and he's just come over to take her back. She won't go, and it's rather a difficult time for her.'

Dornford made a considerate sound.

'I'm very glad you told me. I've been feeling unhappy all dinner.'

'I must go now, I'm afraid, and find out what's happened.'

'Could I come with you?'

'Oh! thank you, but –'

'It would be a real pleasure.'

Dinny stood hesitating. He looked like a present help in

ouble; but she said: 'Thank you, but perhaps my sister ouldn't like it.'

'I see. Any time I can help, please let me know.'

'Your taxi's at the door, Miss.'

'Some day,' she said. 'I'd like to ask you about divorce.'

In the taxi she wondered what she would do if she could not et in; and then what she would do if she could get in and Corven were there. She stopped the cab at the corner of the Mews.

'Stay here, please, I'll let you know in a minute if I want you gain.'

Dark and private loomed that little backwater.

'Like one's life,' thought Dinny, and pulled at the ornamental ell. It tinkled all forlorn, and nothing happened. Again and gain she rang, then moved backward to look up at the win-lows. The curtains – she remembered they were heavy – had een drawn close; she could not decide whether or no there was ight behind them. Once more she rang and used the knocker, lolding her breath to listen. No sound at all! At last, baffled and lisquiet, she went back to the cab. Clare had said Corven was taying at the Bristol, and she gave that address. There might be a dozen explanations; only why, in a town of telephones, had Clare not let them know? Half-past ten! Perhaps she had by low!

The cab drew up at the hotel. 'Wait, please!' Entering its liscreetly gilded hall, she stood for a moment at a loss. The setting seemed unsuitable for private trouble.

'Yes, madam?' said a page-boy's voice.

'Could you find out for me, please, if my brother-in-law, Sir Gerald Corven, is in the hotel?'

What should she say if they brought him to her? Her figure in its evening cloak was reflected in a mirror, and that it was straight filled her with a sort of surprise – she felt so as if she were curling and creeping this way and that. But they did not bring him to her. He was not in his room, nor in any of the public rooms. She went out again to her cab.

'Back to Mount Street, please.'

Dornford and Adrian were gone, her Aunt and Uncle playing piquet.

'Well, Dinny?'

'I couldn't get into her rooms, and he was not in his hotel.'

'You went there?'

'It was all I could think of to do.'

Sir Lawrence rose. 'I'll telephone to Burton's.' Dinny sat down beside her Aunt.

'I feel she's in trouble, Auntie. Clare's never rude.'

'Kidnapped or locked up,' said Lady Mont. 'There was a case when I was young. Thompson, or Watson – a great fuss. Habeas corpus, or something – husbands can't now. Well, Lawrence?'

'He hasn't been in the Club since five o'clock. We must just wait till the morning. She may have forgotten, you know; or got the evening mixed.'

'But she told Mr Dornford that they would meet again.'

'So they will, tomorrow morning. No good worrying, Dinny.'

Dinny went up, but did not undress. Had she done all she could? The night was clear and fine and warm for November. Only a quarter of a mile or so away, was that backwater of Mews – should she slip out and go over there again?

She threw off her evening frock, put on a day dress, hat and fur coat, and stole downstairs. It was dark in the hall. Quietly drawing back the bolts, she let herself out, and took to the streets. When she entered the Mews – where a couple of cars were being put away for the night – she saw light coming from the upper windows of No. 2. They had been opened and the curtains drawn aside. She rang the bell.

After a moment Clare, in her dressing-gown, opened the door.

'Was it you who came before, Dinny?'

'Yes.'

'Sorry I couldn't let you in. Come up!'

She led the way up the spiral stairs, and Dinny followed.

Upstairs it was warm and light, the door into the tiny bathroom open, and the couch in disorder. Clare looked at her sister with a sort of unhappy defiance.

'Yes, I've had Jerry here, he's not been gone ten minutes.'

A horrified shiver went down Dinny's spine.

'After all, he's come a long way,' said Clare; 'good of you to worry, Dinny.'

'Oh! darling!'

'He was outside here when I got back from the Temple. I was an idiot to let him in. After that – oh! well, it doesn't matter! I'll take care it doesn't happen again.'

'Would you like me to stay?'

'Oh! no. But have some tea. I've just made it. I don't want anyone to know of this.'

'Of course not. I'll say you had a bad headache and couldn't get out to telephone.'

When they were drinking the tea Dinny said:

'This hasn't altered your plans?'

'God! no!'

'Dornford was there tonight. We thought it best to tell him you were having a difficult time.'

Clare nodded.

'It must all seem very funny to you.'

'It seems to me tragic.'

Clare shrugged, then stood up and threw her arms round her sister. After that silent embrace, Dinny went out into the Mews, now dark and deserted. At the corner leading into the Square she almost walked into a young man.

'Mr Croom, isn't it?'

'Miss Cherrell? Have you been at Lady Corven's?'

'Yes.'

'Is she all right?'

His face was worried, and his voice anxious. Dinny took a breath before answering:

'Oh! yes. Why not?'

'She was saying last night that man was over here. It worries me terribly.'

Through Dinny shot the thought: 'If he'd met "that man"!' But she said, quietly:

'Walk with me as far as Mount Street.'

'I don't mind your knowing,' he said, 'I'm over head and ears in love with her. Who wouldn't be? Miss Cherrell, I don't think she ought to be in that place alone. She told me he came yesterday while you were there.'

'Yes. I took him away with me, as I'm taking you. I think my sister should be left to herself.'

He seemed to hunch himself together.

'Have *you* ever been in love?'

'Yes.'

'Well, then you know.'

Yes, she knew!

'It's absolute torture not to be with her, able to see that she's all right. She takes it all lightly, but I can't.'

Takes it all lightly! Clare's face looking at her! She did not answer.

'The fact is,' said young Croom, with incoherence, 'people can say and think what they like, but if they felt as I feel, they simply couldn't. I won't bother her, I really won't; but I can't stand her being in danger from that man.'

Dinny controlled herself to say quietly: 'I don't think Clare's in any danger. But she might be if it were known that you —' He met her eyes squarely.

'I'm glad she's got you. For God's sake look after her, Miss Cherrell.'

They had reached the corner of Mount Street, and she held out her hand.

'You may be certain that whatever Clare does I shall stick by her. Good night! And cheer up!'

He wrung her hand, and went off as if the devil were after him. Dinny went in, and slid the bolts quietly.

On what thin ice! She could hardly drag one foot before the other as she went upstairs, and sank down on her bed exhausted.

Chapter Eleven

◄◄·►►

WHEN Sir Lawrence Mont reached Burton's Club the following afternoon he was feeling, in common with many who undertake to interfere in the affairs of others, as uneasy self-importance coupled with a desire to be somewhere else. He did not know what the deuce he was going to say to Corven, or why

he deuce he should say it, since, in his opinion, by far the
best solution would be for Clare to give her marriage another
trial. Having discovered from the porter that Sir Gerald was in
the Club, he poked his nose gingerly into three rooms before
locating the back of his quarry seated in the corner of an apart-
ment too small to be devoted to anything but writing. He sat
down at a table close to the door, so that he could simulate
surprise when Corven came up to leave the room. The fellow
was an unconscionable time. Noting a copy of the British States-
man's vade-mecum beside him, he began idly looking up the
figures of British imports. He found potatoes: consumption
sixty-six million five hundred thousand tons, production eight
million eight hundred and seventy-four thousand tons! Somebody the other day had written to say that we imported forty
million pounds' worth of bacon every year. Taking a sheet of
paper he wrote: 'Prohibition and protection, in regard to food
that we *can* produce here. Annual Imports: Pigs, £40,000,000;
Poultry say, £12,000,000; Potatoes – God knows how much! All
this bacon, all these eggs, and half these potatoes could be produced here. Why not a five-year plan? By prohibition lessen
the import of bacon and eggs one-fifth every year, and the
import of potatoes by one-tenth every year, increasing home production gradually to replace them. At the end of five years our
bacon and eggs and half our potatoes would be all-British. We
should save eighty millions on our Imports Bill and our trade
would practically be balanced.'

Taking another sheet of paper, he wrote:

'To the Editor of *The Times*.
        'The Three P. Plan.
'S I R –
    'A simple plan for the balancing of our trade would seem to merit
the attention of all those not wedded to the longest way round.
There are three articles of food on importing which we expend
annually some ——— pounds, but which could be produced in our
own country without, I venture to think, causing the price of living
to rise to any material extent if we took the simple precaution of
hanging a profiteer at the beginning. These articles are Pigs, Poultry,
Potatoes. There would be no need to put on duties, for all that is
required is –'

o.r. – 4   73

But at this moment, becoming aware that Corven was passing from the room, he said :

'Hello !'

Corven turned and came towards him.

Hoping that he showed as little sign of embarrassment as his nephew twice removed by marriage, Sir Lawrence rose.

'Sorry I didn't see you when you called the other day. Have you got long leave?'

'Another week only, and then I shall have to fly the Mediterranean probably.'

'Not a good month for flying. What do you think of this adverse balance of trade?'

Jerry Corven shrugged.

'Something to keep them busy for a bit. They never see two inches before their noses.'

' *"Tiens! Une montagne!"* Remember the Caran d'Ache cartoon of Buller in front of Ladysmith? No, you wouldn't. It's thirty-two years ago. National character doesn't change much, does it? How's Ceylon? Not in love with India, I hope?'

'Nor with us particularly, but we jog on.'

'The climate doesn't suit Clare, apparently.'

Corven's expression remained watchful and slightly smiling.

'The hot weather didn't, but that's over.'

'Are you taking her back with you?'

'Yes.'

'I wonder if that's wise.'

'To leave her would be less so. One's either married or not.'

Sir Lawrence, watching his eyes, thought : 'Shan't go further. It's hopeless. Besides, he's probably right. Only I would bet –'

'Forgive me,' said Corven, 'I must get these letters off.' He turned and moved away, trim and assured.

'H'm !' thought Sir Lawrence, 'not exactly what you'd call fruitful.' And he sat down again to his letter to *The Times*.

'I must get precise figures,' he muttered. 'I'll turn Michael on to it' ... And his thoughts went back to Corven. Impossible, in such cases, to know where the blame really lay. After all, a misfit was a misfit, no amount of pious endeavour, or even worldly wisdom, would cure it. 'I ought to have been a judge,' he thought, 'then I could have expressed my views. Mr Justice Mont in the course of his judgement said : "It is time to warn the people of this country against marriage. That tie, which was all very well under Victoria, should now only be contracted in cases where there is full evidence to show that neither party has any individuality to speak of ... I think I'll go home to Em.' He blotted the perfectly dry letter to *The Times*, put it into his pocket, and sought the darkening placidity of Pall Mall. He had stopped to look in at the window of his wine merchant's in St James's Street, and consider once more where the extra ten per cent on his surtax was to come from, when a voice said :

'Good evening, Sir Lawrence !' It was the young man called Croom.

They crossed the street together.

'I wanted to thank you, sir, for speaking to Mr Muskham. I've seen him today.'

'How did you find him?'

'Oh ! very affable. Of course I agree it *is* a bee in his bonnet about introducing that cross of Arab blood into our racehorses.'

'Did you show him you thought so?'

Young Croom smiled: 'Hardly ! But the Arab horse is so much smaller.'

'There's something in it, all the same. Jack's only wrong in expecting quick results. It's like politics, people won't lay down for the future. If a thing doesn't work within five years, we think it's no good. Did Jack say he'd take you on?'

'He'll give me a trial. I'm to go down for a week, so that he can see me with horses. But the mares are not going to Royston. He's got a place for them above Oxford near Bablock Hythe. I should be there if I pass muster. It's not till the spring, though.'

'Jack's a formalist,' said Sir Lawrence, as they entered the Coffee House; 'you'll have to mind your p's and q's.'

Young Croom smiled.

'You bet. Everything's simply perfect at his stud farm. Luckily I really am frightfully keen about horses. I didn't feel at sea with Mr Muskham. It's an immense relief to have a chance again; and there's nothing I'd like better.'

Sir Lawrence smiled – enthusiasm was always pleasant.

'You must know my son,' he said, 'he's an enthusiast too, though he must be thirty-seven by now. You'll be in his constituency – no, just out of it. You'll be in Dornford's, I expect. But the way, you know my niece is acting secretary for him?'

Young Croom nodded.

'I don't know,' murmured Sir Lawrence, 'whether that'll go on now Corven's over.' And he watched the young man's expression.

It had perceptibly darkened. 'Oh! it will. She won't go back to Ceylon.'

It was said with frowning suddenness, and Sir Lawrence thought: 'This is where I weigh myself.' Young Croom followed him to the weighing machine, as if he did not know how not to. He was very red.

'What makes you sure of that?' said Sir Lawrence, looking up from the historic chair. Young Croom went even redder.

'One doesn't come away just to go back.'

'Or one does. If Life were a racehorse it'd be always up before the stewards for running in and out.'

'I happen to know Lady Corven won't, sir.'

It was clear to Sir Lawrence that he had lighted on a moment when feeling gets the better of discretion. So the young man *was* in love with her! Was this a chance to warn him off the course? Or was it more graceful to take no notice?

'Just eleven stone,' he said; 'do you go up or down, Mr Croom?'

'I keep about ten twelve.'

Sir Lawrence scrutinized his lean figure.

'Well, you look very fit. Extraordinary what a shadow can be cast on life by the abdomen. However, you won't have to worry till you're fifty.'

'Surely, sir, you've never had any bother there?'

'Not to speak of; but I've watched it darken so many doors. And now I must be getting on. Good night to you!'

'Good night, sir. I really am awfully grateful.'

'Not at all. My cousin Jack doesn't bet, and if you take my advice, you won't either.'

Young Croom said heartily: 'I certainly shan't, sir.'

They shook hands and Sir Lawrence resumed his progress up St James's Street.

'That young man,' he was thinking, 'impresses me favourably, and I can't think why – he appears to be going to be a nuisance. What I ought to have said to him was : "Thou shalt not covet thy neighbour's wife." But God so made the world that one doesn't say what one ought!' The young were very interesting; one heard of them being disrespectful to Age and all that, but really he couldn't see it. They seemed to him fully as well-mannered as he himself had been at their age, and easier to talk to. One never knew what they were thinking, of course; but that might be as well. After all, one used to think that the old – and Sir Lawrence winced on the kerbstone of Piccadilly – were only fit to be measured for their coffins. 'Tempora mutantur et nos mutamur in illis'; but was that true? No more really than the difference in the pronunciation of Latin since one's youth. Youth would always be Youth and Age would be Age, with the same real divergence and distrust between them, and the same queer hankering by Age to feel as Youth was feeling and think as Youth was thinking; the same pretence that it wouldn't so feel and think for the world, and, at the back of all, the instinct that, really given the chance, Age wouldn't have its life over again. Merciful – that! With stealthy quietude Life, as it wore one out, supplied the adjustment of a suitable lethargy. At each stage of existence the zest for living was tailored to what man had before him and no more. That fellow Goethe had attained immortality to the tunes of Gounod by fanning a dying spark into a full-blown flame. 'Rats!' thought Sir Lawrence: 'and very German rats! Would I choose the sighing and the sobbing, the fugitive raptures and the lingering starvations in front of that young man, if I could? I would not! Sufficient unto the old buffer is the bufferism thereof. Is that policeman never going to stop this blamed traffic?' No, there was no real change! Men drove cars now to the same tick as the old horse-bus and the hansom-cab drivers had driven their slipping, clattering gees. Young men and women experienced the same legal or illegal urge towards each other. The pavements were different, and the lingo in which those youthful hankerings were expressed. But – Lord Almighty! – the rules of the road, the collisions and slips and general miraculous avoidances, the triumphs, mortifications, and fulfilments for better for worse, were all the same as ever. 'No,' he thought; 'the Police may make rules, Divines write to the papers, Judges express themselves as they like, but human nature will find its own way about as it did when I was cutting my wisdom teeth.'

The policeman reversed his sleeves, and Sir Lawrence crossed, pursuing his way to Berkeley Square. Here was change enough! The houses of the great were going fast. Piecemeal, without expressed aim, almost shamefacedly, in true English fashion, London was being rebuilt. The dynastic age was gone, with its appendages, feudalism, and the Church. Even wars would now be fought for peoples and their markets. No more dynastic or religious wars. Well, that was something! 'We're getting more like insects daily,' thought Sir Lawrence. And how interesting! Religion was nearly dead because there was no longer real belief in future life; but something was struggling to take its place – service – social service – the ants' creed, the bees' creed! Communism had formulated it and was whipping it into the people from the top. So characteristic! They were always whipping something into somebody in Russia. The quick way, no doubt, but the sure way? No! The voluntary system remained the best, because when once it got hold it lasted – only it was so darned slow! Yes, and darned ironical! So far the sense of social service was almost the perquisite of the older families, who had somehow got hold of the notion that they must do something useful to pay for their position. Now that they were dying out would the sense of service persist? How were the 'people' to pick it up? 'Well,' thought Sir Lawrence, 'after all, there's the bus conductor; and the fellow in the shop, who'll take infinite trouble to match the colour of your socks; and the woman who'll look after her neighbour's baby, or collect for the waifs and strays; and the motorist who'll stop and watch you tinkering at your car; and the postman who's grateful for a tip; and the almost anybody who'll try and pull you out of a pond if he can really see you're in it. What's wanted is the slogan: "Fresh air and exercise for good instincts." One might have it on all the buses, instead of: "Canon's Colossal Crime," or "Strange Sweepstake

Swindle." And that reminds me to ask Dinny what she knows about Clare and that young man.'

So thinking, he paused before his house door, and inserted his key in its latch.

Chapter Twelve

<del>◄◄►►</del>

I N spite of Sir Gerald Corven's assurance, the course before a husband wishing to resume the society of his wife is not noticeably simple, especially if he has but a week wherein to encompass his desire. The experience of that evening had made Clare wary. On leaving the Temple at lunch-time the day after, a Saturday, she took train for Condaford, where she carefully refrained from saying that she had sought asylum. On Sunday morning she lay long in bed, with the windows wide open, watching the sky beyond the tall denuded elms. The sun shone in upon her, the air was mild and alive with sounds surprised into life, the twittering once more of birds, the lowing of a cow, the occasional caw of a rook, the continual cooing of the fantails. There was but little poetry in Clare, but for a moment to her easeful stretched-out being came a certain perception of the symphony which is this world. The lacing of the naked boughs and those few leaves against the soft, gold-bright, moving sky; that rook balancing there; the green and fallow upland, the far line of trees; and all those sounds, and the pure unscented air on her face; the twittering quietude and perfect freedom of each separate thing, and yet the long composure of design – all this for a moment drew her out of herself into a glimpse of the universal.

The vision passed; she thought instead of Thursday night, and Tony Croom, and the dirty little boy outside the restaurant in Soho, who had said in such endearing tones: 'Remember the poor old guy, lady; remember the poor old guy.' If Tony had seen her the next night! How irrelevant was event to feeling, how ignorant were even the closest of each other! She uttered a little discomfited laugh. Where ignorance was bliss, indeed!

The village church bell began ringing now. Marvellous how

her father and mother continued to go every Sunday, hoping – she supposed – for the best; or was it because if they didn't the village wouldn't, and the church would fall into disuse, or at least behind the chapel? It was nice to lie here in one's own old room, feel safe, and warm, and idle, with a dog on one's feet. Till next Saturday she was at bay, like a chased vixen taking advantage of every cover; and Clare drew taut her lips, as a vixen does at sight of hounds. Go back he must – he had said – with her or without. Well, it would be without!

Her sense of asylum was rudely shaken about four o'clock, when, returning from a walk with the dogs, she saw a car outside and was met by her mother in the hall.

'Jerry's with your father.'

'Oh!'

'Come up to my room, dear.'

In that first-floor room adjoining her bedroom Lady Charwell's personality had always more scope than in the rest of the old, tortuous, worn-down house, so full of relics and the past tense. This room's verbena-scented, powder-blue scheme had a distinct if faded elegance. It had been designed; the rest of the house had grown, emerging here and there into small oases of modernity, but for the most part a wilderness strewn with the débris of Time.

Clare turned and turned a china figure, in front of the wood fire. She had not foreseen this visit. Now were conjoined the forces of creed, convention, and comfort, and against them was only a defence that it was hateful to lay bare. She waited for her mother to speak.

'You see, darling, you haven't told us anything.'

But how tell one who looked and spoke like that? She flushed, went pale, and said: 'I can only say there's a beast in him. I know it doesn't show; but there is, Mother, there is!'

Lady Charwell, too, had flushed. It did not suit her, being over fifty.

'Your father and I will help you all we can, dear; only, of course, it is so important to take a right decision now.'

'And I, having made a wrong one already, can only be trusted to make another? You've got to take my word, Mother; I simply can't talk about it, and I simply won't go back with him.'

Lady Charwell had sat down, a furrow between her grey-blue eyes which seemed fixed on nothing. She turned them on her daughter, and said, hesitating:

'You're sure it's not just the beast that is in nearly all men?'

Clare laughed.

'Oh! no. I'm not easily upset.'

Lady Charwell sighed.

'Don't worry, Mother dear; it'll be all right once we've got this over. Nothing really matters nowadays.'

'So they say, but one has the bad habit still of believing that it does.'

At this near approach to irony Clare said quickly:

'It matters that one should keep one's self-respect. Really, with him I couldn't.'

'We'll say no more then. Your father will want to see you. You'd better take your things off.'

Clare kissed her and went out. There was no sound from below, and she went on up to her room. She felt her will-power stiffening. The days when men disposed of their women folk were long over, and – whatever Jerry and her father were concocting – she would not budge! When the summons came, she went to the encounter, blade-sharp, and hard as stone.

They were standing in the General's office-like study, and she felt at once that they were in agreement. Nodding to her husband, she went over to her father.

'Well?'

But Corven spoke first.

'I leave it to you, sir.'

The General's lined face looked mournful and irritated. He braced himself. 'We've been going into this, Clare. Jerry admits that you've got much on your side, but he's given me his word that he won't offend you again. I want to appeal to you to try and see his point of view. He says, I think rightly, that it's more to your interest even than to his. The old idea about marriage may have gone, but, after all, you both took certain vows – but leaving that aside –'

'Yes,' said Clare.

The General twirled his little moustache, and thrust the other hand deep into his pocket.

'Well, what on earth is going to happen to you both? You can't have a divorce – there's your name, and his position, and – after only eighteen months. What are you going to do? Live apart? That's not fair to you, or to him.'

'Fairer to both of us than living together will be.'

The General glanced at her hardened face. 'So you say now; but we've both of us had more experience than you.'

'That was bound to be said sooner or later. You want me to go back with him?'

The General looked acutely unhappy.

'You know, my dear, that I only want what's best for you.'

'And Jerry has convinced you that *is* the best. Well, it's the worst. I'm not going, Dad, and there's an end of it.'

The General looked at her face, looked at the face of his son-in-law, shrugged his shoulders, and began filling his pipe.

Jerry Corven's eyes, which had been passing from face to face, narrowed and came to rest on Clare's. That look lasted a long time, and neither flinched.

'Very well,' he said, at last, 'I will make other arrangements. Good-bye, sir; good-bye, Clare!' And turning on his heel, he went out.

In the silence that followed, the sound of his car crunching away on the drive could be heard distinctly. The General smoking glumly, kept his glance averted; Clare went to the window. It was growing dark outside, and now that the crisis was over she felt unstrung.

'I wish to God,' said her father's voice, 'that I could understand this business.'

Clare did not move from the window: 'Did he tell you he'd used my riding whip on me?'

'What!' said the General.

Clare turned round.

'Yes.'

'On *you*?'

'Yes. That was not my real reason, but it put the finishing touch. Sorry to hurt you, Dad!'

'By God!'

Clare had a moment of illumination. Concrete facts! Give a man a fact!

'The ruffian!' said the General: 'The ruffian! He told me he spent the evening with you the other day; is that true?'

A slow flush had burned up in her cheeks.

'He practically forced himself in.'

'The ruffian!' said the General once more.

When she was alone again, she meditated wryly on the sudden difference that little fact about the whip had made in her father's feelings. He had taken it as a personal affront, an insult to his own flesh and blood. She felt that he could have stood it with equanimity of someone else's daughter; she remembered that he had even sympathized with her brother's flogging of the muleteer, which had brought such a peck of trouble on them all. How little detached, how delightfully personal, people were! Feeling and criticizing in terms of their own prejudices! Well! She was over the worst now, for her people were on her side, and she would make certain of not seeing Jerry alone again. She thought of the long look he had given her. He was a good loser, because for him the game was never at an end. Life itself – not each item of life – absorbed him. He rode Life, took a toss, got up, rode on; met an obstacle, rode over it, rode through it, took the scratches as all in the day's work. He had fascinated her, ridden through and over her; the fascination was gone, and she wondered that it had ever been. What was he going to do now? Well! One thing was certain: somehow, he would cut his losses!

Chapter Thirteen

—◄‹·›►—

O N E who gazes at the Temple's smooth green turf, fine trees, stone-silled buildings, and pouter pigeons, feels dithyrambic, till on him intrudes the vision of countless bundles of papers tied round with pink tape, unending clerks in little outer chambers sucking thumbs and waiting for solicitors, calf-bound tomes stored with reports of innumerable cases so closely argued that the light-minded sigh at sight of them and think of the Café Royal. Who shall deny that the Temple harbours the human mind *in excelsis*, the human body in chairs; who shall gainsay that the human spirit is taken off at its entrances and left outside like the shoes of those who enter a mosque? Not even to its Grand Nights is the human spirit admitted, for the legal mind must not 'slop over,' and warning is given by the word 'Decorations' on the invitation cards. On those few autumn mornings when the sun shines, the inhabitant of the Temple who faces East may possibly feel in his midriff as a man feels on a hilltop, or after hearing a Brahms symphony, or even when seeing first daffodils in spring; if so, he will hastily remember where he is, and turn to: Collister *v*. Daverday: Popdick intervening.

And yet, strangely, Eustace Dornford, verging on middle age, was continually being visited, whether the sun shone or not, by the feeling of one who sits on a low wall in the first spring warmth, seeing life as a Botticellian figure advancing towards him through an orchard of orange trees and spring flowers. At less expenditure of words, he was 'in love' with Dinny. Each morning when he saw Clare he was visited by a longing not to dictate on parliamentary subjects, but rather to lead her to talk about her sister. Self-controlled, however, and with a sense of humour, he bowed to his professional inhibitions, merely asking Clare whether she and her sister would dine with him, 'on Saturday – here, or at the Café Royal?'

'Here would be more original.'

'Would you care to ask a man to make a fourth?'

'But won't you, Mr Dornford?'

'You might like someone special.'

'Well, there's young Tony Croom, who was on the boat with me. He's a nice boy.'

'Good! Saturday, then. And you'll ask your sister?'

Clare did not say: 'She's probably on the doorstep,' for, as a fact, she was. Every evening that week she was coming at half-past six to accompany Clare back to Melton Mews. There were still chances, and the sisters were not taking them.

On hearing of the invitation Dinny said: 'When I left you late that night I ran into Tony Croom, and we walked back to Mount Street together.'

'You didn't tell him about Jerry's visit to me?'

'Of course not!'

'It's hard on him, as it is. He really is a nice boy, Dinny.'

'So I saw. And I wish he weren't in London.'

Clare smiled. 'Well, he won't be for long; he's to take charge of some Arab mares for Mr Muskham down at Bablock Hythe.'

'Jack Muskham lives at Royston.'

'The mares are to have a separate establishment in a milder climate.'

Dinny roused herself from memories with an effort.

'Well, darling, shall we strap-hang on the Tube, or go a bust in a taxi?'

'I want air. Are you up to walking?'

'Rather! We'll go by the Embankment and the Parks.'

They walked quickly, for it was cold. Lamplit and star-covered, that broad free segment of the Town had a memorable dark beauty; even on the buildings, their daylight features abolished, was stamped a certain grandeur.

Dinny murmured: 'London at night *is* beautiful.'

'Yes, you go to bed with a beauty and wake up with a bar-maid. And, what's it all for? A clotted mass of energy like an ant-heap.'

' "So fatiguin'," as Aunt Em would say.'

'But what *is* it all for, Dinny?'

'A workshop trying to turn out perfect specimens; a million failures to each success.'

'Is that worth while?'

'Why not?'

'Well, what is there to *believe* in?'

'Character.'

'How do you mean?'

'Character's our way of showing the desire for perfection. Nursing the best that's in one.'

'Hum!' said Clare. 'Who's to decide what's best within one?'

'You have me, my dear.'

'Well, I'm too young for it, anyway.'

Dinny hooked her arm within her sister's.

'You're older than I am, Clare.'

'No, I've had more experience perhaps, but I haven't communed with my own spirit and been still. I feel in my bones that Jerry's hanging round the Mews.'

'Come into Mount Street, and we'll go to a film.'

In the hall Blore handed Dinny a note.

'Sir Gerald Corven called, Miss, and left this for you.'

Dinny opened it.

DEAR DINNY, –

I'm leaving England tomorrow instead of Saturday. If Clare will change her mind I shall be very happy to take her. If not, she must not expect me to be long-suffering. I have left a note to this effect at her lodgings, but as I do not know where she is, I wrote to you also, so as to be sure that she knows. She or a message from her will find me at the Bristol up to three o'clock tomorrow, Thursday. After that 'à la guerre comme à la guerre.'

With many regrets that things are so criss-cross and good wishes to yourself,

I am,

Very sincerely yours,

GERALD CORVEN

Dinny bit her lip.

'Read this!'

Clare read the note.

'I shan't go, and he can do what he likes.'

While they were titivating themselves in Dinny's room, Lady Mont came in.

'Ah!' she said: 'Now I can say my piece. Your Uncle has seen Jerry Corven again. What are you goin' to do about him, Clare?'

As Clare swivelled round from the mirror, the light fell full on cheeks and lips whose toilet she had not quite completed.

'I'm never going back to him, Aunt Em.'

'May I sit on your bed, Dinny? "Never" is a long time, and – er – that Mr Craven. I'm sure you have principles, Clare, but you're too pretty.'

Clare put down her lipstick.

'Sweet of you, Aunt Em; but really I know what I'm about.'

'So comfortin'! When I say that myself, I'm sure to make a *gaffe*.'

'If Clare promises, she'll perform, Auntie.'

Lady Mont sighed. 'I promised my father not to marry for a year. Seven months – and then your uncle. It's always somebody.'

Clare raised her hands to the little curls on her neck.

'I'll promise not to "kick over" for a year. I ought to know my own mind by then; if I don't, I can't have got one.'

Lady Mont smoothed the eiderdown.

'Cross your heart.'

'I don't think you should,' said Dinny quickly.

Clare crossed her fingers on her breast.

'I'll cross where it ought to be.'

Lady Mont rose.

'She ought to stay here tonight, don't you think, Dinny?'

'Yes.'

'I'll tell them, then. Sea-green *is* your colour, Dinny. Lawrence says I haven't one.'

'Black and white, dear.'

'Magpies and the Duke of Portland. I haven't been to Ascot since Michael went to Winchester – savin' our pennies. Hilary and May are comin' to dinner. They won't be dressed.'

'Oh!' said Clare suddenly: 'Does Uncle Hilary know about me?'

'Broad-minded,' murmured Lady Mont. 'I can't help bein' sorry, you know.'

Clare stood up.

'Believe me, Aunt Em, Jerry's not the sort of man who'll let it hurt him long.'

'Stand back to back, you two; I thought so – Dinny by an inch.'

'I'm five foot five,' said Clare, 'without shoes.'

'Very well. When you're tidy, come down.'

So saying, Lady Mont swayed to the door, said to herself: 'Solomon's seal – remind Boswell,' and went out.

Dinny returned to the fire, and resumed her stare at the flames.

Clare's voice, close behind her, said: 'I feel inclined to sing, Dinny. A whole year's holiday from everything. I'm glad Aunt Em made me promise. But isn't she a scream?'

'Emphatically not. She's the wisest member of our family.

Take life seriously and you're nowhere. She doesn't. She may want to, but she can't.'

'But she hasn't any real worries.'

'Only a husband, three children, several grandchildren, two households, three dogs, some congenial gardeners, not enough money, and two passions – one for getting other people married, and one for French tapestry; besides trying hard not to get fat on it all.'

'Oh she's a duck all right. What d'you advise about these "tendrils," Dinny? They're an awful plague. Shall I shingle again?'

'Let them grow at present, we don't know what's coming; it might be ringlets.'

'Do you believe that women get themselves up to please men?'

'Certainly not.'

'To excite and annoy each other, then?'

'Fashion mostly; women are sheep about appearance.'

'And morals?'

'Have we any? Man-made, anyway. By nature we've only got feelings.'

'I've none now.'

'Sure?'

Clare laughed. 'Oh! well, in hand, anyhow.' She put on her dress, and Dinny took her place at the mirror. . . .

The slum parson does not dine out to observe human nature. He eats. Hilary Charwell, having spent the best part of his day, including meal-times, listening to the difficulties of parishioners who had laid up no store for the morrow because they had never had store enough for today, absorbed the good food set before him with perceptible enjoyment. If he was aware that the young woman whom he had married to Jerry Corven had burst her bonds, he gave no sign of it. Though seated next to her, he never once alluded to her domestic existence, conversing freely on the election, French art, the timber wolves at Whipsnade Zoo, and a new system of building schools with roofs that could be used or not as the weather dictated. Over his face, long, wrinkled, purposeful, and shrewdly kind, flitted an occasional smile, as if he were summing something up; but he gave no indication of what that something was, except that he looked across at Dinny, as though saying: 'You and I are going to have a talk presently.'

No such talk occurred, for he was summoned by telephone to a death-bed before he had finished his glass of port. Mrs Hilary went with him.

The two sisters settled down to bridge with their Uncle and Aunt, and at eleven o'clock went up to bed.

'Armistice day,' said Clare, turning into her bedroom. 'Did you realize?'

'Yes.'

'I was in a bus at eleven o'clock. I noticed two or three people looking funny. How can one be expected to feel anything? I was only ten when the war stopped.'

'I remember the Armistice,' said Dinny, 'because Mother cried. Uncle Hilary was with us at Condaford. He preached on: "They also serve who only stand and wait."'

'Who serves except for what he can get from it?'

'Lots of people do hard jobs all their lives for mighty little return.'

'Well, yes.'

'Why do they?'

'Dinny, I sometimes feel as if you might end up religious. Unless you marry, you will.'

'"Get thee to a nunnery, go!"'

'Seriously, ducky, I wish I could see more of "the old Eve" in you. In my opinion you ought to be a mother.'

'When doctors find a way without preliminaries.'

'You're wasting yourself, my dear. At any moment that you liked to crook your little finger, old man Dornford would fall on his knees to you. Don't you like him?'

'As nice a man as I've seen for a long time.'

'"Murmured she coldly, turning towards the door." Give me a kiss.'

'Darling,' said Dinny, 'I do hope things are going to be all right. I shan't pray for you, in spite of my look of decline; but I'll dream that your ship comes home.'

Chapter Fourteen

⟨✦⟩

YOUNG CROOM's second visit to England's Past at Drury
Lane was the first visit of the other three members of Dornford's
little dinner party, and by some fatality, not unconnected with
him who took the tickets, they were seated two by two; young
Croom with Clare in the middle of the tenth row, Dornford and
Dinny in returned stalls at the end of the third. . . .

'Penny for your thoughts, Miss Cherrell?'

'I was thinking how the English face has changed since
1900.'

'It's the hair. Faces in pictures a hundred to a hundred and
fifty years ago are much more like ours.'

'Drooping moustaches and chignons do hide expression, but
was there the expression?'

'You don't think the Victorians had as much character?'

'Probably more, but surely they suppressed it; even in their
dresses, always more stuff than was needed; frock-coats, high
collars, cravats, bustles, button boots.'

'The leg *was* on their nerves, but the neck wasn't.'

'I give you the woman's necks. But look at their furniture:
tassels, fringes, antimacassars, chandeliers, enormous sideboards.
They *did* play hide-and-seek with the soul, Mr Dornford.'

'And every now and then it popped out, like little Edward
after unclothing himself under his mother's dining-table at
Windsor.'

'He never did anything quite so perfect again.'

'I don't know. He was another Restoration in a mild way.
Big opening of floodgates under him.' . . .

'He *has* sailed, hasn't he, Clare?'

'Yes, he's sailed all right. Look at Dornford! He's fallen for
Dinny completely. I wish she'd take to him.'

'Why shouldn't she?'

'My dear young man, Dinny's been in very deep waters. She's
in them even now.'

'I don't know anyone I'd like better for a sister-in-law.'

'Don't you wish you may get her?'

'God! Yes! Don't I!'

'What do *you* think of Dornford, Tony?'

'Awfully decent, not a bit dry.'

'If he were a doctor he'd have a wonderful bedside manner. He's a Catholic.'

'Wasn't that against him in the election?'

'It would have been, but his opponent was an atheist, so they cried quits.'

'Terrible humbug, politics.'

'But rather fun.'

'Still, Dornford won that Bar point-to-point – he must have guts.'

'Lots. I should say he'd face anything in his quiet way. I'm quite fond of him.'

'Oh!'

'No intention to incite you, Tony.'

'This is like being on board ship, sitting side by side, and – stymied. Come out for a cigarette.'

'People are coming back. Prepare yourself to point me the moral of the next act. At present I don't see any.'

'Wait!' ...

Dinny drew in her breath.

'That's terrible. I can just remember the *Titanic*. Awful, the waste in the world!'

'You're right.'

'Waste of life, and waste of love.'

'Have *you* come up against much waste?'

'Yes.'

'You don't care to talk about it?'

'No.'

'I don't believe that your sister's going to be wasted. She's too vivid.'

'Yes, but her head's in chancery.'

'She'll duck from under.'

'I can't bear to think of her life being spoiled. Isn't there some legal dodge, Mr Dornford; without publicity, I mean?'

'If he would give cause, there need be very little of that.'

'He won't. He's feeling vindictive.'

'I see. Then I'm afraid there's nothing for it but to wait. These things generally disentangle themselves. Catholics are not supposed to believe in divorce. But if *you* feel this is a case for one –'

'Clare's only twenty-four. She can't live alone the rest of her life.'

'Were *you* thinking of doing that?'

'I! That's different.'

'Yes, you're very unlike, but to have you wasted would be far worse. Just as much worse as wasting a lovely day in winter is than wasting one in summer.'

'The curtain's going up.' ...

'I wonder,' muttered Clare: 'It didn't look to me as if their love would have lasted long. They were eating each other like sugar.'

'My God, if you and I on that boat had been –'

'You're very young, Tony.'

'Two years older than you.'

'And about ten years younger.'

'Don't you really believe in love lasting, Clare?'

'Not passion. And after that generally the deluge. Only with those two on the *Titanic* it came too soon. A *cold* sea! Ugh!'

'Let me pull your cloak up.'

'I don't believe I like this show too frightfully, Tony. It digs into you, and I don't want to be dug into.'

'I liked it better the first time, certainly.'

'Thank you!'

'It's being close to you, and not close enough. But the war part of the play's the best.'

'The whole thing makes me feel I don't want to be alive.'

'That's "the satire."'

'One half of him is mocking the other. It gives me the fidgets. Too like oneself.'

'I wish we'd gone to a movie, I could have held your hand.'

'Dornford's looking at Dinny as if she were the Madonna of the future that he wanted to make a Madonna of the past.'

'So he does, you say.'

'He really has a nice face. I wonder what he'll think of the war part. "Weigh-hey! Up she rises!"' ...

Dinny sat with closed eyes, acutely feeling the remains of moisture on her cheeks.

'But she never would have done that,' she said, huskily, 'not waved a flag and cheered. Never! She might have mixed in the crowd, but never that!'

'No, that's a stage touch. Pity! But a jolly good act. Really good!'

'These poor gay raddled singing girls, getting more and more wretched and raddled, and that "Tipperary" whistling! The war must have been *awful!*'

'One got sort of exalted.'

'Did that feeling last?'

'In a way. Does that seem rather horrible to you?'

'I never can judge what people ought to feel. I've heard my brother say something of the kind.'

'It wasn't the "Into Battle" feeling either – I'm not the fighting man. It's a cliché to say it was the biggest thing that will ever be in one's life.'

'You still feel that?'

'It has been up to now. But –! I must tell you while I've a chance – I'm in love with you, Dinny. I know nothing about you, you know nothing about me. That doesn't make any difference. I fell in love with you at once; it's been getting deeper ever since. I don't expect you to say anything, but you might think about it now and then....'

Clare shrugged her shoulders.

'Did people really go on like that at the Armistice? Tony! Did people –?'

'What?'

'Really go on like that?'

'I don't know.'

'Where were you?'

'At Wellington, my first term. My father was killed in the war.'

'Oh! I suppose mine might have been, and my brother. But even then! Dinny says my mother cried when the Armistice came.'

'So did mine, I believe.'

'The bit I liked best was that between the son and the girl. But the whole thing makes you feel too much. Take me out, I want a cigarette. No, we'd better not. One always meets people.'

'Damn!'

'Coming here with you was the limit. I've promised solemnly not to give offence for a whole year. Oh! cheer up! You'll see lots of me....'

'"Greatness, and dignity, and peace,"' murmured Dinny, standing up, 'and the greatest of these is "dignity."'

'The hardest to come by, anyway.'

'That girl singing in the night club, and the jazzed sky! Thank you awfully, Mr Dornford. I shan't forget this play easily.'

'Nor what I said to you?'

'It was very sweet of you, but the aloe only blooms once in a hundred years.'

'I can wait. It's been a wonderful evening for me.'

'Those two!'

'We'll pick them up in the hall.'

'Do you think England ever had greatness and dignity and peace?'

'No.'

'But "There's a green hill far away, without a city wall." Thank you – I've had this cloak three years.'

'Charming it is!'

'I suppose most of these people will go on to night clubs now.'

'Not five per cent.'

'I should like a sniff of home air tonight, and a long look at the stars....'

Clare turned her head.

'Don't, Tony!'

'How then?'

'You've been with me all the evening.'

'If only I could take you home!'

'You can't, my dear. Squeeze my little finger, and pull yourself together.'

'Clare!'

'Look! They're just in front – now vanish! Get a good long
drink at the Club and dream of horses. There! Was that close
enough? Good night, dear Tony!'

'God! Good night!'

Chapter Fifteen

◄‹›►

TIME has been compared with a stream, but it differs – you
cannot cross it, grey and even-flowing, wide as the world itself,
having neither ford nor bridge; and though, according to philo-
sophers, it may flow both up and down, the calendar as yet
follows it but one way.

November, then, became December, but December did not
become November. Except for a cold snap or two the weather
remained mild. Unemployment decreased; the adverse balance
of trade increased; seven foxes escaped for every one killed; the
papers fluttered from the storms in their tea-cups; a great deal of
income tax was paid; still more was not; the question: 'Why
has prosperity gone to pot?' continued to bewilder every mind;
the pound went up, the pound went down. In short, time
flowed, but the conundrum of existence remained unsolved.

At Condaford the bakery scheme was dropped. Every penny
that could be raised was to be put into pigs, poultry and potatoes. Sir Lawrence and Michael were now deep in the 'Three P.
Plan,' and Dinny had become infected. She and the General spent
all their days preparing for the millennium which would follow
its adoption. Eustace Dornford had expressed his adherence to
the proposition. Figures had been prepared to show that in ten
years one hundred millions a year could be knocked off Britain's
purchasing bill by graduated prohibition of the import of these
three articles of food, without increasing the cost of living. With

a little organization, a fractional change in the nature of the Briton, and the increase of wheat offals, the thing was as good as done. In the meantime, the General borrowed slightly on his life assurance policy and paid his taxes.

The new Member, visiting his constituency, spent Christmas at Condaford, talking almost exclusively of pigs, instinct telling him that they were just then the surest line of approach to Dinny's heart. Clare, too, spent Christmas at home. How, apart from secretarial duties, she had spent the intervening time was tacitly assumed. No letter had come from Jerry Corven, but it was known from the papers that he was back in Ceylon. During the days between Christmas and the New Year the habitable part of the old house was full: Hilary, his wife, and their daughter Monica; Adrian and Diana, with Sheila and Ronald, now recovered from the measles – no such family gathering had been held for years. Even Sir Lionel and Lady Alison drove down for lunch on New Year's Eve. With such an overwhelming Conservative majority it was felt that 1932 would be important. Dinny was run off her legs. She gave no sign of it, but had less an air of living in the past. So much was she the party's life and soul that no one could have told she had any of her own. Dornford gazed at her in speculation. What was behind that untiring cheerful selflessness? He went so far as to ask of Adrian, who seemed to be her favourite.

'This house wouldn't work without your niece, Mr Cherrell.'

'It wouldn't. Dinny's a wonder.'

'Doesn't she ever think of herself?'

Adrian looked at him sideways. The pale-brown, rather hollow-cheeked face, with its dark hair, and hazel eyes, was sympathetic; for a lawyer and a politician, he looked sensitive. Inclined, however, to a sheepdog attitude where Dinny was concerned, he answered with caution:

'Why no, no more than reason; indeed, not so much.'

'She looks to me sometimes as if she'd been through something pretty bad.'

Adrian shrugged. 'She's twenty-seven.'

'Would you mind awfully telling me what it was? This isn't curiosity. I'm – well, I'm in love with her, and terrified of butting in and hurting her through ignorance.'

Adrian took a long gurgling pull at his pipe.

'If you're in dead earnest —'

'Absolutely dead earnest.'

'It might save her a pang or two. She was terribly in love, the year before last, and it came to a tragic end.'

'Death?'

'No. I can't tell you the exact story, but the man had done something that placed him, in a sense — or at all events he thought so — outside the pale; and he put an end to their engagement rather than involve Dinny, and went off to the Far East. It was a complete cut. Dinny has never spoken of it since, but I'm afraid she'll never forget.'

'I see. Thank you very much. You've done me a great service.'

'Sorry if it's hurt,' murmured Adrian; 'but better, perhaps, to have one's eyes open.'

'Much.'

Resuming the tune on his pipe, Adrian stole several glances at his silent neighbour. That averted face wore an expression not exactly dashed or sad, but as if contending deeply with the future. 'He's the nearest approach,' he thought, 'to what I should like for her — sensitive, quiet, and plucky. But things are always so damnably perverse!'

'She's very different from her sister,' he said at last.

Dornford smiled.

'Ancient and modern.'

'Clare's a pretty creature, though.'

'Oh, yes, and lots of qualities.'

'They've both got grit. How does she do her work?'

'Very well; quick in the uptak', good memory, heaps of *savoir-faire*.'

'Pity she's in such a position. I don't know why things went wrong, and I don't see how they can come right.'

'I've never met Corven.'

'Quite nice to meet; but, by the look of him, a streak of cruelty.'

'Dinny says he's vindictive.'

Adrian nodded. 'I should think so. And that's bad when it comes to divorce. But I hope it won't — always a dirty business, and probably the wrong person tarred. I don't remember a divorce in our family.'

'Nor in mine, but we're Catholics.'

'Judging by your experience in the Courts, should you say English morality is going downhill?'

'No. On the upgrade, if anything.'

'But surely the standard is slacker?'

'People are franker, not quite the same thing.'

'You lawyers and judges, at all events,' said Adrian, 'are exceptionally moral men.'

'Oh! Where did you get that from?'

'The papers.'

Dornford laughed.

'Well!' said Adrian, rising. 'Let's have a game of billiards. . . .'

On the Monday after New Year's Day the party broke up. In the afternoon Dinny lay down on her bed and went to sleep. The grey light failed and darkness filled her room. She dreamed she was on the bank of a river. Wilfrid was holding her hand, pointing to the far side, and saying: '"One more river, one more river to cross!"' Hand in hand they went down the bank. In the water all became dark! She lost touch of his hand and cried out in terror. Losing her foothold, she drifted, reaching her hands this way and that, and his voice, further and further away, '"One more river – one more river,"' died to a sigh. She awoke agonized. Through the window opposite was the dark sky, the elm tree brushing at the stars – no sound, no scent, no colour. And she lay quite still, drawing deep breaths to get the better of her anguish. It was long since she had felt Wilfrid so close to her, or been so poignantly bereaved once more.

She got up, and, having bathed her face in cold water, stood at her window looking into the starry dark, still shuddering a little from the vivid misery of her dream. 'One more river!'

Someone tapped on the door.

'Yes?'

'It's old Mrs Purdy, Miss Dinny. They say she's going fast. The doctor's there, but –'

'Betty! Does Mother know?'

'Yes, miss, she's going over.'

'No! I'll go. Stop her, Annie!'

'Yes, miss. It's a seizure – nurse sent over to say they can't do nothing. Will you have the light on, miss?'

'Yes, turn it up.'

Thank God they had managed to put the electric light in, at last!

'Get me this little flask filled with brandy, and put my rubber boots in the hall. I shan't be two minutes coming down.'

'Yes, miss.'

Slipping on a jersey and cap, and catching up her mole-skin fur coat, she ran downstairs, stopping for a second at her mother's door to say she was going. Putting on her rubber boots in the hall, and taking the filled flask, she went out. It was groping dark, but not cold for January. The lane was slithery under foot, and, since she had no torch, the half mile took her nearly a quarter of an hour. The doctor's car, with its lights on, stood outside the cottage. Unlatching the door, Dinny went into the ground-floor room. There was a fire burning, and one candle alight, but the crowded homely space was deserted by all but the goldfinch in its large cage. She opened the thin door that shut the stairs off, and went up. Pushing the feeble top door gently, she stood looking. A lamp was burning on the window-sill opposite, and the low, sagging-ceilinged room had a shadowy radiance. At the foot of the double bed were the doctor and village nurse, talking in low tones. In the window corner Dinny could see the little old husband crouched on a chair, with his hands on his knees and his crumpled, cherry-cheeked face trembling and jerking slightly. The old cottage woman lay humped in the old bed; her face was waxen, and seemed to Dinny to have lost already almost all its wrinkles. A faint stertorous breathing came from her lips. The eyes were not quite closed, but surely were not seeing.

The doctor crossed to the door.

'Opiate,' he said. 'I don't think she'll recover consciousness. Just as well for the poor old soul! If she does, nurse has another to give her at once. There's nothing to be done but ease the end.'

'I shall stay,' said Dinny.

The doctor took her hand.

'Happy release. Don't fret, my dear.'

'Poor old Benjy!' whispered Dinny.

The doctor pressed her hand, and went down the stairs.

Dinny entered the room; the air was close, and she left the door ajar.

'I'll watch, nurse, if you want to get anything.'

The nurse nodded. In her neat dark blue dress and bonnet she looked, but for a little frown, almost inhumanly impassive. They stood side by side gazing at the old woman's waxen face.

'Not many like her,' whispered the nurse suddenly. 'I'm going to get some things I'll want – back under the half-hour. Sit down, Miss Cherrell, don't tire yourself.'

When she had gone Dinny turned and went up to the old husband in the corner.

'Benjy.'

He wobbled his pippin head, rubbing his hands on his knees. Words of comfort refused to come to Dinny. Just touching his shoulder, she went back to the bed and drew up the one hard wooden chair. She sat, silently watching old Betty's lips, whence issued that faintly stertorous breathing. It seemed to her as if the spirit of a far-off age were dying. There might be other people as old still alive in the village, but they weren't like old Betty, with her simple sense and thrifty order, her Bible-reading and love of gentry, her pride in her eighty-three years, in the teeth that she ought long since to have parted from, and in her record; with her shrewdness and her way of treating her old husband as if he were her rather difficult son. Poor old Benjy – he was not her equal by any manner of means, but what he would do alone one couldn't think. Perhaps one of his granddaughters would find room for him. Those two had brought up seven children in the old days when a shilling fortunately went as far as three now, and the village was full of their progeny; but how would they like little old Benjy, still argumentative and fond of a grumble and a glass, ensconced by their more modern hearths? Well, a nook would turn up for him somewhere. He could never live on here, alone. Two old age pensions for two old people made just the difference as against one for one.

'How I wish I had money!' she thought. He would not want

the goldfinch, anyway. She would take that, and free and feed it in the old greenhouse till it got used to its wings, and then let it go.

The old man cleared his throat in his dim corner. Dinny started and leaned forward. Absorbed in her thoughts, she had not noticed how faint the breathing had become. The pale lips of the old woman were nearly closed now, the wrinkled lids almost fast over the unseeing eyes. No noise was coming from the bed. For a few minutes she sat looking, listening; then passed round to the side and leaned over.

Gone? As if in answer the eyelids flickered; the faintest imaginable smile appeared on the lips, and then, suddenly as a blown-out flame is dark, all was lifeless. Dinny held her breath. It was the first human death she had seen. Her eyes, glued to the old waxen face, saw it settle into its mask of release, watched it being embalmed in that still dignity which marks death off from life. With her finger she smoothed the eyelids.

Death! At its quietest and least harrowing, but yet – death! The old, the universal anodyne; the common lot! In this bed where she had lain nightly for over fifty years under the low, sagged ceiling, a great little old lady had passed. Of what was called 'birth,' of position, wealth, and power, she had none. No plumbing had come her way, no learning, and no fashion. She had borne children, nursed, fed, and washed them, sewn, cooked, and swept, eaten little, travelled not at all in all her years, suffered much pain, never known the ease of superfluity; but her back had been straight, her ways straight, her eyes quiet, and her manners gentle. If she were not the 'great lady,' who was?

Dinny stood, with her head bowed, feeling this to the very marrow of her soul. Old Benjy in that dim corner cleared his throat again. She started, and, trembling a little, went over to him.

'Go and look at her, Benjy; she's asleep.'

She put her hand under his elbow to help the action of his stiffened knees. At his full height he was only up to her shoulder, a little dried-up pippin of a man. She kept at his side, moving across the room.

Together they looked down at the forehead and cheeks,

slowly uncreasing in the queer beauty of death. The little old husband's face went crimson and puffy, like that of a child who had lost its doll; he said in a sort of angered squeak:

'Eh! She'm not asleep. She'm gone. She won't never speak agen. Look! She an't Mother no more! Where's that nurse? She didn' ought to 'ave left 'er –'

'H'ssh! Benjy!'

'But she'm dead. What'll I do?'

He turned his withered apple face up to Dinny, and there came from him an unwashed odour, as of grief and snuff and old potatoes.

'Can't stop 'ere,' he said, 'with Mother like that. 'Tain't naleral.'

'No; go downstairs and smoke your pipe, and tell nurse when she comes.'

'Tell 'er; I'll tell 'er – shoulden never 'ave left 'er. Oh, dear! Oh, dear! Oh, dear!'

Putting her hand on his shoulders, Dinny guided him to the stairway, and watched him stumbling and groping and grieving his way down. Then she went back to the bed. The smoothed-out face had an uncanny attraction for her. With every minute that passed it seemed the more to proclaim superiority. Almost triumphant it was, as she gazed, in its slow, sweet relaxation after age and pain; character revealed in the mould of that brief interval between torturing life and corrupting death. 'Good as gold!' Those were the words they should grave on the humble stone they would put over her. Wherever she was now, or whether, indeed, she was anywhere, did not matter. She had done her bit. Betty!

She was still standing there gazing when the nurse came back.

Chapter Sixteen

SINCE her husband's departure Clare had met young Croom constantly, but always at the stipulated arm's-length. Love had made him unsociable, and to be conspicuously in his company was unwise, so she did not make him known to her friends; they met where they could eat cheaply, see films, or simply walk. To her rooms she had not invited him again, nor had he asked to come. His behaviour, indeed, was exemplary, except when he fell into tense and painful silences, or gazed at her till her hands itched to shake him. He seemed to have paid several visits to Jack Muskham's stud farm, and to be spending hours over books which debated whether the excellence of 'Eclipse' was due to the Lister Turk, rather than to the Darley Arabian, and whether it were preferable to breed-in to Blacklock with St Simon on Speculum or with Speculum on St Simon.

When she returned from Condaford after the New Year, she had not heard from him for five consecutive days, so that he was bulking more largely in her thoughts.

DEAR TONY, [she wrote to him at the Coffee House:]
Where and how are you? I am back. Very happy New Year!

Yours always,
CLARE

The answer did not come for three days, during which she felt at first huffy, then anxious, and finally a little scared. It was indited from the inn at Bablock Hythe:

DARLING CLARE, —
I was ever so relieved to get your note, because I'd determined not to write until I heard from you. Nothing's further from my thoughts than to bore you with myself, and sometimes I don't know whether I am or not. So far as a person can be who is not seeing you, I'm all right; I'm overlooking the fitting up of the boxes for those mares. They (the boxes) will be prime. The difficulty is going to be acclimatization; it's supposed to be mild here, and the pasture looks as if it

would be tip-top. This part of the world is quite pretty, especially the river. Thank God the inn's cheap, and I can live indefinitely on eggs and bacon. Jack Muskham has been brick enough to start my salary from the New Year, so I'm thinking of laying out my remaining sixty-odd pounds on Stapylton's old two-seater. He's just off back to India. Once I'm down here it'll be vital to have a car if I'm to see anything of you, without which life won't be worth living. I hope you had a splendid time at Condaford. Do you know I haven't seen you for sixteen days, and am absolutely starving. I'll be up on Saturday afternoon. Where can I meet you?

> Your ever devoted
> TONY

Clare read this letter on the sofa in her room, frowning a little as she opened, smiling a little as she finished it.

Poor dear Tony! Grabbing a telegraph form, she wrote:

Come to tea Melton Mews. – C.

and dispatched it on her way to the Temple.

The importance attaching to the meeting of two young people depends on the importance which others attach to their not meeting. Tony Croom approached Melton Mews without thinking of anyone but Clare, and failed to observe a shortish man in horn-rimmed spectacles, black boots, and a claret-coloured tie, who looked like the secretary of a learned society. Unobtrusive and unobserved, this individual had already travelled with him from Bablock Hythe to Paddington, from Paddington to the 'Coffee House', from the 'Coffee House' to the corner of Melton Mews; had watched him enter No. 2, made an entry in a pocket-book, and with an evening paper in his hand was now waiting for him to come out again. With touching fidelity he read no news, keeping his prominent glance on that peacock-blue door, prepared at any moment to close himself like an umbrella and vanish into the street-scape. And while he waited (which was his normal occupation) he thought, like other citizens, of the price of living, of the cup of tea which he would like, of his small daughter and her collection of foreign stamps, and of whether he would now have to pay income tax. His imagination dwelled, also, on the curves of a young woman at the tobacconist's where he obtained his 'gaspers'.

His name was Chayne, and he made his living out of a remarkable memory for faces, inexhaustible patience, careful entries in his pocket-book, the faculty of self-obliteration, and that fortunate resemblance to the secretaries of learned societies. He was, indeed, employed by the Polteed Agency, who made their living by knowing more than was good for those about whom they knew it. Having received his instruction on the day Clare returned to London, he had already been five days 'on the job', and no one knew it except his employer and himself. Spying on other people being, according to the books he read, the chief occupation of the people of these islands, it had never occurred to him to look down on a profession conscientiously pursued for seventeen years. He took a pride in his work, and knew himself for a capable 'sleuth'. Though somewhat increasingly troubled in the bronchial regions owing to the draughts he had so often to stand in, he could not by now imagine any other way of passing his time, or any, on the whole, more knowing method of gaining a livelihood. Young Croom's address he had obtained by the simple expedient of waiting behind Clare while she sent her telegram; but, having just failed to read the message itself, he had started at once for Bablock Hythe, since when until now he had experienced no difficulty. Shifting his position from time to time at the end of the street, he entered the Mews itself when it became dark. At half-past five the peacock door was opened and the two young people emerged. They walked, and Mr Chayne walked behind them. They walked fast, and Mr Chayne, with an acquired sense of rhythm, at exactly the same pace. He soon perceived that they were merely going to where he had twice followed Lady Corven already – the Temple. And this gave him a sense of comfort, because of the cup of tea he pined for. Picking his way in and out among the backs of people large enough to screen him, he watched them enter Middle Temple Lane, and part at Harcourt Buildings. Having noted that Lady Corven went in, and that the young man began parading slowly between the entrance and the Embankment, he looked at his watch, doubled back into the Strand, and bolted into an A.B.C. with the words 'Cup of tea and Bath bun, miss, please.' While waiting for these he made a prolonged entry in his pocket-book. Then, blowing on his tea, he drank it from the saucer, ate half the bun, concealed the other half in his hand, paid, and re-entered the Strand. He had just finished the bun when he regained the entrance to the Lane. The young man was still parading slowly. Mr Chayne waited for his back view, and, assuming the air of a belated solicitor's clerk, bolted down past the entrance to Harcourt Buildings into the Inner Temple. There, in a doorway, he scrutinized names until Clare came out. Rejoined by young Croom, she walked up towards the Strand, and Mr Chayne walked too. When, shortly, they took tickets for a cinema, he also took a ticket and entered the row behind. Accustomed to the shadowing of people on their guard, the open innocence they were displaying excited in him a slightly amused if not contemptuous compassion. 'Regular babes in the wood' they seemed to him. He could not tell whether their feet were touching, and passed behind to note the position of their hands. It seemed satisfactory, and he took an empty seat nearer to the gangway. Sure of them now for a couple of hours, he settled down to smoke, feel warm, and enjoy the film. It was one of sport and travel in Africa, where the two principals were always in positions of danger, recorded by the camera of someone who must surely have been in a position of still greater danger. Mr Chayne listened to their manly American voices saying to each other: 'Gee! He's on us!' with an interest which never prevented his knowing that his two young people were listening too. When the lights went up he could see their profiles. 'We're all young at times,' he thought, and his imagination dwelled more intensively on the young lady at his tobacconist's. They looked so settled-in that he took the opportunity to slip out for a moment. It might not occur again for a long time. In his opinion one of the chief defects in detective stories – for he was given to busmen's holidays – was that authors made their 'sleuths' like unto the angels, watching for days without, so to speak, taking their eyes off the ball. It was not so in real life.

He returned to a seat almost behind his young couple on the other side just before the lights went down. One of his favourite stars was now to be featured, and, sure that she would be placed in situations which would enable him to enjoy her to the full, he put a peppermint lozenge in his mouth and leaned back with a sigh. He had not had an evening watch so pleasant for a long time. It was not always 'beer and skittles' at this season of the year; a 'proper chilly job sometimes – no error'.

After ten minutes, during which his star had barely got into her evening clothes, his couple rose.

'Can't stand any more of her voice,' he heard Lady Corven say; and the young man answering: 'Ghastly!'

Wounded and surprised, Mr Chayne waited for them to pass through the curtains before, with a profound sigh, he followed. In the Strand they stood debating, then walked again, but only into a restaurant across the street. Here, buying himself another paper at the door, he saw them going up the stairs. Would it be a private room? He ascended the stairs cautiously. No, it was the gallery! There they were, nicely screened by the pillars, four tables in!

Descending to the lavatory, Mr Chayne changed his horn spectacles to pince-nez and his claret-coloured tie to a rather floppy bow of black and white. This was a device which had often served him in good stead. You put on a tie of conspicuous colour, then changed it to a quieter one of a different shape. A conspicuous tie had the special faculty of distracting attention from a face. You became 'that man with the awful tie!' and when you no longer wore the tie, you were to all intents someone else. Going up again to a table which commanded a view, he ordered himself a mixed grill and pint of stout. They were likely to be some two hours over their meal, so he assumed a literary air, taking out a pouch to roll himself a cigarette and inviting the waiter to give him a light for it. Having in this way established a claim to a life of his own, he read his paper like any gentleman at large and examined the mural paintings. They were warm and glowing; large landscapes with blue skies, seas, palms, and villas, suggestive of pleasure in a way that appealed to him strongly. He had never been further than Boulogne, and, so far as he could see, never would. Five hundred pounds, a lady, a suite in the sun, and gaming tables handy, was not unnaturally his idea of heaven; but, alas, as unattainable. He made no song about it, but, when confronted with allurements like these on the wall, he could not help hankering. It had often struck him as ironical that the people he watched into the Divorce Court so often went to Paradise and stayed there until their cases had blown over and they could marry and come to earth again. Living in Finchley, with the sun once a fortnight and an income averaging perhaps five hundred a year, the vein of poetry in him was damned almost at source; and it was in some sort a relief to let his imagination play around the lives of those whom he watched. That young couple over there, 'good-lookers' both of them, would go back together in a taxi; as likely as not he'd have to wait hours for the young man to come away. The mixed grill was put before him, and he added a little red pepper in view of his probable future. This bit of watching however, and perhaps another one or two, ought to do the trick; and on the whole 'easy money'. Slowly savouring each mouthful so that it might nourish him, and blowing the froth off his stout with the skill of a connoisseur, he watched them bending forward to talk across the table. What they were eating he could not see. To have followed their meal in detail would have given him some indication of their states of mind. Food and love! After this grill he would have cheese and coffee, and put them down to 'expenses'.

He had eaten every crumb, extracted all the information from his paper, exhausted his imagination on the mural paintings, 'placed' the scattered diners, paid his bill, and smoked three 'gaspers' before his quarry rose. He was into his overcoat and outside the entrance before they had even reached the stairs. Noting three taxis within hail, he bent his attention on the hoardings of an adjoining theatre; till he saw the porter beckon one of them, then, walking into the middle of the Strand, he took the one behind it.

'Wait till that cab starts and follow it,' he said to the driver, 'not too close when it stops.'

Taking his seat, he looked at his watch and made an entry in his pocket-book. Having before now followed a wrong cab at some expense, he kept his eyes glued on the taxi's number, which he had noted in his book. The traffic was but thin at this hour before the theatres rose, and the procession simplicity itself. The followed cab stopped at the corner of the Mews. Mr Chayne tapped the glass and fell back on the seat. Through the window he saw them get out and the young man paying. They walked down the Mews. Mr Chayne also paid and followed to the corner. They had reached the peacock door and stood there, talking. Then Lady Corven put her key into the lock and opened the door; the young man, glancing this way and that, followed her in. Mr Chayne experienced a sensation as mixed as his grill. It was, of course, exactly what he had hoped for and expected. At the same time it meant loitering about in the cold for goodness knew how long. He turned up his coat collar and looked for a convenient doorway. A thousand pities that he could not wait, say half an hour, and just walk in. The Courts were very particular nowadays about conclusive evidence. He had something of the feeling that a 'sportsman' has, seeing a fox go to ground and not a spade within five miles. He stood for a few minutes, reading over the entries in his pocket-book under the lamp, and making a final note; then walked to the doorway he had selected and stood there. In half an hour or so the cars would be coming back from the theatre, and he would have to be on the move to escape attention. There was a light in the upstairs window, but in itself, of course, that was not evidence. Too bad! Twelve shillings the return ticket, ten and six the night down there, cabs seven and six; cinema three and six, dinner six bob – he wouldn't charge the tea – thirty-nine and six – say two pounds! Mr Chayne shook his head, put a peppermint lozenge in his mouth, and changed his feet. That corn of his was beginning to shoot a bit. He thought of pleasant things: Broadstairs, his small daughter's black hair, oyster patties, his favourite 'star' in little but a corset belt, and his own nightcap of hot whisky and lemon. All to small purpose; for he was waiting and waiting on feet that ached, and without any confidence that he was collecting anything of real value. The Courts, indeed, had got into such a habit of expecting the parties to be 'called with a cup of tea' that anything short of it was looked upon as suspect. He took out his watch again. He had been here over half an hour. And here came the first car! He must get out of the Mews! He withdrew to its far end. And then almost before he had time to turn his back there came the young man with his hands thrust deep into his pockets, and his shoulders hunched, hurrying away. Heaving a sigh of relief, Mr Chayne noted in his pocket-book: 'Mr C. left at 11.40 p.m.'; and walked towards his Finchley bus.

Chapter Seventeen

◄◄─►►

THOUGH Dinny had no expert knowledge of pictures, she had, with Wilfrid, made an intensive examination of such as were on permanent show in London. She had also enjoyed extremely the Italian Exhibition of 1930. It was, therefore, natural to accept her Uncle Adrian's invitation to accompany him to the French Exhibition of 1932. After a syncopated lunch in Piccadilly they passed through the turnstile at one o'clock on January the 22nd, and took stand before the Primitives. Quite a number of people were emulating their attempt to avoid the crowd, so that their progress was slow, and it was an hour before they had reached the Watteaus.

' "Gilles," ' said Adrian, resting one leg; 'that strikes me as about the best picture yet, Dinny. It's queer – when a genre painter of the decorative school gets hold of a subject or a type that grips him, how thoroughly he'll stir you up. Look at the pierrot's face – what a brooding, fateful, hiding-up expression! There's the public performer, with the private life, incarnate!'

Dinny remained silent.

'Well, young woman?'

'I was wondering whether art was so conscious. Don't you think he just wanted to paint that white dress, and his model did the rest? It's a marvellous expression, but perhaps he had it. People do.'

Adrian noted her face with the tail of his eye. Yes! People did. Paint her in repose, render her when she wasn't aware of how she was looking, of keeping her end up, or whatever you might call it, and wouldn't you have a face that stirred you with all that lay behind it? Art was unsatisfactory. When it gave you the spirit, distilled the essence, it didn't seem real; and when it gave you the gross, cross-currented, contradictory surface, it didn't seem worth while. Attitudes, fleeting expressions, tricks of light – all by way of being 'real', and nothing revealed! He said suddenly:

'Great books and portraits are so dashed rare, because artists won't high-light the essential, or if they do, they overdo it.'

'I don't see how that applies to this picture, Uncle. It's not a portrait, it's a dramatic moment and a white dress.'

'Perhaps! All the same, if I could paint you, Dinny, as you truly are, people would say you weren't real.'

'How fortunate!'

'Most people can't even imagine you.'

'Forgive impertinence, Uncle, but – can *you*?'

Adrian wrinkled up his goatee.

'I like to think so.'

'Oh, look! There's the Boucher Pompadour!'

After two minutes in front of its expanse Adrian continued:

'Well, for a man who preferred it nude, he could paint what covers the female body pretty well, couldn't he?'

'Maintenon and Pompadour. I always get them mixed.'

'The Maintenon wore blue stockings, and ministered to Louis the XIVth.'

'Oh, yes! Let's go straight from here to the Manets, Uncle.'

'Why?'

'I don't think I shall last much longer.'

Adrian, glancing round, suddenly saw why. In front of the Gilles were standing Clare and a young man whom he did not know. He put his arm through Dinny's and they passed into the next room but one.

'I noticed your discretion,' he murmured, in front of the 'Boy Blowing Bubbles'. 'Is that young man a snake in the grass, or a worm in the bud, or –?'

'A very nice boy.'

'What's his name?'

'Tony Croom.'

'Oh! the young man on the ship? Does Clare see much of him?'

'I don't ask her, Uncle. She is guaranteed to behave for a year;' and, at the cock of Adrian's eyebrow, added: 'She promised Aunt Em.'

'And after the year?'

'I don't know, nor does she. Aren't these Manets good?'

They passed slowly through the room and came to the last.

'To think that Gauguin struck me as the cream of eccentricity in 1910,' murmured Adrian; 'it shows how things move. I went to that post-impressionist exhibition straight from looking at the Chinese pictures in the B. M. Cézanne, Matisse, Gauguin, Van Gogh – the last word then, hoary now. Gauguin certainly *is* a colourist. But give me the Chinese still. I fear I'm fundamentally of the old order, Dinny.'

'I can see these are good – most of them; but I couldn't live with them.'

'The French have their uses; no other country can show you the transitions of art so clearly. From the Primitives to Clouet, from Clouet to Poussin and Claude, from them to Watteau and his school, thence to Boucher and Greuze, on to Ingres and Delacroix, to the Barbizon lot, to the Impressionists, to the Post-Impressionists; and always some bloke – Chardin, Lépicié, Fragonard, Manet, Degas, Monet, Cézanne – breaking away or breaking through towards the next.'

'Has there ever before been such a violent break as just lately?'

'There's never before been such a violent break in the way people look at life; nor such complete confusion in the minds of artists as to what they exist for.'

'And what *do* they exist for, Uncle?'

'To give pleasure or reveal truth, or both.'

'I can't imagine myself enjoying what they enjoy, and – what is truth?'

Adrian turned up his thumbs.

'Dinny, I'm tired as a dog. Let's slip out.'

Dinny saw her sister and young Croom passing through the archway. She was not sure whether Clare had noticed them, and young Croom was clearly noticing nothing but Clare. She followed Adrian out, in her turn admiring his discretion. But neither of them would admit uneasiness. With whom one went about was now so entirely one's own business.

They had walked up the Burlington Arcade, when Adrian was suddenly startled by the pallor of her face.

'What's the matter, Dinny? You look like a ghost!'

'If you don't mind, Uncle, I'd like a cup of coffee.'

'There's a place in Bond Street.' Scared by the bloodlessness of her smiling lips, he held her arm firmly till they were seated at a little table round the corner.

'Two coffees — extra strong,' said Adrian, and with that instinctive consideration which caused women and children to confide in him, he made no attempt to gain her confidence.

'Nothing so tiring as picture-gazing. I'm sorry to emulate Em and suspect you of not eating enough, my dear. That sort of sparrow-pecking we did before going in doesn't really count.' But colour had come back to her lips.

'I'm very tough, Uncle; but food *is* rather a bore.'

'You and I must go a little tour in France. Their grub can move one's senses if their pictures can't move one's spirit.'

'Did you feel *that*?'

'Compared with the Italian — emphatically. It's all so beautifully thought out. They make their pictures like watches. Perfectly art-conscious and thorough workmen. Unreasonable to ask for more, and yet — perhaps fundamentally unpoetic. And that reminds me, Dinny, I do hope Clare can be kept out of the Divorce Court, for of all unpoetic places that is IT.'

Dinny shook her head.

'I'd rather she got it over. I even think she was wrong to promise. She's not going to change her mind about Jerry. She'll be like a bird with one leg. Besides, who thinks the worse of you nowadays!'

Adrian moved uncomfortably.

'I dislike the thought of those hard-boiled fellows playing battledore with my kith and kin. If they were like Dornford — but they aren't. Seen anything more of him?'

'He was down with us for one night when he had to speak.'

He noticed that she spoke without 'batting an eyelid', as the young men called it nowadays. And, soon after, they parted, Dinny assuring him that she had 'come over quite well again'.

He had said that she looked like a ghost; he might better have said she looked as if she had seen one. For, coming out of that Arcade, all her past in Cork Street had come fluttering like some lonely magpie towards her, beaten wings in her face and swerved away. And now, alone, she turned and walked back there. Resolutely she went to the door, climbed the stairs to Wilfrid's rooms, and rang the bell. Leaning against the window-sill on the landing, she waited with clasped hands, thinking: 'I wish I had a muff!' Her hands felt so cold. In old pictures they stood with veils down and their hands in muffs; but 'the old order changeth,' and she had none. She was just going away when the door was opened. Stack! In slippers! His glance, dark and prominent as ever, fell to those slippers and his demeanour seemed to stammer.

'Pardon me, miss, I was just going to change 'em.'

Dinny held out her hand, and he took it with his old air, as if about to 'confess' her.

'I was passing, and thought I'd like to ask how you were.'

'Fine, thank you, miss! Hope you've been keeping well, and the dog?'

'Quite well, both of us. Foch likes the country.'

'Ah! Mr Desert always thought he was a country dog.'

'Have you any news?'

'Not to say news, miss. I understand from his bank that he's still in Siam. They forward his letters to their branch in Bangkok. His lordship was here not long ago, and I understood him to say that Mr Desert was up river somewhere.'

'A river!'

'The name escapes me, something with a "Yi" in it, and a "sang" – was it? I believe it's very 'ot there. If I may say so, miss, you haven't much colour considering the country. I was down home in Barnstaple at Christmas, and it did me a power of good.'

Dinny took his hand again.

'I'm very glad to have seen you, Stack.'

'Come in, miss. You'll see I keep the room just as it was.'

Dinny followed to the doorway of the sitting-room.

'Exactly the same, Stack; he might almost be there.'

'I like to think so, miss.'

'Perhaps he is,' said Dinny. 'They say we have astral bodies. Thank you.' She touched his arm, passed him, and went down the stairs. Her face quivered and was still, and she walked rapidly away.

A river! Her dream! 'One more river!'

In Bond Street a voice said: 'Dinny!' and she turned to see Fleur.

'Whither away, my dear? Haven't seen you for an age. I've just been to the French pictures. Aren't they divine? I saw Clare there with a young man in tow. Who is he?'

'A shipmate — Tony Croom.'

'More to come?'

Dinny shrugged, and, looking at her trim companion, thought: 'I wish Fleur didn't always go so straight to the point.'

'Any money?'

'No. He's got a job, but it's very slender — Mr Muskham's Arab mares.'

'Oh! Three hundred a year — five at the outside. That's no good at all. You know, really, she's making a great mistake. Jerry Corven will go far.'

Dinny said drily: 'Further than Clare, anyway.'

'You mean it's a complete breach?'

Dinny nodded. She had never been so near disliking Fleur.

'Well, Clare's not like you. She belongs to the new order, or disorder. That's why it's a mistake. She'd have a much better time if she stuck to Jerry, nominally at least. I can't see her poor.'

'She doesn't care about money,' said Dinny coldly.

'Oh, nonsense! Money's only being able to do what you want to do. Clare certainly cares about that.'

Dinny, who knew that this was true, said, still more coldly:

'It's no good to try and explain.'

'My dear, there's nothing to explain. He's hurt her in some way, as, of course, he would. That's no reason in the long run. That perfectly lovely Renoir — the man and woman in the box! Those people lived lives of their own — together. Why shouldn't Clare?'

'Would you?'

Fleur gave a little shrug of her beautifully fitted shoulders.

'If Michael wasn't such a dear. Besides — children.' Again she gave that little shrug.

Dinny thawed. 'You're a fraud, Fleur. You don't practise what you preach.'

'My dear, my case is exceptional.'

'So is everybody's.'

'Well, don't let's squabble. Michael says your new Member, Dornford, is after his own heart. They're working together on pigs, poultry, and potatoes. A great stunt, and the right end of the stick, for once.'

'Yes, we're going all out for pigs at Condaford. Is Uncle Lawrence doing anything at Lippinghall?'

'No. He invented the plan, so he thinks he's done his bit. Michael will make him do more when he's got time. Em is screamingly funny about it. How do you like Dornford?'

Asked this question twice in one morning, Dinny looked her cousin by marriage full in the face.

'He seems to me almost a paragon.'

She felt Fleur's hand slip suddenly under her arm.

'I wish you'd marry him, Dinny dear. One doesn't marry paragons, but I fancy one could "fault" him if one tried.'

It was Dinny's turn to give a little shrug, looking straight before her.

Chapter Eighteen

◄‹·›►

THE third of February was a day so bland and of such spring-like texture that the quickened blood demanded adventure.

This was why Tony Croom sent an early wire and set out at noon from Bablock Hythe in his old but newly-acquired two-seater. The car was not his 'dream,' but it could do fifty at the pinch he liked to give it. He took the nearest bridge, ran for Abingdon, and on past Benson to Henley. There he stopped to snatch a sandwich and 'fill up,' and again on the bridge for a glimpse at the sunlit river softly naked below the bare woods. From there on he travelled by the clock, timing himself to reach Melton Mews at two o'clock.

Clare was not ready, having only just come in. He sat in the downstairs room, now furnished with three chairs, a small table, of quaint design, cheap owing to the slump in antiques, and an amethyst-coloured chased decanter containing sloe gin. Nearly half an hour he sat there before she came down the spiral stairs in fawn-coloured tweeds and hat, with a calfskin fur coat over her arm.

'Well, my dear! Sorry to have kept you. Where are we going?'

'I thought you might care to have a look at Bablock Hythe. Then we might come back through Oxford, have high tea there, wander about a bit among the colleges, and be back here before eleven. That do?'

'Perfect. And where will you sleep?'

'I? Oh! tool along home again. I'd be there by one.'

'Poor Tony! A hard day!'

'Oh! Not two hundred and fifty miles. You won't want your fur on yet, the car doesn't open – worse luck.'

They passed out at the westward mouth of the mews, narrowly missing a motor cyclist, and slid on towards the Park.

'She goes well, Tony.'

'Yes, she's an easy old thing, but I always feel she might bust at any moment. Stapylton gave her a terrible doing. And I don't like a light-coloured car.'

Clare leaned back, by the smile on her lips she was enjoying herself.

There was little conversation on that, the first long drive they had taken together. Both had the youthful love of speed, and young Croom got every ounce out of the car that the traffic would permit. They reached the last crossing of the river under two hours.

'Here's the inn where I dig,' he said presently. 'Would you like tea?'

'Not wise, my dear. When I've seen the boxes and paddocks, we'll get out of here to where you're not known.'

'I must just show you the river.'

Through its poplars and willow trees the white way of the river gleamed, faintly goldened by the sunken sun. They got out to look. The lamb's tails on the hazels were very forward.

Clare twisted off a spray.

'False spring. There's a lot to come before the real spring yet.'

A current of chilly air came stealing down the river, and mist could be seen rising on the meadows beyond.

'Only a ferry here, then, Tony?'

'Yes, and a short cut into Oxford the other side, about five miles. I've walked it once or twice: rather nice.'

'When the blossom and meadow flowers come, it'll be jolly. Come along! Just show me where the paddocks lie, and we'll get on to Oxford.'

They got back into the car.

'Won't you see the boxes?'

She shook her head.

'I'll wait till the mares are here. There's a subtle distinction between your bringing me to look at boxes and my coming to look at mares. Are they really from Nejd?'

'So Muskham swears. I shall believe or not when I've seen the syces in charge of them.'

'What colour?'

'Two bays and a chestnut.'

The three paddocks sloped slightly towards the river and were sheltered by a long spinney.

'Ideal drainage and all the sun there is. The boxes are round that corner under the spinney. There's a good deal to do still; we're putting in a heater.'

'It's very quiet here.'

'Practically no cars on this road; motor cycles now and then – there's one now.'

A cycle came sputtering towards them, stopped, wrenched round, and went sputtering back.

'Noisy brutes!' murmured young Croom. 'However, the mares will have had their baptism by the time they get here.'

'What a change for them, poor dears!'

'They're all to be golden something: Golden Sand, Golden Houri, and Golden Hind, these three.'

'I didn't know Jack Muskham was a poet.'

'It stops at horses, I think.'

'Really marvellous, the stillness, Tony!'

'Past five. The men have stopped work on my cottages – they're converting.'

'How many rooms?'

'Four. Bedroom, sitting-room, kitchen, bathroom. But one could build on.'

He looked at her intently. But her face was averted.

'Well,' he said abruptly, 'all aboard. We'll get to Oxford before dark.'

Oxford – between lights, like all towns, at its worst – seemed to say: 'Doomed to villadom, cars, and modernity, I am beyond your aid.'

To those two, hungry and connected with Cambridge, it offered little attraction till they were seated in the Mitre before anchovy sandwiches, boiled eggs, toast, muffins, scones, jam, and a large pot of tea. With every mouthful the romance of Oxford became apparent. This old inn, where they alone were eating, the shining fire, red curtains being drawn, the unexpected cosy solitude, prepared them to find it 'marvellous' when they should set forth. A motor cyclist in leather overalls looked in and went away. Three undergraduates chirped in the doorway, selected a table for dinner, and passed on. Now and again a waitress renewed their toast or fiddled at some table. They were deliciously alone. Not till past seven did they rise.

'Let's scout,' said Clare. 'We've lots of time.'

The Oxford world was dining, and the streets were almost empty. They wandered at random, choosing the narrower ways and coming suddenly on colleges and long old walls. Nothing seemed modern now. The Past had them by the throat. Dark towers, and old half-lit stone-work; winding, built in, glimpsy passages; the sudden spacious half-lighted gloom of a chanced-on quadrangle; chiming of clocks, and the feeling of a dark and old and empty town that was yet brimming with hidden modern life and light, kept them almost speechless; and, since they had never known their way, they were at once lost.

Young Croom had entwined her arm in his, and kept his step in time to hers. Neither of them was romantic, but both just then had a feeling as if they had wandered into the maze of history.

'I rather wish,' said Clare, 'that I'd been up here or at Cambridge.'

'One never got a nooky feeling like this at Cambridge. In the dark this is much more medieval. There the colleges are together in a line. The "backs" lay over anything they've got here, but the old atmosphere here is far stronger.'

'I believe I could have enjoyed the past. Palfreys and buff jerkins. You'd have looked divine, Tony, in a buff jerkin, and one of those caps with a long green feather.'

'The present with you is good enough for me. This is the longest time we've ever spent together without a break.'

'Don't get soppy. We're here to look at Oxford. Which way shall we go now?'

'All the same to me,' said his remote voice.

'Hurt? That's a big college! Let's go in.'

'They'll be coming out of hall. Past eight; we'd better stick to the streets.'

They wandered up the Cornmarket to the Broad, stood before the statues on the right, then turned into a dim square with a circular building in the centre, a church at the end, and colleges for its side walls.

'This must be the heart,' said Clare. 'Oxford certainly has its points. Whatever they do to the outside, I don't see how they can spoil all this.'

With mysterious suddenness the town had come to life; youths were passing with short gowns over their arms, flapping free, or wound round their necks. Of one of them young Croom asked where they were.

'That's the Radcliffe. This is Brasenose, and the High's down there.'

'And the Mitre?'

'To your right.'

'Thanks.'

'Not at all.'

He bent his uncapped head towards Clare and flapped on.

'Well, Tony?'

'Let's go in and have cocktails.'

A motorist, well capped and leathered, standing by his cycle, looked after them intently as they went into the hotel.

After cocktails and biscuits, they came out feeling, as young Croom said: 'Bright and early. We'll go back over Magdalen Bridge, through Benson, Dorchester, and Henley.'

'Stop on the bridge, Tony. I want to see my name-sake.'

The bridge lights threw splashes on the Cherwell's inky stream, the loom of Magdalen lay solid on the dark, and away towards the Christchurch meadows, a few lamps shone. Whence they had come the broad, half-lighted strip of street ran between glimpsed grey frontages and doorways. And the little river over which they were at a standstill seemed to flow with secrecy.

'The "Char" they call it, don't they?'

'In the summer I shall have a punt, Clare. The upper river's even better than this.'

'Will you teach me to punt?'

'Won't I!'

'Nearly ten! Well, I've enjoyed that, Tony.'

He gave her a long side-glance and started the engine. It seemed as if he must always be 'moving on' with her. Would there never be a long and perfect stop?

'Sleepy, Clare?'

'Not really. That was a mighty strong cocktail. If you're tired I could drive.'

'Tired? Gracious, no! I was only thinking that every mile takes me that much away from you.'

In the dark a road seems longer than by day, and so different. A hundred unremembered things appear — hedges, stacks, trees, houses, turnings. Even the villages seem different. In Dorchester they stopped to make sure of the right turning; a motor cyclist passed them, and young Croom called out: 'To Henley?'

'Straight on!'

They came to another village.

'This,' said young Croom, 'must be Nettlebed. Nothing till Henley now, and then it's thirty-five miles. We shall be up by twelve.'

'Poor dear, and you've got to do all this back again.'

'I shall drive like Jehu. It's a good anodyne.'

Clare touched his coat cuff, and there was another silence.

They had reached a wood when he slackened suddenly. 'My lights have gone!'

A motor cyclist skidded past, calling: 'Your lights are out, sir!'

Young Croom stopped the engine.

'That's torn it. The battery must be used up.'

Clare laughed. He got out and moved round, examining the car. 'I remember this wood. It's a good five miles to Henley. We must creep on and trust to luck.'

'Shall I get out and walk ahead?'

'No, it's so pitch dark. I might run over you.'

After a hundred yards or so he stopped again.

'I'm off the road. I've never driven in darkness like this.'

Clare laughed again.

'An adventure, my dear.'

'I've got no torch. This wood goes on for a mile or two, if I remember.'

'Let's try again.'

A car whizzed past, and the driver shouted at them.

'Follow his lights, Tony!' But before he could start the engine the car had dipped or turned and was gone. They crept on slowly.

'Damn!' said young Croom, suddenly, 'off the road again!'

'Pull her right in off the road then, and let's think. Isn't there anything at all before Henley?'

'Not a thing. Besides, recharging a battery can't be done just anywhere; but I expect it's a wire gone.'

'Shall we leave the car and walk in? She'll be all right here in the wood.'

'And then?' muttered young Croom. 'I must be back with her by daylight. I'll tell you what; I'll walk you in to the hotel, borrow a torch and come back to her. With a torch I could get her down, or stay with her till daylight, and then come down and pick you up at the Bridge.'

'Ten miles walking for you! Why not both stay with her and see the sun rise? I've always wanted to spend a night in a car.'

In young Croom a struggle took place. A whole night with her – alone!

'D'you mean you'd trust me?'

'Don't be old-fashioned, Tony. It's much the best thing to do, and rather a lark. If a car came into us, or we were run in for driving without lights, that would be awkward if you like.'

'There's never a moon when you want one,' muttered young Croom. 'You really mean it?'

Clare touched his arm.

'Pull her further in, among the trees. Very slow. Look out! Stop!'

There was a slight bump. Clare said:

'We're up against a tree, and our tail's to the road. I'll get out and see if anyone can see us.'

Young Croom waited, arranging the cushions and rug for her. He was thinking: 'She can't really love me, or she'd never take it so coolly!' Quivering at the thought of this long dark night with her, he yet knew it was going to be torture. Her voice said:

'All right. I should say no one could see the car. You go and have a look. I'll get in.'

He had to feel his way with his feet. The quality of the ground showed him when he had reached the road. It was less densely dark, but he could see no stars. The car was completely invisible. He waited, then turned to feel his way back. So lost was the car that he had to whistle and wait for her answering whistle to find it. Dark, indeed! He got in.

'Window down or up?'

'Half-way down, I should say. I'm comfy, Tony.'

'Thank God for that! D'you mind my pipe?'

'Of course not. Give me a cigarette. This is almost perfect.'

'Almost,' he said in a small voice.

'I should like to see Aunt Em's face. Are you warm?'

'Nothing goes through leather. Are you?'

'Lovely!' There was a silence; then she said: 'Tony! Forgive me, won't you? I did promise.'

'It's quite all right,' said young Croom.

'I can just see your nose by your pipe's glow.'

By the light of her cigarette he, in turn, could see her teeth, her smiling lips, her face lasting just to the eyes, and fading out.

'Take off your hat, Clare. And any time you like, here's my shoulder.'

'Don't let me snore.'

'*You* snore!'

'Everyone snores on occasion. This will be it.'

They talked for a little. But all seemed unreal, except just being beside her in the dark. He could hear now and again a car passing; other noises of the night there were none; too dark even for the owls. His pipe went out, and he put it away. She lay back beside him so close that he could feel her arm against his. He held his breath. Had she dropped off? Oh! He was in for a sleepless night, with this faint perfume from her egging on his senses and the warmth of her arm tingling into his. Even if this were all, it would be sheer waste to sleep. Drowsily she said:

'If you really don't mind, I *will* put my head on your shoulder, Tony.'

'Mind!'

Her head snuggled down on to his scarf; and the faint perfume, which carried with it reminder of a sunny pine wood, increased. Was it credible that she was there against his shoulder, and would be for another six or seven hours? And he shuddered. So still and matter-of-fact! No sign in her of passion or disturbance; he might have been her brother. With the force of revelation he perceived that this night would be a test that he must pass; for if he did not she would recoil and drop away from him. She *was* asleep. Oh! yes. You couldn't counterfeit that little regular cluck, as of the tiniest chicken – a perfect little sound, faintly comic, infinitely precious! Whatever happened to him now, he would have passed a night with her! He sat – still as a mouse, if mice are still. Her head grew heavier and more confiding with the deepening of her slumber. And, while he sat and listened, his feeling for her deepened too, became almost a passion of protection and of service. And the night, cold, dark, still – no cars were passing now – kept him company; like some huge, dark, enveloping, just breathing creature, it was awake. The night did not sleep! For the first time in his life he realized that. Night was wakeful as the day. Unlighted and withdrawn, it had its sentience – neither spoke nor moved, just watched, and breathed. With stars and moon, or, as tonight, lampless and shuttered, it was a great companion.

His arm grew stiff, and, as if that reached her consciousness, she withdrew her head but did not wake. He rubbed his shoulder just in time, for almost at once her head lolled back again. Screwing round till his lips just touched her hair, he heard again, chicklike and bland, that faint rhythmic cluck. It ceased and became the deeper breathing of far-down slumber. Then drowsiness crept on him too; he slept.

Chapter Nineteen

◄◄─►►

YOUNG CROOM awoke, stiff and unconscious of where he was. A voice said :

'It's just getting light, Tony, but I can't see to read the hymn.'

He sat up. 'Heavens! Have I been asleep?'

'Yes, poor dear. I've had a perfect night, just a little achy in the legs. What's the time?'

Young Croom looked at his watch's illumined hands.

'Nearly half past six. Pins and needles. Wow!'

'Let's get out and stretch.'

His voice, far away, even from himself, answered: 'And so it's over.'

'Was it so terrible?'

He put his hands to his head, and did not answer. The thought that next night and all the nights to come he would be apart from her again was like a blow over the heart.

She opened the door.

'I'm going to stamp my feet a bit. Then we might have a stroll to warm ourselves. We shan't get breakfast anywhere till eight.'

He started the engine to warm the car. Light was creeping into the wood; he could see the beech-tree against whose trunk they had passed the night. Then he, too, got out and walked towards the road. Still grey-dark and misty, the wood on either side of its dim open streak looked mournful and mysterious. No wind, no sound! He felt as Adam might have felt, dragging towards the Park Gates of Eden without having earned the right to be expelled. Adam! That quaint, amiable, white, bearded creature. Man before he 'fell,' a nonconformist preacher in a state of nature, with a pet snake, a prize apple, and a female secretary coy and unshingled as Lady Godiva! His blood began to flow again, and he returned to the car.

Clare was kneeling and attending to her hair with a pocket comb and mirror.

'How are you feeling, Tony?'

'Pretty rotten. I think we'll shove along and have breakfast at Maidenhead or Slough.'

'Why not at home? We could be there by eight. I make very good coffee.'

'Fine!' said young Croom. 'I'll do fifty all the way.'

On that very fast drive they spoke little. Both were too hungry.

'While I'm getting breakfast, Tony, you can shave and have a bath. You'll save time and feel comfy driving back. I'll have mine later.'

'I think,' said young Croom, at the Marble Arch, 'I'd better park the car. You go on in alone; it's too conspicuous driving up at this time in the morning; the chauffeurs are sure to be working. I'll slip along in ten minutes.'

When, at eight o'clock, he reached the Mews, she was in a blue wrapper, the little table in the downstair room was set for breakfast, and there was already a scent of coffee.

'I've turned the bath on, Tony, and you'll find a razor.'

'Darling!' said young Croom. 'Shan't be ten minutes.'

He was back again in twelve, and sat down opposite to her. There were boiled eggs, toast, quince jam from Condaford, and real coffee. It was the most delicious meal he had ever eaten, because it was so exactly as if they were married.

'Aren't you tired, darling?'

'Not a bit. I feel thoroughly chirped up. All the same, I don't think we must do it again – too near the hambone altogether.'

'Well, we didn't mean to.'

'No, and you were an angel. Still, it's not exactly what I promised Aunt Em. To the pure all things are not pure.'

'No – blast them! God! How shall I live till I see you again!'

Clare stretched her hand across the little table and gave his a squeeze.

'Now I think you'd better slip off. Just let me look out and see that the coast's clear.'

When she had done this he kissed her hand, got back to his car, and by eleven o'clock was standing alongside a plumber in a horse box at Bablock Hythe. . . .

Clare lay in a very hot bath. It was of the geyser type and not long enough, but it provided a good soak. She felt as when, a little girl, she had done something unpleasing to her governess, without discovery. But poor dear Tony! A pity men were so impatient. They had as little liking for cool philandering as for shopping. They rushed into shops, said: 'Have you such and such? No?' and rushed out again. They hated trying on, being patted here and there, turning their heads to look at their back views. To savour what was fitting was to them anathema. Tony was a child. She felt herself much older by nature and experience. Though much in request before her marriage, Clare had never come into close contact with those, who, centred in London and themselves, were devoid of belief in anything but mockery, motion and enough money to have from day to day a 'good' time. At country houses she had met them, of course, but withdrawn from their proper atmosphere into the air of sport. Essentially an open-air person, of the quick and wiry, rather than the hefty, type, she observed unconsciously the shibboleths of sport. Transplanted to Ceylon, she had kept her tastes, and spent her time in the saddle or on the tennis ground. Reading many novels, she professed, indeed, to keep abreast of the current, with all its impatience of restraint; but, lying in her bath, she was uneasy. It had not been fair to put Tony to such strain as that of last night. The closer she allowed him to come to her, short of the contacts of love, the more she would be torturing him. Drying herself, she made good resolutions, and only with a rush did she reach the Temple by ten o'clock. She might just as well have stayed on soaking in her bath, for Dornford was busy on an important case. She finished what jobs there were, looking idly out over the Temple lawn, whence fine-weather mist was vanishing, and sunlight, brightening to winter brilliance, slanted on to her cheek. And she thought of Ceylon, where the sun was never coolly comforting. Jerry! How, in that horrible, common phrase, was he 'keeping'? And what doing about her? All very well to determine that she would not torture Tony, would keep away from him and spare his senses, but without him – she would be dull and lonely. He had become a habit. A bad habit perhaps – but bad habits were the only ones it was painful to do without.

'I'm naturally a light weight,' she thought. 'So is Tony; all the same he would never let one down!'

And the grass of the Temple lawn seemed suddenly the sea, and this window-sill the ship's bulwark, and he and she leaned there watching the flying fish spring up from the foam and flitter away above the green-blue water. Warmth and colour! Airy shining grace! And she felt melancholy.

'A good long ride is what I want,' she thought. 'I'll go down to Condaford tomorrow, and on Saturday be out all day. I'll make Dinny come out with me; she ought to ride more.'

The clerk entered and said: 'Mr Dornford's going straight from the Courts to the "House" this afternoon.'

'Ah! Do you ever feel hipped, George?'

The clerk, whose face always amused her because it so clearly should have had mutton-chop whiskers on its rosy roundness, replied in his cushiony voice:

'What I miss here is a dog. With my old Toby I never feel lonely.'

'What is he, George?'

'Bull terrier. But I can't bring him here, Mrs Calder'd miss him; besides, if he bit a solicitor –'

'But how perfect!'

George wheezed.

'Ah! you can't have high spirits in the Temple.'

'I should have liked a dog, George, but when I'm out there's no one in.'

'I don't fancy Mr Dornford'll be residential here much longer.'

'Why?'

'He's looking for a house. I've an idea he'd like to marry.'

'Oh! Whom?'

George closed an eye.

'You mean my sister?'

'Ah!'

'Yes. But I don't see how you know.'

George closed the other eye.

'A little bird, Lady Corven.'

'He might do worse, certainly. Not that I'm a great believer in marriage.'

'We don't see the right side of marriage in the Law. But Mr Dornford would make a woman happy – in my opinion.'

'In mine, too, George.'

'He's a very quiet man, but a fund of energy, and considerate. Solicitors like him; judges like him.'

'And wives will like him.'

'Of course he's a Catholic.'

'We all have to be something.'

'Mrs Calder and I've been Anglicans ever since my old dad died. He was a Plymouth Brother – very stiff. Express an opinion of your own, and he'd jump down your throat. Many's the time I've had him threaten me with fire and slaughter. All for my good, you understand. A fine religious old feller. And couldn't bear others not to be. Good red Zummerzet blood, and never forgot it, though he did live in Peckham.'

'Well, George, if Mr Dornford wants me again after all, would you telephone me at five o'clock? I'll look in at my rooms in case.'

Clare walked. The day was even more springlike than yesterday. She went by the Embankment and St James's Park. Alongside the water, clusters of daffodil spikes were pushing up, and tree-shoots swelling into bud. The gentle, warming sunlight fell on her back. It couldn't last! There would be a throwback to winter, for sure! She walked fast out under the chariot, whose horses, not too natural, worried but exhilarated her, passed the Artillery Memorial without a glance, and entered Hyde Park. Warmed up now, she swung out along the Row. Riding was something of a passion with her, so that it always made her restive to see someone else riding a good horse. Queer animals, horses, so fiery and alive at one moment, so dull and ruminative the next!

Two or three hats were raised to her. A long man on a good-looking mare reined up after he had passed and came back.

'I thought it was you. Lawrence told me you were over. Remember me – Jack Muskham?'

Clare – thinking: 'Lovely seat for a tall man!' – murmured: 'Of course!' and was suddenly on her guard.

'An acquaintance of yours is going to look after my Arab mares.'

'Oh! yes, Tony Croom.'

'Nice young chap, but I don't know if he knows enough. Still, he's keen as mustard. How's your sister?'

'Very well.'

'You ought to bring her racing, Lady Corven.'

'I don't think Dinny cares much for horses.'

'I could soon make her. I remember –' he broke off, frowning. In spite of his languid pose, his face seemed to Clare purposeful, brown, lined, ironic about the lips. She wondered how he would take the news that she had spent last night with Tony in a car.

'When do the mares come, Mr Muskham?'

'They're in Egypt now. We'll ship them in April. I might go over for it; possibly take young Croom.'

'I'd love to see them,' said Clare; 'I rode an Arab in Ceylon.'

'We must get you down.'

'Somewhere near Oxford, isn't it?'

'About six miles; nice country. I'll remember. Good-bye!' He raised his hat, touched the mare with his heel, and cantered off.

'My perfect innocence!' she thought. 'Hope I didn't overdo it. I wouldn't like to "get wrong" with him. He looks as if he knew his mind terribly well. Lovely boots! He didn't ask after Jerry!'

Her nerves felt a little shaken, and she struck away from the Row towards the Serpentine.

The sunlit water had no boats on it, but a few ducks on the far side. Did she mind what people thought? Miller of Dee! Only, did he really care for nobody? Or was he just a philosopher? She sat down on a bench in the full sunlight, and suddenly felt sleepy. A night in a car, after all, was not quite the same as a night out of a car. Crossing her arms on her breast, she closed her eyes. Almost at once she was asleep.

Quite a number of people straggled past between her and the bright water, surprised to see one in such nice clothes asleep before lunch. Two little boys carrying toy aeroplanes stopped dead, examining her dark eyelashes resting on her cream-coloured cheeks, and the little twitchings of her just touched-up lips. Having a French governess, they were 'well-bred' little boys without prospect of sticking pins into her or uttering a sudden whoop. But she seemed to have no hands, her feet were crossed and tucked under her chair, and her attitude was such that she had abnormally long thighs. It was interesting; and after they had passed one of them kept turning his head to see more of her.

Thus, for a full hour of elusive spring, Clare slept the sleep of one who has spent a night in a car.

Chapter Twenty

And three weeks passed, during which Clare saw young Croom but four times in all. She was packing for the evening train to Condaford, when the sheep bell summoned her down the spiral stairway.

Outside was a shortish man in horn spectacles, who gave her a vague impression of being connected with learning. He raised his hat.

'Lady Corven?'

'Yes.'

'Pardon me, I have this for you.' Producing from his blue overcoat a longish document, he put it into her hand.

Clare read the words:

In the High Court of Justice
   Probate Divorce and Admiralty Division.
      The Twenty-sixth day of February, 1932.
   In the Matter of the Petition of Sir Gerald Corven.

A weak feeling ran down the back of her legs, and she raised her eyes to the level of those behind the horn-rimmed spectacles.

'Oh!' she said.

The shortish man made her a little bow. She had a feeling that he was sorry for her, and promptly closed the door in his face. She went up the spiral stairs, sat down on the sofa, and lit a cigarette. Then she spread the document on her lap. Her first thought was: 'But it's monstrous – I've done nothing!' Her second: 'I suppose I must read the foul thing!'

She had not read more than: 'The humble petition of Gerald Corven, K. C. B.,' when she had her fourth thought: 'But this is exactly what I want. I shall be free!'

More calmly she read on till she came to the words: 'That your Petitioner claims from the said James Bernard Croom as damages in respect of his said adultery so committed the sum of two thousand pounds.'

Tony! If he had two thousand shillings, it was all! Beast! Revengeful brute! This sudden reduction of the issue to terms of hard cash not only rasped her feelings but brought her a sort of panic. Tony must not, should not be ruined through her! She must see him! Had they – but of course they had served it on him too.

She finished reading the petition, took a long draw at her cigarette and got up.

She went to the telephone, asked for a trunk call and gave the number of his inn.

'Can I speak to Mr Croom? – Gone up to London? – In his car? – When?'

An hour ago! That could only mean that he was coming to see her!

A little soothed, she made a rapid calculation. She could not now catch the train to Condaford; and she got another trunk call through to the Grange.

'Dinny? This is Clare. I can't possibly get down tonight – tomorrow morning instead. ... No! I'm all right; a little worried. Good-bye!'

A little worried! She sat down again, and once more read the 'foul thing' through. They seemed to know everything, except the truth. And neither she nor Tony had ever seen a sign that they were being watched. That man with the horn 'specs,' for instance, evidently knew her, but she'd never seen

im before! She went into the bathroom and washed her face
n cold water. Miller of Dee! The part had become extremely
difficult.

'He'll have had nothing to eat,' she thought.

She set the table downstairs with what she had, made some
coffee, and sat down to smoke and wait. Condaford and the
faces of her people came before her; the face too, of Aunt Em;
and of Jack Muskham; above all the face of her husband, with
its faint, hard-bitten, cat-like smile. Was she to take this lying
down? Apart from the damages, was she to let him triumph
without a fight? She wished now she had taken her father's
and Sir Lawrence's advice and 'clapped a detective on to him.'
Too late now – he would be taking no risks till the case was
over.

She was still brooding by the electric fire when she heard a
car stop outside, and the bell rang.

Young Croom looked chilled and pale. He stood as if so
doubtful of his welcome that she seized both his hands.

'Well, Tony, this is a pleasure!'

'Oh! darling!'

'You look frozen. Have some brandy!'

While he was drinking, she said:

'Don't let's talk of what we ought to have done; only of what
we're going to do.'

He groaned.

'They must have thought us terribly green. I never
dreamed –'

'Nor I. But why shouldn't we have done exactly what we
have done? There's no law against innocence.'

He sat down and leaned his forehead on his hands. 'God
knows this is just what I want; to get you free of him; but I had
no business to let you run the risk. It would be all different if
you felt for me what I feel for you.'

Clare looked down at him with a little smile.

'Now, Tony, be grown-up! It's no good talking about our
feelings. And I won't have any nonsense about its being your
fault. The point is we're innocent. What are we going to do
about it?'

'Of course I shall do whatever you want.'

'I have a feeling,' said Clare, slowly, 'that I shall have to do what my people want me to.'

'God!' said young Croom, getting up: 'To think that if we defend and win, you'll still be tied to him!'

'And to think,' murmured Clare, 'that if we don't defend and win, you'll be ruined.'

'Oh! Damn that – they can only make me bankrupt.'

'And your job?'

'I don't see – I don't know why –'

'I saw Jack Muskham the other day. He looks to me as if he wouldn't like a co-respondent who hadn't given notice of his intentions to the petitioner. You see I've got the jargon.'

'If we *had* been lovers, I would have, at once.'

'Would you?'

'Of course!'

'Even if I'd said "Don't"?'

'You wouldn't have.'

'I don't know that.'

'Well, anyway, it doesn't arise.'

'Except that if we don't defend, you'll feel a cad.'

'God! What a coil!'

'Sit down and let's eat. There's only this ham, but there's nothing like ham when you feel sick.'

They sat down and made motions with their forks.

'Your people don't know, Clare?'

'I only knew myself an hour ago. Did they bring you this same lovely document?'

'Yes.'

'Another slice?'

They ate in silence for a minute or two. Then young Croom got up.

'I really can't eat any more.'

'All right. Smoke!'

She took a cigarette from him, and said:

'Listen. I'm going down to Condaford tomorrow, and I think you'd better come over. They must see you, because whatever's done must be done with open eyes. Have you a solicitor?'

'No.'

'Nor I. I suppose we shall have to have one.'

'I'll see to all that. If only I had money!'

Clare winced.

'I apologize for a husband capable of asking for damages.'

Young Croom seized her hand. 'Darling, I was only thinking of solicitors.'

'Do you remember my answering you on the boat: "Often more damnable, things beginning."'

'I'll never admit that.'

'I was thinking of my marriage, not of you.'

'Clare, wouldn't it be far better, really, not to defend – just let it go? Then you'd be free. And after – if you wanted me, I'd be there, and if you didn't, I wouldn't.'

'Sweet of you, Tony; but I must tell my people. Besides – oh! a lot of things.'

He began walking up and down.

'D'you suppose they'll believe us if we do defend? *I* don't.'

'We shall be telling the exact truth.'

'People never believe the exact truth. What train are you going down by?'

'Ten-fifty.'

'Shall I come too, or in the afternoon from Bablock Hythe?'

'That's best. I'll have broken it to them.'

'Will they mind frightfully?'

'They won't like it.'

'Is your sister there?'

'Yes.'

'That's something.'

'My people are not exactly old-fashioned, Tony, but they're not modern. Very few people are when they're personally involved. The lawyers and the judge and jury won't be, anyway. You'd better go now; and promise me not to drive like Jehu.'

'May I kiss you?'

'It'll mean one more piece of exact truth, and there've been three already. Kiss my hand – that doesn't count.'

He kissed it, muttered: 'God bless you!' and, grabbing his hat, went out.

Clare turned a chair to the unwinking warmth of the electric fire, and sat brooding. The dry heat burned her eyes till they felt as if they had no lids and no capacity for moisture; slowly and definitely she grew angrier. All the feelings she had experienced, before she made up her mind that morning in Ceylon to cut adrift, came back to her with redoubled fury. How dared he treat her as if she had been a 'light of love'? – worse than if she had been one – a light of love would never have stood it. How dared he touch her with that whip? And now how dared he have her watched, and bring this case? She would not lie down under this!

She began methodically to wash up and put the things away. She opened the door wide and let the wind come in. A nasty night, little whirlwinds travelling up and down the narrow Mews!

'Inside me, too,' she thought. Slamming-to the door, she took out her little mirror. Her face seemed so natural and undefended that it gave her a shock. She powdered it and touched her lips with salve. Then, drawing deep breaths, she shrugged her shoulders, lit a cigarette, and went upstairs. A hot bath!

Chapter Twenty-one

THE atmosphere at Condaford into which she stepped next day was guarded. Her words, or the tone of her voice on the telephone, seemed to have seeped into the family consciousness, and she was aware at once that sprightliness would deceive no one. It was a horrible day, too, dank and cold, and she had to hold on to her courage with both hands.

She chose the drawing-room after lunch for disclosure. Taking the document from her bag, she handed it to her father with the words:

'I've had this, Dad.'

She heard his startled exclamation, and was conscious of Dinny and her mother going over to him.

At last he said: 'Well? Tell us the truth.'

She took her foot off the fender and faced them.

'*That* isn't the truth. We've done nothing.'

'Who is this man?'

'Tony Croom? I met him on the boat coming home. He's twenty-six, was on a tea plantation out there, and is taking charge of Jack Muskham's Arab mares at Bablock Hythe. He has no money. I told him to come here this afternoon.'

'Are you in love with him?'

'No. I like him.'

'Is he in love with you?'

'Yes.'

'You say there's been nothing?'

'He's kissed my cheek twice, I think – that's all.'

'Then what do they mean by this – that you spent the night of the third with him?'

'I went down in his car to see his place, and coming back the lights failed in a wood about five miles from Henley – pitch dark. I suggested we should stay where we were till it was light. We just slept and went on up when it was light.'

She heard her mother give a faint gasp, and a queer noise from her father's throat.

'And on the boat? And in your rooms? You say there was nothing, though he's in love, with you?'

'Nothing.'

'Is that absolutely the truth?'

'Yes.'

'Of course,' said Dinny, 'it's the truth.'

'Of course,' said the General. 'And who's going to believe it?'

'We didn't know we were being watched.'

'What time will he be here?'

'Any time now.'

'You've seen him since you had this?'

'Yesterday evening.'

'What does he say?'

'He says he'll do whatever I wish.'

'That, of course. Does *he* think you'll be believed?'

'No.'

The General took the document over to the window, as if the

better to see into it. Lady Charwell sat down, her face very white. Dinny came over to Clare and took her arm.

'When he comes,' said the General suddenly, returning from the window, 'I'll see him alone. Nobody before me, please.'

'Witnesses out of court,' murmured Clare.

The General handed her the document. His face looked drawn and tired.

'I'm terribly sorry, Dad. I suppose we were fools. Virtue is *not* its own reward.'

'Wisdom is,' said the General. He touched her shoulder and marched off to the door, followed by Dinny.

'Does he believe me, Mother?'

'Yes, but only because you're his daughter. He feels he oughtn't to.'

'Do you feel like that, Mother?'

'I believe you because I know you.'

Clare bent over and kissed her cheek.

'Very pretty, Mother dear; but not cheering.'

'You say you like this young man. Did you know him out there?'

'I never saw him till the boat. And, Mother, I may as well tell you that I've not been in the mood for passion. I don't know when I shall be again. Perhaps never!'

'Why not?'

Clare shook her head. 'I won't go into my life with Jerry, not even now, when he's been such a cad as to ask for damages. I'm really much more upset about that than I am about myself.'

'I suppose this young man would have gone away with you, at any moment?'

'Yes; but I haven't wanted to. Besides, I gave Aunt Em a promise. I sort of swore to behave for a year. And I have – so far. It's terribly tempting not to defend, and be free.'

Lady Charwell was silent.

'Well, Mother?'

'Your father is bound to think of this as it affects your name and the family's.'

'Six of one and half-a-dozen of the other, so far as that goes. If we don't defend, it will just go through and hardly be noticed. If we do, it will make a sensation. "Night in a car," and all that, even if we're believed. Can't you see the papers, Mummy? They'll be all over it.'

'I think,' said Lady Charwell slowly, 'it will come back in the end to the feeling your father has about that whip. I've never known him so angry as he was over that. I think he will feel you must defend.'

'I should never mention the whip in court. It's too easily denied, for one thing; and I have some pride, Mother ...'

Dinny had followed to the study, or barrack-room, as it was sometimes called.

'You know this young man, Dinny?' burst out the General.

'Yes, and I like him. He *is* deeply in love with Clare.'

'What business has he to be?'

'Be human, dear!'

'You believe her about the car?'

'Yes. I heard her solemnly promise Aunt Em to behave for a year.'

'Queer sort of thing to have to promise!'

'A mistake, if you ask me.'

'What!'

'The only thing that really matters is that Clare should get free.'

The General stood with head bent, as if he had found food for thought; a slow flush had coloured his cheek-bones.

'She told you,' he said suddenly, 'what she told me, about that fellow having used a whip on her?'

Dinny nodded.

'In old days I could and would have called him out for that. I agree that she must get free, but – not this way.'

'Then you *do* believe her?'

'She wouldn't tell a lie to us like that.'

'Good, Dad! But who else will believe them? Would you, on a jury?'

'I don't know,' said the General, glumly.

Dinny shook her head. 'You wouldn't.'

'Lawyers are damned clever. I suppose Dornford wouldn't take up a case like this?'

'He doesn't practise in the Divorce Court. Besides, she's his secretary.'

'I must get to hear what Kingsons say. Lawrence believes in them. Fleur's father was a member there.'

'Then –' Dinny had begun, when the door was opened.

'Mr Croom, sir.'

'You needn't go, Dinny.'

Young Croom came in. After a glance at Dinny, he moved towards the General.

'Clare told me to come over, sir.'

The General nodded. His narrowed eyes were fixed steadily on his daughter's would-be lover. The young man faced that scrutiny as if on parade, his eyes replying to the General's without defiance.

'I won't beat about the bush,' said the General suddenly. 'You seem to have got my daughter into a mess.'

'Yes, sir.'

'Kindly give me your account of it.'

Young Croom put his hat down on the table, and, squaring his shoulders, said:

'Whatever she has told you is true, sir.'

Dinny saw with relief her father's lips twitching as if with a smile.

'Very correct, Mr Croom; but not what I want. She has told me her version; I should be glad to hear yours.'

She saw the young man moisten his lips, making a curious jerking motion of his head.

'I'm in love with her, sir: have been ever since I first saw her on the boat. We've been going about rather in London – cinemas, theatres, picture galleries, and that; and I've been to her rooms three – no, five times altogether. On February the third I drove her down to Bablock Hythe for her to see where I'm going to have my job; and coming back – I expect she told you – my lights failed, and we were hung up in a pitch-dark wood some miles short of Henley. Well – we – we thought we'd better just stay there until it was light again, instead of risking things. I'd got off the road twice. It really was pitch-dark, and I had no torch. And so – well, we waited in the car till about half-past six, and then came up, and got to her place about eight.' He paused and moistened his lips, then straightened himself again and said with a rush: 'Whether you believe me or not, sir, I swear there was nothing whatever between us in the car; and — and there never has been, except — except that she's let me kiss her cheek two or three times.'

The General, who had never dropped his eyes, said: 'That's substantially what she told us. Anything else?'

'After I had that paper, sir, I motored up to see her at once — that was yesterday. Of course I'll do anything she wants.'

'You didn't put your heads together as to what you would say to us?'

Dinny saw the young man stiffen.

'Of course not, sir!'

'Then I may take it that you're ready to swear there's been nothing, and defend the action?'

'Certainly, if you think there's any chance of our being believed.'

The General shrugged. 'What's your financial position?'

'Four hundred a year from my job.' A faint smile curled his lips: 'Otherwise none sir.'

'Do you know my daughter's husband?'

'No.'

'Never met him?'

'No, sir.'

'When did you first meet Clare?'

'On the second day of the voyage home.'

'What were you doing out there?'

'Tea-planting; but they amalgamated my plantation with some others, for economy.'

'I see. Where were you at school?'

'Wellington, and then at Cambridge.'

'You've got a job with Jack Muskham?'

'Yes, sir, his Arab mares. They're due in the spring.'

'You know about horses, then?'

'Yes. I'm terribly fond of them.'

Dinny saw the narrowed gaze withdraw from the young man's face, and come to rest on hers.

'You know my daughter Dinny, I think?'

'Yes.'

'I'll leave you to her now. I want to think this over.'

The young man bowed slightly, turned to Dinny, and then, turning back, said with a certain dignity:

'I'm awfully sorry, sir, about this; but I can't say I'm sorry that I'm in love with Clare. It wouldn't be true. I love her terribly.'

He was moving towards the door, when the General said:

'One moment. What do you mean by love?'

Involuntarily Dinny clasped her hands: An appalling question! Young Croom turned round. His face was motionless.

'I know what you mean, sir,' he said huskily: 'Desire and that, or more? Well! More, or I couldn't have stood that night in the car.' He turned again to the door.

Dinny moved and held it open for him. She followed him into the hall, where he was frowning and taking deep breaths. She slipped her hand through his arm and moved him across to the wood fire. They stood, looking down into the flames, till she said:

'I'm afraid that was rather dreadful. But soldiers like to have things straight out, you know. Anyway – I know my father – you made what's called a good impression.'

'I felt a ghastly kind of wooden idiot. Where is Clare? Here?'

'Yes.'

'Can I see her, Miss Cherrell?'

'Try calling me Dinny. You can see her; but I think you'd better see my mother too. Let's go to the drawing-room.'

He gave her hand a squeeze.

'I've always felt you were a brick.'

Dinny grimaced. 'Even bricks yield to a certain pressure.'

'Oh! sorry! I'm always forgetting my ghastly grip. Clare dreads it. How is she?'

With a faint shrug and smile, Dinny said:

'Doing as well as can be expected.'

Tony Croom clutched his head.

'Yes, I feel exactly like that, only worse; in those cases there's something to look forward to and – here? D'you think she'll ever really love me?'

'I hope so.'

'You people don't think that I pursued her – I mean, you know what I mean, just to have a good time?'

'They won't after today. You are what *I* was once called – transparent.'

'You? I never quite know what you're thinking.'

'That was a long time ago. Come!'

Chapter Twenty-two

WHEN young Croom had withdrawn into the sleet and wind of that discomforting day, he left behind him a marked gloom. Clare went to her room saying her head was bad and she was going to lie down. The other three sat among the tea-things, speaking only to the dogs, sure sign of mental disturbance.

At last Dinny got up: 'Well, my dears, gloom doesn't help. Let's look on the bright side. They might have been scarlet instead of white as snow.'

The General said, more to himself than in reply:

'They must defend. That fellow can't have it all his own way.'

'But Dad, to have Clare free, with a perfectly clear conscience, would be nice and ironic, and ever so much less fuss!'

'Lie down under an accusation of that sort?'

'Her name will go even if she wins. No one can spend a night in a car with a young man with impunity. Can they, Mother?'

Lady Charwell smiled faintly.

'I agree with your father, Dinny. It seems to me revolting that Clare should be divorced when she's done nothing except been a little foolish. Besides, it would be cheating the law, wouldn't it?'

'I shouldn't think the law would care, dear. However –!' And Dinny was silent, scrutinizing their rueful faces, aware that they set some mysterious store by marriage and divorce which she did not, and that nothing she could say would alter it.

'The young man,' said the General, 'seemed a decent fellow, I thought. He'll have to come up and see the lawyers when we do.'

'I'd better go up with Clare tomorrow evening, Dad, and get Uncle Lawrence to arrange you a meeting with the lawyers for after lunch on Monday. I'll telephone you and Tony Croom from Mount Street in the morning.'

The General nodded and got up. 'Beast of a day !' he said, and put his hand on his wife's shoulder : 'Don't let this worry you, Liz. They can but tell the truth. I'll go to the study and have another shot at that new pigsty. You might look in later, Dinny . .'

At all critical times Dinny felt more at home in Mount Street than she did at Condaford. Sir Lawrence's mind was so much more lively than her father's; Aunt Em's inconsequence at once more bracing and more soothing than her mother's quiet and sensible sympathy. When a crisis was over, or if it had not begun, Condaford was perfect, but it was too quiet for nerve storms or crucial action. As country houses went, it was, indeed, old-fashioned, inhabited by the only county family who had been in the district for more than three of four generations. The Grange had an almost institutional repute. 'Condaford Grange' and 'the Cherrells of Condaford' were spoken of as curiosities. The week-ending or purely sporting existence of the big 'places' was felt to be alien to them. The many families on the smaller 'places' round seemed to make country life into a sort of cult, organizing tennis and bridge parties, village entertainments and looking of each other up; getting their day's shooting here and there, supporting the nearest golf course, attending meets, hunting a bit, and so forth. The Charwells, with their much deeper roots, yet seemed to be less in evidence than almost anyone. They would have been curiously missed, but, except to the villagers, they hardly seemed real.

In spite of her always active life at Condaford Dinny often felt there, as one does waking in the still hours of the night, nervous from the very quietude; and in such troubles as Hubert's, three years before, her own crisis of two years ago, or this of Clare's, she craved at once to be more in the swim of life.

Having dropped Clare at her Mews, she went on in the taxi, and arrived at Mount Street before dinner.

Michael and Fleur were there, and the conversation turned and turned from literature to politics. Michael was of opinion that the papers were beginning to pat the country's back too soon, and that the Government might go to sleep. Sir Lawrence was glad to hear that they were still awake.

Lady Mont said suddenly: 'The baby, Dinny?'

'Frightfully well, thank you, Aunt Em. He walks.'

'I was countin' up the pedigree, and he makes the twenty-fourth Cherrell of Condaford; and before that they were French. Is Jean havin' any more?'

'You bet,' said Fleur. 'I never saw a young woman more like it.'

'There'll be nothin' for them.'

'Oh, she'll wangle their futures all right.'

'Such a singular word,' said Lady Mont.

'Dinny, how's Clare?'

'All right.'

'Any developments?' And Fleur's clear eyes seemed to slide into her brain.

'Yes, but –'

Michael's voice broke the silence.

'Dornford has a very neat idea, Dad; he thinks –'

The neat idea of Dornford was lost on Dinny, wondering whether or not to take Fleur into her confidence. She knew no one of quicker brain, or of a judgement on social matters more cynically sound. Further, she could keep a secret. But it was Clare's secret, and she decided to speak to Sir Lawrence first.

Late that night she did so. He received the news with his eyebrows.

'All night in a car, Dinny? That's a bit steep. I'll get on to the lawyers at ten o'clock tomorrow. "Very young" Roger Forsyte, Fleur's cousin, is there now; I'll get hold of him, he's likely to have more credulity than the hoarier members. You and I will go along too, to prove our faith.'

'I've never been in the City.'

'Curious place; built upon the ends of the earth. Romance and the bank rate. Prepare for a mild shock.'

'Do you think they ought to defend?'

Sir Lawrence's lively eyes came to rest on her face.

'If you ask me whether I think they'll be believed – no. But at least we can divide opinion on the question.'

'You *do* believe them yourself, don't you?'

'I plank on you there, Dinny. Clare wouldn't try to take *you* in.'

Thinking back to her sister's face, and to young Croom's, Dinny had a revulsion of feeling. 'They *are* telling the truth, and they look like it. It would be wicked not to believe them.'

'No end to that sort of wickedness in this wicked world. You look tired, my dear; better go to bed.'

In that bedroom, where she had spent so many nights at the time of her own trouble, Dinny had again that half-waking nightmare, the sense of being close to Wilfrid and unable to reach him, and the refrain: 'One more river, one more river to cross,' kept running in her tired head. . . .

In that quiet and yellow backwater, the Old Jewry, the offices of Kingson, Cuthcott and Forsyte were tribally invaded at four o'clock next day.

'What's become of old Gradman, Mr Forsyte?' Dinny heard her uncle say. 'Still here?'

'Very young' Roger Forsyte, who was forty-two, answered, in a voice which seemed to contradict his jaw: 'I believe he's still living at Pinner, or Highgate, or wherever it was.'

'I should be glad to think so,' murmured Sir Lawrence. 'Old For – er, your cousin thought a lot of him. A regular Victorian piece.'

'Very young' Roger smiled. 'Won't you all sit down?'

Dinny, who had never yet been in a lawyer's office, looked at the law books along the walls, the bundles of papers, the yellowish blind, the repellent black fireplace with its little coal fire that seemed to warm nothing, the map of an estate hanging unrolled behind the door, the low wicker basket on the table, the pens and sealing-wax, and 'very young' Roger, and thought of an album of seaweed, compiled by her first governess. She saw her father rise and place a document in the solicitor's hands.

'We've come about this.'

'Very young' Roger glanced at the heading of the paper and over it at Clare.

'How does he know which of us it is?' thought Dinny.

'There's no truth in the allegations,' said the General.

'Very young' Roger caressed his jaw and began reading.

Dinny, from the side, could see that a sharp and rather bird-like look had come on his face.

Noticing that Dinny could see him, he lowered the paper and said: 'They seem in a hurry. The petitioner signed the affidavit in Egypt, I see. He must have come over there to save time. Mr Croom?'

'Yes.'

'You wish us to represent you as well?'

'Yes.'

'Then Lady Corven and you. Later, perhaps, Sir Conway, you'd come in again.'

'Do you mind if my sister stays?' said Clare.

Dinny met the solicitor's eyes. 'Not at all.' She did not know if he meant it.

The General and Sir Lawrence went out, and there was silence. 'Very young' Roger leaned against the fireplace, and most unexpectedly took a pinch of snuff. Dinny saw that he was lean and rather tall, and that his jaw jutted. There was a faintly sandy tinge in his hair, and in the ruddiness of his hollowed cheeks.

'Your father, Lady Corven, said there was no truth in these – er – allegations.'

'The facts are as stated, the inferences are wrong. There's been nothing between Mr Croom and myself, except three kisses on my cheek.'

'I see. About this night in the car, now?'

'Nothing,' said Clare: 'Not even one of those kisses.'

'Nothing,' repeated young Croom; 'absolutely nothing.'

'Very young' Roger passed his tongue over his lips.

'If you don't mind, I think I should like to understand your feelings for each other – if any.'

'We are speaking,' said Clare, in a clear voice, 'the absolute truth, as we've told it to my people; that's why I asked my sister to stay. Tony?'

'Very young' Roger's mouth twitched. To Dinny he did not seem to be taking it quite as a lawyer should; something in his dress, indeed, was a little unexpected – his waistcoat was it, or his tie? That snuff, too – as if a dash of the artist had been suppressed in him. He said:

'Yes, Mr Croom?'

Young Croom, who had gone very red, looked at Clare almost angrily.

'I'm in love with her.'

'Quite!' said 'very young' Roger, reopening the snuff-box. 'And you, Lady Corven, regard him as a friend?'

Clare nodded – a faint surprise on her face.

Dinny felt a sudden gratitude towards the questioner, who was applying a bandana to his nose.

'The car was an accident,' added Clare quickly; 'it was pitch dark in the wood, our lights had failed, and we didn't want to run any risk of people seeing us together so late at night.'

'Exactly! Excuse my asking, but you're both prepared to go into Court and swear there was absolutely nothing that night or on the other occasions, except – did you say – three kisses?'

'On my cheek,' said Clare; 'one out of doors, when I was in a car and he wasn't, and the others – when were the others, Tony?'

Young Croom said between his clenched teeth: 'In your rooms when I hadn't seen you for over a fortnight.'

'You neither of you knew you were being – er – shadowed?'

'I knew my husband had threatened it, but we'd neither of us noticed anything.'

'About leaving your husband, Lady Corven; any reason you'd care to give me?'

Clare shook her head.

'I'm not going into my life with him, either here or anywhere. And I'm not going back to him.'

'Incompatibility, or worse?'

'I think worse.'

'But no definite charge. You realize the importance?'

'Yes. But I'm not going into it, even privately.'

Young Croom burst out: 'He was a brute to her, of course.'

'You knew him, Mr Croom?'

'Never seen him in my life.'

'Then –'

'He just thinks it because I left Jerry suddenly. He knows nothing.'

Dinny saw 'very young' Roger's eyes rest on herself. 'But you do,' they seemed to say; and she thought: 'He's no fool!'

He had returned from the fireplace, walking with a slight limp; sitting down again, he took up the document, narrowed his eyes, and said:

'This isn't the sort of evidence the Court likes; in fact I'm not sure it's evidence at all. All the same it's not a very bright prospect. If you could show strong cause for leaving your husband, and we could get over that night in the car –' He looked, bird-like, first at Clare and then at young Croom. 'Still, you can't let damages and costs like that go by default, when – er – you've done nothing.' His eyes fell; and Dinny thought:

'Not conspicuous – his credulity!'

'Very young' Roger lifted a paper-knife.

'We might possibly get the damages agreed at a comparatively nominal sum, if you put in a defence and then didn't appear. May I ask your monetary position, Mr Croom?'

'I haven't a bean, but that doesn't matter.'

'What exactly will "defending" mean?' asked Clare.

'You'd both go into the box and deny the charges. You'd be cross-examined, and we should cross-examine the petitioner and the inquiry agents. Candidly, unless you can give good reason for having left your husband, you're almost bound to have the judge against you. And,' he added, in a somewhat human manner, 'a night is a night, especially to the divorce court, even in a car; though, as I say, it's not the sort of evidence generally required.'

'My Uncle thinks,' said Dinny quietly, 'that some of the jury, at all events, might believe them, and that the damages, in any case, would be reduced.'

'Very young' Roger nodded.

'We'll see what Mr Kingson says. I should like to see your father and Sir Lawrence again.'

Dinny went to the door and held it open for her sister and young Croom. Glancing back she saw 'very young' Roger's face. It was as if someone had asked him not to be a realist. He caught her eye, gave a funny little cock of his head, and took out his snuff-box. She shut the door and went up to him.

'You'll make a mistake if you don't believe them. They're speaking the absolute truth.'

'Why did she leave her husband, Miss Cherrell?'

'If she won't tell you, I can't. But I'm sure she was right.'

He considered her for a moment with that sharp glance.

'Somehow,' he said suddenly, 'I wish it were you.' And, taking snuff, he turned to the General and Sir Lawrence.

'Well?' said the General.

'Very young' Roger looked suddenly more sandy.

'If she had good reason for leaving her husband —'

'She had.'

'Father!'

'It appears she isn't prepared to speak of it.'

'Nor should I be,' said Dinny quietly.

'Very young' Roger murmured: 'It might make all the difference, though.'

'Serious thing for young Croom, Mr Forsyte,' put in Sir Lawrence.

'Serious, whether they defend or not, Sir Lawrence. I'd better see them both separately. Then I'll get Mr Kingson's view, and let you know tomorrow. Will that do, General?'

'It revolts me,' said the General, 'to think of that fellow Corven!'

'Quite!' said 'very young' Roger, and Dinny thought she had never heard a more doubtful sound.

Chapter Twenty-three

◄◄►►

DINNY sat in the little bare waiting-room turning over *The Times*. Young Croom stood at the window.

'Dinny,' he said, turning, 'can you think of any way in which I can make this less beastly for her? It's all my fault in a sense, but I have tried to keep myself in hand.'

Dinny looked at his troubled face. 'I can't; except by sticking to the exact truth.'

'Do you believe in that chap in there?'

'I rather do. I like his taking snuff.'

'I don't believe in defending. Why should she be ragged in the witness-box for nothing? What does it matter if they bankrupt me?'

'We must prevent that somehow.'

'D'you think I'd let –'

'We won't discuss it, Tony. Sufficient unto the day! Isn't this a dingy place? Dentists try much harder – Marcus Stone on the walls, all the old *Bystanders*, and you can bring a dog.'

'Could we smoke?'

'Surely.'

'These are only stinkers.'

Dinny took one, and they puffed for a minute in silence.

'It's too foul!' he said, suddenly. 'That fellow will have to come over, won't he? He never can really have cared a scrap for her.'

'Oh! yes he did. *"Souvent homme varie, folle est qui s'y fie!"* '

'Well,' said young Croom grimly, 'I'd better be kept from him.' He went back to the window and stood looking out. Dinny sat thinking of that scene, when two men had not been kept apart, so pitifully like a dog fight and rending to her in its sequel.

Then Clare came in. There were spots of red in her pale cheeks. 'Your turn, Tony.'

Young Croom came from the window, looked hard into her face, and passed into the lawyer's room. Dinny felt very sorry for him.

'Ugh!' said Clare: 'Let's get out of this!'

On the pavement, she went on:

'I wish now we had been lovers, Dinny, instead of in this mock-pretty state that no one believes in.'

'We *do* believe.'

'Oh! you and Dad. But that snuffy rabbit doesn't, and no one else will. Still, I shall go through with it. I won't let Tony down, and I won't give Jerry an inch that I can help giving.'

'Let's have tea,' said Dinny. 'There must be tea somewhere in the City.'

In a crowded thoroughfare they soon saw an A.B.C.

'Then you didn't like "very young" Roger?' asked Dinny from across the small round table.

'Oh! he's all right – rather decent, really. I suppose lawyers simply can't believe. But nothing will shake me, Dinny, about not going into my married life. I will not, and that's flat.'

'I see his point. You start with the battle half won against you.'

'I won't allow the lawyers to work it in. We employ them, and they must do what we want. I'm going straight from here to the Temple, by the bye, and perhaps on to the House.'

'Excuse my reverting for a moment; but what are you going to do about Tony Croom till this comes on?'

'Go on just as we were, except for nights in cars. Though what the difference between day and night – in a car, or anywhere else – is, I don't know.'

'I suppose they go by human nature as a whole.' And Dinny leaned back. So many girls, so many young men, snatching their teas and rolls and buns and cocoa; chatter and silence and a stale effluvium, little tables, and the attendant spirits. What was human nature as a whole? Didn't they say that it had to be changed? The stuffy past wiped out! And yet this A.B.C. was just like the A.B.C. she went into with her mother before the war, and thought so thrilling because the bread was aerated. And the Divorce Court – into which she had never been yet – was that any different?

'Have you finished, old thing?' said Clare.

'Yes. I'll come with you as far as the Temple.'

As they paused to part at Middle Temple Lane, a rather high and pleasant voice said:

'What luck!' and a light momentary grip was laid on her arm.

'If you're going straight to the House,' said Clare, 'I'll run on and get my things and join you here.'

'Tactful,' said Dornford. 'Let's stand against this "portal". When I don't see you for so long, Dinny, I feel lost. Jacob served for Rachel fourteen years — longevity is not what it was, so every month I serve is equal to one of his years.'

'Rachel and he were walking out.'

'I know. Well, I must just wait and hope. I just *have* to wait.'

Leaning against the yellow 'portal' she looked at him. His face was quivering. Suddenly sorry, she said:

'Some day, perhaps, I shall come to life again. I won't wait any more now. Good-bye, and thank you! . . .'

This sudden intrusion of herself was no comfort to her in her homing bus. The sight of his quivering face made her restless and uneasy. She did not want to cause him unhappiness — a nice man, considerate to Clare, a pleasant voice, an attractive face; and in range of interest nearer to her than Wilfrid had ever been. Only, where was that wild, sweet yearning, transmuting every value, turning the world into a single being, the one longed-for, dreamed-of mate? She sat very still in the bus, looking over the head of the woman on the opposite side, who, with fingers crisped on the satchel in her lap, wore the expression of a sportsman about to try a new field or spinney. The lights were coming up in Regent Street of a cold, just not snowy evening. There used to be the low curving roof-line, the rather nice, bilious yellow of the Quadrant. She remembered how on the top of a bus she had differed from the girl Millicent Pole about old Regent Street. Changing, changing, everything changing! And before her suddenly closed eyes came Wilfrid's face, with its lips drawn back, as she had seen it last passing her in the Green Park.

Someone trod on her toe. She opened her eyes, and said: 'I beg your pardon.'

'Granted, I'm sure.'

Very polite! People were more polite every year!

The bus had stopped. Dinny hurried from it. She went down Conduit Street, passing her father's tailors. Poor darling, he never went there now. Clothes were so dear; and, of course, he loathed new clothes! She came to Bond Street.

The traffic staggered to a standstill, the whole street seemed one long line of held-up cars. And England ruined! She crossed into Bruton Street. And then, in front of her, she saw a familiar figure, walking slowly with his head down! She came up with him.

'Stack!'

He raised his head; tears were trickling down his cheeks. He blinked his large dark prominent eyes, and passed his hand over his face.

'You miss? I was just coming to you.' And he held out a telegram.

Holding it up in the dim light, she read:

Henry Stack, 50a Cork Street, London. Very sorry to inform you Honourable Wilfrid Desert drowned on expedition up-country some weeks ago. Body recovered and buried on spot. Report only just come in. No possible doubt. Condolences. British Consulate, Bangkok.

Stonily she stood, seeing nothing. Stack's fingers came up and detached the telegram.

'Yes,' she said. 'Thank you. Show it to Mr Mont, Stack. Don't grieve.'

'Oh, miss!'

Dinny laid her fingers on his sleeve, gave it a little pull, and walked swiftly on.

Don't grieve! Sleet was falling now. She raised her face to feel the tingling touch of those small flakes. No more dead to her than he had already been. But – *dead*! Away over there – utterly far! Lying in the earth by the river that had drowned him, in forest silence, where no one would ever see his grave. Every memory she had of him came to life with an intensity that seemed to take all strength from her limbs, so that she nearly collapsed in the snowy street. She stood for a minute with her gloved hand on the railing of a house. An evening postman stopped and looked round at her. Perhaps some tiny flame of hope – that some day he would come back – had flickered deep down within her; perhaps only the snowy cold was creeping into her bones; but she felt deadly cold and numb.

She reached Mount Street at last and let herself in. And there a sudden horror of betraying that anything had happened to awaken pity for her, interest in her, any sort of feeling, beset her, and she fled to her room. What was it to anyone but her?

And pride so moved within her that even her heart felt cold as stone.

A hot bath revived her a little. She dressed for dinner early and went down.

The evening was one of silences more tolerable than the spasmodic spurts of conversation. Dinny felt ill. When she went up to bed her Aunt came to her room.

'Dinny, you look like a ghost.'

'I got chilled, Auntie.'

'Lawyers! – they do. I've brought you a posset.'

'Ah! I've always longed to know what a posset is.'

'Well, drink it.'

Dinny drank, and gasped.

'Frightfully strong.'

'Yes. Your Uncle made it. Michael rang up.' And taking the glass, Lady Mont bent forward and kissed her cheek. 'That's all,' she said. 'Now go to bed, or you'll be ill.'

Dinny smiled. 'I'm not going to be ill, Aunt Em.'

In pursuance of that resolve she went down to breakfast next morning.

The oracle, it seemed, had spoken in a typewritten letter signed Kingson, Cuthcott and Forsyte. It recommended putting in a defence, and had so advised Lady Corven and Mr Croom. When it had taken the necessary proceedings it would advise further.

And that coldness in the pit of the stomach which follows the receipt of lawyers' letters was felt even by Dinny, the pit of whose stomach was already deadly cold.

She went back to Condaford with her father by the morning train, repeating to her Aunt the formula: 'I'm not going to be ill.'

Chapter Twenty-four

But she *was* ill, and for a month in her conventual room at Condaford often wished she were dead and done with. She might, indeed, quite easily have died if such belief as she had in a future life had grown instead of declining as her strength ebbed. To rejoin Wilfrid, where this world's pain and judgements were not, had fatal attraction. To fade out into the sleep of nothingness was not hard, but had no active enticement; and, as the tide of health turned back within her, seemed less and less natural. The solicitude of people had a subtle, pervasive healing influence. The village required a daily bulletin, her mother had been writing or 'phoning almost daily to a dozen people. Clare had been down every week-end, bringing flowers from Dornford. Aunt Em had been sending twice a week the products of Boswell and Johnson; Fleur bombarding her with the products of Piccadilly. Adrian had come down three times without warning. Hilary began sending funny little notes the moment she had turned the corner.

On March the thirtieth, spring visited her room with south-west airs, a small bowl of the first spring flowers, some pussy willows and a sprig of gorse. She was picking up rapidly now, and three days later was out of doors. For everything in nature she felt a zest such as she had not known for a long time. Crocuses, daffodil clumps, swelling buds, sun on the fantails' wings, shapes and colour of the clouds, scent of the wind, all affected her with an almost painful emotion. Yet she had no desire to do anything or see anybody. In this queer apathy she accepted an invitation from Adrian to go abroad with him on his short holiday.

The memorable things about their fortnight's stay at Argelès in the Pyrenees, were the walks they took, the flowers they picked, the Pyrenean sheep-dogs, the almond blossom they saw, the conversations they held. They were out all day, taking lunch with them, and the opportunities for talk were unlimited. Adrian became eloquent on mountains. He had never got over his climbing days. Dinny suspected him of trying to rouse her from the lethargy in which she was sunk.

'When I went up "the little Sinner" in the Dolomites with Hilary before the war,' he said one day, 'I got as near to God as I ever shall. Nineteen years ago – dash it! What's the nearest to God you ever got, Dinny?'

She did not answer.

'Look here, my dear, what are you now – twenty-seven?'

'Nearly twenty-eight.'

'On the threshold still. I suppose talking it out wouldn't help?'

'You ought to know, Uncle, that talking one's heart out is not in the family.'

'True! The more we're hurt the silenter we get. But one mustn't inbreed to sorrow, Dinny.'

Dinny said suddenly: 'I understand perfectly how women go into convents, or give themselves up to good works. I always used to think it showed a lack of humour.'

'It can show a lack of courage, or too much courage, of the sort fanatical.'

'Or broken springs.'

Adrian looked at her.

'Yours are not broken, Dinny – badly bent, not broken.'

'Let's hope so, Uncle; but they ought to be straightening by now.'

'You're beginning to look fine.'

'Yes, I'm eating enough even for Aunt Em. It's taking interest in oneself that's the trouble.'

'I agree. I wonder if –'

'Not iron, darling. It sews me up inside.'

Adrian smiled. 'I was thinking more of children.'

'They're not synthetic, yet. I'm all right, and very lucky, as things go. Did I tell you old Betty died?'

'Good old soul! She used to give me bulls'-eyes.'

'*She* was the real thing. We read too many books, Uncle.'

'Indubitably. Walk more, read less! Let's have our lunch.'

On the way back to England they stayed two nights in Paris at a little hotel over a restaurant near the Gare St Lazare. They had wood fires, and their beds were comfortable.

'Only the French know what a bed should be,' said Adrian.

The cooking down below was intended for racing men and such as go where they can appreciate food. The waiters, who wore aprons, looked, as Adrian expressed it, 'like monks doing a spot of work,' pouring the wine and mixing the salads with reverence. He and Dinny were the only foreigners in either hotel or restaurant, not far from being the only foreigners in Paris.

'Marvellous town, Dinny. Except for cars in place of *fiacres* and the Eiffel Tower, I don't see any real change by daylight since I was first here in '88, when your grandfather was Minister at Copenhagen. There's the same tang of coffee and wood smoke in the air; people have the same breadth of back, the same red buttons in their coats; there are the same tables outside the same cafés, the same *affiches*, the same funny little stalls for selling books, the same violently miraculous driving, the same pervading French grey, even in the sky; and the same rather ill-tempered look of not giving a damn for anything outside Paris. Paris leads fashion, and yet it's the most conservative place in the world. They say the advanced literary crowd here regard the world as having begun in 1914 at earliest, have scrapped everything that came before the war, despise anything that lasts, are mostly Jews, Poles and Irishmen, and yet have chosen this changeless town to function in. The same with the painters and musicians, and every other extremist. Here they gather and chatter and experiment themselves to death. And good old Paris laughs and carries on, as concerned with reality and flavours and the past as it ever was. Paris produces anarchy exactly as stout produces froth.'

Dinny pressed his arm.

'That was a good effort, Uncle. I must say I feel more alive here than I have for ages.'

'Ah! Paris pets the senses. Let's go in here – too cold to sit out. What'll you have, tea or – absinthe?'

'Absinthe.'

'You won't like it.'

'All right – tea with lemon.'

Waiting for her tea in the quiet hurly-burly of the Café de la Paix, Dinny watched her Uncle's thin, bearded form, and thought that he looked quite 'in his plate,' but with a queer, interested contentment that identified him with the life around.

To be interested in life and not pet oneself! And she looked about her. Her neighbours were neither remarkable nor demonstrative, but they gave an impression of doing what they liked, not of being on the way to somewhere else.

'They dig into the moment, don't they?' said Adrian suddenly.

'Yes, I was thinking that.'

'The French make an art of living. We hope for the future or regret the past. Precious little "present" about the English!'

'Why are these so different?'

'Less northern blood, more wine and oil; their heads are rounder than ours, their bodies more stocky, and their eyes are mainly brown.'

'Those are things we can't alter, anyway.'

'The French are essentially the medium people. They've brought equilibrium to a high point. Their senses and intellects balance.'

'But they get fat, Uncle.'

'Yes, but all over; they don't jut, and they hold themselves up. I'd rather be English, of course; but if I weren't, I'd rather be French.'

'Isn't there anything in having an itch for something better than you've got?'

'Ah! Ever noticed, Dinny, that when we say "Be good!" they say "*Soyez sage!*"? There's a lot in that. I've heard Frenchmen put our unease down to the Puritan tradition. But that's to mistake effect for cause, symptoms for roots. I admit we've got an urge towards the promised land, but Puritanism was part of that urge, so's our wanderlust and colonizing quality; so's our Protestantism, Scandinavian blood, the sea and the climate. None of that helps us in the art of living. Look at our industrialism, our old maids, cranks, humanitarianisms, poetry! We jut in every direction. We've got one or two highly mediumizing institutions – the public schools, 'cricket' in its various forms – but as a people we're chock-full of extremism. The average Briton is naturally exceptional, and underneath his dread of being conspicuous, he's really proud of it. Where, on earth, will you see more diverse bone formation than in England, and all of it peculiar? We do our level best to be average, but, by George, we jut !'

'You're inspired, Uncle.'

'Well, you look about you when you get home.'

'I will,' said Dinny.

They had a good crossing the next day, and Adrian dropped her at Mount Street.

In kissing him good-bye, she squeezed his little finger.

'You're done me a tremendous amount of good, Uncle.'

During those six weeks she had scarcely thought at all about Clare's troubles, and she asked at once for the latest news. A defence had been delivered and issue joined; the case would probably be on in a few weeks.

'I've not seen either Clare or young Croom,' said Sir Lawrence, 'but I gathered from Dornford that they go about as before. "Very young" Roger still harps on the need for getting her to speak about her life out there. Lawyers seem to regard the Court as confessional boxes in which to confess the sins of your opponent.'

'Well, aren't they?'

'Judging by the papers, yes.'

'Well, Clare can't and won't. They'll make a great mistake if they try to force her. Has anything been heard of Jerry?'

'He must have started, if he's to be here in time.'

'Suppose they lose, what is to be done about Tony Croom?'

'Put yourself in his place, Dinny. Whatever happens, he'll probably come in for a slating from the judge. He won't be in a mood to accept favours. If he can't pay up I don't quite know what they can do to him; something unpleasant, no doubt. And there's the question of Jack Muskham's attitude – he's queer.'

'Yes,' said Dinny under her breath.

Sir Lawrence dropped his monocle.

'Your Aunt suggests that young Croom should go gold-digging, come back rich, and marry Clare.'

'But Clare?'

'Isn't she in love with him?'

Dinny shook her head. 'She might be if he's ruined.'

'H'm! And how are *you*, my dear? Really yourself again?'

'Oh, yes!'

'Michael would like to see you some time.'

'I'll go round tomorrow.'

And that, meaning much, was all that was said about the news that had caused her illness.

Chapter Twenty-five

◄◄─►►

DINNY made the effort needed to go round to South Square next morning. Except with Clare on her arrival from Ceylon, she had not been there since the day of Wilfrid's departure to Siam.

'Up in his workroom, miss.'

'Thank you, Coaker, I'll go up.'

Michael did not hear her come in, and she stood for a moment looking at the caricature-covered walls. It always seemed to her so odd that Michael, inclined to over-estimate human virtues, should surround himself with the efforts of those who live by exaggerating human defects.

'Am I interrupting, Michael?'

'Dinny! You're looking a treat! You gave us a bad turn, old thing. Sit down! I was only looking into potatoes – their figures are so puzzling.'

They talked for some time, and then, the knowledge of what she had come for invading both, fell silent.

'You've something to give or tell me, Michael.'

He went to a drawer, and took out a little packet. Dinny unwrapped it in her lap. There was a letter, a little photograph, a badge.

'It's his passport photo, and D.S.O. ribbon. In the letter there's something for you; in fact, the whole letter is really for you. They're all for you. Excuse me, I have to see Fleur before she goes out.'

Dinny sat motionless, looking at the photograph. Yellowed with damp and heat, it had the uncompromising reality that characterizes passport photographs. 'Wilfrid Desert' was written across it, and he looked straight at her out of the paste-board. She turned it face down on her lap, and smoothed the ribbon, which was stained and crushed. Then, nerving herself, she opened the letter. From it dropped a folded sheet, which she set apart. The letter was to Michael.

New Year's Day.

DEAR OLD M. M., —

Greetings to you and Fleur, and many good years! I'm far up north in a very wild part of this country with an objective that I may reach or not – the habitation of a tribe quite definitely pre-Siamese and non-Mongolian. Adrian Charwell would be interested. I've often meant to let you know my news, but, when it came to writing, didn't – partly because if you don't know this part of the world description's no use, and partly because it's difficult for me to believe that anybody can be interested. I'm writing now really to ask you to tell Dinny that I am at peace with myself at last. I don't know whether it's the strength and remoteness of the atmosphere out here, or whether I've gained some of the Eastern conviction that the world of other men does not matter; one's alone from birth to death, except for that fine old companion, the Universe – of which one is the microcosm. It's a kind of queer peace, and I often wonder how I could have been so torn and tortured. Dinny, I think, will be glad to know this; just as I would be truly glad to know that she, too, is at peace.

I've written a little, and, if I come back from this business, shall try and produce some account of it. In three days from now we reach the river, cross it, and follow up a western tributary towards the Himalayas.

Faint echoes of the crisis you've been having trickle out here. Poor old England! I don't suppose I shall ever see her again; but she's a game old bird when put to it, and I can't see her being beaten; in fact, properly moulted, I expect her to fly better than ever.

Good-bye, old man, my love to you both; and to Dinny my special love.

WILFRID

Peace! And she? She rewrapped the ribbon, photograph, and letter and thrust them into her bag. Making no noise, she opened the door, went down the stairs, and out into the sunshine.

Alone by the river, she unfolded the sheet she had taken from the letter, and, under a plane tree as yet bare of leaves, read these verses:

Lie Still!

The sun, who brings all earth to bloom,
Corrupts and makes corruption flower,
Is just a flame that thro' the gloom
Of heaven burns a little hour;

And, figured on the chart of night –
A somewhat negligible star –
Is but a pinpricked point of light
As million-million others are;

And, though it be the all in all
Of my existence and decay,
It has as simple rise and fall
As I have, and as short a day.

But that no unction to my heart
Will lay; the smallest germ in me
Plays just as passionate a part
As I do, in eternity.

The germ and I and sun, we rise,
Fulfil our little lives, and die;
And to all question God replies:
'Lie still! I cannot tell you why!'

Lie still! The Embankment was nearly empty of people and of traffic. She walked on, crossing the main lines of the traffic, and came to Kensington Gardens. There on the Round Pond were many small boats, and many children interested in their vagaries. A bright-haired little boy, something like Kit Mont, was guiding his boat with a stick to a fresh attempt to cross the pond. What blissful unconsciousness of all else! Was that the secret of happiness? To be lost in the moment – to be out of oneself, like a child! He said suddenly:

'It's going! Look!'

The sails filled, the little boat floated away. The small boy stood with arms akimbo, and, quickly looking up at her, said :

'Ha! I must run!'

Dinny watched him stop now and again with a jerk to calculate the landing of his boat.

So one ran through life, watching each venture coming to shore, and at the end lay still! Like birds who uttered their songs, hunted for worms, preened their feathers, flew without seeming cause, unless for joy; mated, built nests and fed their young, and when all was over became little stiffened bundles of feathers, and passed into corruption, and dust.

She followed slowly round the pond, saw him again guiding the boat with his stick, and said: 'What do you call your boat?'

'A cutter. I had a schooner, but our dog ate the rigging.'

'Yes,' said Dinny, 'dogs like rigging – very succulent.'

'Very what?'

'Like asparagus.'

'I'm not allowed asparagus, it's too expensive.'

'But you've tasted it?'

'Yes. See, the wind's catching it again!'

Off went the boat, and off went the small bright-haired boy.

Adrian's words came into her head. 'I was thinking more of children.'

She walked into what in old days would have been called a glade. The ground was covered with crocuses, yellow, violet, white, and with daffodils; the trees had eagerness in every twig, stretching their buds upward to the sun's warmth; the blackbirds were in song. And as she walked she thought: 'Peace! There is no peace. There is life, and there is death!'

And those who saw her thought: 'Nice-looking girl!' 'These little hats!' 'Where's she goin', I wonder, with her head in the air?' or, again, just: 'Coo!' She crossed the road and came to the Hudson Memorial. It was supposed to be a home for birds; but beyond a sparrow or two and a fat pigeon, there were none; nor were more than three people looking at it. She, who had seen it with Wilfrid, glanced at it for a moment and walked on.

'Poor Hudson! Poor Rima!' he had said.

She went down to the Serpentine and walked along it; the sun was bright on the water, and beyond it the grass was springy and dry. The papers were already talking of drought! The sound currents from north and south and west joined in a mild continuous roaring. Where he was lying it would be silent; strange birds and little creatures would be the only visitors, and odd-shaped leaves would drop on his grave. There came into her mind the pastoral scenes in some film pictures of the Normandy home of Briand, that she had seen at Argelès. 'A pity we have to leave all this!' she had said.

An aeroplane droned its way over to the north, a high, silvery, small, noisy shape. *He* had hated them ever since the war. 'Disturbers of whatever Gods there be!'

Brave new world! God no longer in His heaven!

She turned a little north to avoid the place where she used to meet him. The roofless tabernacle of oratory close to the Marble Arch was deserted. She left the Park and went towards Melton Mews. It was over! With a queer little smile on her lips she turned into the Mews and stopped at her sister's door.

Chapter Twenty-six

◄◄─►►

S H E found Clare in. For the first few minutes they avoided each other's troubles, then Dinny said: 'Well?'

'Not at all well. I've split with Tony — my nerves are in rags and his in tatters.'

'But do you mean that he —?'

'No. Only I've told him I can't go on seeing him till this is over. We meet meaning not to talk about the thing; then it crops up, and we get all anyhow.'

'He must be awfully unhappy.'

'He is. But it's only for another three or four weeks.'

'And then?'

Clare laughed — no joyful sound.

'But seriously, Clare?'

'We shan't win, and then nothing will matter. If Tony wants me I suppose I shall let him. He'll be ruined, so I shall owe him that.'

'I think,' said Dinny slowly, 'that I wouldn't let the result affect me.'

Clare stared up at her from the sofa.

'That sounds almost too sensible.'

'It wasn't worth while to plead innocence unless you meant to carry it through, however the case goes. If you win, wait till you can divorce Jerry. If you don't win, wait till you're divorced. It won't do Tony any real harm to wait; and it'll certainly do you no harm to know for certain how you feel.'

'Jerry is quite clever enough to prevent my ever getting evidence against him, if he sets his mind to it.'

'Then we must hope you'll lose. Your friends will still believe in you.'

Clare shrugged. 'Will they?'

'I'll see to that,' said Dinny.

'Dornford has advised telling Jack Muskham before the case comes on. What do you say?'

'I should like to see Tony Croom first.'

'Well, if you come round again this evening, you'll see him. He comes and stares up at me at seven o'clock on Saturday and Sunday evenings. Quaint!'

'No. Very natural. What are you doing this afternoon?'

'Riding with Dornford in Richmond Park. I ride with him in the Row early every morning now. I wish you'd come, Dinny.'

'No things, and no muscles.'

'Darling,' said Clare, springing up, 'it really was awful while you were ill. We felt ever so bad. Dornford was quite potty. You look better now than you did before.'

'Yes, I'm more pneumatic.'

'Oh! you've read that book?'

Dinny nodded. 'I'll come round this evening. Good-bye; bless you!' ...

It was almost seven when she slipped out of Mount Street and walked rapidly towards the Mews. A full moon was up with the evening star in a not yet darkened sky. Coming to the west corner of the deserted Mews, she at once saw young Croom standing below No. 2. Waiting till he began to move away, she ran down the Mews and round the far corner to catch him.

'Dinny! How wonderful!'

'I was told I should catch you looking at the Queen.'

'Yes, that's what the cat has come to.'

'It might be worse.'

'Are you all right again? You must have got a chill in the City that foul day.'

'Let's walk as far as the Park. I wanted to ask you about Jack Muskham.'

'I funk telling him.'

'Shall I do it for you?'

'But why?'

Dinny took his arm.

'He's a connexion, through Uncle Lawrence. Besides, I've had occasion to know him. Mr Dornford is perfectly right; it will depend very much on when and what he's told. Let me!'

'I don't know really – I really don't know.'

'I want to see him again, anyway.'

Young Croom looked at her.

'Somehow I don't believe that.'

'Honest Injun.'

'It's terribly sweet of you; of course you can do it much better than I, but –'

'That's enough then.'

They had reached the Park, and were walking along the rails towards Mount Street.

'Have you been seeing the lawyers much?'

'Yes, our evidence is all taped out. It's the cross-examination.'

'I think I might enjoy that, if I were going to tell the truth.'

'They twist and turn what you say so, and their tones of voice –! I went into that court and listened one day. Dornford told Clare he wouldn't practise in that court for all the gold in France. He's a sound fellow, Dinny.'

'Yes,' said Dinny, looking round at his ingenuous face.

'I don't think our lawyers care about the job either. It's not in their line. "Very young" Roger is a bit of a sportsman. He believes we're telling the truth, because he realizes I'm sorry we are. That's your turning. I shall go and bat round the Park, or I shan't sleep. Wonderful moon!'

Dinny pressed his hand.

When she reached her door, he was still standing there, and raised his hat to her – or to the moon, she could not be quite sure which ...

According to Sir Lawrence, Jack Muskham would be up in Town over the week-end; he now had rooms in Ryder Street. She had not thought twice about going all the way to Royston to see him concerning Wilfrid; but he might well think twice about her going to see him in Ryder Street concerning young Croom. She telephoned, therefore, to Burton's Club at lunch-time the next day.

His voice brought back the shock of the last time she had heard it, close to the York Column.

'Dinny Cherrell. Could I see you some time today?'

The answer came slowly.

'Er – of course. When?'

'Any time that suits you.'

'Are you at Mount Street?'

'Yes, but I would rather come to you.'

'Well – er – would –? How about tea at my rooms in Ryder Street? You know the number?'

'Yes, thank you. Five o'clock?'

Approaching those rooms she needed all her pluck. She had last seen him reeling in the thick of that fight with Wilfrid. Besides, he symbolized to her the rock on which her love for Wilfrid had gone aground. She only did not hate him, because she could not help remembering that this bitterness towards Wilfrid had been due to his queer appreciation of herself. Only by fast walking, and slow thinking, did she arrive.

The door was opened to her by one who obviously bettered his declining days by letting rooms to such as he had valeted in the past. He took her up to the second floor.

'Miss – er – Cherwell, sir.'

Tall, lean, languid, neatly dressed as ever, Jack Muskham was standing by the open window of a not unpleasant room. 'Tea, please, Rodney.' He came towards her, holding out his hand.

'Like a slow-motion picture,' thought Dinny. However surprised at her wanting to see him, he was showing no sign of it.

'Been racing at all since I saw you at Blenheim's Derby?'

'No.'

'You backed him, I remember. Clearest case of beginner's luck I ever knew.' His smile brought out all the wrinkles on his brown face, and Dinny perceived that there were plenty of them.

'Do sit down. Here's tea. Will you make it?'

She gave him his cup, took her own and said :

'Are the Arab mares over yet, Mr Muskham?'

'I expect them the end of next month.'

'You have young Tony Croom to look after them.'

'Oh! Do you know him?'

'Through my sister.'

'Nice boy.'

'He is,' said Dinny. 'It's about him I've come.'

'Oh!'

The thought 'He owes me too much,' darted through her. He could not refuse her this! Leaning back and crossing her knees, she looked him full in the face.

'I wanted to tell you, in confidence, that Jerry Corven is bringing a divorce suit against my sister, and Tony Croom is cited as the co-respondent.'

Jack Muskham moved the hand that held his cup.

'He *is* in love with her, and they *have* been going about together, but there is no truth in the charges.'

'I see,' said Muskham.

'The case is coming on quite soon. I persuaded Tony Croom to let me tell you of it; it would be so awkward for him to talk about himself.'

Muskham was looking at her with unmoved face.

'But,' he said, 'I know Jerry Corven. I didn't realize your sister had left him.'

'We keep it to ourselves.'

'Was her leaving him young Croom's doing?'

'No. They only met on the boat coming over. Clare left Jerry for quite another reason. She and Tony Croom have been in-discreet, of course; they've been watched and seen together in what are known, I believe, as "compromising circumstances." '

'How do you mean exactly?'

'Driving back from Oxford late one evening their lights failed and they spent the rest of the night in the car together.'

Jack Muskham raised his shoulders slightly. Dinny leaned forward with her eyes on his.

'I told you there was no truth in the charges; there is *none*.'

'But, my dear Miss Cherrell, a man never admits –'

'That is why *I* came to you instead of Tony. My sister would not tell me a lie.'

Again Muskham made the slight movement of his shoulders.

'I don't quite see –' he began.

'What it has to do with you? This: I don't suppose they'll be believed.'

'You mean if I just read the case it would put me off young Croom?'

'Yes, I think you would feel he had not "played the game."' She could not quite keep irony out of her voice.

'Well,' he said, 'has he?'

'I think so. He's deeply in love with my sister, and yet he's kept himself in hand. One can't help falling in love, you know.' With those words all the feelings of the past rose up within her, and she looked down so as not to see that impassive face and the provocative set of its lips. Suddenly, by a sort of inspiration, she said:

'My brother-in-law has asked for damages.'

'Oh!' said Jack Muskham, 'I didn't know that was done now.'

'Two thousand, and Tony Croom has nothing. He professes not to care, but if they lose, of course, it's ruin.'

After that there was silence. Jack Muskham went back to the window. He sat on the sill and said:

'Well, I don't know what I can do.'

'You needn't take his job from him – that's all.'

'The man was in Ceylon and his wife here. It's not –'

Dinny rose, took two steps towards him and stood very still.

'Has it ever struck you, Mr Muskham, that you owe me anything? Do you remember that you took my lover from me? Do you know that he is dead out there, where he went because of you?'

'Of me?'

'You and what you stand for made him give me up. I ask you

now, however this case goes, not to sack Tony Croom! Good-bye!' And before he could answer she was gone.

She almost ran towards the Green Park. How far from what she had intended! How fatal – perhaps! But her feelings had been too strong – the old revolt against the dead wall of 'form' and those impalpable inexorable forces of tradition which had wrecked her love life! It could not have been otherwise. The sight of his long, dandified figure, the sound of his voice, had brought it all back too strongly. Ah, well! It was a relief; an escape of old bitterness pent within her spirit!

The next morning she received this note:

Ryder Street.
Sunday.

DEAR MISS CHARWELL, –
    You may rely on me in that matter. With sincere regard,
Yours very faithfully,
JOHN MUSKHAM

Chapter Twenty-seven

WITH that promise to her credit she went back to Condaford the following day and gave herself to mitigation of the atmosphere she found there. Her father and mother, living their ordinary lives, were obviously haunted and harassed. Her mother, sensitive and secluded, was just shrinking from publicity discreditable to Clare. Her father seemed to feel that, however the case went, most people would think his daughter a light woman and a liar; young Croom would be excused more or less, but a woman who allowed circumstance to take such turns would find no one to excuse her. He was clearly feeling, too, a vindictive anger against Jerry Corven, and a determination that the fellow should not be successful if he could help it. Faintly amused at an attitude so male, Dinny felt a sort of admiration at the painful integrity with which he was grasping the shadow and letting the substance go. To her father's generation divorce still seemed the outward and visible sign of inner and spiritual disgrace. To herself love was love and, when it became aversion, ceased to justify sexual relationship. She had, in fact, been more shocked by Clare's yielding to Jerry Corven in her rooms than by her leaving him in Ceylon. The divorce suits she had occasionally followed in the papers had done nothing to help her believe that marriages were made in heaven. But she recognized the feeling of those brought up in an older atmosphere, and avoided adding to the confusion and trouble in her people's minds. The line she took was more practical: The thing would soon be over one way or the other, and probably the other! People paid very little attention to other people's affairs nowadays!

'What!' said the General sardonically. ' "Night in a car" — it's the perfect headline. Sets everybody thinking at once how they themselves would have behaved.'

She had no answer, but: 'They'll make a symposium of it, darling: The Home Secretary, the Dean of St Paul's, the Princess Elizabeth.'

She was disturbed when told that Dornford had been asked to Condaford for Easter.

'I hope you don't mind, Dinny; we didn't know whether you'd be here or not.'

'I can't use the expression "I'm agreeable" even to you, Mother.'

'Well, darling, one of these days you must go down into the battle again.'

Dinny bit her lip and did not answer. It was true, and the more disquieting. Coming from her gentle and unmanaging mother, the words stung.

Battle! Life, then, was like the war. It struck you down into hospital, turned you out therefrom into the ranks again. Her mother and father would hate 'to lose her,' but they clearly wanted her 'to go.' And this with Clare's failure written on the wall!

Easter came with a wind 'fresh to strong.' Clare arrived by train on the Saturday morning, Dornford by car in the afternoon. He greeted Dinny as if doubtful of his welcome.

He had found himself a house. It was on Campden Hill. He had been terribly anxious to know Clare's opinion of it, and she had spent a Sunday afternoon going over it with him.

'"Eminently desirable," Dinny. "South aspect; garage and stabling for two horses; good garden; all the usual offices, centrally heated," and otherwise well-bred. He thinks of going in towards the end of May. It has an old tiled roof, so I put him on to French grey for shutters. Really, it's rather nice, and roomy.'

'It sounds "marvellous." I suppose you'll be going there instead of to the Temple?'

'Yes, he's moving into Pump Court, or Brick Buildings – I can't remember. When you think of it, Dinny, why shouldn't he have been made co-respondent instead of Tony? I see much more of him.'

Otherwise allusion to 'the case' was foregone. It would be one of the first after the undefended suits were disposed of, and calm before the storm was reigning.

Dornford, indeed, referred to it after lunch on Sunday.

'Shall you be in court during your sister's case, Dinny?'

'I must.'

'I'm afraid it may make you very wild. They've briefed Brough, and he's particularly exasperating when he likes with a simple denial like this; that's what they'll rely on. Clare must try and keep cool.'

Dinny remembered 'very young' Roger's wishing it had been herself and not Clare.

'I hope you'll tell her that.'

'I'll take her through her evidence, and cross-examine her on it. But one can't tell the line Brough will take.'

'Shall you be in court yourself?'

'If I can, but the odds are I shan't be free.'

'How long will it last?'

'More than a day, I'm afraid.'

Dinny sighed.

'Poor Dad! Has Clare got a good man?'

'Yes – Instone, very much hampered by her refusal to talk about Ceylon.'

'That's definite, you know. She won't.'

'I like her for it, but I'm afraid it's fatal.'

'So be it!' said Dinny: 'I want her free. The person most to be pitied is Tony Croom.'

'Why?'

'He's the only one of the three in love.'

'I see,' said Dornford, and was silent. Dinny felt sorry.

'Would you care for a walk?'

'Simply love it!'

'We'll go up through the woods, and I'll show you where the Cherrell killed the boar and won the de Campfort – our heraldic myth. Had you any family legend in Shropshire?'

'Yes, but the place has gone – sold when my father died; six of us and no money.'

'Oh!' said Dinny, 'horrible when families are uprooted.'

Dornford smiled.

'Live donkeys are better than dead lions.'

While they were going up through the coverts he talked about his new house, subtly 'pumping' her for expressions of her taste.

They came out into a sunken roadway leading on to a thorn-bush-covered down.

'Here's the place. Virgin forest then, no doubt. We used to picnic here as children.'

Dornford took a deep breath. 'Real English view – nothing spectacular, but no end good.'

'Lovable.'

'That's the word.'

He spread his raincoat on the bank. 'Sit down and let's have a smoke.'

Dinny sat down.

'Come on part of it yourself, the ground's not too dry.'

While he sat there, with his hands hugging his knees and his pipe fuming gently, she thought: 'The most self-controlled man I ever came across, and the gentlest, except Uncle Adrian.'

'If only a boar would come along,' he said, 'it would be prime!'

'Member of Parliament kills boar on spur of Chilterns,' murmured Dinny, but did not add: 'Wins lady.'

'Wind's off the gorse. Another three weeks and it'll be green down there. Pick of the year – this, or the Indian summer, I never know. And yours, Dinny?'

'Blossom time.'

'Um; and harvest. This ought to be glorious then – quite a lot of cornland.'

'It was just ripe when the war broke out. We came up picnicking two days before, and stayed till the moon rose. How much do you think people really fought for England, Mr Dornford?'

'Practically all – for some nook or other of it; many just for the streets, and buses, and smell of fried fish. I fought mainly, I think, for Shrewsbury and Oxford. But Eustace is my name.'

'I'll remember. We'd better go down now, or we shall be late for tea.'

And, all the way home, they contended with birds' songs and the names of plants.

'Thanks for my treat,' he said.

'I've enjoyed it, too.'

That walk had, indeed, a curiously soothing effect on Dinny. So, she could talk with him without question of love-making.

Bank holiday was sou'-westerly. Dornford spent a quiet hour with Clare over her evidence, and then went riding with her in the rain. Dinny's morning went in arranging for spring cleaning and the chintzing of the furniture while the family were up in town. Her mother and father were to stay at Mount Street, she and Clare with Fleur. In the afternoon she pottered with the General round the new pigsties, progressing as slowly as a local builder, anxious to keep his men in work, could make them. She was not alone again with Dornford until after tea.

'Well,' he said, 'I think your sister will do, if she keeps her temper.'

'Clare can be very cutting.'

'Yes, and there's an underlying sentiment among lawyers against being cut up by outsiders in each other's presence; even judges have it.'

'They won't find her a "butterfly on the wheel." '

'It's no good getting up against institutions, you know; they carry too many guns.'

'Oh! well,' said Dinny, with a sigh, 'it's on the knees of the gods.'

'Which are deuced slippery. Could I have a photograph of you, preferably as a little girl?'

'I'll see what we've got – I'm afraid only snaps; but I think there's one where my nose doesn't turn up too much.'

She went to a cabinet, took a drawer out bodily, and put it on the covered billiard table.

'The family snap-board – choose !'

He stood at her side and they turned them over.

'I took most of them, so there aren't many of me.'

'Is that your brother?'

'Yes, and this – just before he went to the war. This is Clare the week before she was married. Here's one of me, with some hair. Dad took that when he came home, the spring after the war.'

'When you were thirteen?'

'Fourteen nearly. It's supposed to be like Joan of Arc being taken in by voices.'

'It's lovely. I shall get it enlarged.'

He held it to the light. The figure was turned three quarters, and the face lifted to the branches of a fruit tree in blossom. The whole of the little picture was very much alive; the sun having fallen on the blossom and on Dinny's hair, which hung to her waist.

'Mark the rapt look,' she said; 'there must have been a cat up the tree.'

He put it into his pocket and returned to the table.

'And this?' he said : 'Could I have this too?'

The snap was one of her a little older, but still with her hair uncut, full face, hands clasped in front, head a little down and eyes looking up.

'No, I'm sorry. I didn't know it was there.' It was the counter-part of one she had sent to Wilfrid.

Dornford nodded; and she realized that in some uncanny way he knew why. Seized with compunction, she said :

'Oh ! yes, you can. It doesn't matter, now.' And she put it into his hand....

After Dornford and Clare had left on Tuesday morning, Dinny studied a map, took the car and set out for Bablock Hythe. She did not care for driving, but she was moved by the thought of Tony Croom deprived of his week-end glimpse of Clare. The twenty-five miles took her well over an hour. At the inn she was told that he would be at his cottage, and, leaving the car, she walked over. He was in shirt-sleeves distempering the walls of the low, timbered sitting-room. From the doorway she could see the pipe wobble in his mouth.

'Anything wrong with Clare?' he said at once.

'Nothing whatever. I just thought I'd like to have a look at your habitat.'

'How terribly nice of you! I'm doing a job of work.'

'Clearly.'

'Clare likes duck's-egg green; this is the nearest I can get to it.'

'It goes splendidly with the beams.'

Young Croom said, looking straight before him, 'I can't believe I'll ever get her here, but I can't help pretending; otherwise the sand would be clean out of my dolly.'

Dinny put her hand on his sleeve.

'You're not going to lose your job. I've seen Jack Muskham.'

'Already? You're marvellous. I'll just wash off and get my coat on, and show you round.'

Dinny waited in the doorway where a streak of sunlight fell. The two cottages, knocked into one, still had their ramblers, wistaria, and thatched roof. It would be very pretty.

'Now,' said young Croom. 'The boxes are all finished, and the paddocks have got their water. In fact, we only want the animals; but they're not to be here till May. Taking no risks. Well, I'd rather have this case over first. You've come from Condaford?'

'Yes. Clare went back this morning. She would have sent her love, but she didn't know I was coming.'

'Why *did* you come?' said young Croom bluntly.

'Fellow feeling.'

He thrust his arm within hers.

'Yes. So sorry! Do you find,' he added suddenly, 'that thinking of other people suffering helps?'

'Not much.'

'No. Wanting someone is like tooth or ear ache. You can't get away from it.'

Dinny nodded.

'This time of year, too,' said young Croom, with a laugh.

'The difference between being "fond of" and "loving"! I'm getting desperate, Dinny. I don't see how Clare can ever change. If she were ever going to love me, she would by now. If she's not going to love me, I couldn't stick it here. I'd have to get away to Kenya or somewhere.'

Looking at his eyes, ingenuously hanging on her answer, her nerve went. It was her own sister; but what did she know of her, when it came to the depths?

'You never know. I wouldn't give up.'

Young Croom pressed her arm.

'Sorry to be talking of my mania. Only, when one longs day and night –'

'I know.'

'I must buy a goat or two. Horses don't like donkeys; and as a rule they shy at goats; but I want to make these paddocks feel homey. I've got two cats for the boxes. What do you think?'

'I only know about dogs, and – pigs theoretically.'

'Come and have lunch. They've got a rather good ham.'

He did not again speak of Clare; and, after partaking together of the rather good ham, he put Dinny into her car and drove her the first five miles of the way home, saying that he wanted a walk.

'I think no end of you for coming,' he said, squeezing her hand hard: 'It was most frightfully sporting. Give my love to Clare,' and he went off, waving his hand, as he turned into a field-path.

She was absent-minded during the rest of the drive. The day, though still south-westerly, had gleams of sunlight, and sharp showers of hail. Putting the car away she got the spaniel Foch and went out to the new pigsties. Her father was there, brooding over their construction like the Lieutenant-General he was, very neat, resourceful, faddy. Doubtful whether they would ever contain pigs, Dinny slipped her arm through his.

'How's the battle of Pigsville?'

'One of the bricklayers was run down yesterday, and that carpenter there has cut his thumb. I've been talking to old Bellows, but – dash it! – you can't blame him for wanting to keep his men in work. I sympathize with a chap who sticks by his

own men, and won't have union labour. He says he'll be
finished by the end of next month, but he won't.'

'No,' said Dinny, 'he's already said that twice.'

'Where have you been?'

'Over to see Tony Croom.'

'Any development?'

'No. I just wanted to tell him that I've seen Mr Muskham,
and he won't lose his job.'

'Glad of that. He's got grit, that boy. Pity he didn't go into
the army.'

'I'm very sorry for him, Dad; he really is in love.'

'Still a common complaint,' said the General drily: 'Did you
see they've more than balanced the Budget? It's an hysterical
age, with these European crises for breakfast every other morning.'

'That's the papers. The French papers, where the print is so
much smaller, don't excite one half so much. I couldn't get the
wind up at all when I was reading them.'

'Papers, and wireless; everything known before it happens;
and headlines twice the size of the events. You'd think, to judge
from the speeches and the "leaders," that the world had never
been in a hole before. The world's always in a hole, only in old
days people didn't make a song about it.'

'But without the song would they have balanced the Budget,
dear?'

'No, it's the way we do things nowadays. But it's not English.'

'Do we know what's English and what isn't, Dad?'

The General wrinkled up his weathered face, and a smile
crept about the wrinkles. He pointed at the pigsties.

'Those are. Done in the end, but not before they must
be.'

'Do you like that?'

'No; but I like this hysterical way of trying to cure it even
less. You'd think we'd never been short of money before. Why,
Edward the Third owed money all over Europe. The Stuarts
were always bankrupt. And after Napoleon we had years to
which these last years have been nothing, but they didn't have it
for breakfast every morning.'

'When ignorance was bliss !'

'Well, I dislike the mixture of hysteria and bluff we've got now.'

'Would you suppress the voice that breathes o'er Eden?'

'Wireless? "The old order changeth, yielding place to new. And God fulfils himself in many ways," ' quoted the General, ' "lest one good custom should corrupt the world." I remember a sermon of old Butler's at Harrow on that text – one of his best, too. I'm not hidebound, Dinny, at least I hope not. Only I think everything's talked out too much. It's talked out so much that it's not felt.'

'I believe in the Age, Dad. It's dropped its superfluous clothes. Look at those old pictures in *The Times* lately. You smelt dogma and flannel petticoat.'

'Not flannel,' said the General, 'in my day.'

'You should know, dear.'

'As a matter of fact, Dinny, I believe *mine* was the really revolutionary generation. You saw that play about Browning? There you had it; but that was all gone before I went to Sandhurst. We thought as we liked, and we acted as we thought, but we still didn't talk. Now they talk before they think, and when it comes to action, they act much as we did, if they act at all. In fact, the chief difference between now and fifty years ago is the freedom of expression; it's so free now, that it takes the salt out of things.'

'That's profound, Dad.'

'But not new; I've read it a dozen times.'

' "You don't think the war had any great influence, then, sir?" They always ask that in interviews.'

'The war? Its influence is pretty well over by now. Besides, the people of my generation were already too set. The next generation was wiped or knocked out –'

'Not the females.'

'No, they ran riot a bit, but they weren't really in the thing. As for your generation, the war's a word.'

'Well, thank you dear,' said Dinny. 'It's been very instructive, but it's going to hail. Come along, Foch !'

The General turned up the collar of his coat and crossed over to the carpenter who had cut his thumb. Dinny saw him examining the bandage. She saw the carpenter smile, and her father pat him on the shoulder.

'His men must have liked him,' she thought. 'He may be an old buffer, but he's a nice one.'

Chapter Twenty-eight

━◄━►━

I F Art is long, Law is longer. The words Corven *v.* Corven and Croom rewarded no eye scanning the Cause List in *The Times* newspaper. Undefended suits in vast numbers occupied the attention of Mr Justice Covell. At Dornford's invitation Dinny and Clare came to the entrance of his court, and stood for five minutes just inside, as members of a cricket team will go and inspect a pitch before playing in a match. The judge sat so low that little but his face could be seen; but Dinny noticed that above Clare's head in the witness-box would be a sort of canopy, or protection from rain.

'If,' said Dornford, as they came out, 'you stand well back, Clare, your face will be hardly visible. But your voice you should pitch so that it always carries to the judge. He gets grumpy if he can't hear.'

It was on the day after this that Dinny received a note delivered by hand at South Square.

Burton's Club: 13.iv.32.

D E A R D I N N Y

I should be very glad if I could see you for a few minutes. Name your own time and place and I will be there. Needless to say it concerns Clare.

Sincerely yours,

G E R A L D C O R V E N

Michael was out, but she consulted Fleur.

'I should certainly see him, Dinny. It may be a death-bed repentance. Let him come here when you know Clare will be out.'

'I don't think I'll risk his seeing her. I'd rather meet him somewhere in the open.'

'Well, there's the Achilles, or the Rima.'

'The Rima,' said Dinny. 'We can walk away from it.'

She appointed the following afternoon at three o'clock, and continued to wonder what he wanted.

The day was an oasis of warmth in that bleak April. Arriving at the Rima, she saw him at once, leaning against the railing with his back to that work of art. He was smoking a cigarette through a short well-coloured holder in meerschaum, and looked so exactly as when she had seen him last that, for no reason, she received a sort of shock.

He did not offer to take her hand.

'Very good of you to come, Dinny. Shall we stroll and talk as we go?'

They walked towards the Serpentine.

'About this case,' said Corven, suddenly, 'I don't want to bring it a bit, you know.'

She stole a look at him.

'Why *do* you, then? The charges are not true.'

'I'm advised that they are.'

'The premises may be; the conclusions, no.'

'If I withdraw the thing, will Clare come back to me, on her own terms?'

'I can ask her, but I don't think so. I shouldn't myself.'

'What an implacable family!'

Dinny did not answer.

'Is she in love with this young Croom?'

'I can't discuss their feelings, if they have any.'

'Can't we speak frankly, Dinny? There's no one to hear us except those ducks.'

'Claiming damages has not improved our feelings towards you.'

'Oh! that! I'm willing to withdraw everything, and risk her having kicked over, if she'll come back.'

'In other words,' said Dinny, gazing straight before her, 'the case you have framed – I believe that is the word – is a sort of blackmailing device.'

He looked at her through narrowed eyes.

'Ingenious notion. It didn't occur to me. No, the fact is, knowing Clare better than my solicitors and the inquiry agents, I'm not too convinced that the evidence means what it seems to.'

'Thank you.'

'Yes, but I told you before, or Clare anyway, that I can't and won't go on with nothing settled, one way or the other. If she'll come back I'll wipe the whole thing out. If she won't, it must take its chance. That's not wholly unreasonable, and it's not blackmail.'

'And suppose she wins, will you be any further on?'

'No.'

'You could free yourself and her at any time, if you liked.'

'At a price I don't choose to pay. Besides, that sounds extremely like collusion – another awkward word, Dinny.'

Dinny stood still.

'Well, I know what you want, and I'll ask Clare. And now I'll say good-bye. I don't see that talking further will do any good.'

He stood looking at her, and she was moved by the expression on his face. Pain and puzzlement were peering through its hardwood browned mask.

'I'm sorry things are as they are,' she said, impulsively.

'One's nature is a hell of a thing, Dinny, and one's never free from it. Well, good-bye and good luck !'

She put out her hand. He gave it a squeeze, turned and walked off.

Dinny stood for some unhappy moments beside a little birch tree whose budding leaves seemed to tremble up towards the sunshine. Queer ! To be sorry for him, for Clare, for young Croom, and be able to do nothing to help !

She walked back to South Square as fast as she could.

Fleur met her with : 'Well?'

'I'm afraid I can only talk to Clare about it.'

'I suppose it's an offer to drop it if Clare will go back. If she's wise she will.'

Dinny closed her lips resolutely.

She waited till bed-time, and then went to Clare's room. Her sister had just got into bed, on the foot of which Dinny sat down, and began at once :

'Jerry asked me to see him. We met in Hyde Park. He says he'll drop the case if you'll go back – on your own terms.'

Clare raised her knees and clasped them with her hands.

'Oh! And what did you say?'

'That I'd ask you.'

'Did you gather why?'

'Partly, I think he really wants you; partly, he doesn't much believe in the evidence.'

'Ah!' said Clare, drily: 'Nor do I. But I'm not going back.'

'I told him I didn't think you would. He said we were "implacable."'

Clare uttered a little laugh.

'No, Dinny. I've been through all the horrors of this case. I feel quite stony, don't care whether we win or lose. In fact, I believe I'd rather we lost.'

Dinny grasped one of her sister's feet through the bed-clothes. She was in two minds whether to speak of the feeling Corven's face had roused in her.

Clare said uncannily:

'I'm always amused when people think they know how husbands and wives ought to behave towards each other. Fleur was telling me about her father and his first wife; she seemed to think the woman made a great fuss for nothing much. All I can say is that to think you can judge anybody else's case is just self-righteous idiocy. There's never any evidence to judge from, and until cine-cameras are installed in bedrooms,' she added, 'there never will be. You might let him know, Dinny, that there's nothing doing.'

Dinny got up.

'I will. If only the thing were over!'

'Yes,' said Clare, tossing back her hair, 'if only –! But whether we shall be any further on, when it is, I don't know. God bless the Courts of Law.'

That bitter invocation went up daily from Dinny, too, during the next fortnight, while the undefended causes, of which her sister's might have been one, were softly and almost silently vanishing away. Her note to Corven said simply that her sister had answered: 'No.' No reply came to it.

At Dornford's request she went with Clare to see his new

house on Campden Hill. To know that he had taken it with the view of having a home for her, if she would consent to share it, kept her expressionless, except to say that it was all very nice, and to recommend a bird shelter in the garden. It was roomy, secluded, airy, and the garden sloped towards the south. Distressed at being so colourless, she was glad to come away; but the dashed and baffled look on his face when she said: 'Goodbye' hurt her. In their bus, going home, Clare said:

'The more I see of Dornford, Dinny, the more I believe you could put up with him. He's got very light hands; he lets your mouth alone. He really is a bit of an angel.'

'I'm sure he is.' And through Dinny's mind, in the jaunting bus, passed and passed four lines of verse:

> 'The bank is steep and wide the river flows —
> Are there fair pastures on the farther shore?
> And shall the halting kine adventure those
> Or wander barren pastures evermore?'

But on her face was that withdrawn expression which Clare knew better than to try and penetrate.

Waiting for an event, even when it primarily concerns others, is a process little desirable. For Dinny it had the advantage of taking her thoughts off her own existence and concentrating them on her people's. The family name, for the first time in her experience, was confronted with a really besmirching publicity, and she the chief recipient of her clan's reaction. She felt thankful that Hubert was not in England. He would have been so impatient and upset. In the publicity attendant on his own trouble, four years ago, there had been much more danger of disaster, but much less danger of disgrace. For however one might say that divorce was nothing in these days, a traditional stigma still clung to it in a country far from being as modern as it supposed itself to be. The Charwells of Condaford, at all events, had their pride and their prejudices, above all they loathed publicity.

When Dinny, for instance, went to lunch at St Augustine's-in-the-Meads, she found a very peculiar atmosphere. It was as if her Uncle and Aunt had said to each other: 'This thing has to be, we suppose, but we can't pretend either to understand or to approve of it.' With no bluff matter-of-fact condemnation, nor anything churchy or shocked about their attitude, they conveyed to Dinny the thought that Clare might have been better occupied than in getting into such a position.

Walking away with Hilary to see a party of youths off to Canada from Euston Station, Dinny was ill at ease, for she had true affection and regard for her overworked unparsonical Uncle. Of all the members of her duty-bound family, he most embodied the principle of uncomplaining service, and however she might doubt whether the people he worked for were not happier than he was himself, she instinctively believed that he lived a real life in a world where not very much was 'real.' Alone with her he voiced his feelings more precisely.

'What I don't like, Dinny, about this business of Clare's is the way it will reduce her in the public eye to the level of the idle young woman who has nothing better to do than to get into matrimonial scrapes. Honestly, I'd prefer her passionately in love and flinging her cap over the windmill.'

'Cheer up, Uncle,' murmured Dinny, 'and give her time. That may yet come.'

Hilary smiled.

'Well! Well! But you see what I mean. The public eye is a mean, cold, parroty thing; it loves to see the worst of everything. Where there's real love I can accept most things; but I don't like messing about with sex. It's unpleasant.'

'I don't think you're being just to Clare,' said Dinny with a sigh; 'she cut loose for real reasons; and *you* ought to know, Uncle, that attractive young women can't remain entirely unfollowed.'

'Well,' said Hilary shrewdly, 'I perceive that you're sitting on a tale you could unfold. Here we are. If you knew the bother I've had to get these youths to consent to go, and the authorities to consent to take them, you'd realize why I wish I were a mushroom, springing up over-night and being eaten fresh for breakfast.'

Whereon, they entered the station, and proceeded towards the Liverpool train. A little party of seven youths in cloth caps, half in and half out of a third-class carriage, were keeping up their spirits in truly English fashion, by passing remarks on each other's appearance and saying at intervals: 'Are we daown-'earted? Naoo!'

They greeted Hilary with the words:

''Ello, Padre! ... Zero hour! Over the top! ... 'Ave a fag, sir?'

Hilary took the 'fag'. And Dinny, who stood a little apart, admired the way in which he became at once an integral part of the group.

'Wish you was comin' too, sir!'

'Wish I were, Jack.'

'Leavin' old England for ever!'

'Good old England!'

'Sir?'

'Yes, Tommy?'

She lost the next remarks, slightly embarrassed by the obvious interest she was arousing.

'Dinny!'

She moved up to the carriage.

'Shake hands with these young men. My niece.'

In the midst of a queer hush she shook the seven hands of the seven capless youths, and seven times said: 'Good luck!'

There was a rush to get into the carriage, a burst of noise from uncouth mouths, a ragged cheer, and the train moved. She stood by Hilary's side, with a slight choke in her throat, waving her hand to the caps and faces stretched through the window.

'They'll all be seasick tonight,' muttered Hilary, 'that's one comfort. Nothing like it to prevent you from thinking of the future or the past.'

She went into Adrian's after leaving him, and was rather disconcerted to find her Uncle Lionel there. They stopped dead in their discussion. Then the Judge said:

'Perhaps you can tell us, Dinny: Is there any chance at all of mediating between those two before this unpleasant business comes on?'

'None, Uncle.'

'Oh! Then seeing as I do rather much of the law, I should suggest Clare's not appearing and letting the thing go unde-fended. If there's no chance of their coming together again, what is the use of prolonging a state of stalemate?'

'That's what I think, Uncle Lionel; but, of course, you know the charges aren't true.'

The Judge grimaced.

'I'm speaking as a man, Dinny. The publicity will be lamentable for Clare, win or lose; whereas, if she and this young man didn't defend, there'd be very little. Adrian says she would refuse any support from Corven, so that element doesn't come in. What *is* all the trouble about? You know, of course.'

'Very vaguely, and in confidence.'

'Great pity!' said the Judge: 'If they knew as much as I do, people would never fight these things.'

'There *is* that claim for damages.'

'Yes, Adrian was telling me – pretty medieval, that.'

'Is revenge medieval, Uncle Lionel?'

'Not altogether,' said the Judge, with his wry smile; 'but I shouldn't have thought a man in Corven's position could afford such luxuries. To put his wife into the scales! Thoroughly unpleasant.'

Adrian put his arm round Dinny's shoulders.

'Nobody feels that more than Dinny.'

'I suppose,' murmured the Judge, 'Corven will at least have them settled on her.'

'Clare wouldn't take them. But, why shouldn't they win? I thought the law existed to administer justice, Uncle Lionel.'

'I don't like juries,' said the Judge abruptly.

Dinny looked at him with curiosity – surprisingly frank! He added:

'Tell Clare to keep her voice up and her answers short. And don't let her try to be clever. Any laughter in court should be raised by the judge.'

So saying, he again smiled wryly, shook her hand, and took himself away.

'Is Uncle Lionel a good judge?'

'Impartial and polite, they say. I've never seen him in court, but from what I know of him as a brother, he'd be conscientious and thorough; a bit sarcastic at times. He's quite right about this case, Dinny.'

'I've felt that all along. It's Father, and that claim for damages.'

'I expect they regret that claim now. His lawyers must be bunglers. Angling for position!'

'Isn't that what lawyers are for?'

Adrian laughed.

'Here's tea! Let's drown our sorrows, and go and see a film. There's a German thing they say is really magnanimous. *Real* magnanimity on the screen, Dinny, think of it!'

Chapter Twenty-nine

OVER was the shuffling of seats and papers, which marks the succession of one human drama by another, and 'very young' Roger said:

'We'll go into the well of the court.'

There, with her sister and her father, Dinny sat down, bastioned from Jerry Corven by 'very young' Roger and his rival in the law.

'Is this,' she whispered, 'the well at the bottom of which truth lies, or *lies?*'

Unable to see the rising 'body' of the court behind her, she knew by instinct and the sense of hearing that it was filling up. The public's unerring sense of value had scented out a fight, if not a title. The Judge, too, seemed to have smelt something, for he was shrouded in a large bandana handkerchief. Dinny gazed upward. Impressively high, and vaguely Gothic, the court seemed. Above where the Judge sat red curtains were drawn across, surprisingly beyond the reach of man. Her eyes fell to the jury filing into their two-ranked 'box'. The foreman fascinated her at once by his egg-shaped face and head, little hair of any sort, red cheeks, light eyes, and an expression so subtly blended between that of a codfish and a sheep that it reminded her of neither. His face recalled rather one of the two gentlemen of South Molton Street, and she felt almost sure that he was a jeweller. Three women sat at the end of the front row, no one of whom, surely, could ever have spent a night in a car. The first was stout and had the pleasant flattish face of a superior housekeeper. The second, thin, dark, and rather gaunt, was perhaps a writer. The third's bird-like look was disguised in an obvious cold. The other eight male members of the jury tired her eyes, so diverse and difficult to place. A voice said :

'Corven versus Corven and Croom – husband's petition,' and she gave Clare's arm a convulsive squeeze.

'If your Lordship pleases –'

Out of the tail of her eye she could see a handsome, small-whiskered visage, winy under its wig.

The Judge's face, folded and far away, as of a priest or of a tortoise, was poked forward suddenly. His gaze, knowing and impersonal, seemed taking her in, and she felt curiously small. He drew his head back, as suddenly.

The slow rich voice behind her began retailing the names and positions of the 'parties,' the places of their marriage and co-habitation; it paused a moment and then went on :

'In the middle of September of last year, while the petitioner was up-country in discharge of official duty, the respondent, without a word of warning, left her home and sailed for England. On board the ship was the co-respondent. It is said by the defence, I believe, that these two had not met before. I shall suggest that they had met, or at all events had had every opportunity of so meeting.'

Dinny saw her sister's little disdainful shrug.

'However that may be,' proceeded the slow voice, 'there is no question that they were always together on the ship, and I shall show that towards the end of the voyage the co-respondent was seen coming out of the respondent's stateroom.' On and on the voice drooled till it reached the words : 'I will not dwell, members of the jury, on the details of the watch kept on the respondent's and co-respondent's movements; you will have these from the mouths of expert and reputable witnesses. Sir Gerald Corven.'

When Dinny raised her eyes he was already in the box, his face carved out of an even harder wood than she had thought. She was conscious of the resentment on her father's face, of the Judge taking up his pen, of Clare clenching her hands on her lap; of 'very young' Roger's narrowed eyes; of the foreman's slightly opening mouth, and the third jurywoman's smothered sneeze; conscious of the brownness in this place — it oozed brownness as if designed to dinge all that was rose, blue, silver, gold, or even green in human life.

The slow voice began its questioning, ceased its questioning; the personable owner of it closed, as it were, black wings; and a different voice behind her said:

'You thought it your duty, sir, to institute these proceedings?'

'Yes.'

'No animus?'

'None.'

'This claim for damages — not very usual, is it, nowadays among men of honour?'

'They will be settled on my wife.'

'Has your wife indicated in any way that she wishes you to support her?'

'No.'

'Would it surprise you to hear that she would not take a penny from you, whether it came from the co-respondent or not?'

Dinny saw the cat-like smile beneath the cut moustache.

'Nothing would surprise me.'

'It did not even surprise you that she left you?'

She looked round at the questioner. So this was Instone, whom Dornford had said was 'very handicapped'! He seemed to her to have one of those faces, with dominant noses, that nothing could handicap.

'Yes, that did surprise me.'

'Now, why? ... Perhaps you would translate that movement into words, sir?'

'Do wives generally leave their husbands without reason given?'

'Not unless the reason is too obvious to require statement. Was that the case?'

'No.'

'What should you say, then, was the reason? You are the person best able to form an opinion.'

'I don't think so.'

'Who then?'

'My wife herself.'

'Still you must have some suspicion. Would you mind saying what it was?'

'I should.'

'Now, sir, you are on your oath. Did you or did you not ill-treat your wife in any way?'

'I admit one incident which I regret and for which I have apologized.'

'What was that incident?'

Dinny, sitting taut between her father and her sister, feeling in her whole being the vibration of their pride and her own, heard the slow rich voice strike in behind her.

'My Lord, I submit that my friend is not entitled to ask that question.'

'My Lord –'

'I must stop you, Mr Instone.'

'I bow to your Lordship's ruling.... Are you a hot-tempered man, sir?'

'No.'

'There would be a certain deliberation about your actions, at all times?'

'I hope so.'

'Even when those actions were not – shall we say – benevolent?'

'Yes.'

'I see; and I am sure the jury also does. Now, sir, let me take you to another point. You suggest that your wife and Mr Croom had met in Ceylon?'

'I have no idea whether they had or not.'

'Have you any personal knowledge that they did?'

'No.'

'We have been told by my friend that he will bring evidence to show that they had met –'

The slow rich voice interposed:

'That they had had opportunity of meeting.'

'We will take it at that. Were you aware, sir, that they had enjoyed such opportunity?'

'I was not.'

'Had you ever seen or heard of Mr Croom in Ceylon?'

'No.'

'When did you first know of the existence of this gentleman?'

'I saw him in London in November last, coming out of a ouse where my wife was staying, and I asked her his name.'

'Did she make any concealment of it?'

'None.'

'Is that the only time you have seen this gentleman?'

'Yes.'

'What made you pitch on him as a possible means of securing divorce from your wife?'

'I object to that way of putting it.'

'Very well. What drew your attention to this gentleman as a ossible co-respondent?'

'What I heard on the ship by which I returned from Port aid to Ceylon in November. It was the same ship as that in which my wife and the co-respondent came to England.'

'And what *did* you hear?'

'That they were always together.'

'Not unusual on board ship, is it?'

'In reason – no.'

'Even in your own experience?'

'Perhaps not.'

'What else, if anything, did you hear to make you so sus- icious?'

'A stewardess told me that she had seen him coming out of ny wife's stateroom.'

'At what time of day or night was that?'

'Shortly before dinner.'

'You have travelled by sea a good deal, I suppose, in the course of your professional duties?'

'A great deal.'

'And have you noticed that people frequently go to each other's staterooms?'

'Yes, quite a lot.'

'Does it always arouse your suspicions?'

'No.'

'May I go further and suggest that it never did before?'

'You may not.'

'Are you naturally a suspicious man?'

'I don't think so.'

'Not what would be called jealous?'

'I should say not.'

'Your wife is a good deal younger than yourself?'

'Seventeen years.'

'Still, you are not so old as to be unable to appreciate the fact that young men and women in these days treat each other with very little ceremony and consciousness of sex?'

'If you want my age, I am forty-one.'

'Practically post-war.'

'I was through the war.'

'Then you know that much which before the war might have been regarded as suspicious has long lost that character?'

'I know that things are all very free and easy.'

'Thank you. Had you ever, before she left you, had occasion to be suspicious of your wife?'

Dinny looked up.

'Never.'

'But this little incident of his coming out of her cabin was enough to cause you to have her watched?'

'That, and the fact that they were always together on the ship, and my having seen him coming out of the house in London.'

'When you were in London you told her that she must come back to you or take the consequences?'

'I don't think I used those words.'

'What words did you use?'

'I think I said she had the misfortune to be my wife, and that she couldn't be a perpetual grass widow.'

'Not a very elegant expression, was it?'

'Perhaps not.'

'You were, in fact, eager to seize on anybody or anything to free yourself?'

'No, I was eager for her to come back.'

'In spite of your suspicions?'

'I had no suspicions in London.'

'I suggest that you had ill-treated her, and wished to be free of an association that hurt your pride.'

The slow rich voice said:

'My Lord, I object.'

'My Lord, the petitioner having admitted —'

'Yes, but most husbands, Mr Instone, have done something for which they have been glad to apologize.'

'As your Lordship pleases. . . . In any case, you gave instructions to have your wife watched. When exactly did you do that?'

'When I got back to Ceylon.'

'Immediately?'

'Almost.'

'That did not show great eagerness to have her back, did it?'

'My view was entirely changed by what I was told on the ship.'

'On the ship. Not very nice, was it, listening to gossip about your wife?'

'No, but she had refused to come back, and I had to make up my mind.'

'Within two months of her leaving your house?'

'More than two months.'

'Well, not three. I suggest, you know, that you practically forced her to leave you; and then took the earliest opportunity open to you to ensure that she shouldn't come back?'

'No.'

'So you say. Very well. These inquiry agents you employed — had you seen them before you left England to return to Ceylon?'

'No.'

'Will you swear that?'

'Yes.'

'How did you come to hit upon them?'

'I left it to my solicitors.'

'Oh! then you had seen your solicitors before you left?'

'Yes.'

'In spite of your having no suspicions?'

'A man going so far away naturally sees his solicitors before he starts.'

'You saw them in relation to your wife?'

'And other matters.'

'What did you say to them about your wife?'

Again Dinny looked up. In her was growing the distaste of one seeing even an opponent badgered.

'I think I simply said that she was staying behind with her people.'

'Only that?'

'I probably said that things were difficult.'

'Only that?'

'I remember saying: "I don't quite know what's going to happen."'

'Will you swear you did not say: "I may be wanting you to have her watched"?'

'I will.'

'Will you swear that you said nothing which conveyed to them the idea that you had a divorce in your mind?'

'I can't tell you what was conveyed to them by what I said.'

'Don't quibble, sir. Was the word divorce mentioned?'

'I don't remember it.'

'You don't remember it? Did you or did you not leave them with the impression that you might be wanting to take proceedings?'

'I don't know. I told them that things were difficult.'

'So you have said before. That is not an answer to my question.'

Dinny saw the Judge's head poked forward.

'The petitioner has said, Mr Instone, that he does not know the impression left on his lawyers' minds. What are you driving at?'

'My Lord, the essence of my case – and I am glad to have this opportunity of stating it succinctly – is that from the moment the petitioner had acted in such a way – whatever it was – as caused his wife to leave him, he was determined to divorce her, and ready to snatch at anything that came along to secure that divorce.'

'Well, you can call his solicitor.'

'My Lord!'

Those simple words were like a shrug of the shoulders put into sound.

'Well, go on!'

With a sigh of relief Dinny caught the sound of finality in the voice of the 'handicapped' Instone.

'You wish to suggest to the jury that although you instituted these proceedings on the first and only gossip you heard, and although you added a claim for damages against a man you have never spoken to – that in spite of all this you are a forbearing and judicious husband, whose only desire was that his wife should come back to him?'

Her eyes went for the last time to the face up there, more hidden by its mask than ever.

'I wish to suggest nothing to the jury.'

'Very well!'

There was a rustling of silk behind her.

'My Lord,' the slow, rich voice intoned, 'since my friend has made so much of the point, I will call the petitioner's solicitor.'

'Very young' Roger, leaning across, said:

'Dornford wants you all to lunch with him . . .'

Dinny could eat practically nothing, afflicted by a sort of nausea. Though more alarmed and distraught during Hubert's case, and at the inquest on Ferse, she had not felt like this. It was her first experience of the virulence inherent in the conduct of actions between private individuals. The continual suggestion that the opponent was mean, malicious and untruthful, which underlay every cross-examining question, had affected her nerves.

On their way back to the court, Dornford said:

'I know what you're feeling. But remember, it's a sort of game; both sides play according to the same rules, and the Judge is there to discount exaggeration. When I try to see how it could be worked otherwise, I can't.'

'It makes one feel nothing's ever quite clean.'

'I wonder if anything ever is.'

'The Cheshire cat's grin did fade at last,' she murmured.

'It never does in the Law Courts, Dinny. They should have it graven over the doors.'

Whether owing to that short conversation, or because she was getting used to it, she did not feel so sick during the afternoon session, devoted to examination and cross-examination of the stewardess and inquiry agents. At four o'clock the petitioner's case was closed, and 'very young' Roger cocked his eye at her, as who should say: 'The Court will now rise, and I shall be able to take snuff.'

Chapter Thirty

-<->

IN the taxi, on the way back to South Square, Clare was silent, till, opposite Big Ben, she said suddenly:

'Imagine his peering in at us in the car when we were asleep! Or did he just invent that, Dinny?'

'If he'd invented it, he would surely have made it more convincing still.'

'Of course, my head *was* on Tony's shoulder. And why not? You try sleeping in a two-seater.'

'I wonder the man's torch didn't wake you.'

'I daresay it did; I woke a lot of times with cramp. No; the stupidest thing I did, Dinny, was asking Tony in for a drink that night after we went to the film and dined. We were extraordinarily green not to realize we were being shadowed. Were there a frightful lot of people in Court?'

'Yes, and there'll be more tomorrow.'

'Did you see Tony?'

'Just a glimpse.'

'I wish I'd taken your advice and let it go. If only I were really in love with him!'

Dinny did not answer.

Aunt Em was in Fleur's 'parlour'. She came towards Clare, opened her mouth, seemed to remember that she shouldn't, scrutinized her niece, and said suddenly:

'Not so good! I do dislike that expression; who taught it me? Tell me about the Judge, Dinny; was his nose long?'

'No, but he sits very low and shoots his neck out.'

'Why?'

'I didn't ask him, dear.'

Lady Mont turned to Fleur.

'Can Clare have her dinner in bed? Go and have a long bath, my dear, and don't get up till tomorrow. Then you'll be fresh for that Judge. Fleur, you go with her, I want to talk to Dinny.'

When they had gone, she moved across to where the wood fire burned.

'Dinny, comfort me. Why do we have these things in our family? So unlike – except your great-grandfather; and he was older than Queen Victoria when he was born.'

'You mean he was naturally rakish?'

'Yes, gamblin', and enjoyin' himself and others. His wife was long-sufferin'. Scottish. So odd!'

'That, I suppose,' murmured Dinny, 'is why we've all been so good ever since.'

'What is why?'

'The combination.'

'It's more the money,' said Lady Mont; 'he spent it all.'

'Was there much?'

'Yes. The price of corn.'

'Ill-gotten.'

'His father couldn't help Napoleon. There were six thousand acres then, and your great-grandfather only left eleven hundred.'

'Mostly woods.'

'That was the woodcock shootin'. Will the case be in the evenin' papers?'

'Certain to be. Jerry's a public man.'

'Not her dress, I hope. Did you like the jury?'

Dinny shrugged. 'I can't ever tell what people are really thinking.'

'Like dogs' noses, when they feel hot and aren't. What about that young man?'

'He's the one I'm truly sorry for.'

'Yes,' said Lady Mont. 'Every man commits adultery in his heart, but not in cars.'

'It's not truth but appearances that matter, Aunt Em.'

'Circumstantial, Lawrence says – provin' they did when they didn't. More reliable that way, he thinks; otherwise, he says, when they didn't you could prove they did. Is that right, Dinny?'

'No, dear.'

'Well, I must go home to your mother. She doesn't eat a thing – sits and reads and looks pale. And Con won't go near his Club. Fleur wants us and them to go to Monte Carlo in her car when it's over. She says we shall be in our element, and that Riggs *can* drive on the right-hand side of the road when he remembers.'

Dinny shook her head.

'Nothing like one's own hole, Auntie.'

'I don't like creepin',' said Lady Mont. 'Kiss me. And get married soon.'

When she had swayed out of the room, Dinny stood looking out into the Square.

How incorrigible was that prepossession! Aunt Em and Uncle Adrian, her father and her mother, Fleur, yes and even Clare herself – all anxious that she should marry Dornford and be done with it!

And what good would it do any of them? Whence came this instinct for pressing people into each other's arms? If she had any use in the world, would that increase it? 'For the procreation of children', went the words of the old order. The world had to be carried on! Why had the world to be carried on? Everybody used the word 'hell' in connexion with it nowadays. Nothing to look forward to but brave new world!

'Or the Catholic church,' she thought, 'and I don't believe in either.'

She opened the window, and leaned against its frame. A fly buzzed at her; she blew it away, and it instantly came back. Flies! They fulfilled a purpose. What purpose? While they were alive they were alive; when they were dead they were dead. 'But not half-alive,' she thought. She blew again, and this time the fly did not come back.

Fleur's voice behind her said:

'Isn't it cold enough for you in here, my dear? Did you ever know such a year? I say that every May. Come and have tea. Clare's in her bath, and very nice she looks, with a cup of tea in one hand and cigarette in the other. I suppose they'll get to the end tomorrow?'

'Your cousin says so.'

'He's coming to dinner. Luckily his wife's at Droitwich.'

'Why "luckily"?'

'Oh! well, she's a wife. If there's anything he wants to say to Clare, I shall send him up to her; she'll be out of her bath by then. But he can say it to you just as well. How do you think Clare will do in the box?'

'Can anyone do well in the box?'

'My father said I did, but he was partial; and the Coroner complimented you, didn't he, at the Ferse inquest?'

'There was no cross-examination. Clare's not patient, Fleur.'

'Tell her to count five before she answers, and lift her eyebrows. The thing is to get Brough rattled.'

'His voice would madden me,' said Dinny, 'and he has a way of pausing as if he had all day before him.'

'Yes, quite a common trick. The whole thing's extraordinarily like the Inquisition. What do you think of Clare's counsel?'

'I should hate him if I were on the other side.'

'Then he's good. Well, Dinny, what's the moral of all this?'

'Don't marry.'

'Bit sweeping, till we can grow babies in bottles. Hasn't it ever struck you that civilization's built on the maternal instinct?'

'I thought it was built on agriculture.'

'By "civilization" I meant everything that isn't just force.'

Dinny looked at her cynical and often flippant cousin, who stood so poised and trim and well-manicured before her, and she felt ashamed. Fleur said, unexpectedly :

'You're rather a darling.'

Dinner, Clare having it in bed and the only guest being 'very young' Roger, was decidedly vocal. Starting with an account of how his family felt about taxation, 'very young' Roger waxed amusing. His Uncle Thomas Forsyte, it appeared, had gone to live in Jersey, and returned indignantly when Jersey began to talk about taxation of its own. He had then written to *The Times* under the *nom de guerre* of 'Individualist', sold all his investments, and reinvested them in tax-free securities, which brought him in slightly less revenue than he had been receiving net from his taxed securities. He had voted for the Nationalists at the last election, and, since this new budget, was looking out for a party that he could conscientiously vote for at the next election. He was living at Bournemouth.

'Extremely well-preserved,' concluded 'very young' Roger. 'Do you know anything about bees, Fleur?'

'I once sat on one.'

'Do you, Miss Cherrell?'

'We keep them.'

'If you were me, would you go in for them?'

'Where do you live?'

'A little beyond Hatfield. There are some quite nice clover crops round. Bees appeal to me in theory. They feed on other people's flowers and clover; and if you find a swarm you can stick to it. What are the drawbacks?'

'Well, if they swarm on other people's ground, ten to one you lose them; and you have to feed them all the winter. Otherwise it's only a question of time, trouble, and stings.'

'I don't know that I should mind that,' murmured 'very young' Roger; 'my wife would take them on.' He cocked his eye slightly: 'She has rheumatism. Apic acid, they say, is the best cure.'

'Better make sure first,' murmured Dinny, 'that they'll sting her. You can't get bees to sting people they like.'

'You can always sit on them,' murmured Fleur.

'Seriously,' said 'very young' Roger, 'half-a-dozen stings would be well worth it, poor thing.'

'What made you take up law, Forsyte?' struck in Michael.

'Well, I got a "blighty" one in the war and had to get something sedentary. I rather like it, you know, in a way, and in a way I think it's —'

'Quite!' said Michael; 'Hadn't you an Uncle George?'

'Old George! Rather! Always gave me ten bob at school, and tipped me the name of a horse to put it on.'

'Did it ever win?'

'No.'

'Well, tell us, frankly: What's going to win tomorrow?'

'Frankly,' said the solicitor, looking at Dinny, 'it depends on your sister, Miss Cherrell. Corven's witnesses have done well. They didn't claim too much, and they weren't shaken; but if Lady Corven keeps her head and her temper, we may pull

through. If her veracity is whittled away at any point, then – I'
he shrugged, and looked – Dinny thought – older. 'There are
one or two birds on the jury I don't like the look of. The foreman's one. The average man, you know, is dead against wives
leaving without notice. I'd feel much happier if your sister
would open up on her married life. It's not too late.'

Dinny shook her head.

'Well, then, it's very much a case of the personal appeal.
But there's a prejudice against mice playing when the cat's
away.'

Dinny went to bed with the sick feeling of one who knows
she has again to watch some form of torture.

Chapter Thirty-one

◂◂►►

DAY by day the Courts of Law are stony and unchanged. The
same gestures are made, the same seats taken; the same effluvium prevails, not too strong, but just strong enough.

Clare was in black on this second day, with a slim green
feather in a close-fitting black hat. Pale, her lips barely touched
with salve, she sat so still that one could not speak to her. The
words 'Society Divorce Suit,' and the 'perfect' headline, 'Night
in a Car,' had produced their effect; there was hardly standing
room. Dinny noticed young Croom seated just behind his
counsel. She noticed, too, that the birdlike jurywoman's cold
was better, and the foreman's parroty eyes fixed on Clare. The
Judge seemed to be sitting lower than ever. He raised himself
slightly at the sound of Instone's voice.

'If it please your Lordship, and members of the jury – the
answer to the allegation of misconduct between the respondent
and co-respondent will be a simple and complete denial. I call
the respondent.'

With a sensation of seeing her sister for the first time, Dinny
looked up. Clare, as Dornford had recommended, stood rather
far back in the box, and the shade from the canopy gave her a
withdrawn and mysterious air. Her voice, however, was clear,

and perhaps only Dinny could have told that it was more clipped than usual.

'Is it true, Lady Corven, that you have been unfaithful to your husband?'

'It is not.'

'You swear that?'

'I do.'

'There have been no love passages between you and Mr Croom?'

'None.'

'You swear that?'

'I do.'

'Now it is said –'

To question on question on question Dinny sat listening, her eyes not moving from her sister, marvelling at the even distinctness of her speech and the motionless calm of her face and figure. Instone's voice today was so different that she hardly recognized it.

'Now, Lady Corven, I have one more question to ask, and, before you answer it, I beg you to consider that very much depends on that answer. Why did you leave your husband?'

Dinny saw her sister's head tilt slightly backwards.

'I left because I did not feel I could remain and keep my self-respect.'

'Quite! But can you not tell us why that was? You had done nothing that you were ashamed of?'

'No.'

'Your husband has admitted that he had, and that he had apologized?'

'Yes.'

'What had he done?'

'Forgive me. It's instinct with me not to talk about my married life.'

Dinny caught her father's whisper: 'By Gad! she's right!' She saw the Judge's neck poked forward, his face turned towards the box, his lips open.

'I understand you to say you felt you could not remain with your husband and keep your self-respect?'

'Yes, my Lord.'

'Did you feel you could leave him like that and keep your self-respect?'

'Yes, my Lord.'

Dinny saw the Judge's body raise itself slightly, and his face moving from side to side, as if carefully avoiding any recipient of his words: 'Well, there it is, Mr Instone. I don't think you can usefully pursue the point. The respondent has evidently made up her mind on it.' His eyes under drooped lids continued to survey what was unseen.

'If your Lordship pleases. Once more, Lady Corven, there is no truth in these allegations of misconduct with Mr Croom?'

'No truth whatever.'

'Thank you.'

Dinny drew a long breath and braced herself against the pause and the slow rich voice to the right behind her.

'You, a married woman, would not call inviting a young man to your cabin, entertaining him alone in your room at half-past eleven at night, spending a night with him in a car, and going about with him continually in the absence of your husband, misconduct?'

'Not in itself.'

'Very well. You have said that until you saw him on the ship you had never seen the co-respondent. Could you explain how it was that from, I think, the second day at sea you were so thick with him?'

'I was not thick with him at first.'

'Oh, come! Always together, weren't you?'

'Often, not always.'

'Often, not always – from the second day?'

'Yes, a ship is a ship.'

'Quite true, Lady Corven. And you had never seen him before?'

'Not to my knowledge.'

'Ceylon is not a large place, is it, from a society point of view?'

'It is not.'

'Lots of polo matches, cricket matches, other functions where you are constantly meeting the same people.'

'Yes.'

'And yet you never met Mr Croom? Odd, wasn't it?'

'Not at all. Mr Croom was on a plantation.'

'But he played polo, I think?'

'Yes.'

'And you are a horsewoman, very interested in all that sort of thing?'

'Yes.'

'And yet you never met Mr Croom?'

'I have said I never did. If you ask me till tomorrow I shall say the same.'

Dinny drew in her breath. Before her sprang up a mental snapshot of Clare as a little girl being questioned about Oliver Cromwell.

The slow rich voice went on:

'You never missed a polo match at Kandy, did you?'

'Never, if I could help it.'

'And on one occasion you entertained the players?'

Dinny could see a frown on her sister's brow.

'Yes.'

'When was that?'

'I believe it was last June.'

'Mr Croom was one of the players, wasn't he?'

'If he was, I didn't see him.'

'You entertained him but you did not see him?'

'I did not.'

'Is that usual with hostesses in Kandy?'

'There were quite a lot of people, if I remember.'

'Come now, Lady Corven, here is the programme of the match – just take a look at it to refresh your memory.'

'I remember the match perfectly.'

'But you don't remember Mr Croom, either on the ground, or afterwards at your house?'

'I don't. I was interested in the play of the Kandy team, and afterwards there too many people. If I remembered him I should say so at once.'

It seemed to Dinny an immense time before the next question came.

'I am suggesting, you know, that you did not meet as strangers on the boat?'

'You may suggest what you like, but we did.'

'So you say.'

Catching her father's muttered: 'Damn the fellow!' Dinny touched his arm with her own.

'You heard the stewardess give her evidence? Was that the only time the co-respondent came to your state-room?'

'The only time he came for more than a minute.'

'Oh! He did come at other times?'

'Once or twice to borrow or return a book.'

'On the occasion when he came and spent — what was it? — half an hour there —'

'Twenty minutes, I should say.'

'Twenty minutes — what were you doing?'

'Showing him photographs.'

'Oh! Why not on deck?'

'I don't know.'

'Didn't it occur to you that it was indiscreet?'

'I didn't think about it. There were a lot of photos — snap-shots and photos of my family.'

'But nothing that you couldn't have shown him perfectly in the saloon or on deck?'

'I suppose not.'

'I take it you imagined he wouldn't be seen?'

'I tell you I didn't think about it.'

'Who proposed that he should come?'

'*I* did.'

'You knew you were in a very dubious position?'

'Yes, but other people didn't.'

'You could have shown him those photographs anywhere? Looking back on it, don't you think it was singular of you to do such a compromising thing for no reason at all?'

'It was less trouble to show them to him in the cabin; besides, they were private photos.'

'Now, Lady Corven, do you mean to say that nothing what-ever took place between you during those twenty minutes?'

'He kissed my hand before he went out.'

'That is something, but not quite an answer to my question.'

'Nothing else that could give you satisfaction.'

'How were you dressed?'

'I regret to have to inform you that I was fully dressed.'

'My Lord, may I ask to be protected from these sarcasms?'

Dinny admired the stilly way in which the Judge said:

'Answer the questions simply, please.'

'Yes, my Lord.'

Clare had moved out from under the shadow of the canopy and was standing with her hands on the rail of the box; spots of red had come into her cheeks.

'I suggest that you were lovers before you left the ship?'

'We were not, and we never have been.'

'When did you first see the co-respondent again after you left him on the dock?'

'I think about a week later.'

'Where?'

'Down near my people's at Condaford.'

'What were you doing?'

'I was in a car.'

'Alone?'

'Yes, I had been canvassing and was going home to tea.'

'And the co-respondent?'

'He was in a car, too.'

'Sprang up in it, I suppose, quite naturally?'

'My Lord, I ask to be protected from these sarcasms.'

Dinny heard a tittering, and heard the Judge's voice addressing nobody:

'What is sauce for the goose is sauce for the gander, Mr Brough.'

The tittering deepened. Dinny could not resist stealing a glance. The handsome face was inimitably wine-coloured. Beside her, 'very young' Roger wore an expression of enjoyment tinctured by anxiety.

'How came the co-respondent to be on this country road fifty miles from London?'

'He had come to see me.'

'You admit that?'

'He said so.'

'Perhaps you could tell us the exact words he used.'

'I could not, but I remember that he asked if he might kiss me.'

'And you let him?'

'Yes. I put my cheek out of the car, and he kissed it, and went back to his car and drove away.'

'And yet you say you were not lovers before you left the ship?'

'Not in your sense. I did not say that he was not in love with me. He was; at least he told me so.'

'Do you suggest that you were not in love with him?'

'I'm afraid I do.'

'But you let him kiss you?'

'I was sorry for him.'

'You think that is proper conduct for a married woman?'

'Perhaps not. But after I left my husband I did not regard myself as a married woman.'

'Oh!'

Dinny had a feeling as if the whole Court had said that word. 'Very young' Roger's hand emerged from his side pocket; he looked at what it contained intently, and put it back. A rueful frown had come on the pleasant broad face of the jurywoman who resembled a housekeeper.

'And what did you do after you had been kissed?'

'Went home to tea.'

'Feeling none the worse?'

'No; better if anything.'

Again the titter rose. The Judge's face went round towards the box.

'Are you speaking seriously?'

'Yes, my Lord. I wish to be absolutely truthful. Even when they are not in love, women are grateful for being loved.'

The Judge's face came round again to gaze at the unseen above Dinny's head.

'Go on, Mr Brough.'

'When was the next occasion on which you saw the co-respondent?'

'At my aunt's house in London where I was staying.'

'Did he come to see your aunt?'

'No, to see my uncle.'

'Did he kiss you on that occasion?'

'No. I told him that if we were to meet, it must be platonically.'

'A very convenient word.'

'What other should I have used?'

'You are not standing there to ask me questions, madam. What did he say to that?'

'That he would do anything I wished.'

'Did he see your uncle?'

'No.'

'Was that the occasion on which your husband said he saw him leaving the house?'

'I imagine so.'

'Your husband came directly he had gone?'

'Yes.'

'He saw you, and asked who that young man was?'

'Yes.'

'Did you tell him?'

'Yes.'

'I think you called the co-respondent Tony?'

'Yes.'

'Was that his name?'

'No.'

'It was your pet name for him?'

'Not at all. Everybody calls him that.'

'And he called you Clare, or darling, I suppose?'

'One or the other.'

Dinny saw the Judge's eyes lifted to the unseen.

'Young people nowadays call each other darling on very little provocation, Mr Brough.'

'I am aware of that, my Lord. . . . Did you call *him* darling?'

'I may have, but I don't think so.'

'You saw your husband alone on that occasion?'

'Yes.'

'How did you receive him?'

'Coldly.'

'Having just parted from the co-respondent?'

'That had nothing to do with it.'

'Did your husband ask you to go back to him?'

'Yes.'

'And you refused?'

'Yes.'

'And that had nothing to do with the co-respondent?'

'No.'

'Do you seriously tell the jury, Lady Corven, that your relations with the co-respondent, or if you like it better, your feelings for the co-respondent, played no part in your refusal to go back to your husband?'

'None.'

'I'll put it at your own valuation: You had spent three weeks in the close company of this young man. You had allowed him to kiss you, and felt better for it. You had just parted from him. You knew of his feelings for you. And you tell the jury that he counted for nothing in the equation?'

Clare bowed her head.

'Answer, please.'

'I don't think he did.'

'Not very human, was it?'

'I don't know what you mean by that.'

'I mean, Lady Corven, that it's going to be a little difficult for the jury to believe you.'

'I can't help what they believe, I can only speak the truth.'

'Very well! When did you next see the co-respondent?'

'On the following evening, and the evening after that he came to the unfurnished rooms I was going into and helped me to distemper the walls.'

'Oh! A little unusual, wasn't it?'

'Perhaps. I had no money to spare, and he had done his own bungalow in Ceylon.'

'I see. Just a friendly office on his part. And during the hours he spent with you there no passages took place between you?'

'No passages have ever taken place between us.'

'At what time did he leave?'

'We left together both evenings about nine o'clock and went and had some food.'

'And after that?'

'I went back to my aunt's house.'

'Nowhere in between?'

'Nowhere.'

'Very well! You saw your husband again before he was compelled to go back to Ceylon?'

'Yes, twice.'

'Where was the first time?'

'At my rooms. I had got into them by then.'

'Did you tell him that the co-respondent had helped you distemper the walls?'

'No.'

'Why not?'

'Why should I? I told my husband nothing, except that I wasn't going back to him. I regarded my life with him as finished.'

'Did he on that occasion again ask you to go back to him?'

'Yes.'

'And you refused?'

'Yes.'

'With contumely?'

'I beg your pardon.'

'Insultingly?'

'No. Simply.'

'Had your husband given you any reason to suppose that he wished to divorce you?'

'No. But I don't know what was in his mind.'

'And, apparently, you gave him no chance to know what was in yours?'

'As little as possible.'

'A stormy meeting?'

Dinny held her breath. The flush had died out of Clare's cheeks; her face looked pale and peaked.

'No; disturbed and unhappy. I did not want to see him.'

'You heard your counsel say that from the time of your leaving him in Ceylon, your husband in his wounded pride had conceived the idea of divorcing you the moment he got the chance? Was that your impression?'

'I had and have no impression. It is possible. I don't pretend to know the workings of his mind.'

'Though you lived with him for nearly eighteen months?'

'Yes.'

'But, anyway, you again refused definitely to go back to him?'

'I have said so.'

'Did you believe he meant it when he asked you to go back?'

'At the moment, yes.'

'Did you see him again before he went?'

'Yes, for a minute or two, but not alone.'

'Who was present?'

'My father.'

'Did he ask you again to go back to him on that occasion?'

'Yes.'

'And you refused?'

'Yes.'

'And after that you had a message from your husband before he left London, asking you once more to change your mind and accompany him?'

'Yes.'

'And you did not?'

'No.'

'Now let me take you to the date of January the – er – third' – Dinny breathed again – 'that is the day which you spent, from five in the afternoon till nearly midnight, with the co-respondent. You admit doing that?'

'Yes.'

'No passages between you?'

'Only one. He hadn't seen me for nearly three weeks, and he kissed my cheek when he first came in to have tea.'

'Oh! the cheek again? Only the cheek?'

'Yes. I am sorry.'

'So I am sure was he.'

'Possibly.'

'You first spent half an hour alone, after this separation, having – tea?'

'Yes.'

'Your rooms, I think, are in the old mews – a room below, a staircase, a room above – where you sleep?'

'Yes.'

'And a bathroom? Besides the tea I suppose you had a chat?'

'Yes.'

'Where?'

'In the ground-floor room.'

'And then did you walk together, chatting, to the Temple, and afterwards to a film and to dinner at a restaurant, during which you chatted, I suppose, and then took a cab back to your rooms, chatting?'

'Quite correct.'

'And then you thought that having been with him nearly six hours, you had still a good deal to say and it was necessary that he should come in, and he came?'

'Yes.'

'That would be past eleven, wouldn't it?'

'Just past, I think.'

'How long did he stay on that occasion?'

'About half an hour.'

'No passages?'

'None.'

'Just a drink and a cigarette or two, and a little more chat?'

'Precisely.'

'What had you to talk about for so many hours with this young man who was privileged to kiss your cheek?'

'What has anyone to talk about at any time?'

'I am asking you that question.'

'We talked about everything and nothing.'

'A little more explicit, please.'

'Horses, films, my people, his people, theatres – I really don't remember.'

'Carefully barring the subject of love?'

'Yes.'

'Strictly platonic from beginning to end?'

'I should say so.'

'Come, Lady Corven, do you mean to tell us that this young man, who on your own admission was in love with you, and who hadn't seen you for nearly three weeks, never once during all those hours yielded to his feelings?'

'I think he told me he loved me once or twice; but he always stuck splendidly to his promise.'

'What promise?'

'Not to make love to me. To love a person is not a crime, it is only a misfortune.'

'You speak feelingly – from you own experience?'

214

Clare did not answer.

'Do you seriously tell us that you have not been and are not in love with this young man?'

'I am very fond of him, but not in your sense.'

In Dinny flamed up compassion for young Croom listening to all this. Her cheeks went hot, and she fixed her blue eyes on the Judge. He had just finished taking down Clare's answer; and suddenly she saw him yawn. It was an old man's yawn, and lasted so long that it seemed never going to end. It changed her mood, and filled her with a sort of pity. He, too, had to listen day after day to long-drawn-out attempts to hurt people, and make them stultify themselves.

'You have heard the inquiry agent's evidence that there was a light in the upstairs room after you returned with the co-respondent from the restaurant. What do you say to that?'

'There would be. We sat there.'

'Why there, and not downstairs?'

'Because it's much warmer and more comfortable.'

'That is your bedroom?'

'No, it's a sitting-room. I have no bedroom. I just sleep on the sofa.'

'I see. And there you spent the time from soon after eleven to nearly midnight with the co-respondent?'

'Yes.'

'And you think there was no harm in that?'

'No harm, but I think it was extremely foolish.'

'You mean that you would not have done so if you had known you were being watched?'

'We certainly shouldn't.'

'What made you take these particular rooms?'

'Their cheapness.'

'Very inconvenient, wasn't it, having no bedroom, and nowhere for a servant, and no porter?'

'Those are luxuries for which one has to pay.'

'Do you say that you did not take these particular rooms because there was no one of any kind on the premises?'

'I do. I have only just enough money to live on.'

'No thought of the co-respondent, when you took them?'

'None.'

'Not even just a sidelong thought of him?'

'My Lord, I have answered.'

'I think she has, Mr Brough.'

'After this you saw the co-respondent constantly?'

'No. Occasionally. He was living in the country.'

'I see, and came up to see you?'

'He always saw me when he did come up, perhaps twice a week.'

'And when you saw him what did you do?'

'Went to a picture gallery or a film; once to a theatre, I think. We used to dine together.'

'Did you know you were being watched?'

'No.'

'Did he come to your rooms?'

'Not again till February the third.'

'Yes, that is the day I am coming to.'

'I thought so.'

'You thought so. It is a day and night indelibly fixed in your mind?'

'I remember it very well.'

'My friend has taken you at length through the events of that day, and except for the hours at Oxford, it seems to have been spent almost entirely in the car. Is that so?'

'Yes.'

'And this car was a two-seater, with what, my Lord, is called a "dicky." '

The Judge stirred.

'I have never been in a "dicky," Mr Brough, but I know what they are.'

'Was it a roomy, comfortable little car?'

'Quite.'

'Closed, I think?'

'Yes. It didn't open.'

'Mr Croom drove and you were seated beside him?'

'Yes.'

'Now when you were driving back from Oxford you have said that this car's lights went out about half-past ten, four miles or so short of Henley, in a wood?'

'Yes.'

'Was that an accident?'

'Of course.'

'Did you examine the battery?'

'No.'

'Did you know when or how it was last charged?'

'No.'

'Did you see it when it was recharged?'

'No.'

'Then why – of course?'

'If you are suggesting that Mr Croom tampered with the battery –'

'Just answer my question, please.'

'I *am* answering. Mr Croom is incapable of any such dirty trick.'

'It was a dark night?'

'Very.'

'And a large wood?'

'Yes.'

'Just the spot one would choose on the whole of that journey from Oxford to London?'

'Choose?'

'If one had designed to spend the night in the car.'

'Yes, but the suggestion is monstrous.'

'Never mind that, Lady Corven. You regarded it as a pure coincidence?'

'Of course.'

'Just tell us what Mr Croom said when the lights went out.'

'I think he said: "Hallo! My lights are gone!" And he got out and examined the battery.'

'Had he a torch?'

'No.'

'And it was pitch dark. I wonder how he did it. Didn't you wonder too?'

'No. He used a match.'

'And what *was* wrong?'

'I think he said a wire must have gone.'

'Then – you have told us that he tried to drive on, and twice got off the road. It must have been *very* dark?'

'It was, fearfully.'

'I think you said it was *your* suggestion that you should spend the night in the car?'

'I did.'

'After Mr Croom had proposed one or two alternatives?'

'Yes; he proposed that we should walk into Henley, and that he should come back to the car with a torch.'

'Did he seem keen on that?'

'Keen? Not particularly.'

'Didn't press it?'

'N – no.'

'Do you think he ever meant it?'

'Of course I do.'

'In fact, you have the utmost confidence in Mr Croom?'

'The utmost.'

'Quite! You have heard of the expression "palming the cards"?'

'Yes.'

'You know what it means?'

'It means forcing a person to take a card that you wish him to take.'

'Precisely.'

'If you are suggesting that Mr Croom was trying to force me to propose that we should spend the night in the car, you are wholly wrong; and it's a base suggestion.'

'What made you think I was going to make that suggestion, Lady Corven? Had the idea been present to your mind?'

'No. When I suggested that we should spend the night in the car, Mr Croom was taken aback.'

'Oh! How did he show that?'

'He asked me if I could trust him. I had to tell him not to be old-fashioned. Of course, I could trust him.'

'Trust him to act exactly as you wished?'

'Trust him not to make love to me. I was trusting him every time I saw him.'

'You had not spent a night with him before?'

'Of course I had not.'

'You use the expression "of course" rather freely, and it seems to me with very little reason. You had plenty of opportunities of passing a night with him, hadn't you – on the ship, and in your rooms where there was nobody but yourself?'

'Plenty, and I did not avail myself of them.'

'So you say; and if you did not, doesn't it seem to you rather singular that you suggested it on this occasion?'

'No. I thought it would be rather fun.'

'Rather fun? Yet you knew this young man was passionately in love with you?'

'I regretted it afterwards. It wasn't fair to him.'

'Really, Lady Corven, do you ask us to believe that you, a married woman of experience, didn't realize the ordeal by fire through which you were putting him?'

'I did afterwards, and I was extremely sorry.'

'Oh, afterwards! I am speaking of before.'

'I'm afraid I didn't before.'

'You are on your oath. Do you persist in swearing that nothing took place between you in or out of the car on the night of February the third in that dark wood?'

'I do.'

'You heard the inquiry agent's evidence that, when about two in the morning he stole up to the car and looked into it, he saw by the light of his torch that you were both asleep and that your head was on the co-respondent's shoulder?'

'Yes, I heard that.'

'Is it true?'

'If I was asleep how can I say, but I think it's quite likely. I had put my head there early on.'

'Oh! You admit that?'

'Certainly. It was more comfortable. I had asked him if he minded.'

'And, of course, he didn't?'

'I thought you didn't like the expression "of course," but anyway he said he didn't.'

'He had marvellous control, hadn't he, this young man, who was in love with you?'

'Yes, I've thought since that he had.'

'You knew then that he must have, if your story is true. But is it true, Lady Corven; isn't it entirely fantastic?'

Dinny saw her sister's hands clenching on the rail, and a flood of crimson coming up into her cheeks and ebbing again before she answered:

'It may be fantastic, but it's entirely true. Everything I've said in this box is true.'

'And then in the morning you woke up as if nothing had happened, and said: "Now we can go home and have breakfast!" And you went? To your rooms?'

'Yes.'

'How long did he stay on that occasion?'

'About half an hour or a little more.'

'The same perfect innocence in your relations?'

'The same.'

'And the day after that you were served with this petition?'

'Yes.'

'Did it surprise you?'

'Yes.'

'Conscious of perfect innocence, you were quite hurt in your feelings?'

'Not when I thought about things.'

'Oh, not when you thought about things? What exactly do you mean by that?'

'I remembered that my husband had said I must look out for myself; and I realized how silly I was not to know that I was being watched.'

'Tell me, Lady Corven, why did you defend this action?'

'Because I knew that, however appearances were against us, we had done nothing.'

Dinny saw the Judge look towards Clare, take down her answer, hold up his pen, and speak.

'On that night in the car you were on a main road. What was to prevent your stopping another car and asking them to give you a lead into Henley?'

'I don't think we thought of it, my Lord; I did ask Mr Croom to try and follow one, but they went by too quickly.'

'In any case, what was there to prevent your walking into Henley and leaving the car in the wood?'

'I suppose nothing really, only it would have been midnight before we got to Henley; and I thought it would be more awkward than just staying in the car; and I always had wanted to try sleeping in a car.'

'And do you still want to?'

'No, my Lord, it's overrated.'

'Mr Brough, I'll break for luncheon.'

Chapter Thirty-two

<del>-←-→-</del>

DINNY refused all solicitations to lunch, and, taking her sister's arm, walked her out into Carey Street. They circled Lincoln's Inn Fields in silence.

'Nearly over, darling,' she said at last. 'You've done wonderfully. He hasn't really shaken you at all, and I believe the Judge feels that. I like the Judge much better than the jury.'

'Oh! Dinny, I'm so tired. That perpetual suggestion that one's lying screws me up till I could scream.'

'That's what he does it for. Don't gratify him!'

'And poor Tony. I do feel a beast.'

'What about a "nice hot" cup of tea? We've just time.'

They walked down Chancery Lane into the Strand.

'Nothing with it, dearest. I couldn't eat.'

Neither of them could eat. They stirred the pot, drank their tea as strong as they could get it, and made their way silently back to the Court. Clare, not acknowledging even her father's anxious glance, resumed her old position on the front bench, her hands in her lap and her eyes cast down.

Dinny was conscious of Jerry Corven sitting deep in confabulation with his solicitor and counsel. 'Very young' Roger, passing to his seat, said:

'They're going to recall Corven.'

'Why?'

'I don't know.'

As if walking in his sleep, the Judge came in, bowed slightly to the Court's presence, and sat down. 'Lower than ever,' thought Dinny.

'My Lord, before resuming my cross-examination of the respondent, I should be glad, with your permission, to recall the petitioner in connexion with the point of which my friend made so much. Your Lordship will recollect that in his cross-examination of the petitioner he imputed to him the intention of securing a divorce from the moment of his wife's departure. The petitioner has some additional evidence to give in regard to that point, and it will be more convenient for me to recall him now. I shall be very short, my Lord.'

Dinny saw Clare's face raised suddenly to the Judge, and the expression on it made her heart beat furiously.

'Very well, Mr Brough.'

'Sir Gerald Corven.'

Watching that contained figure step again into the box, Dinny saw that Clare too was watching, almost as if she wished to catch his eye.

'You have told us, Sir Gerald, that on the last occasion but one on which you saw your wife before you returned to Ceylon – the first of November, that is – you saw her at her rooms in Melton Mews?'

'Yes.'

Dinny gasped. It had come!

'Now on that occasion, besides any conversation that took place between you, what else occurred?'

'We were husband and wife.'

'You mean that the marital relationship between you was re-established?'

'Yes, my Lord.'

'Thank you, Sir Gerald; I think that disposes finally of my friend's point; and it is all I wanted to ask.'

Instone was speaking.

'Why did you not say that when you were first examined?'

'I did not see its relevance until after your cross-examination.'

'Do you swear that you have not invented it?'

'Most certainly I do.'

And still Dinny sat braced against the woodwork with her eyes shut, thinking of the young man three rows behind her. Atrocious! But who would see it, here? People's innermost nerves were torn out of them, examined coldly, almost with enjoyment, and put back lacerated.

'Now, Lady Corven, will you go back to the box?'

When Dinny opened her eyes Clare was standing close up to the rail with her head held high and her gaze fixed on her questioner.

'Now, Lady Corven,' said the slow rich voice, 'you heard that piece of evidence.'

'Yes.'

'Is it true?'

'I do not wish to answer.'

'Why?'

Dinny saw that she had turned to the Judge.

'My Lord, when my counsel asked me about my married life, I refused to go into it, and I do not wish to go into it now.'

For a moment the Judge's eyes were turned towards the box; then strayed from it to stare at the unseen.

'This question arises out of evidence given in rebuttal of a suggestion made by your own counsel. You must answer it.'

No answer came.

'Ask the question again, Mr Brough.'

'Is it true that on the occasion of which your husband spoke the marital relationship was re-established between you?'

'No. It is not true.'

Dinny, who knew that it was, looked up. The Judge's eyes were still fixed above her head, but she saw the slight pouting of his lips. He did not believe the answer.

The slow rich voice was speaking, and she caught in it a peculiar veiled triumph.

'You swear that?'

'Yes.'

'So your husband has gone out of his way to commit perjury in making that statement?'

'It is his word against mine.'

'And I think I know which will be taken. Is it not true that you have made the answer you have in order to save the feelings of the co-respondent?'

'It is not.'

'From first to last, can we attach any more importance to the truth in any of your answers than to the truth in that last?'

'I don't think that is a fair question, Mr Brough. The witness does not know what importance we attach.'

'Very good, my Lord. I'll put it another way. *Throughout* have you told the truth, Lady Corven, and nothing but the truth?'

'I have.'

'*Very* well. I have no more to ask you.'

During the few questions put to her sister, in a re-examination which carefully avoided the last point, Dinny could think only of young Croom. At heart she felt the case was lost, and longed to take Clare and creep away. If only that man behind with the hooked nose had not tried to blacken Corven and prove too much, this last mine would not have been sprung! And yet – to blacken the other side – what was it but the essence of procedure!

When Clare was back in her seat, white and exhausted, she whispered:

'Would you like to come away, darling?'

Clare shook her head.

'James Bernard Croom.'

For the first time since the case began Dinny had a full view, and hardly knew him. His tanned face was parched and drawn; he looked excessively thin. His grey eyes seemed hiding under their brows, and his lips were bitter and compressed. He looked at least five years older, and she knew at once that Clare's denial had not deceived him.

'You name is James Bernard Croom, you live at Bablock Hythe, and are in charge of a horse-breeding establishment there? Have you any private means?'

'None whatever.'

It was not Instone who was examining, but a younger man with a sharper nose, seated just behind him.

'Up to September last year you were superintending a tea plantation in Ceylon? Did you ever meet the respondent in Ceylon?'

'Never.'

'You were never at her house?'

224

'No.'

'You have heard of a certain polo match in which you played,
and after which she entertained the players?'

'Yes, but I didn't go. I had to get back.'

'Was it on the boat, then, that you first met her?'

'Yes.'

'You make no secret of the fact that you fell in love with her?'

'None.'

'In spite of that, is there any truth in these allegations of
misconduct between you?'

'None whatever.'

And as the evidence he gave to the Court went on and on,
Dinny's eyes never left his face, as if fascinated by its con-
strained but bitter unhappiness.

'Now, Mr Croom, this is my last question: You are aware
that if these allegations of misconduct were true, you would be
in the position of a man who has seduced a wife in her husband's absence. What have you to say to that?'

'I have to say that if Lady Corven had felt for me what I feel
for her, I should have written to her husband at once to tell him
the state of things.'

'You mean that you would have given him warning before
anything took place between you?'

'I don't say that, but as soon as possible.'

'But she did *not* feel for you what you felt for her?'

'I am sorry to say, no.'

'So that in fact no occasion to inform the husband ever arose?'

'No.'

'Thank you.'

A slight stiffening of young Croom's figure heralded Brough's
rich slow voice, saying with peculiar deliberation:

'In your experience, sir, are the feelings of lovers towards
each other ever the same?'

'I have no experience.'

'No experience? You know the French proverb as to there
being always one who kisses and the other who offers the cheek
to the kiss?'

'I've heard it.'

'Don't you think it's true?'

'About as true as any proverb.'

'According to the stories you both tell, you were pursuing in her husband's absence a married woman who didn't want you to pursue her? Not a very honourable position – yours – was it? Not exactly what is called "playing the game"?'

'I suppose not.'

'But I suggest, Mr Croom, that your position was not as dishonourable as all that, and that in spite of the French proverb she *did* want you to pursue her?'

'She did not.'

'You say that in face of the cabin incident; in face of her getting you in to distemper her walls; in face of the invitation to tea and to spend over half an hour with her at nearly midnight in those convenient rooms of hers; in face of the suggestion that you should spend the night with her in a car, and come to breakfast the morning after? Come, Mr Croom, isn't that carrying your chivalry rather far? What you say has to convince men and women of the world, you know.'

'I can only say that, if her feelings for me had been what mine were for her, we should have gone away together at once. The blame is entirely mine, and she has only treated me kindly because she was sorry for me.'

'If what you both say is true, she gave you hell – I beg your pardon, my Lord – in the car, didn't she? Was that kind?'

'When a person is not in love I don't think they realize the feelings of one who is.'

'Are you a cold-blooded person?'

'No.'

'But she is?'

'How is the witness to know that, Mr Brough?'

'My Lord, I should have put it: But you think she is?'

'I do not think so.'

'And yet you would have us think that she was kind in letting you pass the night with her head on your shoulder? Well, well! You say if her feelings had been yours, you would have gone away at once. What would you have gone away on? Had you any money?'

'Two hundred pounds.'

'And she?'

'Two hundred a year, apart from her job.'

'Flown away and lived on air, eh?'

'I should have got some job.'

'Not your present one?'

'Probably not.'

'I suggest that both of you felt it would be mad to fling your caps over the windmill like that?'

'*I* never felt so.'

'What made you defend this action?'

'I wish we hadn't.'

'Then why did you?'

'She thought, and her people thought, that as we had done nothing, we ought to defend.'

'But *you* didn't think so?'

'I didn't think we should be believed, and I wanted her free.'

'Her honour didn't occur to you?'

'Of course it did; but I thought for her to stay tied was too heavy a price to pay for it.'

'You say you didn't think you'd be believed? Altogether too improbable a story?'

'No; but the more one speaks the truth, the less one expects to be believed.'

Dinny saw the Judge turn and look at him.

'Are you speaking generally?'

'No, my Lord, I meant here.'

The Judge's face came round again and his eyes studied the unseen above Dinny's head.

'I am considering, you know, whether I should commit you for contempt of Court.'

'I am sorry, my Lord; what I meant was that anything one says is turned against one.'

'You speak out of inexperience. I will let it pass this time, but you mustn't say things of that sort again. Go on, Mr Brough.'

'The question of damages, of course, didn't affect you in making up your mind to defend this action?'

'No.'

'You have said that you have no private means. Is that true?'

'Certainly.'

'Then how do you mean that it didn't affect you?'

'I was thinking so much of other things that bankruptcy didn't seem to matter.'

'Now, you have said in examination that you were not aware of Lady Corven's existence until you were on this ship coming home. Do you know a place in Ceylon called Neurālÿa?'

'No.'

'What?'

Dinny saw a faint smile creep out among the Judge's folds and wrinkles.

'Put the question another way, Mr Brough; we generally call it Neurālÿa.'

'I know Neurālÿa, my Lord.'

'Were you there in June last?'

'Yes.'

'Was Lady Corven there?'

'She may have been.'

'Wasn't she in the same hotel as you?'

'No. I wasn't in an hotel. I was staying with a friend.'

'And you did not meet her playing golf or tennis, or out riding?'

'I did not.'

'Or anywhere?'

'No.'

'Not a large place, is it?'

'Not very.'

'And she's a conspicuous person, isn't she?'

'*I* think so.'

'So you never met her till you were both on this ship?'

'No.'

'When did you first become conscious that you were in love with her?'

'About the second or third day out.'

'Love almost at first sight, in fact?'

'Yes.'

'And it didn't occur to you, knowing that she was a married woman, to avoid her?'

'I knew I ought to, but I wasn't able.'

'You would have been able to if she had discouraged you?'

'I don't know.'

'Did she in fact discourage you?'

'N-no. I don't think she was aware of my feelings for some time.'

'Women are very quick in such matters, Mr Croom. Do you seriously suggest that she was unaware?'

'I don't know.'

'Did you trouble to conceal your feelings?'

'If you mean did I make love to her on the ship – I did not.'

'When did you first make love to her?'

'I told her my feelings just before we left the ship.'

'Was there any real reason why you should have gone to her state-room to see those photographs?'

'I suppose not.'

'Did you look at any photographs at all?'

'Certainly.'

'What else did you do?'

'I think we talked.'

'Don't you know? This was an occasion for you, wasn't it? Or was it only one of several occasions of which we have not been told?'

'It was the only time I was inside her state-room.'

'In that case surely you remember?'

'We just sat and talked.'

'Beginning to remember, eh? Where did you sit?'

'In the chair.'

'And where did she sit?'

'On her bed. It was a small cabin – there was no other chair.'

'An outside cabin?'

'Yes.'

'No chance of being overlooked?'

'No, but there was nothing to overlook.'

'So you both say. I suppose it gave you something of a thrill, didn't it?'

Dinny saw the Judge's face poked forward.

'I don't want to interrupt you, Mr Brough, but the witness has made no secret of his feelings.'

'Very well, my Lord. I will put it to him bluntly. I suggest, sir, that on that occasion there was misconduct between you?'

'There was none.'

'H'm! Tell the jury why it was that when Sir Gerald Corven came to London you did not go to him and frankly avow your relations with his wife.'

'What relations?'

'Come, sir! The fact, on your own showing, that you were seeing all you could of his wife; the fact that you were in love with her, and wanted her to go away with you.'

'She did not want to go away with me. I would willingly have gone to her husband, but I had no right to without her permission.'

'Did you ask for that permission?'

'No.'

'Why not?'

'Because she had told me we could only meet as friends.'

'I suggest she told you nothing of the sort?'

'My Lord, that is asking me if I am a liar.'

'Answer the question.'

'I am not a liar.'

'That is the answer, I think, Mr Brough.'

'Tell me, sir; you heard the respondent's evidence, did it strike you as entirely truthful?'

Dinny saw, and hoped that no one else saw, the quivering of his face.

'Yes, so far as I could judge.'

'It was perhaps not quite a fair question. But I may put it this way : If the respondent were to say that she had done, or not done, this or that, you would feel bound in honour to corroborate her statement, where you could, and to believe it where you could not?'

'I am not sure that is quite fair, Mr Brough.'

'My Lord, I submit that it is vital to my case to establish to the jury what the state of the co-respondent's mind has been throughout this business.'

'Well, I won't stop the question, but there is a limit, you know, to these generalities.'

Dinny saw the first flicker of a smile on young Croom's face.

'My Lord, I don't at all mind answering the question. I do

not know what I should feel bound in honour to do, generally speaking.'

'Well, let us come to the particular. Lady Corven has said that she could trust you not to make love to her. Would you say that was true?'

Dinny saw his face darken.

'Not quite true. But she knew I did my best not to.'

'But now and then you couldn't help it?'

'I don't know what you mean by the expression "making love"; but now and then I know I showed my feelings.'

'Now and then? Mr Croom, didn't you always show your feelings?'

'If you mean did I always show that I was in love with her — of course I did, you can't hide a thing like that.'

'That is a fair admission. I don't want to catch you. I mean more than just showing by your face and eyes that you were in love. I mean downright physical expression.'

'Then, no, except —'

'Yes?'

'Kissing her cheek three times altogether, and holding her hand sometimes.'

'So much she has admitted, and it is all you are prepared to swear to?'

'I will swear there was no more.'

'Tell me, did you sleep at all during that night in the car, when her head was on your shoulder?'

'Yes.'

'Considering the state of your feelings, wasn't that singular?'

'Yes. But I was up at five that morning and I'd driven a hundred and fifty miles.'

'You seriously expect us to believe that after nearly five months of longing you took no advantage of that marvellous opportunity, but just went to sleep?'

'I took no advantage. But I have told you that I do not expect to be believed.'

'I don't wonder.'

For a long time the slow rich voice went on asking questions, and for a long time Dinny's eyes remained fixed on that bitterly unhappy face, till a sort of numbness came over her. She was roused by:

'I suggest to you, sir, that from beginning to end of your evidence you have been actuated by the feeling that you must do everything you can for this lady without regard to your own consciousness of what is true? That your attitude, in fact, has been one of distorted chivalry?'

'No.'

'Very well. That is all.'

Then came the re-examination, and the Judge's releasing remark.

Dinny and Clare arose and, followed by their father, walked out into the corridor, and, as quickly as might be, to open air.

The General said:

'Instone's made a mess of it with that quite unnecessary point of his.'

Clare did not answer.

'I am glad,' said Dinny. 'You'll get your divorce.'

Chapter Thirty-three

◄─►►

T H E speeches were over, and the judge was summing up. From beside her father, on one of the back benches now, Dinny could see Jerry Corven still sitting in front beside his solicitors, and 'very young' Roger sitting alone. Clare was not in Court. Neither was young Croom.

The Judge's voice came slowly, as if struggling past his teeth. It seemed to Dinny marvellous how he remembered everything, for he looked but little at his notes; nor could she detect anything that was not fair in his review of the evidence. Now and again his eyes, turned towards the jury, seemed to close, but his voice never stopped. Now and again he poked his neck forward, priest and tortoise for a moment coalescing; then he would draw it back and speak as it were to himself.

'The evidence not being of the conclusive nature which we

expect of evidence tendered to this Court' – (No 'calling with a cup of tea,' she thought), 'counsel for the petitioner in his able speech laid great stress, and rightly, upon credibility. He directed your attention especially to the respondent's denial that there was any renewal of the marital relationship between the petitioner and herself on the occasion when he went to her rooms. He suggested that there was reason for her denial in her desire to spare the feelings of the co-respondent. But you must consider whether a woman who, as she says, was not in love with the co-respondent, had not encouraged him, or been intimate with him in any way, would go so far as to perjure herself to save his feelings. According to her account, he was from the beginning of their acquaintanceship in the nature of a friend to her and nothing more. On the other hand, if you believe the petitioner on that point – and there seems no sufficient reason for his volunteering perjury – it follows that you disbelieve the respondent, and she has deliberately denied evidence which was in her favour rather than against her. It seems difficult to believe that she would do that unless she had feelings for the co-respondent warmer than those of mere friendship. This is, in fact, a very crucial point, and the decision you come to as to which is true – the husband's statement or the wife's denial of it – seems to me a cardinal factor in your consideration of whether or not to accept the respondent's evidence in the rest of the case. You have only what is called circumstantial evidence to go upon; and in such cases the credibility of the parties is a very important factor. If on one point you are satisfied that one of the parties is not speaking the truth, then the whole of his or her evidence is tinged with doubt. In regard to the co-respondent, though he conveyed an impression of candour, you must remember that there is a traditional belief in this country, regrettable or not, that a man whose attentions have involved a married woman in a situation of this kind must not, in vulgar parlance, "give her away." You must ask yourselves how far you can treat this young man, who is quite obviously, and by his own admission, deeply in love, as a free, independent, truthful witness.

'On the other hand, and apart from this question of general credibility, you must not let appearances run away with your judgement. In these days young people are free and easy in their association with each other. What might have seemed conclusive indication in the days of my youth is now by no means conclusive. In regard to the night, however, that was spent in the car, you may think it well to pay particular attention to the answer the respondent gave to my question: Why, when the lights went out, they did not simply stop a passing car, tell the occupants what had happened, and request to be given a lead into Henley. Her answer was: "I don't think we thought of it, my Lord. I did ask Mr Croom to follow a car, but it was going too fast." It is for you to consider, in the light of that answer, whether the respondent really wanted that simple solution of the difficulty they were in, namely, a lead into Henley, where no doubt the damage could have been repaired; or whence at least she could have returned to London by train. It is said by her counsel that to have gone into Henley at that time with a damaged car would have made them too conspicuous. But you will remember that she has said she was not aware that she was being watched. If that was so, you will consider whether the question of conspicuosity would have been present to her mind.'

Dinny's gaze by now had left the Judge's face and was fixed upon the jury. And, while she searched the lack of expression on those twelve faces, a 'cardinal factor' was uppermost in her mind: It was easier to disbelieve than to believe. Remove whatever tempering influence there might be from a witness's voice and face, and would not the spicier version of events prevail? The word 'damages' took her eyes back to the Judge's face.

'Because,' he was saying, 'if you should come to a decision in favour of the petitioner, the question of the damages he claims will arise. And in regard to that I must draw your attention to one or two salient considerations. It cannot be said that claims for damages in divorce suits are common in these days, or indeed looked on with any great favour in this Court. It has become disagreeable to think of women in terms of money. Not much more than a hundred years ago it was actually not unknown – though illegal even then – for a man to offer his wife for sale. Such days – thank God! – are long past. Though damages can still be asked for in this Court, they must not be what is called "vindictive," and they must bear reasonable relation to the co-respondent's means. In this case the petitioner has stated that if any damages are awarded him, they will be settled on the respondent. That is, one may say, the usual practice nowadays where damages are claimed. In regard to the co-respondent's means, if it should become necessary for you to consider the question of damages, I would remind you that his counsel stated that he has no private means, and offered to provide evidence of the fact. One has never known counsel to make a statement of that sort without being sure of his ground, and I think you may take the co-respondent's word for it that his only means of subsistence are derived from his – er – "job," which appears to carry a salary of four hundred pounds a year. Those, then, are the considerations which should guide you if you should have to consider the amount, if any, of damages to be awarded. Now, members of the jury, I send you to your task. The issues are grave for the future of these people, and I am sure that I can trust you to give them your best attention. You may retire if you wish to do so.'

Dinny was startled by the way he withdrew almost at once into contemplation of a document which he raised from the desk in front.

'He really is an old ducky,' she thought, and her gaze went back to the jury rising from their seats. Now that the ordeals of her sister and Tony Croom were over, she felt very little interest. Even the Court today was but sparsely filled.

'They only came to enjoy the suffering,' was her bitter thought.

A voice said:

'Clare is still in the Admiralty Court when you want her.' Dornford, in wig and gown, was sitting down beside her. 'How did the Judge sum up?'

'Very fairly.'

'He *is* fair.'

'But barristers, I think, might wear: "Fairness is a virtue, a little more won't hurt you," nicely printed on their collars.'

'You might as well print it round the necks of hounds on a scent. Still, even this Court isn't as bad in that way as it used to be.'

'I'm so glad.'

He sat quite still, looking at her. And she thought:

'His wig suits the colour of his face.'

Her father leaned across her.

'How long do they give you to pay costs in, Dornford?'

'A fortnight is the usual order, but you can get it extended.'

'It's a foregone conclusion,' said the General glumly. 'Well, she'll be free of him.'

'Where is Tony Croom?' asked Dinny.

'I saw him as I came in. At the corridor window – quite, close. You can't miss him. Shall I go and tell him to wait?'

'If you would.'

'Then will you all come to my chambers when it's over?' Receiving their nods, he went out and did not come back.

Dinny and her father sat on. An usher brought the Judge a written communication; he wrote upon it, and the usher took it back to the jury. Almost immediately they came in.

The broad and pleasant face of her who looked like a house-keeper had a mortified expression as if she had been over-ridden; and, instantly, Dinny knew what was coming.

'Members of the jury, are you agreed on your verdict?'

The foreman rose.

'We are.'

'Do you find the respondent guilty of adultery with the co-respondent?'

'Yes.'

'Do you find the co-respondent guilty of adultery with the respondent?'

'Isn't that the same?' thought Dinny.

'Yes.'

'And what damages do you say the co-respondent should be ordered to pay?'

'We think that he should pay the costs of all the parties to the action.'

Through Dinny passed the thought: 'The more one loves the more one pays.' Barely listening to the Judge's words, she whispered to her father, and slipped away.

Young Croom was leaning against the stone that framed the

window, and she thought she had never seen so desolate a
figure.

'Well, Dinny?'

'Lost. No damages, just all the costs. Come out, I want to
talk to you.'

They went in silence.

'Let's go and sit on the Embankment.'

Young Croom laughed. 'The Embankment! Marvellous!'

No other word passed between them till they were seated
under a plane tree whose leaves were not yet fully unfurled in
that cold spring.

'Rotten!' said Dinny.

'I've been a complete fool all through, and there's an end of
it.'

'Have you had anything to eat these last two days?'

'I suppose so. I've drunk quite a lot, anyway.'

'What are you going to do now, dear boy?'

'See Jack Muskham, and try and get another job somewhere
out of England.'

Dinny felt as if she had grasped a stick by the wrong end.
She could only be helpful if she knew Clare's feelings.

'No one takes advice,' she said, 'but couldn't you manage to
do nothing at all for a month or so?'

'I don't know, Dinny.'

'Have those mares come?'

'Not yet.'

'Surely you won't give that job up before it's even begun?'

'It seems to me I've only got one job at the moment – to keep
going somehow, somewhere.'

'Don't I know that feeling? But don't do anything desperate!
Promise! Good-bye, my dear, I must hurry back.'

She stood up and pressed his hand hard.

When she reached Dornford's chambers, her father and Clare
were already there, and 'very young' Roger with them.

Clare's face looked as though the whole thing had happened
to someone else.

The General was saying:

'What will the total costs come to, Mr Forsyte?'

'Not far short of a thousand, I should say.'

'A thousand pounds for speaking the truth! We can't possibly let young Croom pay more than his own share. He hasn't a bob.'

'Very young' Roger took snuff.

'Well,' said the General, 'I must go and put my wife out of her misery. We're going back to Condaford this afternoon, Dinny. Coming?'

Dinny nodded.

'Good! Many thanks, Mr Forsyte. Early in November, then – the decree? Good-bye!'

When he had gone Dinny said in a low voice:

'Now that it's over, what do you really think?'

'As I did at first: If you'd been your sister we should have won.'

'I want,' said Dinny coldly, 'to know whether you believe them or not?'

'On the whole – yes.'

'Is it impossible for a lawyer to go further than that?'

'Very young' Roger smiled.

'No one tells the truth without mental reservations of some kind.'

'Perfectly true,' thought Dinny. 'Could we have a taxi?'

In the cab Clare said: 'Do something for me, Dinny. Bring me my things to the Mews.'

'Of course.'

'I don't feel like Condaford. Did you see Tony?'

'Yes.'

'How is he?'

'Rotten.'

'Rotten!' repeated Clare, bitterly. 'How could I help what they sprung on me? I lied for him, anyway.'

Dinny, looking straight before her, said:

'When you can, tell me exactly what your feeling towards him is.'

'When I know myself, I will.'

'You'll want something to eat, darling.'

'Yes, I'm hungry. I'll stop here in Oxford Street. I shall be cleaning up when you come with my things. I feel as if I could sleep the clock round, and probably I shan't sleep a wink. When you're divorced, Dinny, don't defend — you keep on thinking of better answers.'

Dinny squeezed her arm, and took the taxi on to South Square.

Chapter Thirty-four

M O R E deadly than the atmosphere during a fight is that when it is over. You 'keep on thinking of better answers,' and you feel that life is not worth living. The primary law of existence having been followed to its logical and — win or lose — unsatisfying conclusion, the sand is out of your dolly, you loll and droop. Such were the sensations of Dinny, who had but understudied. Unable to feel that she could be of any real help, she fell back on pigs, and had been for a good week in this posture when she received a letter headed:

> Kingson Cuthcott & Forsyte,
> Old Jewry.
> May 17th, 1932.

MY DEAR MISS CHARWELL, —

I write to tell you that we have succeeded in coming to an arrangement by which the costs of the action will be met without making any call upon either Mr Croom or your sister. I shall be grateful if you could take an opportunity of relieving their minds and also your father's mind in the matter.

> Believe me, my dear Miss Charwell,
> Very faithfully yours,
> ROGER FORSYTE

Reaching her on a really warm morning, to sound of mowing machine and to scent of grass, it would have 'intrigued' her if she had not detested the word. She turned from the window and said:

'The lawyers say we need none of us worry any more about those costs, dad; they've come to an arrangement.'

'How?'

'They don't say, but they want your mind relieved.'

'I don't understand lawyers,' muttered the General, 'but if they say it's all right, I'm very glad. I've been worrying.'

'Yes, dear. Coffee?'

But she resumed her meditations on that cryptic letter. Did something in Jerry Corven's conduct force him to agree to this 'arrangement'? Was there not someone called 'The King's Proctor' who could stop decrees being granted? Or – what?

Abandoning her first idea of driving over to Tony Croom because of the questions he might ask, she wrote to him and to Clare instead. The more, however, she pondered over the wording of the solicitor's letter, the more convinced she became that she must see 'very young' Roger. There was that at the back of her mind which refused quietus. She, therefore, arranged to see him at a teashop near the British Museum on his way homeward from the City, and went there direct from her train. The place was an 'artifact,' designed, so far as a Regency edifice could be, to reproduce such a 'coffee house' as Boswell and Johnson might have frequented. Its floor was not sanded, but looked as if it should be. There were no long clay pipes, but there were long cardboard cigarette-holders. The furniture was wooden, the light dim. No record having been discovered of what the 'staff' should look like, they looked sea-green. Prints of old coaching inns were hung on walls panelled by the Tottenham Court Road. Quite a few patrons were drinking tea and smoking cigarettes. None of them used the long cardboard holders. 'Very young' Roger, limping slightly, and with his customary air of not being quite what he ought to be, uncovered his sandyish head and smiled above his chin.

'China or Indian?' said Dinny.

'Whatever you're having.'

'Then two coffees, please, and muffins.'

'Muffins! This *is* a treat, dear papa. Those are quite good old copper bed-warmers, Miss Cherrell. I wonder if they'd sell them.'

'Do you collect?'

'Pick things up. No use having a Queen Anne house unless you can do something for it.'

'Does your wife sympathize?'

'No, she's all for the T.C.R., bridge, golf, and the modernities. *I* never can keep my hands off old silver.'

'I *have* to,' murmured Dinny. 'Your letter was a very pleasant relief. Did you really mean that we should none of us have to pay?'

'I did.'

She considered her next question, scrutinizing him through her lashes. With all his æsthetic leanings, he looked uncommonly spry.

'In confidence, Mr Forsyte, how did you manage to make that arrangement? Had it to do with my brother-in-law?'

'Very young' Roger laid his hand on his heart.

'"The tongue of Forsyte is his own," *cf.* Marmion. But you needn't worry.'

'I need, or shall, unless I know it wasn't that.'

'Make your mind easy, then; it had nothing to do with Corven.'

Dinny ate a muffin in complete silence, then spoke of period silver. 'Very young' Roger gave an erudite dissertation on its mark – if she would come down for a weekend, he would turn her into a connoisseur.

They parted cordially, and Dinny went towards her Uncle Adrian's. That uneasiness was still at the back of her mind. The trees had leaved enticingly these last warm days; the Square wherein he dwelled had an air quiet and green, as if inhabited by minds. Nobody was at home. 'But,' said the maid, 'Mr Cherrell is sure to be in about six, miss.'

Dinny waited in a small panelled room full of books and pipes and photographs of Diana and the two Ferse children. An old collie kept her company, and through the opened window seeped the sounds of London streets. She was crumpling the dog's ears when Adrian came in.

'Well, Dinny, so it's over. I hope you feel better.'

Dinny handed him the letter.

'I know it's nothing to do with Jerry Corven. You know Eustace Dornford, Uncle. I want you to find out from him quietly whether it's he who is paying these costs.'

Adrian pulled at his beard.

'I don't suppose he'd tell me.'

'Somebody must have paid them, and I can only think of him. I don't want to go to him myself.'

Adrian looked at her intently. Her face was concerned and brooding.

'Not easy, Dinny; but I'll try. What's going to happen to those two?'

'I don't know, they don't know; nobody knows.'

'How are your people taking it?'

'Terribly glad it's over, and don't care much now it is. You'll let me know soon, won't you, Uncle dear?'

'I will, my dear; but I shall probably draw blank.'

Dinny made for Melton Mews, and met her sister on the doorstep. Clare's cheeks were flushed; there was febrility in her whole manner and appearance.

'I've asked Tony Croom here this evening,' she said, when Dinny was leaving to catch her train. 'One must pay one's debts.'

'Oh!' murmured Dinny, and for the life of her could say no more.

The words haunted her in the bus to Paddington, in the refreshment room while she ate a sandwich, in the railway carriage going home. Pay one's debts! The first canon of self-respect! Suppose Dornford had paid those costs! Was she as precious as all that? Wilfrid had had all of her according to her heart and her hope and her desire. If Dornford wanted what was left over – why not? She dropped thinking of herself and went back to thought of Clare. Had she paid her debt by now? Transgressors by law – ought to transgress! And yet – so much future could be compromised in so few minutes!

She sat very still. And the train rattled on in the dying twilight.

Chapter Thirty-five

◄—►►

TONY CROOM had spent a miserable week in his converted cottages at Bablock Hythe. The evidence given by Corven on his recall to the box had seared him, nor had Clare's denial anointed the burn. In this young man was an old-fashioned capacity for jealousy. That a wife should accept her husband's embrace was not, of course, unknown; but, in the special circumstances and states of feeling, it had seemed to him improper, if not monstrous, and the giving of his own evidence, directly after such a thrust at his vitals, had but inflamed the wound. A sad unreason governs sex; to be aware that he had no right to be suffering brought no relief. And now, a week after the trial, receiving her note of invitation, he had the impulse not to answer, to answer and upbraid, to answer 'like a gentleman' – and, all the time, he knew he would just go up.

With nothing clear in his mind and that bruise still in his heart, he reached the Mews an hour after Dinny had gone. Clare let him in, and they stood looking at each other for a minute without speaking. At last she said with a laugh:

'Well, Tony! Funny business – the whole thing, wasn't it?'

'Exquisitely humorous.'

'You look ill.'

'You look fine.'

And she did, in a red frock open at the neck, and without sleeves.

'Sorry I'm not dressed, Clare. I didn't know you'd want to go out.'

'I don't. We're going to dine in. You can leave the car out there, and stay as long as you like, and nobody the worse. Isn't it nice?'

'Clare!'

'Put your hat down and come upstairs. I've made a new cocktail.'

'I take this chance to say I'm bitterly sorry.'

'Don't be an idiot, Tony.' She began to mount the spiral stairway, turning at the top. 'Come!'

Dropping his hat and driving gloves, he followed her.

To the eyes of one throbbing and distraught, the room above had an air of preparation, as if for ceremony, or – was it sacrifice? The little table was set out daintily with flowers, a narrow-necked bottle, green glasses – the couch covered with some jade-green stuff and heaped with bright cushions. The windows were open, for it was hot, but the curtains were nearly drawn across and the light turned on. He went straight across to the window, stifled by the violent confusion within him.

'In spite of the Law's blessing, better close the curtains,' said Clare. 'Would you like a wash?'

He shook his head, drew the curtains close, and sat on the sill. Clare had dropped on to the sofa.

'I couldn't bear to see you in the box, Tony. I owe you a lot.'

'Owe! You owe me nothing. It's I – !'

'No! I am the debtor.'

With her bare arms crossed behind her neck, her body so graceful, her face a little tilted up – there was all he had dreamed about and longed for all these months! There she was, infinitely desirable, seeming to say: 'Here I am! Take me!' and he sat staring at her. The moment he had yearned and yearned for, and he could not seize it!

'Why so far off, Tony?'

He got up, his lips trembling, every limb trembling, came as far as the table, and stood gripping the back of a chair. His eyes fixed on her eyes, searched and searched. What was behind those dark eyes looking up at him? Not love! The welcome of duty? The payment of a debt? The toleration of a pal? The invitation of one who would have it over and done with? But not love, with its soft gleam. And, suddenly, there came before his eyes the image of her and Corven – *there!* He covered his face with his arm, rushed headlong down those twisting iron stairs, seized hat and gloves, and dashed out into his car. His mind did not really work again till he was far along the Uxbridge Road; and how he had got there without disaster he could not conceive. He had behaved like a perfect fool! He had behaved exactly as he had to! The startled look on her face! To be treated as a creditor! To be paid! *There!* On that sofa! No! He drove again with a sort of frenzy, and was brought up sharply by a lorry lumbering along in front. The night was just beginning, moonlit and warm. He turned the car into a gateway and got out. Leaning against the gate, he filled and lit his pipe. Where was he going? Home? What use? What use going anywhere? His brain cleared suddenly. Drive to Jack Muskham's, release himself, and — Kenya! He had money enough for that. A job would turn up. But stay here? No! Lucky those mares hadn't come! He got over the gate and sat down on the grass. Relaxed against the bank he looked up. Lot of stars! What had he — fifty pounds — sixty — nothing owing! An East African boat — go steerage! Anything — anywhere away! Close to him on the bank were ox-eyed daisies slowly brightening in the moonlight; the air was scented by ripening grass. If in her eyes there had been one look of love! He let his head fall back on the grass. Not her fault she didn't love him! His misfortune! Home — get his kit together, lock up, straight to Muskham's! It would take all the night! See those lawyers — Dinny, too, if possible! But Clare? No! His pipe ceased to draw; the moon and stars, the ox-eyed daisies, the grassy scent, the shadows creeping out, the feel of the bank, lost all power to soothe. Get on, do something, go on doing something, till he was again on shipboard and away. He got up, climbed back over the gate, and started his engine. He kept straight on, instinctively avoiding the route through Maidenhead and Henley. He passed through High Wycombe and approached Oxford from the north. The old town was lit up and in evening feather when he dropped down on it from Headington and threaded into the quiet Cumnor road. On the little old New Bridge over the Upper Thames he stopped. Something special about this upper river, quiet and winding, and withdrawn from human blatancy! In full moonlight now the reeds glistened and the willows seemed to drip silver into the water, dark below their branches. Some windows in the inn beyond were lamp-lit, but no sound of gramophone came forth. With the moon riding so high, the stars now were but a pricking of the grape-coloured sky; the scent from the reedy banks and the river fields, after a whole week of warmth, mounted to his nostrils, sweet and a little rank. It brought a sudden wave of sheer sex-longing – so often and so long had he dreamed of Clare and himself in love on this winding field-scented stream. He started the car with a jerk, and turned past the inn down the narrowed road. In twenty minutes he stood in the doorway of his cottage, looking into the moonlit room he had left sunlit seven hours before. There was the novel he had been trying to read, tipped on to the floor; the remains of his cheese and fruit lunch not cleared away; a pair of brown shoes which he had been going to shine up. The big black beams across the low ceiling and around the big old fireplace rescued from Victorian enclosure and brown varnish, the copper fire-dogs and pewter plates and jugs and bowls he had hardily collected, hoping they would appeal to Clare, all his *res angusta domi*, welcomed him dimly. He felt suddenly exhausted, drank half a tumbler of whisky and water, ate some biscuits, and sank into his long wicker armchair. Almost at once he fell asleep, and awoke in daylight. He woke remembering that he had meant to spend the night in action. Level sunlight was slanting in at the window. He finished the water in the jug, and looked at his watch. Five o'clock. He threw open the door. Early haze was bright over the fields. He went out past the mares' boxes and their meadows. A track, sloping down towards the river, led over grass broken by bushy scoops and green banks covered with hazel and alders. No dew had fallen, but the grass and every shrub smelled new.

About fifty yards from the river he threw himself down in a little hollow. Rabbits and bees and birds – nothing else as yet awake. He lay on his back staring at the grass and the bushes and the early sky, blue and lightly fleeced. Perhaps because he could see so little from that hollow all England seemed to be with him. A wild bee close to his hand was digging into a flower, there was a faint scent, as of daisy-chains; but chiefly it was the quality of the grass – its close freshness, its true greenness. 'Greatness and dignity and peace!' That play! Those words had given him a choke. Other people had laughed, Clare had laughed. 'Sentimental!' she had said. 'No country ever had, or will have "Greatness and dignity and peace."' Probably not, certainly not – a country, even one's own, was a mish-mash of

beauties and monstrosities, a vague generalization that betrayed
dramatists into over-writing, journalists into blurb. All the
same, you couldn't anywhere else in the world get just such a
spot, or just such grass to feel and see, a scent that was well-
nigh none, a tender fleecy sky, tiny flowers, birds' songs, age and
youth at once! Let people laugh – you couldn't! Leave grass
like this! He remembered the thrill he had felt six months ago,
seeing again English grass! Leave his job before it had begun;
chuck it back at Muskham, who had been so really decent to
him! He turned over on to his face and laid his cheek to that
grass. There he got the scent better – not sweet, not bitter, but
fresh, intimate and delighting, a scent apprehended from his
earliest childhood – the scent of England. If only those mares
would come, and he could get at it! He sat up again, and
listened. No sound of train or car or airplane, no human sound,
no sound of any four-footed thing; just birds' songs, and those
indistinguishable and a little far – a long meandering tune wide
above the grass. Well! No use making a song! If one couldn't
have a thing, one couldn't!

Chapter Thirty-six

THE moment Dinny had left, Adrian made the not uncommon
discovery that he had promised what would need performance.
To get one of His Majesty's Counsel to commit himself – how?
Too pointed to go to him! Impossible to pump a guest! Em, if
he prompted her, would ask them both to dinner, especially if
made to understand that the matter concerned Dinny; but even
then –? He waited to consult Diana, and, after dining, went
round to Mount Street. He found them playing piquet.

'Four kings,' said Lady Mont. 'So old-fashioned – Lawrence
and I and Mussolini. Have you come for something, Adrian?'

'Naturally, Em. I want you to ask Eustace Dornford to
dinner, and me to meet him.'

'That'll be Dinny. I can't get Lawrence to be chivalrous;
when I have four kings he always has four aces. When?'

'The sooner the better.'

'Ring, dear.'

Adrian rang.

'Blore, call up Mr Dornford and ask him to dinner – black tie.'

'When, my lady?'

'The first evenin' not in my book. Like dentists,' she added, as Blore withdrew. 'Tell me about Dinny. She hasn't been near us since the case.'

'The case,' repeated Sir Lawrence, 'went much as one expected, didn't you think, Adrian? Any repercussions?'

'Someone has settled the costs, and Dinny suspects Dornford.'

Sir Lawrence laid down his cards. 'Bit too like a bid for her, that !'

'Oh, he won't admit it, but she wants me to find out.'

'If he won't admit it, why should he do it?'

'Knights,' murmured Lady Mont, 'wearin' a glove, and gettin' killed, and nobody knowin' whose glove. Yes, Blore?'

'Mr Dornford will be happy to dine on Monday, my lady.'

'Put him in my book, then, and Mr Adrian.'

'Go away with him after dinner, Adrian,' said Sir Lawrence, 'and do it then – not so pointed; and, Em, not a hint, not even a sigh or a groan.'

'He's a nice creature,' said Lady Mont, 'so pale-brown . . .'

With the 'nice creature so pale-brown' Adrian walked away the following Monday night. Their directions were more or less the same, since Dornford was not yet in his new house. To Adrian's relief, his companion seemed as glad of the opportunity as himself, for he began at once to talk of Dinny.

'Am I right in thinking something's happened to Dinny lately – I don't mean that case – but when she was ill and you went abroad together?'

'Yes. The man I told you of that she was in love with two years ago was drowned out in Siam.'

'Oh !'

Adrian stole a look. What should Dornford's face express – concern, relief, hope, sympathy? It only wore a little frown.

'There was a question I wanted to ask you, Dornford. Someone had settled the costs granted against young Croom in that case.' The eyebrows were raised now, but the face said nothing. 'I thought you might have known who. The lawyers will only say that it wasn't the other side.'

'I've no idea.'

'So!' thought Adrian. 'No nearer, except that, if a liar, he's a good one!'

'I like young Croom,' said Dornford; 'he's behaved decently, and had hard luck. That'll save him from bankruptcy.'

'Bit mysterious, though,' murmured Adrian.

'It is.'

'On the whole,' Adrian thought, 'I believe he did. But what a poker face!' He said, however:

'How do you find Clare since the case?'

'A little more cynical. She expressed her views on my profession rather freely when we were riding this morning.'

'Do you think she'll marry young Croom?'

Dornford shook his head.

'I doubt it, especially if what you say about those costs is true. She might have out of a sense of obligation, but otherwise I think the case has worked against his chance. She's no real feeling for him – at least that's my view.'

'Corven disillusioned her thoroughly.'

'I've certainly seldom seen a more disillusioning face than his,' murmured Dornford. 'But she seems to me headed for quite an amusing life on her own. She's got pluck and, like all these young women now, she's essentially independent.'

'Yes, I can't see Clare being domestic.'

Dornford was silent. 'Would you say that of Dinny, too?' he asked suddenly.

'Well, I can't see Clare as a mother; Dinny I can. I can't see Dinny here, there and everywhere; Clare I can. All the same – "domestic" of Dinny! It's not the word.'

'No!' said Dornford fervently. 'I don't know what it is. You believe very much in her, don't you?'

Adrian nodded.

'Enormously.'

'It's been tremendous for me,' said Dornford, very low, 'to

have come across her; but I'm afraid so far it's been nothing to her.'

'Much to allow for,' suggested Adrian. ' "Patience is a virtue," or so it used to be before the world went up in that blue flame and never came down again.'

'But I'm rising forty.'

'Well, Dinny's rising twenty-nine.'

'What you told me just now makes a difference, or – doesn't it?'

'About Siam? I think it does – a great difference.'

'Well thank you.'

They parted with a firm clasp, and Adrian branched off northwards. He walked slowly, thinking of the balance-sheet that confronts each lover's unlimited liability. No waterings of capital nor any insurance could square or guarantee that shifting lifelong document. By love was man flung into the world; with love was he in business nearly all his days, making debts or profit; and when he died was by the results of love, if not by the parish, buried and forgotten. In this swarming London not a creature but was deeply in account with a Force so whimsical, inexorable, and strong, that none, man or woman, in their proper senses would choose to do business with it. 'Good match', 'happy marriage', 'ideal partnership', 'life-long union', ledgered against 'don't get on', 'just a flare up', 'tragic state of things', 'misfit' ! All his other activities man could insure, modify, foresee, provide against (save the inconvenient activity of death); love he could not. It stepped to him out of the night, into the night returned. It stayed, it fled. On one side or the other of the balance sheet it scored an entry, leaving him to cast up and wait for the next entry. It mocked dictators, parliaments, judges, bishops, police, and even good intentions; it maddened with joy and grief; wantoned, procreated, thieved, and murdered; was devoted, faithful, fickle. It had no shame, and owned no master; built homes and gutted them; passed by on the other side; and now and again made of two hearts one heart till death. To think of London, Manchester, Glasgow without love appeared to Adrian, walking up the Charing Cross Road, to be easy; and yet without love not one of these passing citizens would be sniffing the petrol of this night air, not one grimy brick would have been laid upon brick, not one bus be droning past, no street musician would wail, nor lamp light up the firmament. A somewhat primary concern! And he, whose primary concern was with the bones of ancient men, who but for love would have had no bones to be dug up, classified and kept under glass, thought of Dornford and Dinny, and whether they would 'click' . . .

And Dornford, on his way to Harcourt Buildings, thought even more intensively of himself and her. Rising forty! This overmastering wish of his – for its fulfilment it was now or never with him! If he were not to become set in the groove of a 'getter-on', he must marry and have children. Life had become a half-baked thing without Dinny to give it meaning and savour. She had become – what had she not become? And, passing through the narrow portals of Middle Temple Lane, he said to a learned brother, also moving towards his bed:

'What's going to win the Derby, Stubbs?'

'God knows!' said his learned brother, wondering why he had played that last trump when he did, instead of when he didn't . . .

And in Mount Street Sir Lawrence, coming into her room to say 'Good night', found his wife sitting up in bed in the lace cap which always made her look so young, and, on the edge of the bed, in his black silk dressing-gown, sat down.

'Well, Em?'

'Dinny will have two boys and a girl.'

'Deuce she will! That's counting her chickens rather fast.'

'Somebody must. Give me a nice kiss.'

Sir Lawrence stooped over and complied.

'When she marries,' said Lady Mont, shutting her eyes, 'she'll only be half there for a long time.'

'Better half there at the beginning than not at all at the end. But what makes you think she'll take him?'

'My bones. We don't like being left out when it comes to the point, Lawrence.'

'Continuation of the species. H'm!'

'If he'd get into a scrape, or break his leg.'

'Better give him a hint.'

'His liver's sound.'

'How do you know that?'

'The whites of his eyes are blue. Those browny men often have livers.'

Sir Lawrence stood up.

'My trouble,' he said, 'is to see Dinny sufficiently interested in herself again to get married. After all, it *is* a personal activity.'

'Harridge's for beds,' murmured Lady Mont.

Sir Lawrence's eyebrow rose. Em was inexhaustible!

Chapter Thirty-seven

SHE whose abstinence from interest in herself was interesting so many people, received three letters on Wednesday morning. That which she opened first said:

DINNY DARLING, –

I tried to pay, but Tony would have none of it, and went off like a rocket; so I'm a wholly unattached female again. If you hear any news of him, let me have it.

Dornford gets more 'interesting-looking' every day. We only talk of you, and he's raising my salary to three hundred as compensation.

Love to you and all,
CLARE

That which she opened second said:

MY DEAR DINNY, –

I'm going to stick it here. The mare arrives on Monday. I had Muskham down yesterday, and he was jolly decent, didn't say a word about the case. I'm trying to take up birds. There is one thing you could do for me if you would – find out who paid those costs. It's badly on my mind.

Ever so many thanks for always being so nice to me.

Yours ever,
TONY CROOM

That which she read last said:

DINNY, MY DEAR, –

Nothing doing. He either didn't, or else played 'possum,' but if so it was very good 'possum.' All the same, I wouldn't put it past him that it *was* 'possum.' If you really set store by knowing, I think I should ask him point-blank. I don't believe he would tell *you* a lie, even 'a little one.' As you know, I like him. In my avuncular opinion he is still on the gold standard.

> Your ever devoted
> ADRIAN

So! She felt a vague irritation. And this feeling, which she had thought momentary, she found to be recurrent. Her state of mind, indeed, like the weather, turned cold again and torpid. She wrote to Clare what Tony Croom had written of himself, and that he had not mentioned her. She wrote to Tony Croom, and neither mentioned Clare nor answered his question about the costs; she concentrated on birds – they seemed safe, and to lead nowhere. She wrote to Adrian: 'I'm feeling I ought to be wound-up, only there'd be no dividend for the shareholders. It's very cold and dull, my consolation is that little "Cuffs" is beginning to "sit up and take real notice" of me.'

And then, as if by arrangement with the clerk of the course at Ascot, the weather changed to 'set warm'; and, suddenly, she wrote to Dornford. She wrote on pigs, their breeds and sties, the Government and the farmers. She ended with these words:

'We are all very worried by not knowing who had settled the costs in my sister's case. It is so disquieting to be under an obligation to an unknown person. Could you by any means find out for us?' She debated some time how to sign herself in this her first letter to him, and finally wrote 'Yours always, Dinny Charwell.'

His answer came very quickly:

MY DEAR DINNY, –

I was delighted to get a letter from you. To answer your last question first. I will do my best to get the lawyers to 'come clean,' but if they won't tell *you*, I can't imagine their telling me. Still, I can try. Though I fancy that if your sister or young Croom insisted they'd have to tell. Now about pigs – [there followed certain information, and a lamentation that agriculture was still not being properly tackled.] If only they would realize that all the needed pigs, poultry, and potatoes, nearly all the vegetables, much of the fruits, and much more than the present dairy produce, can really be produced at home, and by a graduated prohibition of foreign produce encourage, and indeed force, our home growers to supply the home market, we should, within ten years, have a living and profitable native agriculture once more, no rise to speak of in the cost of living, and a huge saving in our imports bill. You see how new I am to politics! Wheat and meat are the red herrings across the trail. Wheat and meat from the Dominions, and the rest (bar hot climate fruits and vegetables) home-grown, is my motto. I hope your father agrees. Clare is becoming restive, and I'm wondering if she wouldn't be happier in a more active job than this. If I can come across a good one, I shall advise her to take it. Would you ask your mother whether I should be in the way if I came down for the last weekend this month? She was good enough to tell me to let her know any time I was coming to the constituency. I was again at *Cavalcade* the other night. It wears well, but I missed you. I can't even begin to tell you how I missed you.

> Your ever faithful
> EUSTACE DORNFORD

Missed her! After the faint warmth those wistful words aroused, she thought almost at once of Clare. Restive! Who would be otherwise in her anomalous position? She had not been down at Condaford since the case. And that seemed to Dinny very natural. However one might say it didn't matter what people thought, it did, especially in a place where one had grown up, and belonged, as it were, to the blood royal of the neighbourhood. And Dinny thought, unhappily: 'I don't know what I want for her – and that's lucky, because one day she'll see exactly what she wants for herself.' How nice to see exactly what one wanted for oneself! She read Dornford's letter again, and suddenly faced her own feelings for the first time. Was she or was she not ever going to marry? If so, she would as soon marry Eustace Dornford as anyone – she liked, admired, could talk to him. But her – past! How funny it sounded! Her 'past', strangled almost from birth, yet the deepest thing she would ever know! 'One of these days you'll have to go down into the battle again.' Unpleasant to be thought a shirker by one's own mother! But it wasn't shirking! Spots of colour rose in her cheeks. It was something no one would understand – a horror of being unfaithful to him to whom she had belonged in soul if not in body. Of being unfaithful to that utter surrender, which she knew could never be repeated.

'I am not in love with Eustace,' she thought; 'he knows it, he knows I can't even pretend it. If he wants me on those terms, what is it fair for me – what is it possible for me to do?' She went out into the old yew-hedged rose garden, where the first burst of roses had begun, and wandered round, smelling at this and that, followed half-heartedly by the spaniel Foch, who had no feeling for flowers.

'Whatever I do,' she thought, 'I ought to do now. I can't keep him on tenterhooks.'

She stood by the sundial, where the shadow was an hour behind its time, and looked into the eye of the sun over the fruit trees beyond the yew hedges. If she married him, there would be children – without them it would not be possible. She saw frankly – or thought she did – where she stood in the matter of sex. What she could not see was how it would all turn for herself and for him in the recesses of the spirit. Restless, she wandered from rose-bush to rose-bush, extinguishing the few greenfly between her gloved fingers. And, in a corner, with a sort of despair, the spaniel Foch sat down unnoticed and ate a quantity of coarse grass.

She wrote to Dornford the same evening. Her mother would be delighted if he would come for that weekend. Her father quite agreed with his views on agriculture, but was not sure that anyone else did, except Michael, who, after listening to him carefully one evening in London, had said: 'Yes. What's wanted is a lead, and where's it coming from?' She hoped that when he came down he would be able to tell her about those costs. It must have been thrilling to see *Cavalcade* again. Did he know a flower called meconopsis, if that was the way to spell it, a sort of poppy of a most lovely colour? It came from the Himalayas, and so would be suitable for Campden Hill, which she believed had much the same climate. If he could induce Clare to come down it would rejoice the hearts of the aborigines. This time she signed herself 'always yours', a distinction too subtle to explain even to herself.

Telling her mother that he was coming, she added:

'I'll try and get Clare; and don't you think, mother, that we ought to ask Michael and Fleur? They were very sweet to put us up so long.'

255

Lady Charwell sighed.

'One gets into a way of just going on. But do, dear.'

'They'll talk tennis, and that'll be so nice and useful.'

Lady Charwell looked at her daughter, in whose voice something recalled the Dinny of two years back.

When Dinny knew that Clare was coming, as well as Michael and Fleur, she debated whether to tell Tony Croom. In the end she decided not to, sorrowfully, for she had for him the fellow feeling of one who had been through the same mill.

The camouflage above her father's and mother's feelings touched her. Dornford – high time, of course, he was down in the constituency again! Pity he hadn't a place of his own – didn't do to get out of touch with the electors! Presumably he'd come by car, and bring Clare; or Michael and Fleur could call for her! By such remarks they hid their nervousness about Clare and about herself.

She had just put the last flower in the last bedroom when the first car slid up the driveway; and she came down the stairs to see Dornford standing in the hall.

'This place has a soul, Dinny. It may be the fantails on the stone roof, or perhaps the deep way it's settled in, but you catch it at once.'

She left her hand in his longer than she had meant to.

'It's being so overgrown. There's the smell, too – old hay and flowering verbena, and perhaps the mullions being crumbled.'

'You look well, Dinny.'

'I am, thank you. You haven't had time for Wimbledon, I suppose?'

'No. But Clare's been going – she's coming straight from it with the young Monts.'

'What did you mean in your letter by "restive"?'

'Well, as I see Clare, she must be in the picture, and just now she isn't.'

Dinny nodded.

'Has she said anything to you about Tony Croom?'

'Yes. She laughed and said he'd dropped her like a hot potato.'

Dinny took his hat and hung it up.

'About those costs?' she said, without turning.

'Well, I went to see Forsyte specially, but I got nothing out of him.'

'Oh! Would you like a wash, or would you rather go straight up? Dinner's at quarter-past eight. It's half-past seven now.'

'Straight up, if I may.'

'You're in a different room; I'll show you.'

She preceded him to the foot of the little stairway leading to the priest's room.

'That's your bathroom. Up here, now.'

'The priest's room?'

'Yes. There's no ghost.' She crossed to the window. 'See! He was fed here at night from the roof. Do you like the view? Better in the spring when the blossom's out, of course.'

'Lovely!' He stood beside her at the window, and she could see his hands clenched so hard on the stone sill that the knuckles showed white. A bitter wind swept through her being. Here she had dreamed of standing with Wilfrid beside her. She leaned against the side of the embrasured window and closed her eyes. When she opened them he was facing her, she could see his lips trembling, his hands clasped behind him, his eyes fixed on her face. She moved across to the door.

'I'll have your things brought up and unpacked at once. Would you answer me one question: Did you pay those costs yourself?'

He gave a start and a little laugh, as if he had been suddenly switched from tragedy to comedy.

'*I?* No. Never even thought of it.'

'Oh!' said Dinny again. 'You've lots of time.' And she went down the little stairway.

Did she believe him? Whether she believed him or not, did it make any difference? The question would be asked and must be answered. 'One more river — one more river to cross!' And at the sound of the second car she went hurrying down the stairs.

Chapter Thirty-eight

⇥⇤

D U R I N G that strange week-end, with only Michael and Fleur at ease, Dinny received one piece of enlightenment as she strolled in the garden.

'Em tells me,' said Fleur, 'you're all worked up about those costs – she says *you* think Dornford paid them, and that it's giving you a feeling of obligation?'

'Oh? Well, it *is* worrying, like finding you owe nothing to your dressmaker.'

'My dear,' said Fleur, 'for your strictly private ear, *I* paid them. Roger came to dinner and made a song about hating to send in such a bill to people who had no money to spare, so I talked it over with Michael and sent Roger a cheque. My Dad made his money out of the Law, so it seemed appropriate.'

Dinny stared.

'You see,' continued Fleur, taking her arm, 'thanks to the Government converting that loan, all my beautiful gilt-edgeds have gone up about ten points, so that, even after paying that nine hundred-odd, I'm still about fifteen thousand richer than I was, and they're still going up. I've only told *you*, in confidence, because I was afraid it would weigh with you in making up your mind about Dornford. Tell me : Would it?'

'I don't know,' said Dinny dully; and she didn't.

'Michael says Dornford's the freshest egg he's come across for a long time; and Michael is very sensitive to freshness in eggs. You know,' said Fleur, stopping suddenly, and letting go her arm, 'you puzzle me, Dinny. Everybody can see what you're cut out for – wife and mother. Of course, I know what you've been through, but the past buries its dead. It is so, I've been through it, too. It's the present and the future that matter, and we're the present, and our children are the future. And you specially – because you're so stuck on tradition and continuity and that – ought to carry on. Anybody who lets a memory spoil her life – forgive me, old thing, but it's rather obviously now or never with you. And to think of you with "never" chalked against you is too bleak. I've precious little *moral* sense,' continued Fleur, sniffing at a rose, 'but I've a lot of the commoner article, and I simply hate to see waste.'

Dinny, touched by the look in those hazel eyes with the extraordinarily clear whites, stood very still, and said quietly:

'If I were a Catholic, like him, I shouldn't have any doubt.'

'The cloister?' said Fleur sharply: 'No! My mother's a Catholic, but – No! Anyway, you're not a Catholic. No, my dear – the hearth. That title was wrong, you know. It can't be both.'

Dinny smiled. 'I do apologize for worrying people so. Do you like these *Angèle Pernets*?'

She had no talk with Dornford all that Saturday, preoccupied as he was with the convictions of the neighbouring farmers. But after dinner, when she was scoring for the four who were playing Russian pool, he came and stood beside her.

'Hilarity in the home,' she said, adding nine presented by Fleur to the side on which she was not playing: 'How did you find the farmers?'

'Confident.'

'Con –?'

'That whatever's done will make things worse.'

'Oh! Ah! They're so used to that, you see.'

'And what have *you* been doing all day, Dinny?'

'Picked flowers, walked with Fleur, played with "Cuffs", and dallied with the pigs. . . . Five on to your side, Michael, and seven on to the other. This is a very Christian game – doing unto others as you would they should do unto you.'

'Russian pool!' murmured Dornford: 'Curious name nowadays for anything so infected with religion.'

'*Apropos*, if you want to go to Mass tomorrow, there's Oxford.'

'You wouldn't come with me?'

'Oh! Yes. I love Oxford, and I've only once heard a Mass. It takes about three-quarters of an hour to drive over.'

His look at her was much as the spaniel Foch gave when she returned to him after absence.

'Quarter past nine, then, in my car . . .'

When next day they were seated side by side, he said:

'Shall we slide the roof back?'

'Please.'

'Dinny, this is like a dream.'

'I wish my dreams had such a smooth action.'

'Do you dream much?'

'Yes.'

'Nice or nasty?'

'Oh! like all dreams, a little of both.'

'Any recurrent ones?'

'One. A river I can't cross.'

'Ah! like an examination one can't pass. Dreams are ruthlessly revealing. If you could cross that river in your dream, would you be happier?'

'I don't know.'

There was a silence, till he said:

'This car is a new make. You don't have to change gears in the old way. But you don't care for driving, do you?'

'I'm an idiot at it.'

'You're not modern, you see, Dinny.'

'No. I'm much less efficient than most people.'

'In your own way I don't know anybody so efficient.'

'You mean I can arrange flowers.'

'And see a joke; and be – a darling.'

It seemed to Dinny the last thing she had been able to be for nearly two years, so she merely replied:

'What was your college at Oxford?'

'Oriel.'

And the conversation lapsed.

Some hay was stacked and some still lying out, and the midsummer air was full of its scent.

'I'm afraid,' said Dornford suddenly, 'I don't want to go to Mass. I don't get so many chances to be with you, Dinny. Let's make for Clifton and sit in a boat.'

'Well, it *is* rather lovely for indoors.'

They turned off to the left, and, passing through Dorchester, came to the river by the bend and bluffs at Clifton. Leaving the car, they procured a punt and after drifting a little, moored it to the bank.

'This,' said Dinny, 'is a nice exhibition of high purpose, I don't think. "Something done" isn't always what was attempted, is it?'

'No, but it's often better.'

'I wish we'd brought Foch; he likes any kind of vehicle where he can sit on one's feet and get a nice sick feeling.'

But in that hour and more on the river they hardly talked at all. It was as if he understood – which, as a fact, he did not – how, in that drowsing summer silence, on water half in sunlight, half in shade, she was coming closer to him than ever before. There was, indeed, to Dinny something really restful and reassuring in those long lazing minutes, when she need not talk, but just take summer in at every pore – its scent, and hum, and quiet movement, the careless and untroubled hovering of its green spirit, the vague sway of the bulrushes, and the clucking of the water, and always that distant calling of the wood pigeons from far trees. She was finding, indeed, the truth of Clare's words, that he could 'let one's mouth alone'.

By the time they were back at the Grange, it had been one of the most silent and satisfactory mornings she had ever known. But between his: 'Thank you, Dinny, a heavenly time,' and his real feelings, she could tell from his eyes there was a great gap fixed. It was unnatural the way he kept his feelings in check! And, as became a woman, compassion soon changed in her to irritation. Anything better than his eternal repression, perfect consideration, patience, and long waiting! And all that afternoon she saw as little of him as she had seen much all the morning. His eyes, fixed on her with longing and a sort of reproach, became an added source of vexation, and she carefully refrained from seeming to notice them. 'Verra pavairse,' her old Scottish nurse would have said.

Bidding him 'Good night' at the foot of the stairs, she felt a keen pleasure at the dashed look on his face, and an equally keen sense that she was 'a beast'. She entered her bedroom in a curious turmoil, at odds with herself, and him, and all the world.

'Damn!' she muttered, feeling for the switch.

A low laugh startled her. Clare, in her pyjamas, was perched on the window-seat, smoking a cigarette.

'Don't turn up, Dinny; come and sit here with me, and let's puff out of the window together.'

Three wide-opened casements laid bare the night under a teazle-blue heaven trembling with stars. Dinny, looking out at it, said:

'Where have you been ever since lunch? I didn't even know you were back.'

'Have a gasper? You seem to want soothing.'

Dinny expelled a puff of smoke.

'I do. I'm sick of myself.'

'So was I,' murmured Clare, 'but I feel better.'

'What have you been doing, then?'

Again Clare laughed, and in the sound was something that made Dinny say:

'Seeing Tony Croom?'

Clare leaned back and her throat showed pale.

'Yes, my dear. The Ford and I went over. Dinny, we've justified the law. Tony no longer looks like a bereaved orphan.'

'Oh!' said Dinny, and again: 'Oh!'

Her sister's voice, warm and languid, and satisfied, made her cheeks go hot and her breath come quickly.

'Yes, I prefer him as lover to a friend. How sane is the law – it knew what we ought to have been! And I like his converted cottages. Only there's a fireplace upstairs that still wants opening up.'

'Are you going to get married, then?'

'My dear, how can we? No, we shall live in sin. Later, I suppose, we shall see. I think this "nisi" period is very thoughtful. Tony will come up in the middle of the week, and I shall go down at the week-end. And all so legal.'

Dinny laughed. Clare sat up, suddenly, clasping her knees.

'I'm happier than I've been for ever so long. It doesn't do to make other people wretched. Also, women ought to be loved, it suits them somehow. Men, too.'

Dinny leaned out of the window, and the night slowly cooled her cheeks. Beautiful and deep it was, out there, the shapes unstirring, dark and as if brooding. Through the tense stillness came a far drone, swelling to the rightful sound of a passing car, and, between the trees, she could see its travelling light burnish up the hedgerows for flying moments, and die beyond the angle of vision. Then the drone grew faint and fainter, and stillness recommenced. A moth flew by, and a little white feather from a fantail on the roof floated down, turning over in the quiet air. She felt Clare's arm come round her waist.

'Good night, old thing! Rub noses.'

Withdrawing from the night, Dinny clasped that slim pyjamaed body. Their cheeks touched, and to each the warmth of the other's skin was moving – to Clare a blessing, to Dinny an infection, as though the lingered glow from many kisses was passing into her.

When her sister had gone, she moved restlessly up and down her dark room.

'It doesn't do to make people wretched! ... Women ought to be loved. ... Men, too.' Quite a minor prophet! Converted by lightning, like Paul on his way to wherever it was. Up and down, up and down, till at last, quite tired, she turned on the light, threw off her clothes, and sat down in a wrapper to brush her hair. Brushing away at it, she stared at her image in the glass with fascination, as if she had not seen herself for a long time. The fever with which she had been infected seemed still in her cheeks and eyes and hair, she looked unnaturally vivid to herself; or was it that the sun, while she and Dornford were sitting in that punt, had left her with this hot feeling in the veins? She finished brushing, shook back her hair, and got into bed. She had left the casements open, the curtains undrawn; and the starry night confronted her lying on her back in the darkness of her narrow room. The hall clock struck midnight faintly – only three hours or so before it would be light! She thought of Clare sunk in beauty sleep close by. She thought of Tony Croom, deep-drugged with happiness, in his converted cottages, and the old tag from *The Beggars' Opera* ran in her mind: 'With bliss her kisses dissolve us in pleasure and soft repose.' But she! She could not sleep! She felt, as sometimes when a little girl, that she must roam about, explore the strangeness of the dead of night, sit on the stairs, peep into rooms, curl up in some armchair. And, getting up, she put on her dressing-gown and slippers and stole out. She sat on the top stair, clasping her knees and listening. Not a sound in the old dark house, except a little scraping noise, where some mouse was at work. She rose, clutched the banister, and crept downstairs. The hall smelled musty already, too much old wood and furniture to stand enclosure by the night. She groped across to the drawing-room door and opened it. Here flowers and last year's pot-pourri and stale cigarette smoke scented the air with a heavy reek. She made her way to one of the French windows, drew the curtains back, and opened it. She stood there a minute taking deep breaths. Very dark, very still, very warm. By starlight she could just see the sheen on the magnolia leaves. Leaving the window open, she sought her favourite old armchair, and curled up in it with her feet tucked under her. There, hugging herself, she tried to recapture the feeling that she was a child again. The night air came in, the clock ticked, and the hot feeling in her veins seemed to cool away in measure with its rhythm. She shut her eyes fast, and the sort of cosiness she used to feel in that old chair, as if she were all clasped and protected, stole upon her; but still she did not sleep. Behind her from the window with the rising of the moon a presence had stolen in, a sort of fingering uncanny light, slowly lifting each familiar object into ghostly semblance of itself. It was as if the room had come awake to keep her company; and the feeling she had sometimes had, that the old house had a life of its own, felt, saw, knew its spells of wakefulness and of slumber, tingled once more within her. Suddenly, she heard footsteps on the terrace and sat up startled.

Someone said: 'Who is that! Is anyone there?'

A figure stood in the open window; by the voice she knew that it was Dornford, and said:

'Only me.'

'*Only* you!'

She saw him come in and stand beside the chair, looking down. He was still in his evening clothes, and, with his back to the faint light, she could hardly see his face at all.

'Anything the matter, Dinny?'

'Just couldn't sleep. And you?'

'I've been finishing a bit of work in the library. I went out on the terrace for a breath, and saw this window open.'

'Which of us is going to say: "How marvellous"?'

Neither of them said anything. But Dinny unclasped herself and let her feet seek the ground.

Suddenly, Dornford put his hands to his head and turned his back on her.

'Forgive my being like this,' she murmured, 'I naturally didn't expect –'

He turned round again, and dropped on his knees besides her. 'Dinny, it's the end of the world, unless –'

She put her hands on his hair and said quietly: '– it's the beginning.'

Chapter Thirty-nine

ᐊ←◦→➤

ADRIAN sat writing to his wife.

Condaford: August 10.

MY VERY DEAR, –

I promised to give you a true and particular account of how Dinny went off. Look in *The Lantern* for their conception of 'the bride and bridegroom leaving the church.' Fortunately, the lens of that inquiring organ caught them just before they pushed off – except in movies the camera simply cannot record movement; it always get the sole of one foot cocked towards the eye, flannelizes the knee of the other leg, and upsets the set of the trousers. Dornford looked quite good value – in this style, fourteen-and-six; and Dinny – bless her! – without the 'bride's smile,' almost as if she saw the joke. Ever since the engagement, I've wondered what she's really feeling. Love such as she gave Desert it certainly is not, but I don't believe there's any physical reluctance. When, yesterday, I said to her: 'In good heart?' her answer was: 'No half heart, anyway.' We both of us have reason to know that she can go all out in what she does for other people. But she's really doing this for herself. She'll be carrying on – she'll have children – and she'll count. That's as it should be, and so I believe she feels. If she hasn't what hopeful youth calls 'a crush on' Dornford, she admires and respects him, and I think quite rightly. Besides, he knows from me, if not from her, what she's capable of, and won't expect more until he gets it. The weather held up all right, and the church – wherein, by the way, your special correspondent was baptized – in the word of Verdant Green never looked 'berrer.' The congregation was perhaps a trifle Early English, though it seemed to me you could have got most of the faces at Woolworth's.

At the top of the nave, in the more holy positions, came our own gang, County and would-be County. The more I looked at County the more I thought how merciful that the states of life into which it has pleased God to call us have prevented the Charwells of our generation from looking County. Even Con and Liz, who have to stick down here all the time, haven't got quite the hang of it. Remarkable, if you think, that there is such a thing as 'County' left; but I suppose it'll last while there's 'huntin' and shootin' '. I remember, as a boy, out hunting (when I could screw a mount out of our stables or somebody else's), I used to lurk out of reach of people for fear of having to talk to them, their words and music were so trying. Better to be human than County or even would-be County. I must say that Clare, after all her jollification in the courts, carried it off amazingly, and so far as I could see, nobody had the nerve to show any of the feelings which, as a fact, at this time of day, they probably hadn't got. Then, a little less holy, came the village in force – Dinny's a great favourite with them – quite a show of oldest inhabitants. Some real faces; an old chap called Downer, in a Bath chair, all 'Whitechapel' whiskers and beard, and shrewd remaining brown spaces. He perfectly remembered Hilary and me falling off a hay-cart we oughtn't to have been on. And old Mrs Tibwhite – a sweet old witch of a thing, who always let me eat her raspberries. The schoolchildren had a special holiday. Liz tells me not one in twenty of them has ever seen London, or indeed been ten miles out of the village, even now. But there's a real difference in the young men and maidens. The girls have most excellent legs and stockings and quite tasteful dresses; and the youths good flannel suits and collars and ties – all done by the motor bike and the film. Lots of flowers in the church, and a good deal of bell-ringing and blowy organ-playing. Hilary did the swearing in with his usual rapidity, and the old rector, who held the sponge, looked blue at the pace he went and the things he left out. Well, you want, of course, to hear about those dresses. The general effect, as they stood in the aisle, was what you might call delphinian. Dinny, even in white, has that look, and, consciously or not, the bridesmaids were togged up according; and what with Monica and Joan and two young Dornford nieces being slim and tall, they really looked like a planting of blue delphiniums, preceded by four blue tots, sweet, but none as pretty as Sheila. Really, that chickenpox was very perverse; you and your two were terribly missed, and Ronald as a page would just have topped everything up. I walked back to the Grange with Lawrence and Em, an imposing steel-grey presence slightly marred where 'tears had got mixed with her powder sometimes.' In fact, I had to stop her under a stricken tree and do some good work with one of those silk handkerchiefs you gave me. Lawrence was in feather – thought the whole show the least gimcrack thing he had seen for a long time, and had now more hope of the pound going still lower. Em had been to see the house on Campden Hill; she predicted that Dinny would be in love with Dornford within a year, which started another tear, so I called her attention to the tree which had in fact been struck by lightning while she and I and Hilary were standing under it. 'Yes,' she said, 'you were squits – so providential; and the butler made a penholder out of the wood; it wouldn't hold nibs, so I gave it to Con for school, and he cursed me. Lawrence, I'm old.' Whereon Lawrence took her hand, and they walked hand in hand the rest of the way.

The reception was held on the terrace and lawn; everybody came, schoolchildren and all, a quaint mix-up, but jolly, it seemed to me. I didn't know I was so fond of the old place. However much one may believe in levelling-up chances, there's something about old places. They can't be re-created if they're once let slip, and they focus landscape in a queer kind of way. Some villages and land-scapes seem to have no core – you can't explain why, but they feel hollow, and shallow and flat. A real old place puts heart into a neighbourhood. If the people who live in it are not just selfish pigs, it means a lot in a quiet way to people who have no actual owner-ship in it. The Grange is a sort of anchor to this neighbourhood. I doubt if you'd find a single villager, however poor, who grudged its existence, or wouldn't feel the worse for its ruination. Generations of love and trouble, and goodness knows not too much money, have been spent on it, and the result is something very hand-made and special. Everything's changing, and has got to change, no doubt, and how to save the old that's worth saving, whether in landscape, houses, manners, institutions, or human types, is one of our greatest problems, and the one that we bother least about. We save our works of art, our old furniture, we have our cult – and a strong one – of 'antiques,' and not even the most go-ahead modern thought objects to that. Why not the same throughout our social life? 'The old order changeth' – yes, but we ought to be able to preserve beauty and dignity, and the sense of service, and manners – things that have come very slowly, and can be made to vanish very fast if we aren't set on preserving them somehow. Human nature being what it is, nothing seems to me more futile than to level to the ground and start again. The old order had many excrescences, and was by no means 'all werry capital,' but, now that the housebreakers are in, one does see that you can smash in an hour what has taken centuries to produce; and that, unless you can see your way pretty clearly to replace what admittedly wasn't perfect with something more perfect, you're throwing human life back instead of advancing it. The thing is to pick on what's worth preserving, though I don't say there's very much that is. Well, that's all very portentous! To come back to Dinny – they're going to spend their honeymoon in Shropshire, round about where Dornford comes from. Then they come back here for a bit, then settle in on Campden Hill. I hope this weather will last for them. Honeymooning in wet weather, especially when one is keener on the other than the other is on the one, should be very trying. Dinny's 'going away' frock, you may like to know, was blue, and suited her not quite down to the ground. We had a minute together. I gave her your love, and she sent you hers, and said: 'Well, I'm very nearly over, Uncle dear. Wish me luck!' I felt like piping my eye. Over what? Well, anyway, if wishes for luck will help, she goes wreathed with them; but all that kissing business is hard to get through. Con and Liz took theirs down at the car. I felt rather a brute, looking at their faces when she'd gone. They went away in Dornford's car, with himself driving. After that I confess that I slunk off. They're all right, I know, but it didn't feel like it. There's such cursed finality about a wedding, however easy divorce is or may become; besides, Dinny is not the sort who would take someone who loved her and then let him down; it's the old-fashioned 'for better for worse' there, but I think it'll be 'for better' – in the long run, anyway. I sneaked out of sight into the orchard and then up through the fields to the woods. I hope it was as gorgeous a day with you as it was here. These beechwoods on the slopes are more beautiful than the careful beech-clumps they plant on downs, though even those have a sort of temple-like effect, in spite of being meant as landmarks or to give shade to sheep. I can assure you that wood about half-past five was enchanted. I went up the slope and sat down and just enjoyed it. Great shifting shafts of sunlight coming in below and splashing the trunks; and ever-so-green cool spaces between – only one word for it, holy. The trees, many of them, go up branchless for a long way, and some of the trunks looked almost white. Not much undergrowth and very little 'life' except jays and a brown squirrel. When you're in a wood as lovely as that, and think of death duties and timber, your heart turns over and over as if you'd supped entirely off Spanish onions. Two hundred years in His sight may be as yesterday, but in mine I confess they're like eternity. These woods are no longer 'shot,' and anybody can come into them. I suppose the young folk do – what a place to wander about in, lovering! I lay down in a patch of sunlight and thought of you; and two small grey wood-doves perched about fifty yards off and talked cosily to each other, so that I could have done with my field-glasses. Willow-herb and tansy were out where trees have come down and been cleared away – foxgloves don't seem to flourish round here. It was very restful, except that one ached a bit because it was green and beautiful. Queer, that 'beauty' ache! Lurking consciousness of mortality, perhaps knowledge that all things must slip away from one in time, and the greater their beauty the greater the loss in store! Mistake in our make-up, that. We ought to feel: The greater the earth's beauty, the more marvellous the screen of light and wind and foliage, the lovelier nature, in fact – the deeper and sweeter our rest in her will be. All very puzzling! I know the sight of a dead rabbit out in a wood like that affects me more than it does in a poulterer's shop. I passed one as I was going back – killed by a weasel; its soft limpness seemed saying: 'Pity I'm dead!' Death may be a good thing, but life's a better. A dead shape that's still a shape moves one horribly. Shape *is* life, and when life's gone one can't see why shape should remain even for the little time it does. I'd have liked to stay and see the moon come up and peer about in there, and slowly fill it all up with ghostly glistening; then I might have caught the feeling that shape lives on in rarefied form, and all of us, even the dead rabbits and birds and moths, still move and have their being – which may be the truth, for all I know or ever shall. But dinner was at eight, so I had to come away with the light still green and golden – there flows alliteration again like a twopenny brook! Outside, on the terrace, I met Dinny's spaniel, Foch. Knowing his history, it was like meeting a banshee – not that he was howling; but it reminded me sharply of what Dinny has been through. He was sitting on his haunches and looking down at nothing, as dogs – especially spaniels – will when things are beyond them, and the one and only scent is no more, for the time being. He'll go with them, of course, to Campden Hill when they come back. I went up and had a bath, and dressed, and stood at my window, listening to the drone of a tractor still cutting corn, and getting a little drunk on whiffs from the honeysuckle that climbs and flowers round my window. I see now what Dinny meant by: 'Over.' Over the river that she used to dream she couldn't cross. Well, all life is crossing rivers, or getting drowned on the way. I hope – I believe – she's touching shore. Dinner was just like dinner always is – we didn't talk of her, or mention our feelings in any way. I played Clare a game of billiards – she struck me as softer and more attractive than I've ever seen her. And then I sat up till past midnight with Con, in order, apparently, that we might say nothing. They'll miss her a lot, I'm afraid.

The silence in my room, when I got up here at last, was stunning, and the moonlight almost yellow. The moon's hiding, now, behind one of the elms, and the evening star shining above a dead branch. A few other stars are out, but very dim. It's a night far from our time, far even from our world. Not an owl hooting, but the honey-suckle still sweet. And so, my most dear, here endeth the tale! Good night!

Your ever loving

ADRIAN

MORE ABOUT PENGUINS

Penguin Book News, which appears every month, contains details of all the new books issued by Penguins as they are published. From time to time it is supplemented by *Penguins in Print*, which is a complete list of all books published by Penguins which are in print. (There are nearly three thousand of these.)

A specimen copy of *Penguin Book News* will be sent to you free on request, and you can become a subscriber for the price of the postage – 3s. for a year's issues (including the complete lists). Just write to Dept EP, Penguin Books Ltd, Harmondsworth, Middlesex, enclosing a cheque or postal order, and your name will be added to the mailing list.

Some other volumes in the Forsyte Chronicles are described overleaf.

Note : *Penguin Book News* and *Penguins in Print* are not available in the U.S.A. or Canada

Also in 'The End of the Chapter'

MAID IN WAITING

The 'Maid in Waiting' is Dinny Cherrell, daughter of the Grange, friend of Fleur Mont. Her squirearchal duties are palling on her when a threat to deport her brother Hubert on a murder charge challenges Dinny's string-pulling skill and the Cherrell family influence as never before. . . .

FLOWERING WILDERNESS

Wilfrid Desert, a wandering war poet, has been forced, at pistol point, to renounce Christianity and embrace Islam. On his return to England, he meets Dinny Cherrell . . . but, during their whirlwind romance, the gossip of the bazaars reaches the London clubs. Soon Dinny's engagement is in the balance, tragically undermined by sheer weight of outraged opinion.

The other titles in Galsworthy's Forsyte Chronicles already available in Penguins

*THE MAN OF PROPERTY

IN CHANCERY

TO LET

THE WHITE MONKEY

THE SILVER SPOON

SWAN SONG

NOT FOR SALE IN THE U.S.A. OR CANADA
* NOT FOR SALE IN THE U.S.A.